"Something's wrong," Feril said in a hush. Her nostrils quivered, trying to pick up the scent that was making the mounts nervous.

Fury sensed a problem, too. The wolf threw back his head and howled, just as a bolt of lightning cut through the air—sideways, like a thrown spear. It pierced the neck of Feril's horse, which slumped and died before it hit the ground.

"Everyone down!" Dhamon shouted as he leapt from his mount and drew his sword.

Crouched on the muddy ground, Feril concentrated and her keen elven vision parted the darkness, helping her distinguish the shadowy, moving shapes from the stationary ones of the low hills nearby. As she focused on the black forms in the distance, the bushes in front of her suddenly started to move forward. She scrambled backward and Dhamon raised his sword.

Pointed white teeth stood out from the inky background.

THE DRAGONLANCE® SAGA

Read these books by Margaret Weis and Tracy Hickman

DRAGONS OF AUTUMN TWILIGHT
DRAGONS OF WINTER NIGHT
DRAGONS OF SPRING DAWNING

TIME OF THE TWINS
WAR OF THE TWINS
TEST OF THE TWINS

THE SECOND GENERATION

DRAGONS OF SUMMER FLAME

DRAGONS OF A FALLEN SUN
DRAGONS OF A LOST STAR
DRAGONS OF A VANISHED MOON

. . . and more than one hundred other DRAGONLANCE
novels and anthologies by dozens of
authors.

The DAWNING of a NEW AGE

THE DAWNING OF A NEW AGE

Cover art by Matt Stawicki
Interior art by Karolyn Guldan
Cartography by Dennis Kauth
First Printing: September 1996
Library of Congress Catalog Card Number: 2001012345

9 8 7 6 5 4 3 2 1

US ISBN:0-7869-2842-5
UK ISBN: 0-7869-2843-3
620-88210-001-EN

U.S., CANADA,
ASIA, PACIFIC, & LATIN AMERICA
Wizards of the Coast, Inc.
P.O. Box 707
Renton, WA 98057-0707
+1-800-324-6496

EUROPEAN HEADQUARTERS
Wizards of the Coast, Belgium
P.B. 2031
2600 Berchem
Belgium
+32-70-23-32-77

Visit our web site at www.wizards.com/books

Acknowledgment

The Fifth Age of the DRAGONLANCE® world and the awesome dragons who populate it were shaped by many individuals at TSR, Inc. They include: Harold Johnson, game design team leader, Krynn scholar, and kender creator; William Connors, author of the FIFTH AGE™ game rules; Sue Weinlein Cook, FIFTH AGE game editor; Skip Williams, sounding board and Legion of Steel creator; and Steve Miller, Krynn on-line liaison.

Thanks also to Margaret Weis and Tracy Hickman for their novel *Dragons of Summer Flame*, which served as the foundation for the Age of Mortals. And to Steve Glimpse, who breathed life into Blister.

Dedication

For Brian and Lorraine—
for believing in me enough to let me wander through Krynn.

And for Margaret—
for shaping such a grand world to believe in.

Northern Wastes

Hinterlund

Palanthas

Nightlund

Schallsea Island

Abanasinia

Newports

Prologue

Palin's Descent

Palin Majere stood near a broken altar in the midst of a fire-ravaged forest. He was tall and spindly, like the handful of scorched birch trees that clung to life around him. A staff topped by a hammered silver dragon's claw was tucked under one arm and his white robe whipped about his legs in the strong breeze. His long, chestnut-colored hair fluttered annoyingly against his neck and face and streamed into his eyes. Nevertheless, he wouldn't remove his fingers from the book he cradled to brush away the bothersome strands.

He glanced down at the cover. The red leather binding was cracked and faded, and it nearly matched the rosy shade of Lunitari, the moon emerging overhead—the moon named for one of Krynn's gods of magic. There was magic in the book. Palin could sense it. He could feel a tingling in his slender fingers, feel the pulse of arcane energy that seemed at first erratic but now beat in time with his heart.

The gold lettering on the tome's cover was faint. "Magius," was the only word Palin could make out.

Still, that word, the name of the greatest war-wizard of Krynn, revealed the importance of what he was holding. The ancient tome was the most treasured of the collection of spellbooks in the Tower of Wayreth. Palin knew the tome had never been allowed outside that august building until now, until the enchantments penned on its flaking pages were so desperately needed. Yet would they be enough against Chaos, who had been unleashed by the Graygem and who was threatening to destroy the world? And would he, little more than an apprentice, be up to the task of invoking the enchantments against the all-powerful deity who raged in the Abyss?

Raistlin, who stood nearby, had placed the book in Palin's hands. In so doing, he had placed an immeasurable amount of trust in his young nephew's ability to use the spells wisely. Palin considered himself a mere fledgling next to his Uncle Raistlin and the other revered and powerful sorcerers of Krynn. He had not made the sacrifices in the name of magic that they had, though the challenge before him could make up for that. It could end his young life.

"I am ready," he told Raistlin. I am ready to make my sacrifice, he added silently.

The black-robed sorcerer nodded and backed away. Usha, a child of the Irda who was at Raistlin's side, opened her mouth to say something but her words were lost in the quickening, howling wind. The growing magical gust overtook Palin and swept him up above the forest floor like a weightless leaf, carrying him from the land of the Irda and from Raistlin and beautiful Usha with the golden eyes.

He floated, suspended like a marionette on invisible strings, buffeted by what was now a caterwauling gale. The whites and greens of the birch trees, the blacks of the charred firs, gyrated around him and blended into a dizzying array of swirls and splotches. Then a moment later he felt himself falling, the strings cut, the wind gone. All sound ceased except for the pounding of his heart. The magic sucked him down into a silent, seemingly bottomless vortex of quivering energy that sent sparks dancing and biting across his skin like thousands of ravenous insects.

After several interminable moments, the irritating sensation lessened and became a mere tingling on his arms and face, on his fingers that still clasped the book. But the sensation of falling continued.

The colors shifted before his eyes as the rose of Lunitari, the gold of Usha's mesmerizing eyes, and the silvery white of his Uncle Raistlin's hair chased away the hues of the birches and the burned firs. The red, gold, and white worked themselves together like yarn on a spinning wheel, blended into one by the spell that was transporting him between dimensions and to the plane named the Abyss.

He blinked, and the colors changed again, for an instant becoming a brilliant blue that swelled and receded as if it were a thing alive, a great being inhaling and exhaling. Then the blue was gone, replaced by a foglike, wispy gray that felt damp and oppressive. Gray tendrils like spidery lengths of an old man's hair, curled and wrapped about his wrists and ankles, circled his waist and tugged him ever onward toward his frightening destination. Above and below him there was only this grayness, this perpetual fog that filled his senses, this fog that carried him toward Chaos, and perhaps to his doom.

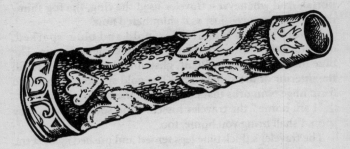

Chapter 1

The Storm Over Krynn

In Nightlund, far from the land of the Irda, a dense fog clung to a broad swatch of tall rye grass and stretched toward a lush forest canopy high overhead. The fog's milk-white tendrils writhed about the trunks of the oldest oaks, circling ever tighter.

The fog was thickest against the earth, palpable, practically obscuring the gentle rise and fall of the land. It flowed toward a clearing on the horizon, where it embraced a ring of ancient stones.

The fog never left the ring, which marked the heart of Nightlund. The sun couldn't chase it away, and the fiercest wind couldn't drive it away. It was part of the primal, unfailing magic that pulsed through the carved stones and reached beyond Krynn—to other worlds and the dimensions that lay between. The fog shrouded the ring of stones from the curious, keeping it safe for those few who knew how to use it as a portal. And whenever a traveler used the ring, the fog shimmered with energy—just as it shimmered now.

Inside the ring bits of color, gold and blue, sparked, danced, and shimmered, then faded and coalesced again. The blue intensified to a brilliant, glistening hue, growing to fill the interior of the stone circle. The gold sparks expanded to form huge twin orbs that cut through the fog like beacons.

"I am home," the traveler hissed. "And soon, Kitiara, very soon, I shall bring you home, too."

The traveler's thick blue legs tensed and pushed against the ground, propelling him above the ring and the fog, above the forest's highest canopy and into Nightlund's cloudless early evening sky.

He swept his enormous wings out to his sides and beat them almost imperceptibly, just enough to keep himself aloft. Then the traveler craned his long, scaly neck, and his cavernous nostrils quivered and sniffed and took in the heady scent of the land below.

The blue dragon was immense, a great ancient wyrm. Each of his scales was as large as a knight's shield, though they all lay sleek and gleaming against his body, making it seem as if he was made of molten sapphires. His serpentine tail trailed behind him and undulated slowly.

"Ah, Kitiara, to have finally found you!" he cried. "To have touched you after so many years!" He threw back his head and a joyous rumble started deep in his belly. The sound raced up his throat, and he opened wide his gigantic jaws. A bolt of white-hot lightning shot from between his fangs and arced high into the sky, streaking toward Lunitari. "Soon, Kitiara, we shall be together again!"

The dragon beat his wings faster now, whipping the air

into a frenzy, forcing away all of the fog except that which eternally clung to the ring. His jaws clacked open and shut rhythmically, and his tail jerked and twitched. He closed his eyes. Seemingly from out of nowhere, clouds gathered and blotted out the pale red moon. The clouds quickly turned dark and thickened, grew heavy with rain.

A bolt of lightning shot from the dragon's mouth and buried itself deep into the largest cloud. The sky reverberated in response, and a myriad of lightning strokes flashed down to tease the treetops and dance erratically toward the earth.

A bolt struck the dragon's wings, raced to his shoulder blades, then played along the spiked ridge of his back. It crackled up his neck and along the length of his silver-white horns, and it darted toward the tip of his tail and sparked across his massive haunches. Then another bolt struck him, and another. He relished its tingling touch. He was its master.

The dragon closed his eyes in ecstasy, and his roar was echoed by the storm's booming thunder. Then the rain began, splashing against the dragon's hide, against the shrouded, ancient ring of stones far below. He flew higher, until he was just below the clouds, and then unleashed his lightning breath again and again. He was illuminated by the bolts, his rain-shiny scales acting as bits of mirrors that reflected the lightning and made him glow.

He lashed his tail about like a whip. In response, the storm grew fiercer still, and the rain came in torrents, battering the trees and flattening the grass.

The deluge intensified as the dragon swooped to hover above the ring of stones, still hidden by the immutable magical fog, but not from him.

"Hear me!" he cried in a voice that sounded like a keen wind. "Khellendros, the Portal Master . . . Khellendros, the Storm Over Krynn . . . has returned! Khellendros, once called Skie by Kitiara, is home!"

The lightning and thunder rocked the ground, the rain hammered against the trees, and the sky grew black as midnight.

Chapter 2

The Abyss

The falling sensation stopped, and the fog pulled away from Palin, leaving him on a barren rock floor in what seemed to be an immense cavern. The air was hot and fetid. Dozens upon dozens of knights mounted on dragons flew high above him, skimming just below the ceiling and streaking toward something. Palin could hear the sounds of battle, the faint screams of the dying, the roar of war cries and the whoosh of dragonbreath. Chaos was somewhere ahead.

Palin's lungs burned. It was difficult to breathe here, and the warmth of the place surged upward from the rock, through the leather of his boots, and into the very soles of his feet. He swallowed hard and glanced down at his hands to make sure he still held the book. He'd been clutching it so fiercely his fingers had gone numb. The book was there, he noted with relief, as was his magical staff.

The next several moments were a blur to the young sorcerer. Like bits and snatches from a nightmare, events began unfolding around him. He spied Steel Brightblade, his cousin, on the back of a blue dragon overhead. He motioned to him, and within several heartbeats Palin was sitting behind the young Knight of Takhisis. The dragon's wings closed the distance to Chaos, taking Palin and his cousin toward the father of everything and nothing.

"He need only be wounded," Palin whispered to Steel.

Then he was on the ground again, the battle raging about him, the sea of men and dragons—of blood and flame—filling the air surrounding Chaos's giant form.

Somehow Usha was here, on the ground at the far rim of the battle, and Tasslehoff, too. Palin saw them as he lifted his eyes from the book, spotted them at the edge of his vision. The last words of the spell tumbled from his lips and his eyes locked onto Usha's. Chaos swatted a dragon overhead as if it were a gnat and the creature tumbled from the sky and struck Palin.

He felt the crushing weight of the creature's tail over his chest, felt the book fall from his fingers, and the staff slip from his grasp. A sudden wave of cold washed over him. He, the knights and dragons, and the form of Chaos that reached to the cavern's rocky ceiling were all swallowed by a sheet of impenetrable blackness.

Chapter 3

Spawn

The warm sand felt good against the pads of the creature's clawed feet as it plodded across the desert toward the north-west, angling away from the dawning sun.

Hours ago the creature had an urgent purpose, a reason for being in this seemingly endless desert. It was supposed to locate its mistress's allies—the blue dragons who laired in this hot desolation, and the lesser creatures like itself which milled about. Once gathered, they would be transported to the battle that was brewing in the Abyss.

But the creature had received those instructions many hours ago, the evening before in fact, and now it had lost touch with its mistress, the Queen of Darkness—Takhisis. It could no longer feel her powerful presence. Not knowing what to do, it continued its monotonous course and enjoyed the feel of the sand.

The creature walked upright like a man, but more resembled a dragon. Its coppery-hued scales and skin proclaimed it a kapak, one of the most dull-witted of Krynn's draconians. It had a lizardlike snout, reptilian eyes, and hunks of scraggly and matted dun-colored hair that hung from its mottled jowls. It sported leathery wings that it flapped occasionally to cool itself. The spiky ridge on its back ran from the base of its thick skull to the tip of its stubby tail, which twitched with nervous uncertainty.

What to do? it wondered. Despite its simple mind, the kapak sensed something was wrong. Perhaps the battle had begun earlier than expected and the Queen of Darkness was occupied.

Should I continue to search for the dragons? It had already discovered two empty lairs. Maybe the queen's other draconian minions, dispatched at the same time, had found all the dragons that lived in the Wastes and the lot of them had been spirited away by the queen. Or perhaps the battle was called off and the Dark Queen had neglected to inform her loyal kapak minion.

Maybe I have been forgotten, it thought. Abandoned. The kapak paused and stared across the barren expanse, which was broken only occasionally by patches of scrub grass and piles of rocks. It scratched its scaly head, then resumed its journey, deciding to abide by its orders until it again felt the touch of Takhisis's mind.

* * * * *

Khellendros continued to revel in the summer storm as he banked toward the northwest and left Nightlund behind. The rain was warm and sang to him, pattering out a soft melody

eyes. A~~~~~~~~~~~~~
again be joined ~~~~~~

"I made a promise ~~~~~
miles passed beneath his enor~~~~~
you safe. But I failed you, and your bo~~~~
appeared from Ansalon, though I know it i~~~~
bers me."

The dragon remembered, too. He remembered what it wa~
like to be teamed with the only human whom he believed
possessed the heart of a dragon. Ambitious and crafty,
Kitiara had led him on successful strikes and rode him into
one glorious battle after another. Together, there was nothing
they would not dare to do and no force that could stand up
to them.

Khellendros felt complete in those long-ago years, always
purposeful and always content in the company of his trusted,
calculating partner. He remembered the overwhelming exhil-
aration they shared in the midst of a fight, remembered the
dizzying sense of victory afterward.

And he remembered the frustration of not being able to
save Kitiara one rare day when she was alone and far from his
side. Even across the miles, he had felt her body die, had felt
the instant of her death as if an incredible blow had been
landed against his own stomach. He had flown to her then
and seen the crumpled, weak human shell that once housed
her remarkable mind. And through a haze of anger and tears
he had watched her spirit slip free and rise above its useless
shell. Her spirit still lived!

Khellendros had vowed to snare her essence and find
another shell—one that he would guard more carefully—for
his partner. The dragon had chased Kitiara's spirit above
Ansalon's plains and valleys, losing touch with it from time to

The Dawning of a New Age

...ndros
to ... turned
slippe... s spirit had
gateway... ess through the
ancient po... gh the mystical,
... the hazy dimensions
where faeries ... s drift.

For what seem... him, he searched. In that
time he grew, beco... ncient wyrm of immense pro-
portions and awesom...wer. He memorized the foggy pas-
sages and slipstreams between realms and planes, discovered
races unknown to Krynn, and grasped enchantments long
forgotten by mortals. When he believed there was nowhere
else for him to search, no dusky dimension left to be explored, he had stumbled upon The Gray.

It was a land without land, a misty domain filled with
swirling gray vapors and teeming with spirits. Few creatures
of any substance seemed to dwell there—save Khellendros
the Portal Master. The great blue dragon hadn't intended to
stay there very long, but he had sensed something precious
and familiar to him, a hint of Kitiara. So he continued to
search, perhaps for another century. Time passed differently
beyond the portals, speeding by as it crawled on Krynn, and

the only way the dragon knew this was his increasing growth rate. But time was irrelevant to Khellendros—only Kitiara and mending his shattered pledge mattered.

Finally he had found her, touching her spirit briefly, as if his mind were a hand caressing a loved one's cheek. She had acknowledged his presence, had asked him to stay at her side in The Gray that had become her home. "Soon we shall be together. Always," he had whispered. Then he had departed to return through the portal to Krynn.

"We shall be partners again," Khellendros said as he drew his thoughts back to the present and watched his shadow pass over the twisting Vingaard River. "I shall find suitable flesh for your spirit."

The expansive grasslands of Hinterlund spread out below him, the wind from his wings rippling the grass. A large herd of deer stopped grazing and glanced up. Panicked at the sight of the dragon, they bolted in a dozen different directions. Khellendros was hungry, and the herd was tempting, but filling his belly would have to wait. First, he would tend to Kitiara's new form.

During his trip through the portals he had learned a powerful enchantment that would allow him to displace the spirit from a body and put a different one inside. He would choose the body of a warrior, young and healthy, well-muscled and satisfying to the eye—something Kitiara would be happy with.

An elf warrior, Khellendros decided. Elves lived much longer than humans and the other races of Krynn, and the dragon, virtually immortal himself, wanted a body for Kitiara that would weather the decades. When the elven form finally grew feeble and old, he would get her another. He would not let her die again.

The morning and Hinterlund dissolved behind him, with no sign of elves anywhere. The desolate stretches of the Northern Wastes came into view. Waves of blessed afternoon heat rose up from the ground and stroked the underside of his wings. He loved the pulsing warmth of the Wastes' desert, and he would have enjoyed stretching out on the sand and letting the sun caress his scales. But he hadn't the time to squander on personal pleasures, and he knew there were no elves in the Wastes.

Though elves come and go from Palanthas, he mused. I need only wait outside the city until I see an acceptable one. Perhaps I shall snare a few and experiment.

He angled his great form toward the west. The country of Palanthas lay beyond the desert, and the city of Palanthas sat on the far coast, nestled between a harbor on the Turbidus Ocean and a range of mountains. It would not take him too long to get there, probably no more than three days if he continued to push himself. Or perhaps he could find another portal and get there faster.

He would eat and rest after he found a few elves. Then he would—

Khellendros's thoughts were interrupted by something he spied on the sand far below. The figure jumped and glided, flapped its small wings and waved its arms to get the dragon's attention.

Khellendros focused his keen eyes on the creature. A witless kapak. What could it want? The blue dragon soared past the beckoning creature, but questions about the draconian intruded on his thoughts. Why would it dare bother me? Could it be important? Maybe I should . . . .

Curiosity finally overcoming him, he folded his wings close to his side, reversed his course, and dropped to the desert floor. One brief interruption would not matter. He welcomed the chance to feel the hot sand—if only for a few moments.

The kapak did not fear the dragon. All draconians respected dragons, were in awe of them and their wondrous abilities. The kapak was especially impressed by Khellendros's size. The moment Khellendros landed, the draconian rushed toward him, waving its arms about to ward off the shower of sand stirred up from the blue's massive wings. It started chattering.

"Slower," Khellendros ordered.

"The Dark Queen," the kapak hoarsely barked. Its voice was scratchy, its mouth and throat dry from being in the Wastes for so long. "My mistress, *our* mistress, Takhisis, wants the dragons to gather."

Khellendros raised his massive brow in an unspoken question.

The kapak pursed its cracked lips and struggled to remember its orders. "Here," it said finally. "Takhisis wants the blue dragons to gather here . . . in the desert. Draconians, too, if I find any. Gather them together in the desert, the Dark Queen said. In the desert—"

"Why?" Khellendros interrupted before the kapak could continue.

"A battle in the Abyss," it huffed. "Takhisis wants the blue dragons to gather here in the desert. Others are gathering elsewhere. She will call us all to the Abyss. There will be a glorious battle."

Khellendros growled, and the kapak stepped back. "I haven't the time for battles," the dragon spat. He raised his lips in a sneer, and lightning flickered across his teeth.

"But Takhisis . . ."

Khellendros closed his eyes, concentrated, and stretched his thoughts outward in an effort to touch the Queen of Darkness's mind, to verify what the fool draconian was saying. The great blue pictured his multiheaded dragon goddess as clearly as if she were before him, but he could not establish contact with her. He surmised that his goddess was preoccupied with divine concerns, and he suspected the kapak didn't know what it was blathering about. A battle in the Abyss? Unlikely. If there was one, the all-powerful dragon goddess would not need help. What was more likely was that the heat had driven the simple kapak mad. But its body is in good condition. The blue dragon scrutinized the kapak.

"Takhisis wants the blue dragons to gather in the desert," it repeated.

The kapak's body had a hint of magic about it—and the essence of a dragon. Suitable for a woman with the heart of a dragon, Khellendros mused. More suitable than the body of an elf.

"There will be a battle in the Abyss," the kapak droned, unaware that the dragon was scarcely listening. "Takhisis says the Irda broke the Graygem and released Chaos. The all-father is angry, wants to destroy Krynn. Everyone must fight Chaos in the Abyss, Takhisis says."

Khellendros's mind buzzed with thoughts. Draconians are immune to human diseases. They live a thousand years. Kitiara would approve. The great blue dragon knew that the kapak, and all other draconians, were created by the Queen of Darkness to serve as her minions—messengers, spies, assassins, soldiers.

From the eggs of good dragons she fashioned these sterile draconian forms and encased the essence of tanar'ri, evil spirits of the Abyss, inside them. This kapak came from the egg of a copper dragon. It was a superior form.

Khellendros edged closer until his huge snout was inches from the kapak. He snaked a paw forward, and his claws closed gingerly about the surprised draconian.

"What?" it snapped.

"You're coming with me," Khellendros replied.

"To the Abyss?"

"To my lair."

"But Takhisis! Chaos! No!" With the kapak's last word it spit a gob of saliva on the dragon's claw and began struggling.

Venomous and caustic, the liquid hissed and popped. With a growl, Khellendros released the kapak and thrust his paw into the sand to soothe the annoying sensation.

The kapak stepped back and stared, finally realizing that the dragon was not going to follow its precious instructions. It whirled and dashed across the sand, intending to tell Takhisis, whenever she touched his mind, that this insolent blue dragon had disobeyed her. The draconian madly flapped its wings and leapt into the air, and glided about a dozen feet before it landed on the sand and leapt upward again, still flapping furiously.

A rumble started in Khellendros's belly as he watched the draconian try to flee. Only one type of draconian could truly fly, he knew, those made from the eggs of silver dragons. The kapak's attempts at flight were pitiful, laughable.

But you shall be able to fly, Kitiara, the blue dragon thought, as the rumble raced up his throat and he unfurled his wings. Khellendros rose from the sand as he opened his maw, and the rumble erupted as a lightning bolt that struck the ground in front of the fleeing kapak.

The startled draconian twisted to the right and pumped its legs harder, sending a shower of sand behind its stubby tail.

Another bolt landed several yards in front of it, spewing sand everywhere as the desert sky boomed with thunder. The kapak shuddered as a bolt landed behind it. The creature cringed and swung again to the right, its feet churning over the ground. But it was instantly overtaken by Khellendros's shadow, and skidding to a stop, looked up to see the blue dragon's belly.

Khellendros's claw reached down, snatched the kapak by a leathery wing, and climbed high into the sky. The dragon sped to the north with its struggling, spitting prize, uninterested in its banter about the Abyss and concentrating instead on the sound of the wind whistling merrily about his blue wings.

When night brought its cooling touch to the desert, and the stars began to wink into view, Khellendros descended toward the base of a slight rocky ridge. There was a single moon in the sky, a large pale one. It was unlike any of the three moons that had revolved around Krynn since the world's creation—the red Lunitari, the white Solinari, and the black Nuitari. But the dragon was thinking only of Kitiara and the draconian in its grasp, and the pale moon went unnoticed.

There was little fight left in the kapak, so the blue dragon tossed it on the sand and set about digging near a recess in the ridge. His long claws stabbed into the desert floor and ripped upward, pulling with them dirt, sand, and rocks. The kapak cowered, afraid the blue dragon meant to bury it alive. But as the night grew older, the hole grew bigger. The moon rose higher and its light exposed an immense cavern.

Not long after, dawn found the Northern Wastes, but the shadow created by the ridge effectively hid the entrance to the dragon's reclaimed lair. Khellendros quickly shoved the kapak toward the opening and followed it inside.

"The Dark Queen—" the draconian started to say. Its voice was soft and cracked after each word, its leathery lips swollen from lack of moisture.

"Created you," Khellendros finished, as he looked about his home. The blue dragon was pleased that nothing had been disturbed while he was gone, that no other dragon had discovered the huge underground cave and seized it along with its vast treasures. Piles of coins and gems feebly flickered and sparkled in the faint light that spilled in from the entrance. His hoard, covered by a faint layer of sand and dust, was intact, and soon he would share it with Kitiara.

"Takhisis—"

"Gave you a weak mind," the blue dragon interrupted. "But she gave you a fine, strong body, and I shall use it well."

The kapak trembled. Its lips formed pleas, but no sound came out, and its heart beat wildly in its chest. A dragon threatening one of Takhisis's minions? It isn't right, the kapak's mind screamed. The creature watched in horror as Khellendros settled himself nearby. With a sharp talon, the blue dragon began to etch a pattern into the stone, his gaze drifting between his work and his kapak prisoner.

The minutes stretched by until finally Khellendros was finished, and he crooked a claw toward the draconian, beckoning it. Numbly, the kapak complied, shuffling forward until it stood in the center of the design.

"I learned spells," Khellendros hissed, talking to himself more than to the draconian. "I learned ancient enchantments that Krynn's pathetic human sorcerers would barter all they own for." The dragon extended a talon until it touched the kapak's breastbone. The draconian cringed and inhaled sharply as it was dragged downward. Blood and coppery scales spilled on the stone floor. "I learned how to displace minds."

As Khellendros withdrew the talon, the draconian clutched at its wounded chest, forced itself not to cry out and reveal pain and weakness. The dragon began mumbling words that were foreign, rich and deep. They filled the underground cavern and added to the kapak's fear. The blue dragon's sonorous voice quickened, and he looked straight into the draconian's eyes as the spell ended.

The kapak's resolve melted into a single, piercing scream. It dropped to its knees, and threw its clawed hands up to the sides of its throbbing head. Its tail lashed madly about, and the muscles along its legs and arms jumped and quivered. A thin sheen of sweat formed over its scaly hide.

Khellendros waited, heedless of his captive's agony, watching as the kapak fell forward. It gasped for air, twitched wildly, and retched. After several long moments, its writhing movements slowed, then stopped. Its chest heaving, it slowly picked itself up off the floor and fearfully regarded the dragon.

"Takhisis—"

"No!" Khellendros cried. He batted at the kapak, sending it careening into the cavern's wall. The thing's mind should have been gone, its spirit displaced. It should have been unable to think or speak. The draconian should have been nothing more than an empty husk, immobile, but living. It should've been awaiting Kitiara's essence. "Takhisis's magic is too strong!"

The dragon crawled forward as a lone tear of frustration spilled from his eye. The drop rolled down his azure cheek and dripped onto the diagram, mingling with the kapak's blood and scales. Khellendros stared at the etching as it began to spark and shimmer with blue and pale gold.

"But my magic is strong, too," the blue dragon said. "Perhaps a cloning enchantment might work." Again he started mumbling, old words from another spell learned from his portal-hopping. As his voice increased in intensity, the shimmering brightened. The glow expanded and formed a column of scintillating copper and blue lights. It sputtered and sparked, then a shard of bright blue light flew from the column and struck the kapak. The draconian screamed again.

Khellendros concentrated on the column, which had begun to take on a different shape. Through the gleam of lights the dragon could see muscular limbs, a thick chest and a dragonlike head taking shape. As the lights faded, wings sprouted from the creature's back, and a long tail grew to the floor. The creature vaguely resembled the kapak, but was sleeker, with dark blue scales the color of the sea at sunset. Its eyes were golden, like the blue dragon's, and a spiked ridge ran from the crest of its high forehead to the tip of its tail. Miniature lightning bolts crackled about the thing's claws, and its breath sounded like soft rain.

"My tear," Khellendros said in a hushed tone. "It altered the spell, created something *different*."

"Master," the blue creation croaked.

The dragon's eyes grew wide and he cast his glance between the cowering kapak and the new creature. The kapak, huddled like a frightened child, glanced at the dragon, then lowered its gaze.

"Spawn of Khellendros," the dragon pronounced. He decided to call the creature a khellspawn. He was tremendously pleased with himself. His ego soared.

Then it crashed with the realization that naming the creature after himself might give away his secret prematurely. "For now, I shall just call you . . . spawn." He grimaced at the meager word and looked at his creation, which resembled him so in beauty and bearing. He was swept up in his own magnificence and the words rushed from his sizeable maw, "Perhaps I shall call you blue spawn." He figured he deserved that much credit, at least.

"Master," the spawn said again. The word was stronger this time. The creature balled its fists, rotated its reptilian head, and crouched to test its rippling leg muscles. Its wings flapped slightly, disturbing the faint layer of sand and dust in the cavern and rising a few inches above the stone floor.

I could not displace the mind of the kapak because Takhisis's magic is too strong, Khellendros mused. But perhaps I could displace the mind of the spawn. Kitiara's spirit would have an exquisite form then.

"Master?" a pained expression crossed the spawn's scaly face. The creature's eyes dulled, and its form grew transparent. Its body quavered and rippled, like waves of heat above hot desert sand. Then it disappeared, leaving behind a faint blue glow that folded in about itself and extinguished.

Khellendros's angry roar rocked the cavern. "I shall not be defeated!" the great dragon spat. He rose on his haunches until his head grazed the stony roof.

The kapak clung to the shadows and crept away from Khellendros, edging toward the exit from the lair.

"I shall succeed!" the blue dragon bellowed as a massive

paw shot forward and trapped the kapak. "I shall experiment with you again—and again."

* * * * *

Many months later Khellendros was well-rested, sated, and pleased. A quartet of blue spawn stood deep in his lair, and he had spent the past few hours admiring them.

The kapak that helped fuel their creation lay on the cavern floor, exhausted and sore. Its thirst had been quenched, and it, too, had recently eaten. The blue dragon was making sure it stayed reasonably healthy so he could use it again.

Khellendros knew his blue spawn, his children, were more powerful than the kapak, possibly more powerful than even the auraks—the greatest of the Dark Queen's draconians. It had taken the ancient spell coupled with the kapak's blood and scales, his own tears, and four humans gathered from a nomadic barbarian tribe north of his lair. The bodies gave substance to the spawn, kept the forms from fading. The human minds were blended with the kapak's to create a new creature, one that was thoroughly and magically loyal to Khellendros.

"One of you shall have the honor of housing Kitiara," the blue dragon whispered. He padded from his lair, spread his wings, and headed toward Nightlund.

Behind him and forgotten, the kapak struggled to its clawed feet. For several long moments it studied the blue-scaled spawn. They returned its stare, but said nothing, did nothing. Khellendros had not given them any orders, had not told them they could speak. Miniature lightning bolts crackled about their sharp black claws, and their eyes seemed to glow like smoldering embers.

They are beautiful, the kapak thought. It was angry and astonished that a bit of its own mind, and some of its scales, kindled the magic that birthed them. Birth. The word hung in its dense head.

"Auraks should know," it said, referring to its brother draconians that were made from the corrupted eggs of gold dragons. "They should know about this. And the sivaks." The kapak knew that the auraks and the sivaks were the smartest and most cunning of the draconians. Perhaps they could use this magic to make draconians procreate, to make them no longer sterile. Perhaps they would reward the kapak for this information.

The scheming kapak stumbled from Khellendros's lair, a self-appointed mission powering its uneven steps.

* * * * *

The miles melted beneath Khellendros's wings. It was dark when he reached Nightlund, and the pale moon that hung in the clear sky overhead illuminated a scene that was the same—yet different—than what he had observed many months ago. The great blue dragon skimmed over the tops of the old trees and dropped toward the ground. He glided to a stop near a small hillock, and stared at the circle of stones that sat there. The fog was gone, the ancient stones visible to anyone.

Khellendros was puzzled, but he strode forward, his footfalls sounding like muffled thunder. His body too large to fit between the stones, he pushed off with his legs and landed in their center. Catlike, he wrapped his tail about his haunches.

He closed his eyes and concentrated, pictured the misty realm of The Gray, thought about Kitiara. Khellendros saw himself floating through the haze, moving closer to his once-partner, calling out to her, being reunited, telling her about his blue spawn and her new body. But when he opened his eyes he was still inside the ring.

"No!" The blue dragon's scream cut across the Nightlund countryside. A deep sound raced up his throat and formed a

25

bolt of lightning that shot out from his mouth and sped far into the sky.

Khellendros slammed his eyes shut, concentrating again. He repeated the spell over and over in his head, pictured himself moving beyond Krynn, to other dimensions. Again nothing happened.

In anger, he thrashed his tail about, striking one of the stones and toppling it. "The magic!" he hissed. "The magic does not come! The portal does not open!"

He breathed another bolt of lighting, striking a stone and sending it into a shower of pebbles that harmlessly bounced off his thick hide. Then he called clouds to form, heavy black ones that quickly filled the sky and yielded a terrible storm to match his raging temper. The wind picked up and was soon howling. Rain smacked into the earth, lightning flashed, and thunder rocked the landscape.

"Another portal," he hissed over the storm's wailing. "I shall fly to another portal." His legs tensed, ready to push him into the sky.

"Another portal will not work."

The voice sounded hollow, little more than a whisper, but it froze the great dragon in place. He cast his massive head about, looking for the speaker who would dare intrude on his portal. His keen eyes saw nothing but the rain, the storm-flattened grass, and the ancient stones.

"The magic is gone from this portal, from all of the portals."

"Who are you?" the dragon boomed in a voice that could be heard above the thunder.

"No one of consequence," the voice replied.

"*How* do you know this?"

"I know there is little magic left on Krynn."

"Reveal yourself!" Khellendros snapped, as his tail lashed out again and knocked over two more stones.

"Careful!" the speaker cautioned, at last showing himself.

One of the ancient stones pulled back from the circle, shimmered dully, shrank, and, like clay being worked by a skilled potter, formed itself into a small, humanlike image. The man was little more than a foot tall, naked and gray. He had no ears, only tiny holes on the sides of his head, and his eyes were large and black, without pupils. His fingers were reed thin and pointed, like his small teeth.

The dragon moved forward, raised a paw, and drove it down to squash the little man. But the speaker was fast. He darted to the side, clung to one of the stones, and made "*tsk-tsk*" sounds.

"Killing me will not make the portals work."

"What are you?" Khellendros boomed.

"A huldrefolk," the man replied.

"A faerie," the blue dragon hissed, his eyes narrowing.

"You know of us?"

Khellendros lowered his head until his nose was mere inches from the huldrefolk's small form. "One of Krynn's lost races," the dragon intoned flatly. "A shapeshifter, a master of elements. A master of earth?"

The gray man nodded his bald head.

"You live in The Gray."

"Or wherever suits my tastes. *Suited*," he quickly corrected himself.

"I want to access The Gray," Khellendros growled.

"As do I," the huldrefolk said. "I prefer it to other realms. But the magic is gone from this world. The battle in the Abyss saw to that."

"The Abyss?" Khellendros's golden eyes grew wide. The kapak had mentioned a battle in the Abyss, but the dragon had paid no attention to the creature and its ramblings.

"Weren't you there?" the huldrefolk began. "I thought all the dragons were in the Abyss, summoned by Takhisis."

"I was . . . elsewhere." The blue dragon's words were iced with menace. "What happened to provoke such a battle?"

"The Graygem—the stone that held the essence of Chaos, the all-father—was shattered. He was released, and he was furious he'd been imprisoned for so many centuries. He threatened to destroy Krynn as punishment to his children, who had trapped him in the gem. So his children, the lesser gods, joined together to fight him. The dragons helped, as well as many humans—plus elves, kender, and the like."

"Takhisis?"

"She's gone," the small man said.

"How could she abandon her children, especially if they fought at her behest?"

"In the end all the gods abandoned their children. Chaos could not be truly bested, though somehow his essence was captured again in the Graygem. The lesser gods vowed to leave Krynn if Chaos would promise not to destroy it. And when he agreed, they left, taking the three moons and magic with them. There's only one moon now."

Khellendros stared up at the large orb so unlike the other moons. "All the magic is gone?"

The huldrefolk shrugged. "The magic that powers the portals—that's gone. The magic sorcerers call on to cast their spells is gone too. There's a little magic left here and there in the earth, in old weapons and baubles, and in creatures like you and me," he continued. "But that's all. They call this the Age of Mortals, but I call it the Age of Despair."

Khellendros stared beyond the huldrefolk, through the sheets of rain that continued to drive against the ground. "Magical items still have power?"

The huldrefolk nodded.

"The tower in Palanthas," the dragon said. "There are magical items stored there, lots of them. Kitiara told me about them once, and about a portal below the tower that leads to the Abyss."

"The fight in the Abyss is over," the small man interrupted. "You missed it, remember? Which was probably a good thing, because you might have died. At least half the dragons who fought are dead. The men who fought there are dead or gone. And there's nothing you could do there now except pick over the bones."

Khellendros seemed not to hear him. "I shall use the magical items in the tower to open the portal, and from the Abyss I can access The Gray. I shall yet succeed and save Kitiara."

"Aren't you listening to me?" the gray man persisted. "The gods are gone. The world is different. Doesn't any of this matter to you?"

Only Kitiara matters, Khellendros thought. He tensed his legs, pushed off from the ground, and joined the terrible storm.

Chapter 4

The Vision

Palin awoke in a sweat, the sheets drenched and his long auburn hair plastered to the sides of his face. His chest heaved, and he took in great gulps of air trying to calm himself.

Usha stirred next to him. He tried to get out of bed without waking her, but he didn't succeed.

"What's wrong?" she whispered. She sat up and ran her fingers across Palin's forehead. "You've a fever! You've had that dream again."

"Yes," he replied softly. "But this time it was worse than before." His feet stretched to the cold stone floor, and he stood and padded to the window. He pulled back the heavy curtain and peered toward the east, where the sun was just starting to show itself. "This time I'm convinced it's more than a dream."

Usha shuddered and climbed out of bed, drawing a silk robe about her. She glided toward him and rested her head on his bare shoulder. "It was the blue dragon?"

He nodded. "I saw him flying toward Palanthas again. This time he reached the city." He turned toward her, wrapped his arms around her slight frame, and bent his head down and brushed his lips over her cheek. He stared into her golden eyes and combed his fingers through her disheveled silvery hair. The strands caught the first rays of the sun and glimmered. Even just roused from sleep, she was beautiful. "I think you've married a madman, Usha."

She hugged him tightly. "I think I married a wonderful man," she returned. "And I think, husband, you might have inherited your Uncle Raistlin's ability to see the future."

They were married less than a month ago, after Usha had convinced Palin she was no relation to Raistlin, though she had golden eyes and silvery white hair. Raistlin had not been seen for some time. The two had taken up residence in Solace, though Palin visited the Tower of Wayreth frequently.

Palin edged away from her. His intense green eyes peered out the window and over the Solamnian countryside. The tower sat just outside the city of Solanthus now, as it had for several weeks. Tomorrow it might be somewhere else. The tower never stayed in one spot too long, and it sometimes moved at Palin's behest. The tower's ability to manipulate space was one of the enchantments that remained with Krynn despite the disappearance of the gods of magic. Palin had learned that things imbued with magic before the war against Chaos, retained their magic.

"Let's see if I can give this dream . . . this premonition," he corrected himself, "a little more substance." He walked over to a large oak bureau in one corner of the room, retrieved a pewter hand mirror from the top drawer, and returned to

Usha's side. Turning his back to the window, he drew his concentration to a spot in the center of the mirror's glassy surface as she intently leaned forward, her elbows resting on the sill.

There was a flash of light as the sun struck the mirror, and then the air shimmered and sparkled and a large, pale green oval frame materialized within the glass. Inside the frame, a picture took shape. At first the hues ran together like watercolors, but then the image sharpened and came into lifelike focus. The sun was setting on the Palanthas harbor, and a large bird was skimming across the top of the gentle waves, angling itself toward the western shoreline.

The young sorcerer cringed as he watched the creature come closer, revealing itself as a dragon. He heard Usha gasp behind him, felt her smooth fingertips on his back. Palin concentrated on the beast's visage. It was an immense blue, a male with long white horns and bright golden eyes. It was the one that had been filling his dreams for the past three nights, and it was one he hadn't seen in the Abyss during the war against Chaos. Though there had been so much going on, so many dragons filling the air during that fight, he would have remembered a dragon that big. It was larger than any who fought there.

"What's the dragon want with Palanthas?" Usha said in a hushed tone.

They watched the blue dragon fade to a shadow that glided silently over the city like a hawk.

"The dragon must want something *in* Palanthas," Palin whispered.

The shadow of the dragon banked toward a wraithlike view of the city's Great Library. Pulling its wings close to its side and descending heavily to the roof, the dragon broke through the tiles and disappeared. Palin directed his attention to the hole the beast had created, peered through the dust and broken masonry.

The view shifted to accommodate him, revealing the

building's interior. The dragon sat atop the crushed and bloody bodies of monks. With his huge claws, he was tearing down shelf upon shelf, retrieving rare manuals here and there. It was evident the blue dragon was after specific tomes, magical ones. Finished with his grim work, the dragon clutched his prizes in a claw, departed the ruins, and soared into the sky. His course took him toward a tower.

"The Tower of High Sorcery," Usha murmured.

Palin's voice grew weaker, and his lanky frame shuddered.

The dragon paid no heed to the Shoikan Grove that surrounded the Tower of High Sorcery and kept most at bay. Poised above the tower, he appeared to enact some sort of spell before he lighted agilely atop the tall building. With his rear claws, the beast started tearing at the tower. Pale stones the color of parchment flew like chunks of dirt scattered by a digging beast. The rocks rained down on the city, crushing the curious who'd come out of their homes and businesses to see what was happening.

When the image of the tower was reduced to rubble, the dragon thrust his claws into the chambers below and began retrieving chests and coffers filled with magical items, scrolls saturated with powerful arcane spells, and more. Then the dragon's golden eyes fixed on the portal to the Abyss.

"No!" Palin hoarsely barked. "I must stop him."

The wavering image dissipated, leaving the reflection of Palin's ashen face and the cloudless morning sky in its place.

"But what can you do?" Usha tugged her husband away from the window and drew the curtain. "What can you do against a dragon that size?"

"I don't know." He cupped her chin. "But I have to do something—and soon. If my dream is in truth a vision, a glimpse into the future, the dragon could mean to strike soon, perhaps today at sunset. I can't let him kill those people. And I can't let him claim the tower's magic and access the portal."

"There's nothing in the Abyss but the bodies of dragons and rubble," Usha said. "What could the dragon want there?"

"It doesn't matter," Palin replied. "To get there, the dragon would have to ruin the tower and the precious magic inside." He moved toward the end of the bed, where his white robe lay. Quickly donning it, he glanced back at his wife. "I've got a contact in Palanthas. I can alert him, share my dream. He can do something. He can contact someone in the Tower of High Sorcery."

"I thought with Chaos and the gods gone, we were safe," Usha whispered. "I thought we'd finally know peace."

Chapter 5

The Master of the Tower

Deep in the Tower of High Sorcery in Palanthas, a dark-clad man separated himself from the shadows. He stood before a moisture-slick wall from which jutted a lone, guttering torch. The flickering light danced over his black robe—a garment hanging in thick folds that looked much too large for his slight frame.

"You call to me," he said in a voice that was little more than a whisper. "You rouse me from my rest." He sighed, and a train of heavy fabric trailed on the floor behind him as he lost himself once more in the darkness. His course took him up a winding stone staircase, chipped and crumbling from age. He didn't need light to see where he was going. He knew every musty corner, expansive room, and secret corridor of the ancient tower by heart. He ran his fingertips along the cool stone walls that were covered with ornamental weapons and shields and portraits of old, long-dead wizards. He didn't need to see the faces in the portraits, either. He knew the sorcerers when they breathed and studied in this tower, and he preferred his memories to the painted canvas—they did his friends more justice.

His measured steps took him ever higher, until he emerged in a room filled with bright morning sunlight that spilled in from several evenly-spaced windows. He glided toward the one overlooking the palace in the center of the sprawling city. In the distance was the Bay of Branchala, its brilliant blue-green waters beckoning invitingly. To the north was the massive Library of Ages, the grandest library on all of Krynn, and to the south was the Temple of Paladine. He idly wondered whether the latter would receive any more visitors now that the gods had abandoned the world.

He gazed at the city, at the many buildings that were in ruins—damaged by the battle against Chaos, by the energy and magic that had expanded beyond the Abyss. It looked to the watcher as if the battle had been fought here. No doubt, he suspected, other cities likewise had felt the repercussions of the war, their buildings and citizens scarred.

"What do you want?" he said to the air. He felt a soft breeze wash over his skin, and looked upon the translucent visage of a young man's face.

"To warn you," the image replied. "To share a dream."

The black-cloaked sorcerer closed his eyes, and his mind relived Palin's vision, blue scales and golden eyes filling his senses. After several long moments the haze vanished, the wispy cloud disappeared, and the sorcerer rushed away from the window. He hurried down the twisting stairs, stopping on each level to retrieve a few priceless baubles and magical trinkets.

The sorcerer worked diligently for many hours, collecting scrolls, magical weapons and armor, crystal balls and the like. All the while he mulled over the dragon from Palin's dream and wondered why it wanted access to the Abyss.

All of the Tower of High Sorcery's magic wouldn't necessarily allow him to open the portal. Such an act would devastate the city, flatten all the buildings within at least a mile of the tower. Hundreds could be killed. Worse could happen if the dragon first turned the power of the magical items loose on Palanthas before using them to open the portal.

The battle with Chaos was over. Only death hovered in the Abyss now. What could the dragon want there, hope to accomplish there? Palin had told the sorcerer it didn't matter. But it did, the sorcerer knew. He vowed to consider the matter later—after the magic was saved.

Not used to strenuous physical labor, the sorcerer was nearly exhausted by the time he had an impressive pile of objects gathered in one place deep below ground. His chest heaved as he regarded the hoard that twinkled in the torchlight.

"It is not everything," he whispered, brushing a strand of sweat-soaked hair away from his eyes. "But it is the best and the most powerful, and it will have to do." His slight frame shuddered and he leaned against the damp stone wall. "Old friend," he said to the stone. "I shall miss you. We've . . . what's that?" He cocked his head, ran his fingers along a seam between the bricks. "The dragon. He's coming."

He reached into the deep folds of his robe and produced a staff of polished mahogany. It was topped by a bronze dragon claw clutching a faceted crystal and fairly pulsed with energy. He traced his fingertips over the staff's smooth surface, then raised it high before twice driving its end down against the stone floor.

A blinding blue flash filled the underground chamber. As the glow receded, the guttering torch illuminated the crumpled form of the sorcerer. The horde of arcane treasure was gone. "Safe," the man whispered. His breathing was labored, and he used the staff for support as he slowly rose.

He struggled up the steps, his robes tangling his feet and causing him to falter. His trembling fingers brushed against the cool stones in a gesture of farewell.

"We have been together so long, you and I," he whispered to the walls.

Outside, the first rays of the setting sun were touching the rooftops of the city and the trees in the Shoikan Grove. The guardians in the grove let him pass unchallenged. "Flee," he whispered to them as he made his way to the gate and out onto the bustling city streets. "Flee or die."

"Flee!" he called to the people, his voice rising.

At first the passersby ignored him, prattling amongst themselves about their purchases or discussing what they would cook for dinner. A few hovered outside the door to an inn, ogling a menu board in the window. But those nearest the sorcerer saw him lift the staff high into the air. They heard him speak words they couldn't understand, and they felt a tremor beneath their feet.

"Run!" someone called.

The people moved back like a wave receding from the sand, leaving the dark-clad man standing alone before the tower. But few ran so far away that they couldn't watch what was transpiring, their curiosity overcoming their common sense. Most took cover inside buildings, their faces pressed against the windows. Some huddled in doorways or under awnings.

His fist clenched the staff in a death grip and the words flowed furiously from his lips. His eyes glowed with an intense light, and the tower shuddered like a pained old man.

The sorcerer sobbed. His breath came in uneven rasps and tears welled up in his eyes. "Fall," he urged. "Please, fall."

Somewhere behind him he heard the loud chatter of a

Palanthas group that had refused to take shelter.

"What's he doing?" a woman cried.

"It's magic!" a man barked.

"But magic is dead!" another called.

"It must be the staff!" retorted the man.

"Flee!" the sorcerer called to them. He drove the staff down into the ground repeatedly. "Down!" he shouted, "down!" And, as if in response, the cobblestones shook beneath his knees, and the tower quaked and groaned.

Screams erupted from behind the sorcerer. He barely heard the sound of retreating footsteps. The gawkers were no longer brave enough to watch. Then he heard nothing but the moaning of the tower as it started to fall. He looked up to see cracks appear in the sky above the tower; its invisible barrier was shattering like an egg. Shards of glass from the tower's windows burst into the air and pelted the street below.

A spiderweb-fine crack appeared in the cobblestones between the sorcerer's knees. It spread, racing toward Shoikan Grove and through the open gate. The crack began to widen. The ground vibrated, and the sorcerer watched through a haze of tears as stones from the grove's wall were pitched into the still-widening fissure. The trees of the grove heaved and toppled into the crevice. The grass flowed into the crack like water, taking with it the wildflowers and berry bushes the sorcerer had once so carefully tended.

Pops and hisses cut through the cacophony, evidence that the tower's magical wards and guards were being simultaneously released and obliterated by the quake.

The sorcerer grabbed his side, screaming. The sound was echoed by the tower as it collapsed upon itself. The blood-red minarets fell inward first, swallowed whole as the black marble ruins began to melt down to the ground.

Glass shattered from somewhere behind him, and he heard a child wail. An awning flapped and tore free from a building facade, flying past him to disappear into the black, molten mass.

He tried to stand, but the vibrating ground threw him onto his back. Looking up at the dust-heavy sky, he saw a shape that he could barely make out.

A large bird? No. The dragon.

The sorcerer rolled onto his stomach. Digging his thin fingers into the cracks between the cobblestones, he pulled himself along, away from the inward pull of the tower.

A great boom rocked Palanthas then, signaling the end of the Tower of High Sorcery. The reverberations continued to damage the building facades, shaking free balconies, chimneys, and roof tiles.

The sorcerer reached the side of a building and turned to see the large crevice in the ground seal itself, burying the remnants of the grove. His eyes followed the line of the fissure as it closed, racing toward the tower. But the line led his eyes only to a round spot of mirrorlike obsidian material. That was all that remained of the Tower of High Sorcery.

Coughs racked his body as he tried to steady himself. For an instant he wondered if the damage he had unleashed was worse than what the dragon would have done. But he knew otherwise. No one had died, that he was sure of. Not only was the tower's magic beyond the dragon's grasp now, but the contents of the Great Library had also disappeared. At the moment of the tower's demise, the books simultaneously departed.

He looked at the flat, shiny black spot and thought of all it contained, the remnants of the tower and the paintings of the old wizards who had once studied there and walked by the sorcerer's side.

"Goodbye," the sorcerer whispered to the ruins as he huddled against the building's cold stone wall.

* * * * *

In the sky above Palanthas, Khellendros raged. The tower was destroyed and its remains buried. His path to the Abyss was lost.

"Kitiara!" he cried.

Lightning streaked the sky and darted down to Palanthas's cobblestones, shattering the sidewalk in front of an inn where a crowd huddled. Dark clouds gathered to blot out the setting sun, and a fierce storm began. Frightened citizens barred their doors as the rain started. It was soft at first, but its force quickly grew until the rain was pummeling the city. It washed away the dust and dirt from the magical earthquake and mingled with the sorcerer's tears.

Chapter 6

The Coming of Malystryx

The warrior stood on a peak overlooking Palanthas and watched Khellendros bank away from the city. He was drenched by the blue dragon's storm.

"I thought he was the one. Pity."

The warrior looked vaguely like a man, but he was solid black and featureless, as if cut from a piece of wet slate or obsidian. His glowing, ruby eyes followed the retreating form of the dragon until it was a speck on the horizon. Then he peered down through the sheets of rain at the black puddle that was once the Tower of High Sorcery.

"The blue was too soft," he growled. "When he did not get what he wanted, he should have destroyed the city. He had the power and the right to seek revenge."

The warrior balled his black fists, which for an instant glowed orange like hot coals. "There was no one in Palanthas who could have challenged him. Only the sorcerer, and he spent all his energy destroying the tower. They are all such silly, pathetic fools."

A large crowd milled about on the street, humans primarily, though the warrior could pick out a handful of elves and several kender in the bunch. They were commoners for the most part, clad in simple tunics and leggings of brown and gray. Their clothes and their expressions were haggard and worn.

Curiosity helped a few of them brave the potential danger and slowly approach the area where the Tower of High Sorcery had stood several minutes ago. Finally, a pair of eager kender rushed forward and when the two got close enough to look down into the reflection of the hard obsidian surface, they saw a reflection of the tower locked inside. All remained still, but their fellows held back for a brief moment, waiting to see what might happen.

When it was clear that nothing more would occur, the warrior began to watch another pair of overly-curious kender as they searched the area that was once the Shoikan Grove. The warrior suspected the others in the crowd had heard the tales of the creatures lurking in the tower's surroundings and decided to stay away. The kender weren't so easily cowed.

After glancing behind himself, the warrior returned his attention to the kender in the decimated grove. He couldn't see them, though he noticed twin wisps of orange smoke twisting upward from the spot where they had stood before.

"Fools," he whispered again. "They don't know what they trifle with."

As more townsfolk gathered excitedly, the level of noise grew. The warrior could hear only some of what they said.

"It was magic that destroyed the tower," a tired-looking

man proclaimed suddenly. "Earthquakes aren't so selective that they only swallow one building."

"There were probably sorcerers in the tower," another interjected. "They experimented with something they shouldn't have. I saw one running from the place. Dressed all in black, like a piece of coal, he was. He told me to flee."

"I think it was the gods." The new speaker was a butcher. He wiped his hands on his bloodied apron and shook his head. "The gods were angry at the sorcerers."

"The gods are gone, and so's magic," an old woman sighed. "And I think neither will ever be back. But I bet what little magic might have been hanging on in that tower caused the quake."

"Did you see the dragon?" asked a kender who tugged on her skirt.

The old woman said nothing.

A haggard-looking young man answered. "I saw the dragon. It was a great blue one. Never saw anything so big."

"He could have killed us," the kender uttered with a hint of awe.

"He *should* have killed you," the warrior whispered. "All of you. Chaos wanted you dead."

The warrior was birthed during the recent war in the Abyss. In the heat of the struggle, Chaos, father of the gods, called a star down from the heavens and demolished it with but an impulse. From the flaming fragments of rock that resulted, the deity shaped the watcher and his evil brethren, worked them into magical, manlike images in much the same way a sculptor would create a series of statues. Chaos breathed life into his creations by tugging memories from the knights who swarmed about him, drawing out their worst nightmares and using them to inspire his daemon warriors, to start their dark hearts beating. The evil constructs fought in Chaos's defense and by his command.

Most of them died in the battle. The daemon warrior overlooking Palanthas saw most of his brethren perish and fail. He had been spared when the mortals won. And he and a handful of others like him felt their creator pull away from them, abandon them. Without orders, and without Chaos to guide them, the surviving daemon warriors left the Abyss and found their way to Ansalon. They were forced to find a new reason to keep living.

This one was obsessed with revenge. He vowed to make the humans pay for chasing away the all-father. The warrior shifted his shape to a conical, swirling mass and grew foggy claws and a snakelike tail that whipped about. Chaos had gifted his warriors with the ability to alter their bodies, to ride the winds, and to move through water or the earth as effortlessly as the mortals walked upon the ground.

"Everyone should be dead, moldering in their pathetic graves," the warrior hissed. "They should be food for the worms."

The daemon warrior knew the people of Palanthas were already starting to rebound from the war. The people were mourning the many heroes who died in the battle against Chaos, crying over the pitiful Knights of Solamnia and Knights of Takhisis who fought side by side. The bodies that had been recovered were buried. Those forever lost beneath the carcasses of the dead dragons and the collapsed caverns of the Abyss were honored with markers and kind words.

No one mourned for Chaos and his lost shapeshifting children. No one mourned except his brethren. The daemon warrior's piercing red eyes turned toward the expansive Palanthas harbor. A soft breeze sent ripples across the bay. The setting sun coated the water with a fiery orange glow that reminded the creature of smoldering embers, of the bits of the broken star that had birthed it. Some of the docks had been damaged by the backlash of energy from the Abyss, and he could see teams of men laboring to replace them.

"The blue could have destroyed the harbor," the daemon

warrior ranted. "But the blue is too weak and fosters a spark of respect for these ants. Fortunately, I sense another who is not so weak, who has no attachments. She will bring her raging fire to this world. And I will help to kindle it."

* * * * *

Thousands of miles from Palanthas, a young black dragon stalked deer on the rain-soaked plain of Misty Isle.

He paused in his hunt when the sky grew dark. An enormous red dragon, one larger than any he had seen before, was blotting out the sunset. With scales colored a deep crimson, she hovered in the sky and returned the black's stare. The dragon's wings were stretched out to her sides, billowed like the sails of a schooner. The black had to turn his head from side to side just to take in all of her.

Her glistening ivory horns rose tall and curved gently from atop her massive ridged head. Her amber eyes were unblinking orbs that held him mesmerized. Steam curled upward from her cavernous nostrils. The hunt forgotten, the black dragon rose on his hind legs.

She is as large as Takhisis was, perhaps even larger, he thought. *Only a god could be so huge.* His heart leapt with that thought. *Perhaps the red is Takhisis—the Dark Queen of the evil dragons—returned to Krynn to lead her children!*

His mind had touched hers once, many months ago, when she was summoning her children for the battle in the Abyss. The black had begged to be chosen to be among those dragons who would fight for their Dark Queen. But Takhisis had passed him over, saying he was too small and would not be able to contribute. The black had not felt her presence since, nor had he seen many other dragons. The black so badly wanted to know about everything that had transpired in the Abyss. Perhaps Takhisis would tell him now.

He breathed a stream of acid into the air in tribute, and the great red glided forward. The luminous rays of the dying sun touched her scales and made them glimmer like flickering flames, made her look as if she were a bonfire brought to life.

He reverently bowed his head as she landed. The ground trembled from her weight, and the black squinted as mud showered all about him, thrown everywhere by the draft from her wings.

A gout of flame arced through the sky above him, fanning out to touch the forests on both sides of the plain. The searing heat of the red's dragonbreath was intense and painful, and he heard the snap and crackle of the trees around him that had caught fire despite the dampness of the Misty Isle. The black looked up and opened his mouth to speak and saw a red claw stretching out toward him.

The claw struck him hard, sending him flying several yards toward the old forest. The impact knocked the air from his lungs. Dazed, he shook his head to clear his senses and stared at her.

The red dragon's massive claw raked his side. The talons slashed through his thick dark scales and dug into the softer flesh beneath. Then another claw pinned him to the ground and threatened to pierce his ribs.

"Takhisis, my queen!"

The black dragon's blood flowed from the wound. He cried in surprise and pain, struggling futilely beneath the weight. Through a haze of tears he looked up, his eyes locking onto hers, pleading with her, questioning.

Her immense head filled his vision as it bore down on him. And the smell of her breath was hot and sulphurous like the fire that was now raging in the forest.

She opened her mouth, and her enormous tongue snaked out to touch the tip of his nose, then retreated to lick her lips.

"No!" the black screamed. "Takhisis would not slay one of her own!" He summoned all his strength and fought to budge the claw that held him to the ground. But the black couldn't move, the red was too massive.

"Please!" he cried as he gasped for air. "Please!" he called again, surprised to hear such a human word escape his jaws, but desperate to make himself heard.

The black's heart beat frantically in his chest and his back legs jerked spasmodically. He tried desperately to find purchase in the mud, something his claws could grasp to serve as an anchor and keep him away from her. He swiveled his head about, and breathed a stream of his acid. The acid splashed against the side of the red dragon's head and made a sickening popping noise. Her jaws relaxed their grip, and the black launched himself away.

He was stopped by a paw that slammed down on his tail. Another slammed against his rump, then he felt sharp teeth close over the ridge on his back. He felt himself being lifted. The red carried him toward the beach and threw him down harshly. Laying in a heap, the black had little energy left. He labored to rise, and almost succeeded, but the red's lengthy tailed whipped about and struck him soundly across the snout, stunning him.

He concentrated, hoping to summon one final stream of acid—something, anything that might drive her off so he could rise above the cliff and escape into the trees. He was so much smaller than she, perhaps he could hide among the ancient willows. He opened his maw, breathed, but only a rivulet of acid rose from his throat. It sloshed onto the sand. The red's jaws loomed closer, sank deep into the black's throat, and she began to feast.

* * * * *

The dawning sun found the shore of the Misty Isle. None of the verdant forests remained—only charred, broken remains that stretched upward at twisted, odd angles. The red had destroyed everything.

Yawning, the great dragon rose from the beach, stretched, and shook off her sleep. Last night's meal of the big black lizard gave her some energy and she had feasted on a herd of deer, though they had been so small.

But she was still ravenous—and disturbed. Had she imagined the black lizard talking to her? Calling her . . . what was the word . . . Takhisis? Had she dreamed the words? Or had the lizard really spoken? In a fit of privation had she dined on a sentient reptile?

She glanced at the tide pool where she had left the lizard's head and a few of its rib bones. The carcass looked different in the morning light. She was able to make out more of the subtleties. The great red shuddered. It wasn't the head of a large black lizard that lay at a grotesque angle against the slope. It was the head of a black dragon.

How could her hunger have blinded her so, made her devour a baby, a hatchling? Padding to the water's edge, she glanced at her own scowling visage. She noted that a few of the scales near her jaw were melted and distorted from the baby black's acid breath.

She reached a claw up and dug the blemished scales loose. They fell on the sand with dull thuds. She grimaced. Others would grow to take their place, and she would be beautiful again, but it would take a few weeks.

At least it was a black, an inferior dragon, she told herself, trying to mollify her conscience somewhat. Blacks aren't as smart as reds. If it had been smart, it wouldn't have waited for her on the plain.

What had it meant when it called her Takhisis? What did the word mean?

By the time the sun had reached its zenith, the red dragon was high in the sky, the ruins of Misty Isle far below her. The island seemed small, like the black dragon had been small.

Maybe she should go back home. She didn't care for the brutish company of the other reds, but perhaps she would try to put up with them again. She could force herself. One more try. She hated this sensation of hunger. Raising a wing, she banked toward home.

"You cannot leave."

The red's eyes focused on the swirling gray image of a tiny man that hovered in the air before her. She drew her wings back and squinted so she could see him better. He looked like a shadow, which shouldn't be possible given the brightness of the morning sun. His eyes were unblinking crimson dots. Not a man, she decided. But what?

The red hissed. Steam rose from her nostrils, the wispy tendrils curling like chimney smoke and drifting toward the clouds overhead. Her lips twisted upward and she snarled. She could eat him, but he was so small her belly would scarcely acknowledge the offering. It would hardly be worth the effort of swallowing.

"What are you?" she growled.

"I am a daemon warrior, a creation of the all-father Chaos," the shadow man answered. "I will have my revenge against the mortals who caused my father to leave Krynn. And you will be my means of achieving it." The shadowy image grew horns and darkened itself to a glossy black shade.

The creature should be begging for mercy, the red thought. Instead he was shifting his form and chatting with her as if she were his friend. She had no friends.

"Where are you from?" The warrior's voice was gravelly and at the same time hollow, like an echo. "You are not from Ansalon, and you have not been here long. Someone would have noticed a dragon your size before. Heroes would have been dispatched to slay you. Are there more like you?"

The red narrowed her eyes to thin slits and glowered at him. A lick of flame flickered out between her pointed teeth. "My homeland is none of your concern," the dragon finally answered.

"But where you are going is. You must go toward Ansalon,

not away from it. You must kill them all, but not all at once. They must be made to fear for their lives, realize they are all doomed. They must wait inexorably for the end."

"They?"

"The people," the shadow man replied. "The humans and elves. The dwarves, gnomes, kender."

"Enough!" A growl sounded from deep in the dragon's chest. She opened her mouth and fire raced out of it, cutting through the crisp morning air and forming a great ball of searing flame. The fire rushed toward him, roaring and crackling, then it parted just inches before reaching him. It flowed like water around him and joined again behind his back.

"I am a creature of fire, sired in the Abyss. Flames cannot touch me, no matter how intense." The daemon warrior displayed glowing eyes like hot coals. "Now listen to me. Down there is the Misty Isle, the island you slept on last night and treated as so much kindling. To the north is Kothas, perched on the edge of the Blood Sea of Istar."

The dragon glared at him, a hint of curiosity creeping across her huge visage. She decided to listen to him just a little bit longer.

"Kothas is not so important as the rest of the world," the daemon warrior continued. "Neither are Mithas and Karthay. But the Dairly Plains . . ." The glow of the shadow man's eyes softened. "There are herds of cattle to satisfy your appetite, villages ripe for terrorizing, and there are smaller dragons."

Does he know about the black? she wondered.

"That is where I want you to begin."

"I go where I want, hunt what I want. I do what I want."

"You will teach them they should not have defied Chaos," the warrior replied. "They should not have forced my father to leave."

"No one tells me what to do."

"I am telling you," the shadow man hissed. "I am telling

you to devastate Ansalon, to slay the humans and elves. The people will no longer be the dominant force in the land. You will—under my direction."

"And the dragons?"

"The dragons are scattered. With their goddess Takhisis gone—"

"So Takhisis is a goddess," the red mused. *The black thought me a goddess.*

"The gods are gone. All of them," the daemon warrior continued, irate that the red had interrupted him. "The dragons have no leader. A few of them challenge the people from time to time, but not many. Yesterday I watched a great blue fly over a city and claim not one life."

I could lead the dragons, the red thought. *I could rule this Ansalon.*

"The Dairly Plains . . ." The words seeped out of her mouth like steam.

"That is where I want you to start. The people on the Dairly Plains are unsuspecting. Unprepared."

"There is land beyond these Dairly Plains?" the red hissed.

"Of course," the shadow man replied. "After you strike against the Dairly Plains, I will instruct you where to travel next. Do you have a name? I would know what to call my impressive pawn."

The dragon furrowed her considerable scarlet brow. "Malystryx. My name is Malystryx."

"Malys," the shadow man voiced, finding the shorter word more accommodating. Again the daemon warrior gestured toward the Dairly Plains.

The dragon's eyes followed the shadow man's foggy fingers, then she looked up and met his hollow gaze. All of a sudden her paw shot out, swiftly striking the warrior. Claws raked through his nebulous image.

Malys saw the surprise on his face, and she felt a surprisingly cold sensation when what passed for his blood trickled over her paws. As the daemon warrior gasped, she brought her massive head in closer, her breath scalding the air.

"Fire might not harm you," Malys uttered. "But there are other ways to slay." Opening her maw, she edged nearer, and her teeth closed about the daemon warrior. She felt his cold, heavy body slide down her throat, then she folded her wings close to her body, and angled herself toward the coastline of the Dairly Plains.

She spread her wings as the land rushed up to meet her, and glided south along the eastern shore, following a rocky coastline. Shards of obsidian and quartzlike stones jutted up from the water like teeth. Not as sharp or deadly as my teeth, she thought.

Reaching the tip of the land, she turned and started north, skimming across the treetops this time and inhaling deeply. Lush and heady scents tickled her nostrils—unusual flowers, exotic herbs, plants she was unfamiliar with. Birds scattered, and her keen, darting eyes took them in. They were too small to eat; she simply watched them.

The forest ended and a verdant plain stretched before her. Tall grass formed a dark green carpet that ranged toward a clearing that was the site of a small village. Malys trained her eyes on the thatched huts and the antlike people milling about. Oblivious to the red dragon, they were busying themselves with chores and games.

They all look so peaceful, unsuspecting, unprepared, she mused, using the daemon warrior's words.

Something cooked over a central fire, some tiny creature being roasted on a spit. The smell reminded the red dragon that she was famished. She swooped closer. As her shadow touched the edge of the village, she spied one of the people as he glanced up. He pointed at her, began waving a fleshy arm and shouting.

In a heartbeat, all of the people were looking up. Some dropped baskets of fruit they had been carrying. Others cried and ran toward the false safety of their huts. A few grabbed spears and shook them at her. They were yelling words she couldn't quite make out because too many of them were shouting at the same time. Their voices sounded like the buzzing of insects.

Curious, and knowing that she would have to get closer to feast upon them anyway, she landed at the edge of the village. The impact of her weight sent tremors that knocked some of the humans to the ground.

An especially brave one advanced on her. His eyes fixed on her massive head, and he boldly thrust a spear. For an instant, the red dragon considered slaying him with her claw and granting him the honor of being killed by her touch. But curiosity got the better of her, and she called forth a gout of flame. It sped up her throat and raced outward from her mouth in a cone-shaped pattern that first engulfed the brave villager, and then struck at the huts directly behind.

So they are not all like the daemon warrior, she mused. Fire hurts these people.

The brave villager's screams were brief, and the fire so hot that Malys barely smelled the burning flesh. Striding forward over the charred form, she flapped her wings to fan the flames, causing them to leap to other huts.

She felt something nudge her haunch. She twisted her head and saw two spearmen thrusting at her back leg. Their spears couldn't penetrate her thick scales.

She shot her right claw forward to topple one of the few huts not on fire. Three young cowered inside. Malys smashed them with a footfall.

She thrust her neck forward and opened her maw and scooped up a handful of villagers trying to flee. Their struggling forms disappeared quickly down her throat, and she turned her attention to another group, which also helped to appease her appetite.

More warriors joined the pair at her haunches. They yelled

curses and poked their spears futilely at her. Through the stench of burned flesh and thatch, she picked up the delightful scent of sweat mingled with fear. She twitched her tail and swatted them, crushing their chests and ending their lives.

There were still a few left, and these were running toward the forest on the other side of the village. She pushed against the ground, and leapt toward them. She coaxed forth another blast of fire. The flames streaked beyond the runners, scorching the trees beyond.

The people spun on their heels and started back toward the village, but Malys landed in their path. They didn't plead with her. She surmised they were smart enough to know their lives were over. Her mouth snapped open and shoveled up the closest few, then she moved in and slowly savored the rest.

As the sated red dragon vaulted into the air, the forest fire rose. She banked toward the south, soaring past the burning village and the grassy plain.

Soon her wings carried her over another forest. The trees were tall and inviting, their canopy massive enough to cloak her presence.

Descending, her feet crashed through the topmost branches, toppled a few of the oldest oaks, and struck the rich loam.

I will rest here, she thought. This will be my home for a time—as long as I stay in these Dairly Plains. But I will not stay here forever.

Chapter 7

The Dragon Purge Begins

Malys raided more villages to help appease her considerable appetite. But she was careful not to consume every last one of those she found. She didn't want to deplete her food supply too quickly, and she needed to keep some people alive so she could scrutinize them, and learn about her adopted territory. Besides, she savored the thought of people from other villages living in terror of her, wondering if they would be the next to burn, spreading word of her attacks, and gifting her with an august reputation.

She alternately feasted on cattle and various unusual forest creatures she tired of studying, and on occasion she devoured the crews of ships sailing too close to the rocky eastern shore of the Dairly Plains.

Nothing offered her any significant threat—until the other red came. He was only half the size of Malys, stretching perhaps a little more than two hundred feet from nose to tail. She'd seen him skirting the edges of villages she had decimated, picking through the ruins. She'd watched him slithering through the forest, stopping in clearings she'd made when she ripped up trees to corner particularly tasty animals. He had been watching her, apparently wanting to learn from the best.

One day she spotted him approaching the lair she had created along the coastline, a steep rise perched on a cliff overlooking the Southern Courrain Ocean. She'd carefully sculpted the lair and the surrounding terrain during the past few months. Like a determined potter, she was continually modifying the land, making the rise bigger, craggier, more imposing with jutting peaks and shadowy recesses.

She had carved a massive cave into the inland side of the Dairly Plains, a hole just large enough for her scaly body and the few chests of coins she'd taken from ships. From inside of her comfortable niche, she watched him come closer.

"What do you want?" she hissed as he approached.

"I had to see you," he snarled. The male growled low and soft, flames licking out of his nostrils. "I heard talk of a large red on the Plains, one who was not in the Chaos War in the Abyss. One who was, perhaps, afraid to fight with the rest of us alongside Takhisis."

"I am Takhisis," Malys spouted, remembering the word the young black dragon and the daemon warrior had used. "I am your goddess. Bow to me."

The male laughed, and a low growl started deep in his belly. "You're big," he snapped. "But you're not Takhisis. You're not a goddess. Gods don't have to eat, and they don't live in caves. All the gods are gone. Bow to *me*."

Malys heard the sharp intake of his breath, smelled a trace

of sulphur, and knew he was about to send a gout of flame her way. But she didn't move from her spot. She knew his breath wouldn't hurt her. It would only prove how foolish he was.

He opened his mouth and a ball of yellow and orange fire raced from between his glistening fangs. It rushed toward Malys, but not directly at her. Instead, it struck the rocky hillside just above her head. The male rumbled again, and Malys felt her lair shake. The male red was not so witless after all. Dirt and rocks cascaded down on her head, sealing her in. Again she heard the crackling of fire, felt the heat, and sensed the crevice closing, the earth baking, and the softer rocks melting beneath the male's intense breath. The ground pressed against her sides.

"You mean to bury me?" she hissed as the earth coffin squeezed her massive form tighter and pushed ever more uncomfortably against her ribs.

Like a wet dog shaking water from its back, Malys tossed her head from side to side, pushed out with her wings, and lashed backward with her muscular tail. A rumble ignited deep inside her, sounding like an earth tremor. The noise grew as she flailed about, then she took a deep breath and exhaled.

The rocky rise exploded. Stones, earth and white flames shot outward in all directions. Some rocks fell far out into the Southern Courrain, others flew toward the impudent red male and pelted his thick vermillion hide.

He snarled and charged her, unaffected by the fan of fire that continued to pour from her mouth. His claws slammed into her chest, and the impact pushed her back. She wrapped her tail around his rear leg, and they grappled for a moment on the edge of the cliff. Then the ground gave way beneath their weighty bodies and they tumbled down toward the jagged stone teeth that jutted upward along the coastline.

Malys knew her land by heart, had committed to memory

the location of every pond and village, every obsidian and quartzlike spike that stuck above the water and threatened ships. In mid-fall she pivoted, twisting the male's body beneath hers. She dug her claws into his sides, and pulled her wings in close, so she would drop like a stone.

He flapped madly, trying to stop his descent, but she was too heavy. His neck coiled about like an angry serpent, and he brought his head in close. The male's jaws jerked open wide and closed about Malys's neck. She screamed in surprise and pain and raked her claws against his side. The male's warm blood flowed over her talons, while her own blood ran in hot rivulets down her neck. She lashed her tail back and forth, brought it up to slash at his wings, then whipped it against his snout in an effort to make him release his grip.

But his teeth sunk in deeper, and for an instant Malys found it difficult to breathe. She felt dizzy, her lungs tight. Then she felt a jarring impact as the male struck the jagged rocks below. Spikes of obsidian impaled him, pushing through his back and pinning him in place.

In the same instant that he released his hold on her neck, Malys thrust her wings out to her sides and beat them frantically to keep from joining him on the sharp rocks. Hovering only a few feet above him, her talons grazing his heaving belly, she watched him futilely struggle to free himself. Steam rose from the water where his mouth touched it and he began to shake violently.

"You're no god," he gasped.

"But I am alive," she replied huskily.

Malys landed behind him, as close to the cliff face as she could, where the water was shallow and where there were no obsidian spikes. Creeping forward, she lashed out at his underside with a claw. Her sharp talons cut through his scaly flesh and drew parallel lines of blood.

As the male drew his last breath, Malys inhaled deeply. A shimmering crimson aura lifted from the dead dragon's body and drifted toward Malys as if it were being pulled there. The red essence dropped down over Malys and slid smoothly over every contour of her massive body like a cloak. Then it seemed to cling tightly to her slightly protruding scales before sinking into her body and disappearing altogether.

Malys looked down at the dead male, who was now no more than a dry husk that was quickly dashed upon the rocks and washed out to sea. She had meant to feast upon him in order to sate her hunger.

Her regret at the missed opportunity was outweighed by the new feeling of power that crackled through her body and danced along the edge of her talons. She felt vital and superior, infused with a heady sense of power. It made her wish she had been part of the battle in the Abyss, the Chaos War he had chattered about. And it made her crave another violent encounter, another chance to prove herself.

* * * * *

"Tell me more about this Chaos War, what led to it." Malys was snout to snout with a green dragon, another curious visitor to the Dairly Plains. This one she had elected not to kill, as she might have a use for him later—if nothing more than as a source of information about another part of Krynn or as a puppet for her plans. She didn't trust the green dragon, didn't trust anyone or anything, but she knew how to feign cooperation and friendship. She settled on conquering the green with silky words and unaccustomed politeness.

The green was a little larger than the red Malys slaughtered better than a month ago. He was the color of the Misty Plains' forests, with small scales that were supple like spring twigs, not thick and rigid like other dragons. He was handsome for a green, Malys thought, but not so regal or beautiful as a red.

"The Chaos War is a tribute to mortals' stupidity and their

disregard for the gods," the green began. "The Irda, also known as the high ogres, were the first to show their ignorance. The Graygem was in their possession, and it contained enough of Chaos to keep him at bay and away from Krynn, which he had sworn to destroy. With Chaos restricted, Takhisis could act as she pleased."

The green regaled Malys with tales he had heard of how the Dark Queen carefully deployed her charges—loyal dragons and unwitting human pawns dubbed Knights of Takhisis—in every country on Krynn. She waited for the proper moment to order a strike and then hoped to bring all of the land under her control.

"But the Irda ruined her plans. They somehow thought the Graygem would better serve them if it was shattered. They thought with its power released, the outside world would leave them alone," the green sneered. "They didn't know the power inside was Chaos."

"So Takhisis's plan to rule Krynn ended because the gem broke?" Malys asked.

"Once freed, Chaos intended to keep his pledge to destroy the world. If our Dark Queen did nothing to stop him, she would have nothing left to rule. So she, and the less powerful gods who agreed to cooperate with her, challenged him. Chaos made his stand in the Abyss. Takhisis called her most powerful dragons to her side and permitted them to join her. Hundreds of dragons fought at our queen's side."

The green paused, staring at nothing. "But so few lived through it. We are scattered now, for the most part keeping to ourselves."

"Only the dragons fought?" Malys pressed. "And Takhisis and the other gods, of course."

"Humans were there, too—the Knights of Takhisis. There were other armored men, elves, dwarves—all of the mortal races. Even a kender. But they were gnats, nothing next to Chaos. Only the dragons were strong enough to weaken him, wear him down and distract him so a drop of his blood could be gathered within the broken halves of the Graygem. Had it not been for the dragons, there would be no Krynn. Sealing the stone again was enough to force him to leave. But his godchildren had to go with him—and all the magic, too. They say this is the Age of Mortals now."

"I think it is the Age of Dragons," Malys said.

The green flicked his tail lazily like a cat and shook his head sadly. He reached a talon up to scratch his angular jaw. "No. The time of dragons is passing. There are not near so many of us now. We are creatures of magic. And with magic gone, how long will it take for us to fade from Krynn?"

It was a statement, really, not a question, and the green hadn't expected an answer. But Malys gave him one.

"We do not have to fade at all." She fixed her eyes on the green, and the corner of her massive scarlet lip curled upward in a slight smile. "A red challenged me recently, and though it pained me, I was forced to fight him. I was victorious, of course. As he died, I felt stronger. I became more powerful. I knew that by slaying him I had absorbed his magical essence. I am not going to fade."

The green rose on his haunches and backed away from Malys. "Are you suggesting dragons purposely kill each other to survive?"

"You don't want to fade from Krynn, do you?" she asked, turning the green's words back on him. "Better some die, rather than all. Better you live."

The green silently regarded Malys. Then after several silent moments he spoke. "The coppers, the brass, the bronzes. The draconians."

"Those who are smaller and weaker, those who would not pose much of a challenge in a fight. Those who have a hint of magic about them. Kill them and gain their power."

"They are my enemies anyway," the green mused, his conscience tossed soundly out the door.

"Perhaps even smaller green dragons."

"No!"

"Of course not," Malys was quick to apologize. "Forgive me. I was merely thinking you might want to eliminate those beneath you, those who could present a threat and who might grow more powerful as they killed *their* enemies—and eventually turned on you."

The green stared at her, thinking. He drummed a claw against the earth. "I would presume that smart dragons would use the magical essence they gained to establish domains, claim tracts of Krynn and shape the land to suit them."

Malys glanced over her shoulder at her new lair, which was part of a small mountainous area she was landscaping. "The Dairly Plains are mine," she hissed. "And soon I will take the land to the west of them."

The green dragon nodded. Malys had provided him with an excellent plan. He couldn't wait to share it with all of his other allies.

* * * * *

One year later, Khellendros became dragon overlord of a realm consisting of the Northern Wastes, Hinterlund, Gaardlund, and the Plains of Solamnia—those lands touched by the Turbidus Ocean as far south as Solamnia's new border. The Blue likely could have claimed more territory, but that would have taken more time, and would require that many more hours be devoted to patrolling his realm.

He selected a lesser blue dragon, Gale, to keep an eye on the farthest edges of his territory. Gale, knowing it was better to ally himself with Khellendros than to be trampled by him, loyally served the Storm Over Krynn.

Khellendros preferred to spend his time trying to perfect blue spawn. He selected the best human candidates to become his nightmarish creations, and found the occasional draconian that was needed to power the transformations. He preferred to spend time thinking about Kitiara and how he would ultimately find a way to bring her back.

* * * * *

The inhabitants of New Coast were occupied with worries about their land, which was becoming wetter than was normal for fall. The rains had increased dramatically and the water was not being absorbed by the ground as fast as usual. Deep pools of water lay about inland villages, drowning crops and threatening homes. Rivers were spreading out and threatening to swallow farms. The temperature was climbing and swarms of insects were becoming as thick as clouds.

The unseasonable fall warmth was making the coastline steamy, hotter than it was in the summer. And the coastline itself was shifting. The water in the fingerlike bay of New Sea that reached between New Coast and Blödehelm was rising and becoming choked by lilies. People who lived along the shore were being forced farther inland.

A concerned silver dragon had taken to the skies in search of an answer. On this day he dipped low over the land, inspecting a fetid bog. It hadn't been there a few weeks ago when he had visited. He made another pass over it and landed nearby. A hundred yards away was the edge of a copse of trees, and nestled between the largest willows was a reedy marsh that stretched toward the horizon. The trees had been there a long time, but the thick vines and moss that hung from their branches were new. Their roots were submerged in the brackish water.

The dragon didn't remember the marsh either, though he had to admit he was not thoroughly conversant with this stretch of New Coast. A haze of mosquitoes hovered above the stagnant surface and wet roots. A fat, contented frog had partly submerged itself in a patch of mud and now rotated its eyes in the dragon's direction.

"It is wet here," the dragon began. "Too wet for this season." The words sounded more like grunts and croaks. Silvers had a knack for being able to communicate with most species, and the young dragon enjoyed animal banter, often finding the conversations enlightening. Unlike people, and some other dragons he knew, animals didn't lie.

"Never too wet," the frog belched in tones the dragon understood. "Wet. Warm. Many insects to eat. Wonderful."

"It has not been like this long."

"Less than a moon," the frog replied.

"Less than a month," the dragon whispered.

"Forever," the frog added. "It will be wet forever."

The silver cocked his head closer. "What do you know about the water?"

"The master likes the water, too. And the heat. Wonderful heat."

"The master?"

"The master makes it rain. She makes the ground hard so the rain stays on top, doesn't sink in and run away. Wonderful rain."

"Who is this master?"

"I am."

The voice wasn't the frog's. It was deep and rich, feminine, and it came from behind the silver, from the insect-plagued marsh.

"And you are trespassing."

The dragon slowly turned his head, and his eyes narrowed. Peering into the copse of moss-draped trees, he saw a pair of large, dull yellow eyes gleaming just above ground level, shining through the fog of mosquitoes.

The silver slipped away from the wallowing frog and moved closer to the marsh.

"What you are doing here is wrong, unnatural," the silver

lectured. "The land was not meant to be like this. You have no right to change it."

"The land is mine, all of New Coast and Blödehelm."

The silver edged its head past a curtain of vines so he could see the Black better. The Black was lying in the marsh. Only the top crest of her head and her eyes were visible above the reedy water.

Suddenly the vines nearby twisted like writhing serpents. At the Black's unspoken command, they wrapped about the silver's head and jaws, muzzling him, spinning around his neck. Tree roots rose from the water and circled his legs.

The silver struggled. He was immensely strong, and the vines could not hold him. In the instant the silver broke free, the Black rose from the marsh and breathed a gout of acid, striking the silver on his snout.

The caustic liquid sizzled and hissed, and the silver dragon recoiled in pain and surprise. The Black pressed her attack, breathing on him again. The harsh acid melted the scales around the silver's head. The Black rushed forward and slammed her shoulder into a willow. The tree groaned and toppled, striking the silver.

The silver backed quickly away from the marsh's edge, and the Black followed him. Now, in the light, he could see better. She was covered with black thick scales and had midnight-blue ridged plates on the underside of her neck and her belly. Her wings were smooth and the color of the night sky, and her horns grew out of a crest just above and behind her slanted eyes. The ivory horns were menacing hooks, cruelly curving up a bit at the tips.

Her tongue snaked out repeatedly, and the saliva that dripped from her mouth sizzled as it struck the grassy carpet.

The Black was only a little larger than the silver, and in a fair fight she could not have bested him. But she had gained the advantage, and she worked to keep it. This time she directed her acid breath at his front claws.

The silver rose on his back legs and opened his mouth to retaliate. He inhaled sharply, then exhaled, expelling a stream of quicksilver. But the Black was too quick. She dashed forward, under him.

The Black lashed upward at the silver's belly. Her talons and teeth cut through his mirror scales, and she released another stream of acid. It splashed into his wound and he began to crumple and twitch. She moved in to finish him.

"I am Onysablet," she hissed as she brought her jaws toward his face. Her horns pricked the scaly flesh beneath his eyes. "This is my realm."

* * * * *

Six years later, the inhabitants of Southern Ergoth, an island continent six hundred miles north to south and nearly as wide, found themselves experiencing a change in climate thanks to one new resident.

Throughout the land's history, Southern Ergoth boasted diverse climates. Now it was perpetually cold. Snow covered the desolate plains in the north. Snow blanketed the old forests and the mountains. A thick sheet of ice lay sparkling over the grasslands and lakes. The deep waters of the Bay of Darkness were so choked with ice and snow that they, and the surrounding coast, had become a glacier. In the Straits of Algoni and in the Sirrion Sea beyond, icebergs floated and menaced the shipping lanes.

It was winter—and would stay winter—because Southern Ergoth's dragon overlord, Gellidus, was partial to the cold. Gellidus had spent the better part of a year sculpting the land to suit his needs. He was particularly fond of deep, hard-packed snow that he could glide across at amazing speeds. He also fancied thick drifts in which he'd hide and wait for unsuspecting prey. To him, the frigid wind was as cherished as a lover's caress, and its howl blew down the mountainsides and across the frozen lakes as welcomed as a whispered kiss.

The dragon was known as "Frost." An immense white dragon with glistening scales, his wings were smooth like oiled leather and tinged with pale blue edges. His head was covered with an angular, ridged carapace.

Gellidus had spent the past several months sculpting the climate to suit him, and dining on those dragons who protested. He'd also acquired a taste for the Kagonesti, Qualinesti, and Silvanesti, though it took a lot of them to fill his cavernous stomach.

The ogres and goblins claimed the mountains—or rather the mountain caves and niches that were too small to accommodate the White's massive body. The elves who were able, abandoned the land. Those who remained did their best to hide from Gellidus and to adapt to the unnatural environment.

Southern Ergoth no longer held the promise of being a sovereign state for elvenkind where the Kagonesti, Qualinesti, and Silvanesti could exist side by side in peace. Shivering and weeping, most of the elves were driven from their homes and forced to flee west.

* * * * *

As the years passed, Krynn's dragon population dwindled. Only a few dozen remained, and these were great, fearsome beasts of incredible size and power who firmly established their territories.

Some smaller dragons survived, those who knew how to hide from their huge brethren and who had no desire to challenge any of them for territory.

One such dragon was Brynseldimer. He had previously lived in the troubled waters of the Blood Cup, but laid claim to Dimernesti—the easterly sunken land of the sea elves.

He was a sea dragon, an ancient one who'd seen more than four hundred years. His blue and green scales had long ago lost their iridescent shine, and were flat and dull and covered with barnacles, dark like the bottom of the sea. His horns rose twisting from the top of his head, and when he nestled himself on the ocean floor, he looked like a craggy coral ridge. His tail was thin and smooth like a sea snake, and it was tipped with a barbed point that he often used to skewer large fish—or to spear the occasional overly-curious sea elf.

Brynseldimer had abandoned his northern home in self-preservation. The sea dragon wanted to avoid fights with larger dragons who had moved in and begun to battle in the area. He feared those who were his size and larger. He was not especially crafty or clever, and he did not want to fall victim to well-planned attacks.

The blue-skinned Dimernesti elves were more of an annoyance than a threat, and he did not think they tasted especially good. But from time to time armed bands of them would swim out of their coral-towered homes and challenge him. He swallowed them because he did not know what else to do with them.

Those few who tried to swim toward the land of the Silvanesti, to seek help from their air-breathing kin in the forests, were crushed beneath the dragon's claws. Eventually the Dimernesti elves learned to keep to themselves and to stay in their homes, which had become their prison cells. The dragon, whom they dubbed Brine, usually left them alone if they did not wander.

Isolated, they didn't know that elsewhere on Krynn dragons were establishing realms and tormenting people— that as the months and years passed the dragons claimed more and more of Krynn and changed the land to suit their temperaments.

The sea elves didn't know that despite their seemingly-quarantined state, humans and elves in many other places were faring much worse. They didn't know that Brynseldimer kept busy capsizing ships that got too close to his domain, concentrating on keeping the elves in their underwater communities, preventing visitors from reaching them. He swallowed other intelligent sea life, especially otters because the Dimernesti elves could shapechange into them.

And they didn't know that his actions centered on squelching news of his presence. Though Brynseldimer was not the brightest of Krynn's massive dragons, he knew that if he didn't want his large, scaly brethren to hunt him, he would have to keep them from finding him. He would have to keep his presence a secret.

* * * * *

Almost twenty years after Malys shared her secret plan with the green male, another larger green dragon digested the powerful information (as well as the unfortunate green male) and set about claiming her own domain. Her name was Beryllinthranox and by the time she had slain more than two dozen draconians with her devastating poisonous breath, she was also known as The Green Peril.

The windswept plain of Kharolis, the land surrounded by Ice Mountain Bay and the Sirrion Sea, was hers. She directed her efforts to ferreting out draconians in hiding and hatchling blue and copper dragons who relished the dry land of Kharolis's sloughs. She spent her captured energy transforming the land, creating an environment for trees and streams, where before only sporadic patches of scrub weeds grew.

She eventually edged her way north, to the grasslands south of the Qualinesti forest, where she added three young brass dragons to her list of victories and feasted on a patrol of elves.

Beryl grew larger, more powerful, more belligerent, and within the span of three years, she claimed the home of the

Qualinesti elves and became dragon overlord of Qualinesti and its surroundings.

* * * * *

Malys's realm included Kendermore, Balifor, Khur, and the Dairly Plains. The latter was no longer flat. She had expended her energies on crafting a rugged mountain range that stretched from the far south to the north and curved toward the Kender homeland. The rich forests were thinned, both from her extensive hunting and from the toll her sculpting of the land took on the earth.

Her lair, the Peak of Malys, was now just south of a place called Flotsam. It was a massive, high plateau ringed on all sides by spiky rocks. She met with other dragon overlords there, and they shared news of conquests. Malys was always interested in learning about the humans the other dragons encountered. She wanted to know all about them, their drives and passions, their weaknesses and faults.

"It is the Age of Dragons, not the Age of Mortals," the great Red hissed to Khellendros. The Blue was visiting her, answering a summons out of curiosity, not respect. "Powerful magic is beyond them."

"But not beyond us," Khellendros interjected. "We are magical creatures, and magic will not fade from us. We grow stronger."

The Blue looked intently at her, as if he were studying her. For an instant Malys wondered if Khellendros suspected that she had initiated the fights between the dragons. Did he know dragons didn't need to kill each other or the draconians to hold onto their magical essence and ensure their place in Krynn? She thought him clever, but it was hard to believe he was smart enough to figure her out. Impossible, really.

"Now is the time to strike," she softly growled. "While men are at their weakest. They can't stand up to us. They can't defeat us as they defeated other dragons in decades past. We must subjugate them."

Khellendros continued to stare at her for several long moments. Finally he nodded his great head. "Now is the time to strike," he agreed.

Chapter 8

A Meeting of Minds

"What are you thinking about?" The voice was soft and feminine, coming from behind Palin as he stood at the window and gazed out over Wayreth Forest.

"I was wondering what you were doing this fine afternoon, Usha."

"You're a terrible liar, husband." She laid a gentle hand on his shoulder, as he slowly turned to face her.

The three decades that had passed since the Chaos War had been especially kind to Usha Majere. Her long hair was white and shiny, the same color as the day he met her. Her figure was shapely and turned the heads of men half her age. And the few lines on her face were at the edges of her golden eyes and were noticeable mainly when she smiled.

But Usha had not smiled often as of late. She knew Palin was troubled. He was getting less and less sleep these days. The dreams had returned, and he often awoke sweating and unwilling to talk about them.

Age and worry had painted silver streaks in Palin Majere's auburn, shoulder-length hair. The years had put a few creases in his brow and thin lines on his handsome face, and they'd slowed his gait a little. The years hadn't stooped his shoulders or dulled his wits, however, nor had they lessened his determination.

Palin was in his mid-fifties now. He still wore long ivory robes, as he had since he was chosen to be the head of the Order of the White Robes. And he still often thought about his Uncle Raistlin, the most formidable Wizard of the Black Robes ever to walk upon Krynn.

With magic apparently gone, Palin was feeling frustrated and useless. He had served as the head of the Conclave of Wizards for the past four years, but nothing had changed. Wizards could not cast even simple spells and could only use some magical items. The elves of Qualinesti were in dire need of some means to battle against the powerful dragon overlord Beryl and the wizards had come up with nothing.

"What are you *really* thinking about?" Usha persisted.

Palin reached up and twirled a finger in her soft hair, moving it around and around until it formed a curl. He released the strand and cupped her face. She smelled of lilacs this morning, and he inhaled her fragrance deeply.

"I was thinking about the dragons," he said finally.

"You're always thinking about the dragons."

"It's hard to think about much else these days. I have to do something about them before the situation gets any worse. But I just don't know what I *can* do. Things we've tried, the other sorcerers and myself, have done nothing and have gone unnoticed."

Usha stepped back, balled her fists, and placed them against her hips. "The dragons frighten me, too, Palin Rinta-laisin Majere. But the entire fate of Krynn is not on your shoulders. You hardly sleep anymore. Up so late, studying, thinking. Up so early too. I'm concerned about you."

"I'm fine."

"Not if you keep this up."

"I've a lot to do. I've made a discovery that—"

"Whatever it is you've been working on can wait for one day," Usha insisted. "Just *one* day. We promised to have din-ner with our children. What about the grandchildren? We promised. Tomorrow you can . . ."

Palin made a face. "I want to see them. I really do," he began. There was a hint of exasperation in his voice. "But it will have to be a very quick dinner. And a late one, I'm afraid. I've things to tend to here that can't be put off. "

"Palin!" his wife chided.

"Palin," a deeper voice called. "We're ready."

Usha drew her lips into a thin, tight line and stared into her husband's eyes. "I just wish I didn't have to share you with the dragons and this tower," she softly huffed. "And I wish I didn't have to share you with those . . . men." She ges-tured behind her, to a silvery-robed man whose face was hid-den by his hood.

Palin gently drew her into his arms. "I'm the one who called this meeting. They came because I asked them to." His lips brushed her forehead and lingered there for a moment. "I have to go now."

* * * * *

They met in the topmost room in the Tower of Wayreth. Palin sat at the head of a long ebonwood table. The afternoon sun gleamed warmly on its polished surface.

To his right sat the silvery-robed sorcerer, who looked

about thirty, only a few years older than Palin's son, Ulin. But Palin suspected the man was much older than himself. The sorcerer's smooth, black-gloved hands edged out of his voluminous sleeves and his fingers traced the whorls in the table-top. He brushed the cowl away from his unblemished, ebony-skinned face.

"I had hoped more sorcerers would have answered your summons, Majere," he stated. "Or in their answers had not declined. This conclave you've called could well be the last on Ansalon." The man was known as the Master of the Tower. He was caretaker of the Tower of Wayreth and a bit of a mystery. No one remembered having seen him before the Chaos War.

"Some said they were too preoccupied to attend. Others claimed they simply did not have the means to get here," said the speaker who sat to Palin's left, the one called the Shadow Sorcerer. It was impossible to discern if the voice was male or female because it was muted as it came from behind a metal-lic face mask that only sported eye slits. The speaker was a slight figure dressed entirely in black. The hood of the sor-cerer's cloak seemed to swallow the expressionless metal face inside it. "But I believe the other sorcerers did not come because they've lost faith in what little magic is left. It seems no one studies magic anymore. Apprentices are rare. And the dragons have killed the spellcasters who dared to stand up to them."

"I think we're all frightened of the dragons," Palin said.

"We should be," the Master said.

"Then this meeting is pointless." The Shadow Sorcerer pushed away from the table, the chair legs screeching against the stone floor. "I doubt that the dragons can be stopped. *We* certainly don't have the means to do so."

"But there are so few of the dragons left, at least compared to their numbers before the Chaos War—and before they started fighting each other," the Master offered.

"I'll grant that their so-called Dragon Purge seems to be at an end," the Shadow Sorcerer replied. The sorcerer's shoulders were hunched, hinting at age or despair. "But the ones we are left to deal with are more cunning. Deadlier. Perhaps undefeatable."

Palin sighed and silently looked to his companions.

"You've been having visions again," the Master prompted.

"The dragon I saw in my dreams was a tremendous blue. The same one as before. It had to be Khellendros," Palin stated. "If someone hadn't destroyed the Tower of High Sorcery, the dragon would've claimed it, taken the magic inside and done who knows what with it. Maybe Palanthas wouldn't be here today."

"The dragon would have turned the magic against someone, no doubt," the Master agreed.

"Have you had any dreams about the Red to the east— Malystryx? About any other dragon?" the Shadow Sorcerer asked softly.

Palin shook his head. "Just the Blue." He took a deep breath and ran his fingers through his hair. "He is near Palanthas, but he hasn't threatened the city. Not since thirty years ago, the day the tower was destroyed. But until I can understand the visions, determine what he is up to, let us attend to other urgencies."

"Your discovery, Majere?" the Master asked.

"Yes. I believe it might have an impact on whatever we try against the dragons." Palin stood and steepled his fingers on the table. "I think I've learned how to cast spells."

"How is it possible?" the Shadow Sorcerer's voice was laced with intrigue.

"I kept thinking it was up to me to figure out how to bring magic back to Krynn. I refused to accept that it was simply gone. And then it occurred to me that maybe *I* could do it, me personally, and that maybe magic hadn't left our world."

"We've all wished the same. We've all tried," said the Master.

"Yes, but we've only tried to use magic in the same way we always have. This is not the same Krynn that it was some thirty years ago. We've always used the magic of High Sorcery given to us by the gods millenia ago, but they are gone now. We don't have their help now, so, of course, we can't access Krynn's magic the way we used to."

"*Krynn's* magic," said the Shadow Sorcerer, nodding his head.

"Yes! It's still here in our world, an innate, primordial magic that still permeates Krynn—*Krynn's* magic."

"But how do you use it without written or memorized spells?" asked the Master, leaning forward in his chair.

"Find your own way!" shouted Palin enthusiastically.

The two seemed to take offense at this and they leaned back in their chairs.

"I mean reach out for Krynn's magic in *your* way, weave your own unique spells," Palin said quietly.

"If one can *feel* the magic, he can shape it to his will," remarked the Shadow Sorcerer in an off-handed way that surprised Palin.

The three stared at each other, and for several long minutes the only sound heard was the wind whistling through the spiral staircase beyond the chamber.

"This new sorcery of yours could never be as powerful as the old wizardry," said the Master with a tone of regret.

Palin reluctantly agreed. "It's true that it is less powerful, at least, for now."

The room fell silent again.

"Perhaps one could draw out the energy from a magical item to enhance his spell," said the Sorcerer.

Palin smiled, nodding his head in affirmation as the idea grew more and more plausible to him. His smile faded when he saw the worried look on the Master's dark face.

"If it is possible to boost a spell by exhausting a magical item, no one must know."

Palin glared at him. "To keep such a thing a secret!"

"Indeed!" the Master said. "To keep it a secret is the best course. What would you have us do, Majere, declare open season on Ansalon's most precious artifacts? We only just now came up with the idea. Who's to say if it will even work? What do you think, Sorcerer?"

"I think it is best if I consider this matter for a while," said the Shadow Sorcerer quietly.

Palin sat heavily in his chair. "Let's concentrate on what we *can* do."

"Quite right," said the Shadow Sorcerer. "This new sorcery ought to come as quite a surprise to the dragons. I vote we launch an attack on Beryl."

"Your enthusiasm is commendable, colleague, but don't you think we need to learn how to cast spells first?" asked the Master.

"It's just that the elves are in such dire need. That's one of the reasons we came here," said the Shadow Sorcerer.

The discussion went late into the evening, past the hour when Palin was supposed to go to dinner with his children. Usha went ahead without him, whispering that she understood and that Linsha and Ulin would, too.

* * * * *

Palin was unable to sleep that night. His restlessness came more from excitement than worry. The Master of the Tower had declared that their meeting constituted the Last Conclave and had instructed Palin to dissolve the old Orders of Magic and open a school to teach the new sorcery. And, though they didn't have enough magic to destroy Beryl, they were going to try to drive her off. The future of elvenkind depended on them at least giving the Green a setback.

Palin was finally equipped with the means to *do* something. He was glad, but he also felt somewhat alone, burdened with a great deal of responsibility. Where were all the good dragons? Where were the brasses and the bronzes, the golds, silvers, and coppers? Where were the ones who always helped men in the past?

His thoughts drifted back a few decades, to the Chaos War. He had witnessed blues flying next to golds, some with riders, some alone, all united under the same banner. There were no evil dragons then, as far as Palin was concerned. There were simply dragon champions who fought to save Krynn. More humans died than dragons that day. Knights of Solamnia and Knights of Takhisis both—their loyalties were cast aside during the fight. And when the battle was over, the knights, once enemies, were buried side by side in a tomb in Solace that honored fallen heroes.

Krynn needs new champions, Palin thought. If this is indeed the Age of Mortals, then mortals must reclaim the land. Perhaps Goldmoon will help us find them.

Chapter 9

Tears of an Army

"They remind me of cattle." Malys's voice was tinged with scorn.

"Humans?" Khellendros posed.

The majestic Red nodded her head. "And the elves, dwarves, gnomes. All of them. Even the kender. Especially the cheerful, pitiful kender. The contemptible kender with their puny weapons, impudent grins, and their endless, annoying banter. I took this land from them, and they could do nothing to stop me."

Malys was stretched out on her belly in her plateau lair south of Flotsam, letting the late afternoon sun bake her scales. She closed her eyes and softly, contentedly growled.

She loved the heat. Khellendros sat in front of her.

"Some aspire to greatness," he began. "Some *humans*, anyway."

"You are soft to think so," she hissed.

"I am wise to *know* so," Khellendros rebuked. "Humans and their allies have been responsible for chasing dragons from the face of Krynn before. They should not be taken lightly."

Malys raised a scaly brow, opened one eye, and silently urged him to continue.

"This world has seen three dragon wars, four if the last could be called a war," the Blue explained. "Each was glorious—and devastating—to our kind. In the first war, nearly four thousand years past, the elves tried to drive us from what they believed were their lands. They were *our* lands, and we would have won, as the elves did not have the numbers to stand up to us. But the gods of magic aided the elves, giving them a handful of enchanted stones. The stones captured the dragons' spirits and drew their strength inside, then the elves buried the stones deep in the tallest mountains. The dragons were weakened and exiled from the world."

"But they returned," Malys purred.

"The second war was not quite a thousand years later. The stones had been planted in the Khalkist Mountains, where a clan of dwarves was mining. Dwarves do not trust magic. So when their new tunnel broke into the chamber where the stones were held and they sensed the powerful magic, they cast the stones out onto the surface. They thought they were keeping themselves safe, protecting their mine."

"Returning dragons to the world?" Malys asked. Her voice was thick with disbelief and she kept both eyes open and on him now.

Khellendros nodded. "The unsuspecting dwarves freed the dragons. The dragons gathered great armies of lizard people, called bakali, and invaded the Silvanesti forests to seek revenge against the elves. The oldest trees were trampled and the elven casualties were staggering. The dragons hoped to slaughter the entire race, cast them into extinction. And the dragons might have succeeded. *Should* have succeeded. But, again, it was not to be."

"What happened? Were you there?"

"No. I was not yet born. And I suspect none of the dragons who walk Krynn now were alive then, save our Queen, Takhisis," Khellendros replied. "But all dragons—all the dragons of Ansalon—know what happened and share our common history. I am revealing it to you so you can better understand your new kin."

"Go on," she urged.

"Three sorcerers and a scion, one of the world's more magical creatures, summoned powerful forces and demanded that the very earth swallow the dragons for all eternity. The dragons were not buried, but they were defeated and driven away. And the smug elves went on with their lives and again took our land."

"But the dragons obviously rose to power again," Malys stated.

"Yes. Takhisis would not let it be otherwise. She called on the lizard people, and with their help planted eggs deep in the mines of Thoradin. When the eggs hatched, the young dragons devoured their caretakers and grew strong, and they hid in the mines for a few centuries—until they were large enough to strike in the Dark Queen's name. That time was called the Third Dragon War, the bloodiest of the struggles and the most costly. The humans barely survived. Wave upon wave of dragons swooped down on them, breathing fire, lightning, acid, poison, and frost. Victory should have belonged to us. But the good dragons, the meddlesome silvers and golds, intervened. The humans crafted enchanted lances, and from the backs of their dragon allies they flew against us. In the end, Takhisis fell. She agreed to leave

Krynn, taking her children with her."

"And this happened . . . "

"More than fifteen hundred years after the second war, which was about two thousand years ago."

"A long time," Malys mused.

"But not so long as far as history is concerned. Or dragons." The Red snarled and flicked her tail. It was clear she didn't like being corrected. "And the dragons . . . "

"Reawakened once more about four hundred years ago. Takhisis discovered a gate and returned to the world to lead us. I was there." Khellendros paused for a moment, wondering if Malys would realize he was much larger and more formidable than a four hundred-year-old dragon should be. But he decided Malys probably did not know about the portals, and about how time passes between them. And she surely did not know much about the age and size of dragons in Ansalon.

"What happened?" she persisted.

"As time passed, we made a pact with ogres and wicked humans, beings who had no compunction against killing their own. The Dark Queen's armies grew, draconians were born, and the land finally came under our control." Khellendros stared at a spot on the plateau, his mind drifting back to those days. "The time was dubbed the War of the Lance. It was a time unlike any other. Dragon Highlords, select humans with military minds, led us into one superb battle after the next. From atop our backs, they helped us achieve victory over their brethren."

"You were partnered with a *human*?" She spit the last word out as if it were a spoiled piece of meat.

"Kitiara." Khellendros spoke the name softly, almost reverently.

"And where is she now, this Kit-ee-ar-ah?"

"Human bodies are frail."

"My point," Malys hissed.

"But human minds are extraordinary," Khellendros continued. "As the battle raged, a lone human, another wizard, sacrificed himself to seal the Abyss—with the Dark Queen inside. Men rebuilt their world, and we dragons schemed in the background."

"But we are not in the background any longer. And men are without magic now," Malys growled. "They are without their gods, without power. They are cattle. And I have plans for them."

Now it was Khellendros's turn to listen. The great Blue looked into her eyes and saw the hint of a smile.

"Some will be kept in pens," Malys began, "just like they keep cattle. They'll breed for us, giving us a constant food supply. Humans, elves, dwarves. All of them." Malys studied Khellendros, gauging if he was appalled by the idea. But his expression held steady, and the Red was pleased. "The smartest and the easiest to dominate will be used as spies. I want to know what is going on in their cities, and the loyal spies that I cultivate will tell me."

The Blue reached a talon up and idly scratched at his lower jaw. "I warned you that humans are clever. You will not find many who will cooperate with you."

"But I will find enough. And those who dare to stand up to me will be slaughtered." Malys rose on her haunches until her eyes were level with those of Khellendros. "Hundreds, thousands of them must be slaughtered anyway. Their population must be held in check, kept down. They must be kept under control. This time the humans will not be able to chase us from the face of Krynn because we will not give them the opportunity."

Khellendros silently regarded her. He was impressed with her drive for power, yet he was more than a little concerned by it. Malys was determined. If she managed to realize her goals of dominating people, what would she consider next?

"You need me," she hissed, interrupting his thoughts. "You

need me as an ally."

"I would not want you as a foe."

"And I need you," the Red continued. "You are powerful, larger than the other dragon overlords. Together, you and I can orchestrate the taking of Krynn," she said silkily. "And when the time is right, you and I can breed a new race of dragons to walk on the face of the world."

* * * * *

Khellendros agreed to Malys's scheme. As he flew toward his desert home, he recalled his exact words to her. "There is no other on Krynn I would ally myself with. I am honored, Malystryx, you chose to include me in your plans."

The pact sealed, he left her to return to the Northern Wastes. Khellendros hadn't lied to her. There was no one on Krynn he would consider as a partner. Kitiara's essence was in The Gray, so Malys would do as an ally for the time being. It was safer to be with her than to stand against her. She was greedy, ambitious, manipulative, powerful—she had the traits he admired. But she was not Kitiara. And she could never take Kitiara's place.

"I shall use humans as cattle, Malys," he whispered, as his course took him over Neraka's tallest mountains. "But not in the manner you would suspect."

The Blue spent most of his days entrenched in his lair beneath the Northern Wastes' vast desert. Khellendros had enlarged his cavern, using Malys's techniques for molding the terrain. There were several underground chambers now, and a few of them held humans—barbarians he snatched from their villages along the Shark Reef.

They stared at him with frightened eyes. They knew better than to talk to him, ask what would happen to them, dare to challenge him. Humans are more intelligent than you give them credit for, dear Malys, Khellendros thought.

The Blue worked with his captives, separating them, playing upon their fears and weaknesses. He had to corrupt them, turn them against each other or drive them insane. Through the process of creating spawn, Khellendros learned that only evil humans, or those who had been rendered near-mindless, made suitable offspring. Strong-willed humans with good hearts always seemed to die in the process or result in empty blue husks that lacked the comprehension to follow even the simplest of orders.

But I shall find a way to overcome that obstacle, he thought. *I shall find a way to transform any human, regardless of its nature.*

At the end of a month he had a dozen suitable candidates for the process, and an angry captive sivak draconian that would fuel their transformation. But the dragon's tears wouldn't come, and he needed a tear—a bit of himself—to complete the transformation of each of his offspring.

The dragon paced in his expansive underground lair. He concentrated on Kitiara, thought about her body's death, about how he had failed her. A great sense of sadness overcame him, but at the back of his mind he couldn't deny that a trace of hope, of bringing her back and giving her the body of a spawn, still remained. And that trace of hope kept him from producing that vital tear.

The Blue's curses reverberated like thunder in the cavern, causing the walls to shake and crack. The ominous rumble in his belly began, and only the gasps of his human prisoners kept him from releasing a lightning bolt.

His great claws pounded over the stone floor and carried him out into the desert. It was night. The stars winked down at him as if they were mocking him. The sand was cool beneath his feet, signaling that it was late, that the ground had been given hours to cast off its heat. Khellendros had lost track of time, and he howled in frustration. He sent a bolt of lightning skyward and roared deafeningly.

"No!" he screamed. "I shall not be defeated!" He spit another bolt of lightning, this time toward the horizon, blasting a patch of offending scrub grass. He thrust his claws into the sand, digging and scratching to vent his anger. The grains flew all about him, as if tossed by a violent wind. Suddenly he stopped his tirade and stared at the hole he created.

"The sand," he whispered. "The blessed sand."

Khellendros opened his eyes wide and shoved his head into the hole. The coarse grains of sand worked their way beneath his eyelids, rubbing, irritating, causing tears to well up. He pushed his head in deeper, ground his eyes and nostrils against the desert floor until the sensation was overwhelming and he could scarcely breathe. Then at last he pulled back, raised his face to the sky, and turned toward his lair. The sand forced his eyes to water, forced the tears he so desperately needed for his spawn.

He hurried into his underground chamber and began muttering the words to the enchantment he had learned in the portals beyond Krynn. His teardrops splashed onto the rocky floor and shimmered.

* * * * *

The dozen blue spawn that stood before Khellendros were his first successful ones. Corrupted before their metamorphosis, their eyes gleamed evilly in the dark chamber beneath the desert. Diminutive bolts of lightning crackled around their jet black claws, and their sapphire wings fluttered gently. The spawns' scales were tiny, looking like dark blue chainmail that had been oiled and well cared for. Their forms were manlike, with broad-chested torsos, long legs, and muscular arms. But their heads looked more like the snouts of lizards, and each had a jagged ridge that ran from between their eyes down to the tips of their stubby tails. Their feet were webbed and clawed, resembling Khellendros's, but in

miniature. Their noses flared as they alertly sniffed their surroundings.

Khellendros sat back against the far wall of his lair and
intently studied them. He was as proud of them as any father
would be of his young children. But these children were not
soft and cuddly, they were warriors, and they would do the
Blue's bidding without argument or question. One of them
would be chosen to become Kitiara's body, perhaps the one
that distinguished itself most in battle.

"Soon there shall be more of you," Khellendros gushed to
his attentive pupils. "Many more. You shall be an impressive
force, and you shall ravage the desert and, after that, the
sweet countryside of Palanthas. Together we shall steal the
humans' precious magical items—their scrolls and swords,
anything that pulses with enchantment. We shall somehow
find enough magic to force open a portal. And no one shall
stop us. Your very appearance shall so frighten every living
creature that—"

As one, the spawns' eyes flashed to the right, toward the
entrance of the lair. Khellendros growled and padded past
them, curious to see what or who might have wandered into
his cavern, hoping it wasn't Malystryx. He had not intended
to share news of his creation with her, and it was critical that
she not learn about his plans to open a portal and bring
Kitiara back to life.

"Hello?" a small voice called.

Not Malys, Khellendros realized. But who? He peered into
the darkness, his acute vision seeing only shadows and a hint
of light.

"May I join you?" One of the shadows separated from the
wall, or rather a portion of the wall split off. The small block
of rock shuffled forward, changing its shape as it neared
Khellendros. "Remember me?". the rock queried as it continued its transformation. "I know it's been almost thirty years
since we met, but I like to think that I'm hard to forget."

"Fissure," the Blue growled. It was the huldrefolk, the one he saw at the circle of stones portal, the one who explained why Khellendros could not return to The Gray. The Blue rumbled, hostilely preparing to blast the creature who so arrogantly strolled into his lair.

"Wait!" Fissure cried, sensing the dragon's intent. "I came here to help you."

The rumble caught in Khellendros's throat, the energy remained poised, ready to be released.

"I was listening in. Bad habit of mine," Fissure babbled. "I heard that you still want access to the portals—even after all this time. Well, I suppose it's really no time at all to you."

"Insolent creature!" Khellendros spat.

"Yes, maybe I am," Fissure continued. "But I still want access to the portals, too. You've got the right idea about gathering magic to force one open. But not just any magic will do. I have an idea . . . "

The rumble died, and Khellendros moved aside, allowing the huldrefolk to step deeper into his lair.

TASSLEHOFF BURRFOOT

Chapter 10

The Calling

The tomb stood in a field near Solace. It was built a few decades past by the people of Ansalon. A stark building, simple in design, it was nonetheless impressive and elegant, made of fine black obsidian and polished white marble that had been hauled by dwarven artisans from the kingdom of Thorbardin.

Inside it lay the bodies of the Knights of Solamnia and the Knights of Takhisis who fought and fell in the Abyss. Their names were engraved on the blocks that made up the tomb's outer walls, as were the names of knights whose bodies could not be recovered. Tanis Half-Elven also rested here.

The tomb had two exquisitely crafted doors. One was gold

and carried the image of a rose; the other was silver and had an etching of a lily in the center. Above the sealed doors the name Tasslehoff Burrfoot had been painstakingly carved. But the kender's body was not inside—it had vanished in the Abyss after Tas nicked Chaos and drew the necessary drop of blood to save Krynn. A hoopak, the kender's favorite possession, was chiseled beneath his name.

All around the tomb grew trees that had been brought by elves from the Silvanesti and Qualinesti forests. They were saplings when the tomb's construction began. Now they were tall and could stand against unpredictable weather and shade the shrine's frequent visitors.

On the tomb's low steps a bouquet of flowers had begun to wilt in the warm, still air. There were always flowers at the tomb because there were always pilgrims to bring them. The pilgrims consisted of elves, dwarves, kender, gnomes, humans, and an occasional centaur. And though they were respectful, the visitors were rarely grim. The tomb wasn't a place of sadness and grief, it was a place of reflection and introspection. It honored life. It was also sometimes the site of family gatherings, particularly when the families involved were kender.

Two kender stood outside the tomb now. They were not related. In fact, they had only just met. But they were quickly becoming friends, as kender had a tendency to do.

"See this spoon?" the smaller boasted. "It's just like the one Tasslehoff had, the one he used to chase away undead. It's a magical spoon of undead turning."

"That's a fine spoon. And quite valuable I suspect," the taller replied. She was attempting to read the names on the stones, while at the same time trying to pay at least a modicum of attention to the young man. "I wish I had one like it."

"Now you do!" he exclaimed, as he thrust the spoon toward her. "Consider it an early birthday present. Or a late one. Happy birthday, Blister!"

"Thank you." Blister grinned and reached out a gloved hand. Her fingers slowly closed about the handle and she grimaced. It hurt to use her hands much—the result of an unfortunate accident of her youth that she preferred not to think about. She dropped the spoon in one of the many pouches at her side, and resumed reading the names of the honored dead.

"How old are you, anyway?" The small one asked as he fussed over a daisy.

"Old enough."

"Older than me?"

"By quite a lot."

"Thought so. You've got almost as much gray hair as you do blonde."

"Thanks."

"You're welcome."

His hair was red and was a snarled mess that was tied in a poor semblance of a topknot. Blister suspected his unruly mane was the source of half his name—Raph Tanglemop. Her topknot was neat, every hair in place. It took her a long time to arrange it, and she used modern methods to do so. No need to make her fingers ache when a gnomish invention would do the trick. Blister's clothes were also a contrast to her new-found companion's. His orange shirt seemed to collide with his bright green pants that had mismatched blue patches on the knees. And he wore a dark purple vest that had a half-dozen lighter purple pockets sewn on it with yellow thread. Blister wore tan leggings and a rose-colored tunic that hung a few inches above her knobby ankles. Her brown leather boots matched her pouches, and nearly complemented the wood of the hoopak she laid next to Raph's flowers.

"I bet Tas had one just like that," Raph said, as he closely admired her offering.

"No. I suspect his wasn't broken." Blister nodded toward a crack in the haft.

"So why are you leaving this one, if I may be so imperti-
nent to ask?"

"This was my favorite," she replied wistfully. "Besides,
those inside have no need of weapons—functional or otherwise. This is just a token of respect."

"Oh." Raph's attention drifted from the tomb to a tall man
who was standing several yards away, under the branches of a
shaggybark tree.

"Wonder what token that fellow'll leave?" Raph speculated
out loud. "Maybe a bag of seeds. I think he looks like a
farmer."

Blister glanced over her shoulder. "What he leaves, if anything, should be none of our business."

Raph scowled. "Just curious," he said.

"Let's be polite." Blister tugged the smaller kender away
from the steps. She sat against the trunk of an Errow elm, the
closest tree to the tomb. Raph slumped at her side.

"You're pouting," she observed.

"I never pout," he said, his lower lip protruding noticeably.

The stranger glanced in their direction, then strode toward
the tomb. He stopped a few feet from the doors and knelt. He
could have been a farmer or a common laborer. His gray shirt
was thin and worn at the elbows, and laced with a plain white
cord. His black leather breeches also showed some age, and
the heels of his boots were pitted. He wiggled his shoulders to
free a canvas backpack, and let it fall to the ground behind
him.

"Wonder who he is?" Raph whispered. "Wonder what's in
his pack?"

The stranger's skin was tanned and slightly weathered
from the sun, and his long blond hair was neatly tied at the
base of his neck with a black leather thong. His shoulders
were broad, and Blister saw muscles ripple beneath the thin
fabric of his shirt. He drew a long sword from a battered
scabbard at his side and laid it on the ground in front of him.

Then he bowed his head, whispering.

"Do you think he's going to leave that sword? It looks old. I bet it's valua . . . er, sharp. And I bet it would be dangerous just to leave it there. Children could get hurt."

"Shhh!"

"If he's going to leave it, I'm going to go pick it up. Just to keep the children safe, of course."

"It would be too big for you to carry," Blister admonished.

"I could drag it."

The man could hear the kender quibbling nearby, but pushed their voices aside and gazed up at the tomb. He had walked to the tomb from Crossing, a port city to the north. It had taken him more than a week to reach the site, and he'd pushed himself, especially in the foothills near Solace. He was tired and hot, and he intended to find an inn and rest right after he paid his respects. Then he'd come back again tomorrow.

"Forgive me," he spoke softly and stared at the silver door, his eyes fixed on the lily. "The battles I fought, the blood on my hands, those I killed—" He stopped. A breeze had picked up, washing over his face and cooling him.

His skin began to tingle, slightly at first, but then more pervasively. The hair on the back of his neck rose, and a shiver raced down his spine.

"You spoke of battles," he thought he heard the breeze whisper. "Are you a warrior?"

The man glanced about, spied the kender chattering to themselves. It wasn't one of them. He looked over his shoulder. Perhaps another visitor to the tomb had arrived and overheard him. But no one else was here.

"Are you a warrior?" the wind persisted.

"I was," the man answered softly.

Perhaps someone was behind the tomb. He made a motion to rise, but his legs felt as if they were rooted to the ground. Suddenly the double doors to the tomb shimmered, became translucent for an instant, and a ghostly woman with golden hair stepped through them. A flowing robe of pale blue mist clung to her ethereal form. Golden curls whipped softly about her radiant face. And when she moved, the stranger felt a soft breeze flow over him.

"Perhaps you could be a warrior again," she stated. Her voice was musical. She closed her eyes and extended a ghostly hand toward him.

The man's skin tingled even more, and a chill coursed through his body. He shivered, but the sensation quickly passed, and he swallowed hard and stared at the image.

"I've looked into your heart," the ghostly woman said.

"Are you a ghost? A specter of someone who died in the Abyss? Why show yourself to me?"

"I'm no ghost. I show myself to warriors, strong men and women with the ability and willingness to make a difference in the world."

"Who are you?"

"Names are for another time, for when we meet on Schallsea." Her hair settled about her shoulders, and her diaphanous blue eyes locked onto his. "I sense that you are searching for a cause, one to heal your wounded soul. I can give you a grand one."

"How do you know what I'm searching for?"

"I know your heart. Perhaps better than you do," the ghostly image replied to the man. "Come to the Silver Stair on the island of Schallsea."

"Where the Citadel of Light is?"

"Where your destiny lies."

"My destiny?"

"And Krynn's."

The stranger watched the image quaver and disappear.

"Excuse me," Raph blurted. "Are you all right?"

The man shook his head, trying to clear his senses. The door looked solid. The ghost was gone. "Did you hear what that woman said?" he asked, standing and retrieving his sword.

Raph scowled as he watched the man thrust the old blade into the scabbard. "What woman?"

"The one who came out of the tomb."

"No one came out of the tomb," Blister interjected.

"The woman who stepped through the door."

"Maybe you'd better rest," Blister suggested. "I think you have a fever."

"Here's a spoon of wellness!" Raph exclaimed as he reached into his pouch and pulled out a tarnished silver soupspoon.

"How many of those do you have?" Blister asked.

"A couple dozen or so. But they're all different."

"I don't need to rest," the man stammered. "I'm fine. I just need to get to Schallsea."

"I've never been to Schallsea," Blister said. "I've always wanted to go there. I know a ship runs a trade route from New Ports to the island."

"Thank you." The stranger nodded to Blister, declined Raph's spoon, and brushed by the kender.

"I've never been to Schallsea, either," Raph announced. "Wonder what it's like?"

"I don't have anything better to do at the moment," Blister mused.

"So let's go!"

Blister hurried to keep up with Raph, who hurried to keep up with the tall human.

Chapter 11

Ghostly Tidings

Again the ghostly image of the woman appeared, though this time it was to hover above the top of a long, dark table in a room high in the Tower of Wayreth. The sun was setting and the orange glow that spilled into the room created a soft halo about the translucent woman.

The apparition glided toward Palin, who sat alone and unaware at the head of the table. Stacks of parchment were carefully arranged in front of him, and he was staring at one curled and yellowed page that was covered with notes written in a near-incomprehensible scrawl. The page fluttered in the breeze created by the phantom, and he glanced up.

Palin's lips edged upward into a slight smile. "You have

good news, I hope," he said.

The apparition drifted until her fair, blue eyes were even with Palin's. She stretched out an insubstantial hand, and he extended his own, until solid and incorporeal fingers touched in a sort of greeting.

"It is not as good as I had hoped," the female image replied. "But it is a start. I've called out to many suitable warriors, though only one so far seems to be a likely prospect. He makes his way toward Schallsea as we speak."

Palin shook his head. "Only one?"

"There will be others," the apparition said. "Remember, I was alone at the beginning, in the time of the War of the Lance. But your father joined me, and your uncle. And then more were added to our ranks. I will continue calling to people at the tomb. More will answer. It might just take more time than expected."

"I haven't given up hope," Palin said softly.

"I know. And neither have I."

"This one who comes to you," Palin began, "if he is willing . . ."

"I will send him to the Lonely Refuge, in the Northern Wastes near Palanthas."

"The handle is there."

"Waiting for the pennant," the ghostly image added. She nodded and disappeared.

Chapter 12

Company

"What's your name?" Raph huffed.

"Dhamon."

"That's it? Just Dhamon?"

"Dhamon Grimwulf."

"Hmm. Not a very cheery name. Why'd your folks call you that? Must have been in a bad mood, huh? Maybe it was raining. Or maybe a wolf killed all the cows on their farm. Where're you from?"

Dhamon didn't answer. Though exhausted, he in fact lengthened his stride, and it was all the two kender could do to stay within several yards of him. The vision of the phantom woman kept playing over in his mind, spurring him on and raising question after question.

"A grand quest," he muttered half under his breath. "Schallsea. My destiny. Maybe I'm crazy to be doing this, going after a ghost. Maybe I imagined the whole thing."

"He's talking to himself again, Blister."

"Hush. Walk faster, Raph."

Dhamon had a map of the country. He'd purchased it from a scribe in Crossing and used it to find the tomb. He had intended to stay at the tomb longer, a few days maybe, to meditate, consider what had brought him there, and to think about what he would do with the rest of his life. He hadn't counted on the ghost.

He looked at the map as he walked. It was an artfully-rendered one, and the mapmaker had taken considerable care to ink sites of historical interest and paths through the woods south of Solace, near the cities of Haven and Qualinost. But Beryl ruled there, and Dhamon was glad the vision was directing him away from the creature and not to it.

The map also showed a road from Solace to New Ports, and unfortunately it looked like a considerable distance. If the mapmaker's scale was accurate, it would take at least a couple of days to get there.

Maybe I can lose them by then, he thought. He yawned, glanced over his shoulder, and saw the two kender huffing. They'll have to sleep sometime.

So did Dhamon. Early that evening he selected a clearing by the side of the road, one with a stream nearby so he could bathe and clean the dirt from his clothes. Just a few hours of rest, he told himself. I'll be up before dawn, and the kender will still be snoring. Maybe I'll rethink this whole thing then and decide to turn back.

Dhamon's dreams were filled with images of battlefields, the twisted corpses of men left behind in shallow, unmarked graves, pools of sticky blood scattered across the ground. It was always the same. But tonight was a *little* different. The phantom woman intruded and floated above the carnage. She neared him and lessened the nightmare. "Schallsea," she repeated. "Your destiny." The words echoed in his head until his fatigue took over. He awoke midmorning, to the smell of roast rabbit and fresh berries.

"He even talks to himself in his sleep," Raph whispered. "I was wondering if he'd ever wake up. And I thought farmers were s'posed to get up with the sun."

"Hope you slept well!" Blister chirped. "We left the best part of breakfast for you! It's still plenty warm."

"Caught it myself," Raph interjected. "With my spoon of rabbit grabbing!"

"And your snare," Blister added quietly.

Dhamon's stomach rumbled. The rabbit smelled better than the dried venison in his pack. "Thank you," he said, as he helped himself. While he ate, the kender continued to chatter.

"We haven't been properly introduced." Raph puffed out his chest and gestured at his companion. "This is Blister Nimblefingers. She's a lot older than I am. I'm Raph Tanglemop. I'm originally from Zhea Harbor in Southern Ergoth. I don't know if Zhea Harbor is still called Zhea Harbor, or even if it's a harbor. There's lots of ice around it now. I doubt ships could get in. And what's a harbor without ships? See, this big white dragon moved in—a really big dragon—and the whole country started getting terribly cold. I don't like the cold. I don't have warm enough clothes for it. And I'm not particularly fond of dragons—even though I've never actually seen one before. I suspect if I saw one I wouldn't be here. Anyway, I decided I should move out before I froze. So I got on this ship and came here. Well, actually I came to Solace—after landing in Crossing—because the name Solace sounded like it would be a nice place. And I would've stayed in Solace for a while. I saw some other kender there. They told me about the tomb and Tasslehoff and everything. That's where I met you and Blister. I've never been to Schallsea. That sounds like it could be a nice place, too."

"I'm originally from Kendermore," Blister interrupted as Raph took a gulp of air. "I left home when Malys came. I had to warn the Knights of Solamnia about the Red. After I accomplished my mission, I found I had no home left to return to, thanks to Malys. So, I decided to see the world."

Dhamon offered her a weak smile between the last few bites of the delicious rabbit.

"How about you?" Raph persisted. "Are you a farmer? Blister thinks you're a farmer. Well, I do anyway, and she probably would agree with me. Do you raise pigs or cows? Or maybe corn? I haven't figured that part out yet. How'd you come to be at the tomb? And why do you always talk to yourself?"

"I'd better be on my way," Dhamon said as he reached for his backpack. He stood and strapped on his sword. "I suppose you're joining me?"

"Of course!" Blister and Raph answered practically in unison.

"You're not going anywhere—yet."

The three whirled to see a pair of grisly men, bandits from the looks of them. The pair had snuck up behind Dhamon and the two kender during the steady stream of conversation. Their clothes were worn and dirty, but they had on expensive new boots and carried clean satchels, spoils of their previous victims perhaps. The swords they waved were in good repair. The taller one's blade had a fine filigreed hilt edged in gold that hinted it once belonged to a gentleman.

"There's a toll for using this road," the tall one said. A fresh scar ran from just below his eye to the bottom of his jaw, and he was missing the little finger on his right hand. "The toll is whatever you have that's valuable."

"Then, provided we're satisfied, you can be on about your business," the other sneered. He was several years younger than his companion, and his scars were less noticeable.

"I have spoons," Raph offered nervously. He fumbled in his pouch and held up a tarnished one.

The tall man was quick. He spun forward and kicked the pouch from Raph's grasp. A dozen spoons went flying, spinning in the air and clattering to the ground. Raph scooted back and tried to hide behind Blister.

"We don't want spoons!" the younger bandit shouted. He grinned, revealing a row of yellowed teeth. "We want steel coins. Give them up—Now!"

"No!" As the word erupted from Dhamon's mouth, he leapt backward and drew his long sword. The blade arced above his head, flashing in the morning sun, and came down hard on the older bandit's sword hand. He struck with only the flat of the blade, but the force was enough to disarm the man, whom Dhamon guessed was the greater threat.

The younger bandit stepped forward, slicing the air to keep Dhamon at a distance. But Dhamon brought his sword up to arrest the swing, and the blades met loudly.

"I like a challenge!" the young man jeered.

"I'd have thought you'd like to live," Dhamon retorted. "We can end this now, and you and your friend can leave. No one will get hurt. And I'll forget this happened."

The young man laughed and darted in, slashing at Dhamon's legs and cleaving only air.

"Look out!" Blister cried. She fluttered her short arms in the direction of the older bandit, who'd stooped to retrieve his weapon.

A growl escaped Dhamon's lips. He pivoted to his right and swept his blade in a wide arc. The young bandit was unprepared, still moving forward. Dhamon's weapon passed over his opponent's sword and sliced deep into the young bandit's chest. An expression of surprise etched on his face, the bandit dropped his blade and fell to his knees, clutching at the growing line of red on his tunic. A moment later he pitched forward, his face falling in the dying embers of the cookfire.

Dhamon stepped over the body to meet the charge of the older man. "I'll repeat my offer," he hissed between clenched teeth. He brought his blade up to parry a vicious stroke. "End this now and walk away."

"I'll end it by killing you!" The bandit pushed forward, trying to make Dhamon trip over the dead man behind him.

But Dhamon jumped to the side. The bandit was so close Dhamon could smell the pungent, old sweat that clung to the man's clothes.

The bandit pressed again, and Dhamon held his breath to avoid the stench. He dropped to a crouch, watching the fancy sword pass over his head. In that moment, he brought his own blade up, thrusting it hard through the man's stomach. He pulled it free as the body fell heavily.

Dhamon shook his head sadly, then knelt between the bodies. He hung his head, laid his sword on the ground, and clasped his hands in front of him. The soft breeze teased the stray strands of hair that had come loose from his ponytail. He mumbled reverently.

"Is he praying?" Raph whispered.

"I think so," Blister said.

"Doesn't he know the gods are gone? There's no one to hear him."

Blister drew a gloved finger to her mouth, encouraging Raph to be quiet.

"There's not a scratch on Dhamon," Raph whispered. "He just killed two men and he didn't even get dirty. And now he's praying over them. They were evil, and he's praying."

Dhamon rose, picked up his sword, and strode toward the stream. He washed the blood off the old blade, sheathed it, then retied his hair.

"You're not a farmer, are you?" Blister asked.

"No," Dhamon answered.

Behind him Raph was chattering again and rummaging through the dead men's possessions. He pocketed most of the coins and the other interesting odds and ends that were pulled from the bodies.

"You want this fancy sword, Dhamon?" Raph asked. "You earned it. And it's too long for me."

Dhamon shook his head.

"Bet it's worth something," Raph mumbled softly.

"It's probably at least worth passage to Schallsea," Blister said. "Look, Dhamon's leaving! Let's go."

"Wait! I gotta get my spoons!"

Chapter 13

The Path to the Silver Stair

New Ports was perched on a thumb-shaped bay of the New Sea. It was a bustling town, growing with the addition of elves who'd left the Qualinesti forest when the Green moved in. Not all the elves left the forest, nor did all those who left come here. But those who did swelled the population and made it look as if the town was thriving.

The town was built like a wheel. The oldest residential section formed the hub, and from it radiated spokelike streets filled with homes and businesses. The newest buildings were those farthest from the center of town, except for a stretch of old buildings on the coast.

It was easy to distinguish the older section of town from

the new. The center of the city was comprised of sturdy stone buildings with thatch roofs. The shutters and window boxes were worn and covered with chipping paint. To the west, the buildings were smaller, made of wood, and covered in new paint—or no paint at all. Some looked like they had been thrown together, and their walls smelled of freshly cut pine. Between them were shacks and lean-tos, occupied by people who did not yet have permanent homes. It looked like a city that was swelling, prospering, perhaps growing too quickly.

But despite appearances, New Ports wasn't flourishing. Beggars clustered between buildings. Urchins played by the back doors of inns, hoping to find tasty morsels amid the trash or to receive handouts from the cooks. Several businesses were closed or looked dusty and vacant inside.

Raph struck up a conversation with a street merchant who explained that most businesses were faring poorly, and some closed their doors because it took more coins to stay open than they could make in a day. People were simply saving their money in the event the Green expanded her territory east to the town and they needed to buy passage to another land where it might be safer. Most of the residents were uneasy, though they hid it well under smiling facades.

The fishermen were the only truly happy folk around, the merchant said. Now that the far part of New Sea was a marsh due to the Black's alteration of the climate, the warm weather had extended to the west and touched this stretch of the water and fishing was considerably better. People had to eat, so the fishermen were profiting because New Ports had more mouths to feed.

Dhamon paused at a corner and bought an apple from a gnome. The kender did likewise, then they were quick on his heels toward the waterfront.

The salty sea air was strong and not unpleasant. The breeze stirred it with the scents of freshly-caught fish, crabs, and lobster. Dhamon spied several men fishing with nets and poles from an old, narrow dock that stretched out into the sparkling bay. A few ships were moored to the larger docks where the water was darker and deeper. It was midday, so most of the fishing boats would be out for several more hours.

It didn't take the trio long to find a ship that made somewhat regular runs to Schallsea Island. It was a small coastal trader called the *Wind Chaser*. Made of poplar and pine, it was not quite fifty feet long and had only one mast and a square sail. The captain was a handsome, dark-skinned man with short black hair. He was tall and muscular and bedecked in a crisp yellow shirt with voluminous sleeves that snapped in the wind. His tan breeches were baggy and gathered at the knees, just above his black snakeskin boots.

"Schallsea, huh?" the captain asked as he strode from the center of the deck and peered over the low rail at Dhamon. He had a deep, melodious voice that carried well and was pleasant to listen to. His dark eyes locked onto the kender, and he pursed his lips. "I only go when I've enough passengers—and enough coin. That will probably be sometime tomorrow or maybe the day after that."

Raph produced the filigreed long sword he'd been dragging. "Will this buy us a ride?"

The captain grinned, his eyes surveying the weapon in admiration and lingering on the pommel. Dhamon glanced at the cutlass that hung from the dark man's right hip. It was well-oiled and had a keen edge that flashed in the sunlight, but it wasn't as valuable as the sword Raph had offered him. Several daggers were strapped about his waist, and the pommels of more daggers peaked out from beneath his shirt and from the tops of his boots.

"That's a fine blade. How'd you come by it, little one?" The speaker was a woman, as dark as the captain, but with even shorter hair. It almost appeared as if she'd shaved her head. She wore an ivory satin vest that nearly matched the color of the lowered sail she'd stepped from behind. Her brown breeches hugged her long legs like a tight glove, and the green silk sash she wore low around her hips waved animatedly in the strong breeze.

Dhamon suspected they were from the race of sea barbarians far to the northeast, black mariners from the lands around the Blood Cup, or the Blood Sea.

"My uncle gave me the sword," Raph began. "It's been in the family for years. I'm just too short to use it, and I'm tired of hauling it around."

"That'll buy passage for *you*," the captain stated.

"For *all* of us," Blister said.

The dark man raised an eyebrow. "All right. For all of you. The sword's valuable enough. Come back tomorrow. Before noon."

"Today," Dhamon insisted. "I need to go to Schallsea Island today."

"Well, you'll not get there in a day—no matter how early we leave. It's about three hundred miles to the main port on the island. Come back tomorrow and we'll see if there's enough passengers to make the trip."

"I've some coin," Dhamon continued. "I could make it worth your while to leave now."

"Someone after you?" the captain probed. "You a wanted man?"

Dhamon shook his head. "I'm just in a hurry."

"The coin *and* the sword," the woman said. She moved up behind the captain, gliding silently like a cat. "And then you'll have yourself a deal. I'm Shaon." She extended a slender, calloused hand to Dhamon to help him aboard. Her grip was forceful. "This is Rig. He's in charge of the *Wind Chaser*. We've two other crewmen, and they'll be here soon. They're picking up some supplies." She pivoted on her sandaled feet and brushed by Rig. "The men won't be happy about this," she whispered. "They thought we'd be in town at least one night."

"It'll cost you a hundred steel coins *and* the sword," Rig snapped.

Dhamon sighed and reached for his backpack. Raph's eyes grew wide.

"He's got that much steel?" the young kender whispered as he tugged on Blister's tunic.

"We could practically buy a boat for that," Blister cut in, ignoring her curious companion. "Fifty, and not a coin more. Fifty's too much anyway, but we're in a hurry. Take it, or we'll find another boat."

Rig grumbled as he glared at the two kender, who scrambled onto the deck. But he nodded and cupped his hands.

"Heard of the Silver Stair?" Dhamon asked as he paid the coins.

The dark man nodded. "The Citadel of Light. Pilgrims have been visiting the site for years." He passed the coins to Shaon, then pointed to a pair of benches near the center of the deck.

"That's where I need to go. The Silver Stair."

"It's farther up the coast. It'll cost you more."

"How much more?" Raph piped up.

"Twenty."

"Ten," Blister countered. The kender put her hands on her hips and scowled.

"Done." The dark man laughed and strode toward the bow.

"You would've really paid him twenty—and the hundred he asked for before that?" Blister asked.

Dhamon drew his lips into a straight line. "It's all the coin I have. But, yes, I would have."

"You've got to learn to bargain, Mr. Grimwulf," Blister lectured. "If you don't, you'll end up without a coin in your pocket. And then you'll starve."

Dhamon and the kender hadn't quite settled themselves on an old bench when two sailors laden with fresh water and fruit climbed aboard. They seemed surprised at the ship's imminent departure, and started to object, explaining their plans for the evening. But a cross look from Rig and a couple of barked orders cut them off and sent them scurrying to work on the sail. Moments later they were untying the ropes that held the *Wind Chaser* to the dock and the boat was moving slowly away.

"Stop! Wait for me!" called a voice accompanied by the hurried stomping of bootsteps. Dhamon looked over the rail at the hopeful passenger. "Rig Mer-Krel, you told me you weren't leaving until tomorrow at the earliest! What do you think you're doing?"

The captain motioned to Shaon, who rushed to the side and stretched to reach a slender arm over the railing. Dhamon noticed Raph's filigreed sword hung from Shaon's hip. Within a heartbeat she had helped aboard a russet-haired, panting dwarf.

"Sorry, Jasper," Shaon said, as she ruffled her fingers through the curls on his head. "We must've got our days mixed up."

"It was a good thing I saw your sail open," the dwarf huffed. He grumbled and fished around in his pocket, eventually producing seven steel coins. "The usual place, the Citadel. Just drop me up the coast as close as you can get."

Blister and Raph opened their mouths, a protest at the dwarf's small fee playing on their lips. But a glare from Dhamon silenced them. Dhamon inwardly fumed that he'd paid so much more than the dwarf, but he had the sense to keep quiet. At least he had a ride to his rendezvous with the ghost.

The dwarf shuffled toward the bench opposite them and settled onto it, directly across from Blister. Dhamon caught Raph staring at the newcomer. The dwarf did indeed look a little unusual and worth a second glance. The hair on his head was short, no more than a few inches long, and it grazed the tops of his ears. His beard was neatly trimmed, too, and was short—undwarflike. Dhamon guessed him to be about a hundred years old, in his prime, and fit for his stunted race, wearing a leather tunic over a bright blue shirt and trousers. He lacked the paunch of many of his kind, but not the dour expression. The dwarf grimaced at them.

"Who're you?" Raph asked.

The dwarf glowered at the kender. "Jasper Fireforge. Shaon says you're going to Schallsea, too."

"The Silver Stair," Raph announced. "Mr. Grimwulf thinks he has to go there, and Blister and me are going too."

It was Dhamon's turn to grimace.

The dwarf's eyes narrowed and he cocked his head. A shrug of his stout shoulders parted the neck of his leather tunic, showing a heavy gold chain and a piece of jasper.

"You're going there," the young kender persisted. "I over-heard you tell the lady—just as you paid her only seven steel."

"Where I go is my business," the dwarf returned.

Raph opened his mouth to ask another question.

"And when I go somewhere," the dwarf interrupted, "I pre-fer to go there quietly." He crossed his stubby arms, closed his eyes, and continued to glower.

The rest of the trip passed in an uneasy silence, with the two kender often at the bow, where they could chatter with-out bothering the dwarf.

* * * * *

The sight of the Citadel of Light left even the noisy kender speechless. The sunlight bouncing off of the Citadel's many huge crystalline domes made it hard to look directly at the structure, but its beauty drew them closer. Arcs of water from two grand fountains followed the curves of the sparkling buildings and drew attention to the central dome of the citadel. A figure stood in its entryway, waiting.

"She greets all who come here to learn the powers of the

heart," said the dwarf, his mood brightening considerably. He eagerly moved forward and the kender followed him.

Dhamon looked back toward the sea. Rig had agreed to wait just offshore until late afternoon tomorrow—for the promise of another ten pieces of steel. He said he'd bring the rowboat back for them when they signaled. If they took longer than that, the dark man said they'd have to catch him on his return trip next week. Dhamon grudgingly accepted the terms. He didn't want the *Wind Chaser* out of sight. He had no desire to be stranded, even though he had no particular place to go.

When Dhamon turned back to face the citadel, he found his companions had left him behind. The figure standing in the entry of the central crystalline dome beckoned to him. He was unsure of what waited for him. He rushed to catch up with his cohorts and found himself breaking into a run, suddenly swept up by an exhilirating wave of emotion that carried him forward.

Chapter 14

The Faces of Goldmoon

**Dhamon heard the hurried footsteps of the dwarf and
the kender behind him and briefly wondered if he should
have slowed his pace to accommodate them. He wasn't sure
of what had come over him. He had sped right by. It wasn't
like him to be pointedly rude. He turned to retrace his steps
and apologize to them.**

"I've been waiting for you."

The voice was familiar. He turned to see a small woman
with pale, wrinkled skin. Her white robe fluttered in the sea
breeze and outlined her slight frame.

"I have been calling out to many warriors who visited the
tomb, but you were the first to answer my summons."

It was the phantom woman, but her voice sounded softer than when he'd heard her near Solace and she looked much older than the young woman he saw at The Last Heroes Tomb. Her blond hair was wispy, and contained thick streaks of white. Her blue eyes were dull and rheumy. The strong sunlight revealed the lines on her face, and Dhamon could see that the flesh on her arms and along her jaw sagged slightly.

She was an old woman, seventy or eighty, he guessed, though she exuded a matronly air and carried herself with a quiet grace and dignity. Her gait was slow, but he could tell she was not infirm. There was a presence about her, a sensation of power.

"Please, come closer." Her voice was soft, not much above a whisper.

Dhamon's eyes locked onto hers, but he held his place. "I can see you well enough from here," he said.

"Tell me what brought you to the tomb."

Dhamon gave a slight shrug. "I came to the tomb to pay my respects to the knights. That's why most people go there, isn't it? But the tomb has nothing to do with why I'm here." He paused and pursed his lips. "And just why am I here?"

"I go to the tomb to honor my friends," she replied, ignoring his questions.

"Who are you?"

"I am Goldmoon of the Qué-Shu."

He stared at her as he searched his memory. Was this *the* Goldmoon, a Hero of the Lance? Was she the woman who fought in the War of the Lance and helped to restore healing magic to Krynn? The age would be about right, he mused.

"How were you able to call me?" was the only question he voiced.

"There is still some magic left in the world and in me. I sent my thoughts to the tomb in Solace. A place that honors fallen heroes should attract living ones, don't you think? I believed the tomb would be the best place to find new champions."

"Did you have to use your magic to make yourself look like a young woman? Did you think you needed that to get my attention?" Dhamon snapped. "Did you think I'm only interested in helping—"

"Goldmoon!" Jasper came rushing forward, panting from his long, hurried run. He regarded Dhamon. "His legs! They go on forever."

The dwarf's stubby legs carried him past Dhamon. The old woman smiled and extended a hand, and the dwarf shook it. Jasper looked into Goldmoon's starlike blue eyes. They were bright and full of warmth and surprisingly youthful.

"Sorry I've been away so long," he muttered. "I tried to get into Thorbardin, but you know they sealed the mountain. I thought I could find a way in, visit my relatives. Maybe I could have if I would've looked harder. But I remembered my promise and came back here."

Jasper watched her brush a strand of thick, silky hair away from her unblemished face. Her ruddy complexion nearly matched his, and the skin on her hand felt soft and smooth against his calloused fingers. The dwarf wasn't looking at an elderly woman. He saw Goldmoon as an ageless beauty full of life and filled with a sense of hope and faith. There were no age lines when he looked at her. There were no wrinkles or white hairs, no slowness of motion. Her voice and her manner were strong, as she was at the time of the War of the Lance.

"It's all right, Jasper," she said. She reached a finger down and touched the tip of his nose. "And I'm glad you escorted our visitor. I sent for him."

The dwarf looked at her quizzically, stroking his short beard. "A new student? Should I leave?"

"I want you to stay," she added.

"Can we stay, too?" Raph panted, as he edged forward.

"Raph, slow down! I told you not to barge into things.

You could get hurt!" Blister huffed and puffed up behind him, staring at Goldmoon. She straightened her tunic, brushed the sand off her shoes, and offered Goldmoon a smile. "Excuse us for coming to your home uninvited. My companions are rather headstrong. They didn't mean to be impolite."

"No apology needed," Goldmoon replied. "You are all welcome here."

She glided toward Dhamon. "There is a grand adventure in the offing," she said. "And it is an adventure one person alone should not undertake, Dhamon Grimwulf."

"You know my name?" The moment after Dhamon spoke the words, he wished he could draw them back into his mouth. If a woman could project an image over hundreds of miles and through a tomb door, she no doubt could learn the identity of whom she was projecting to.

"I know a lot about you, Dhamon. But do you know anything of me?"

He didn't answer.

"Decades past, my companions and I sought to stop the Dragonarmies. In droves, the evil men and creatures came west from the Khalkist Mountains, sweeping into Balifor and beyond. It was the start of the War of the Lance. Our struggle lasted five years, and in that time we witnessed the fall of eastern Ansalon."

Dhamon knew the stories of the Heroes of the Lance by heart. There were few on Ansalon who didn't know about the exploits of Caramon and Tika Majere, Raistlin, Goldmoon and the rest.

"The dragonlances were the key," Goldmoon said, interrupting his thoughts. "The secret of creating dragonlances was rediscovered during a time when many people had given up hope—like many have now. We used the newly forged weapons to drive back the Blue Dragonarmy. The good dragons, once held at bay because their eggs had been stolen, entered the war. The tide turned, and Takhisis's forces scattered. The evil dragons fled to remote parts of Ansalon and became weaker. Some of my companions who fought in that war have passed beyond this world—the kender Tasslehoff Burrfoot, Tanis Half-Elven, Flint Fireforge, Sturm Brightblade, dear Riverwind. Those few of us left . . . "

She paused and took a step closer. "We can only watch and believe the future will brighten. This is your world now, your time. We bested the dragons once. Perhaps they can be bested again. The gods are gone, and the threat of the dragons is greater than ever before. And you're looking for a cause, Dhamon Grimwulf, though you may not realize it. You're looking for something to lighten your heart. It seems a cause has found you."

She touched his shoulder. "Now is an age when men must gaze into their hearts and find the strength and faith to overcome the obstacles placed before them. They cannot look to the gods anymore for worldly salvation. They can only look to themselves. I've stared into your heart, Dhamon, and it's much stronger than you believe it to be."

"But what can I do?" Dhamon stared at the old woman. "Can one man really make a difference?"

"Not just one," Goldmoon replied. "Jasper will go with you. And others will eventually follow. I will continue contacting visitors to the tomb."

The dwarf scowled and shook his head. He shuffled toward Dhamon. "Flint Fireforge was my uncle. I promised him once that I'd help Goldmoon whenever she asked." Under his breath he added "I just never thought she'd ask."

"It might be exciting," Raph whispered. "We might get to see a dragon. And I've never seen one of them before."

"I think we should stay out of this," Blister calmly returned. "This isn't our concern. We only tagged along. This is Dhamon's business, not ours."

"So we'll tag along again."

"No, we won't," Blister scolded.

"Well, *I* will."

"No, you won't."

Dhamon ignored the chatter behind him. "What do you want me to do?" he asked Goldmoon.

"You must travel north to Palanthas. Evil breeds there, and it must be stopped. It will be a long journey, but a necessary one. I have friends nearby. The sorcerer Palin Majere will meet you in a place called the Lonely Refuge. It's in the Northern Wastes. Jasper can tell you how to get there. Palin will help. You must give him this." She reached into the folds of her robe and produced a tattered piece of blue and yellow silk.

"A piece of cloth?"

Goldmoon pressed it into his hand and motioned for the kender and Jasper to leave. The dwarf's grumbles were heard above the kender's banter, and Goldmoon waited until they were situated in front of one of the Citadel's large fountains.

"The cloth is a banner that was tied to a dragonlance. Palin has the lance's handle, or haft. When you've joined these two pieces, Palin will tell you where the lance rests. Unite the weapon's parts, Dhamon Grimwulf. It was one of the original dragonlances, rumored to be the most powerful of all. It might be our only hope against the dragon overlords."

"One weapon?"

"A single weapon maybe, but, more importantly, a symbol. Something to give the people of Ansalon hope. Something they can stand behind, be united by. There are a few other original lances left, but most of them are inaccessible to us right now. What you will join together will be a start. Perhaps subsequent visitors to the tomb who answer my summons can retrieve the other weapons."

Dhamon took a deep breath. Should he go to Palanthas and the Lonely Refuge, or travel wherever he wanted? Was she giving him a choice? Or was she giving him an order?

Could he walk away and take his life elsewhere? Or had he already decided at the tomb in Solace to let this woman chart his destiny, help him cleanse his heart?

"There are many ships in New Ports. I'll see if one will take us to Palanthas," he said.

"Hurry," Goldmoon urged.

Chapter 15

A Growing Evil

"It was my idea to come here," the creature snarled. "I said we should do it. It was me! Do you hear?"

The young goblin, a manlike thing less than four feet tall, had a flat face and a broad nose that looked as if it had been smashed with a hard object. His dark mouth was wide, and small yellow fangs peeked out from below his thin upper lip. His forehead sloped back, giving his bright red eyes more prominence, and his hairy arms almost dangled down to his knees, making him look apelike. He was a fine specimen of his race.

The sun that was starting to drop toward the horizon was only a shade lighter than the goblin's burnt orange skin. He squinted into the offensive light as he ranted. "I should get the credit for the idea! Do you hear?"

His fellows appeared roughly the same type, though they were older, less muscular, and had skin tones ranging from dirty yellow to deep vermillion. All of them were wearing crude leather boots and mismatched pieces of armor that had been pathetically fastened together. Most of the armor had been stolen from the graves of kender and elven warriors. Only a few pieces had been claimed in fair fights. And to the goblins, a fair fight usually meant a carefully planned ambush or a well-constructed pit trap laden with sharp spikes.

Several carried crude shields fashioned from boards and bearing designs of clenched fists or bashed heads. A few had impressive metal shields looted from fallen foes. Their weapons included primitive stone axes, clubs with metal spikes pounded into them, and maces.

"It was *not* your idea," the largest of the goblins barked. He carried a dented metal shield that bore the emblem of three roses—two buds and one full bloom—indicating it had at one time belonged to a knight from the Order of the Rose. "We were summoned."

The large goblin was called M'rgash, and he was the chieftain of the three dozen who were slowly picking their way through what was left of the forest. At one time the dense forest covered about half of Kendermore and bordered on Balifor. But a mountain range had sprung up where the two countries met and had obliterated a considerable number of trees.

M'rgash's entire tribe numbered more than four hundred, and they laired in tunnels deep beneath Wendle Woods to the south in kender territory. These three dozen were among his favorite and most loyal warriors. He handpicked them for this journey, and they'd set out five days ago.

The goblins stopped at the base of a rocky embankment

that formed the base of the mountain ridge and looked up. It hadn't been there a few months ago.

"We might have been summoned, M'rgash," the orange-skinned goblin retorted. "But it was *my* idea to answer the call." He was called Dorgth, and he was M'rgash's lieutenant.

M'rgash growled and slapped Dorgth's face with enough force to send the young lieutenant reeling. It was necessary for M'rgash to show a little force every now and then in order to keep his lofty position. "It was *my* decision. You merely agreed with me."

M'rgash was an old goblin, having seen nearly forty summers, and he knew goblin protocol better than any in the tribe. He cast a baneful look at Dorgth, who had risen in the ranks only because of his brashness and fearlessness. Then he motioned the entourage to follow him. Dorgth, properly chastised, took up the rear.

The goblins wound their way ever higher, quickly clawing their way up the sheer surface until they found what amounted to a path. M'rgash knelt and traced a footprint in a small patch of dirt. "Hobgoblins," he muttered. "I suspect our large cousins were summoned, too. But why?" He stepped onto the path and glanced to his right. The path snaked around the far side of the mountain. To his left it curved upward, leading to a large crevice. The spiky rocks at the very top were dark, indicating the sun had sunk lower. It would be blessed twilight within several minutes. M'rgash had timed the journey well.

The goblin chieftain strode toward the crevice, his tribesmen shuffling single file behind. Beyond the crevice stretched a plateau, and on it sat Malys, who took up nearly half of the space. The Red was impressive, and M'rgash stood in the heavy shadows of the opening and heard the sharp intake of the dragon's acrid breath. The warriors behind him heard it as well, and M'rgash heard the nervous chattering of their teeth.

"Don't run," the goblin chieftain mumbled. "Show no fear."

The dragon sat on her rear haunches, her horns even with the top of the rocky ridge that surrounded her plateau. The last bit of the sun's rays poked through the crevice and made her scales look molten. Her dark eyes gleamed malevolently at M'rgash. Wisps of steam curled upward from her great nostrils as she slightly nodded her head, deigning to acknowledge him.

To her right stretched a line of two dozen barbarians. Savages, they wore strips of fur and leather. Their tangled hair hung past their shoulders, and their skin was tanned and weathered from living above ground. Their muscles were thick, sweat-slick cords that stood out along their arms and legs with veins that twisted around them like rope. The goblin chieftain picked out their leader immediately. He held the largest spear and wore a heavy silver chain around his neck with a large golden charm dangling from it. The lead barbarian's eyes met M'rgash's glance, but only for a moment. The barbarian returned his attention to the dragon.

To Malys's left was a gathering of nearly fifty hobgoblins. M'rgash softly growled when he noted that Illbreth the Untrusting was leading this particular clan. The hobgoblins were clustered together, whispering and skittishly pointing at the dragon. M'rgash chuckled to himself. His cousins, nearly double his size, had little military training and didn't know how to stand at attention. The hobgoblins were a dark reddish brown, their hide a mixture of tough skin and hair. They carried maces and spears that were in far better repair than their black leather armor.

M'rgash, seeing that he had Illbreth's attention, strode through the opening so his soldiers could follow. He ordered them to form three lines directly behind him. Standing shoulder to shoulder, they looked like a reasonably well-polished military unit. However, the goblin chieftain smelled the strong scent of fear they gave off. He hoped the Red and Illbreth did not also recognize the odor.

Malys idly drummed a claw against the plateau's slate floor. "We will begin," her voice boomed. "Know that I could destroy you all if I wanted."

The fear scent grew stronger, and M'rgash heard the gasps of his hobgoblin cousins.

"But if I wanted to kill you, I wouldn't have summoned you here so your bodies could litter my lair. I have need of you." Her voice reverberated off the stone walls.

The silence that followed was long and uncomfortable, and finally the goblin chieftain found the courage to break it.

"Tell us what you need, dragon." His tone was strong and steady, filled with respect. "If it is within our power, we will give it to you."

"It is." The dragon lowered her head until her chin grazed the ground. Her neck snaked forward until her face was mere feet from M'rgash's. He could feel her hot breath. "I want your allegiance and the allegiance of your tribe. I want the allegiance of all the tribes represented here. Understand?"

Then she pulled her head in close to her chest and glanced from the barbarians to the hobgoblins, and finally back to M'rgash and his soldiers.

"You have our allegiance!" The barbarian leader took a step forward and bowed to the dragon. "I, Harg Darkaxe, so swear!"

M'rgash saw Illbreth step forward, too. The hobgoblin's knees wobbled, and his jaw trembled. M'rgash was pleased that though he was frightened, his cousin was even more afraid.

"I-I-I am Illbreth, leader of the Bloodridge Band. I promise the allegiance of my men here, as well as that of all my tribe in The Desolation. We number more than two hundred. We are yours."

It was M'rgash's turn. He puffed out his small chest, took a deep breath, and bowed to Malys. "I am M'rgash, chief of the mighty Tunnel Tribe. Our numbers are more than four hundred. And we pledge our—"

"What does our allegiance entail?" The words were Dorgth's. The young lieutenant had left the third rank and strolled forward to stand even with M'rgash.

The chieftain growled and stretched an arm out to strike his insolent lieutenant. Dorgth leapt forward to avoid the blow, moving closer to the Red.

"What do we have to do? I want to know before I make any promises," the brash goblin persisted. "I won't blindly swear allegiance to anybody."

Behind Dorgth, M'rgash muttered a quiet string of foul curses.

"You dare question me?" Malys hissed. A growl started deep in her belly, and the slate floor trembled in response. "I could slay you before your next breath!"

Dorgth held his place and stared up at her. The sun had set, and he could see much better now. The offending light no longer troubled his eyes.

"I was curious," the goblin lieutenant answered. "That's all." He didn't offer her an apology. According to goblin protocol, an apology was an acknowledgment of weakness.

"Stand away from your fellows," the dragon spat. "Come closer to me. That's it. Closer. Closer."

M'rgash clenched his hands and pursed his lips as he watched his lieutenant inch nearer to Malys. He would be needing a new lieutenant now. Who should he choose? Thornthumb? Perhaps Snargath? None of them were as brave, but they certainly weren't as foolish, either.

The Red's gaze drifted from the barbarians to the hobgoblins, back to M'rgash and his charges. "Do you have any others so audacious, goblin?" The rumble in her belly was growing louder still, and flames flickered out between her fangs.

"No, dragon!" M'rgash bellowed. "Dorgth is an impudent dog. He is not like the rest of my men!"

"Pity," Malys hissed. The rumble crescendoed until the plateau shook. She opened her maw and a column of flame rushed out. The searing lance of fire streaked over the head of Dorgth and hit M'rgash first. The goblin chieftain's screams were drowned out by the wild crackling of flames. The fire spread to engulf the three ranks behind him. The air on the plateau was instantly filled with the scent of charred bodies and the overpowering odor of fear from those who still lived.

She closed her mouth and stared down at the sole remaining goblin.

"Chieftain Dorgth," she began, "I trust you will return to your tribe and explain that they are working for me—all four hundred of them. All without question."

The goblin swallowed hard and nodded. He touched the top of his head where his hair had been singed off and then cast a quick look over his shoulder to see the smoking piles of ashes that had been his comrades. "Y-y-yes. I swear my allegiance—and theirs!"

"Hear me!" Malys snarled. "In exchange for all of your pitiful lives, you and your brethren in the mountains, plains, and tunnels will serve me. You will begin by gathering humans—villagers, farmers, wanderers—in the nearby lands you call Khur and Balifor. Age is unimportant. Take the old, as well as the young—even the infants."

"A-a-alive?" Dorgth stammered.

"Of course, I want them alive!"

"A-a-and when we have them? What do you want us to do with them?"

The dragon rumbled again, and the tremors sent shivers racing up and down the spines of the hobgoblins, barbarians, and Dorgth. "Cage them. Pen them up. Keep them weak and submissive, but keep them alive. Treat them like cattle, and show them no respect. And when you've collected more than the number in your tribe, return to me for instructions."

After dutifully cleaning up the ashes of his vanquished tribesmen, Dorgth led the procession from the Red's plateau lair.

None of them spoke until the sky was black and until they were deep in what was left of the forest between Kendermore and Balifor. Then the silent woods were filled with shared ideas for carrying out the Red's orders.

Chapter 16

Flint's Anvil

A few days later found Dhamon and Jasper back at the harbor in New Ports.

Rig Mer-Krel laughed loud and long and shook his finger at Dhamon. "Let me see if I understand you correctly. You want to pay me—and Shaon—and whoever else I can drag along sixty coins to sail to Palanthas on some scow you've managed to buy?" The dark mariner slapped his thigh. "Sixty coins wouldn't get one of us there as a deck hand."

"You've a good reputation," Dhamon began. He thought if money didn't work, perhaps compliments might do the trick. "We need a captain, and I hear you're the best. You certainly did a good job on our trip to the Silver Stair."

"He is a good captain!" Shaon beamed. She swept her hand out to her side, indicating the harbor. "He's got more experience on open waters than most of the folks here put together. Why, he sailed the Blood Sea of Istar and piloted a galleon through the Eye of the Bull. He was first mate on . . ."

Rig's glare kept her from spouting about more of his attributes and sailing accomplishments.

She gave him a sly wink. "But sixty coins are an insult," she admitted. "We'll have to brave the Gale—the storm that brews constantly in the Straits of Algoni. The money would have to be a lot better for us to give up our jobs here and risk our necks."

"How about the ship as payment?" Jasper offered. "She's at the third dock. Look her over. You take us to Palanthas, wait around for a few weeks, and then she's yours."

The big mariner leaned forward and studied the dwarf. "The green carrack?" Rig asked.

Jasper nodded. "I bought it yesterday. And I'm none too fond of water, so I wouldn't mind parting with it—after it takes us where we want to go."

"You'll take care of the supplies?"

Dhamon nodded.

"Then we'll leave in the morning, while the weather's still holding. I'm going to pick up a couple of extra men—if you don't mind. I doubt the pair of you would be much help on a ship."

* * * * *

Rig and Shaon had thoroughly inspected the carrack by the time Dhamon and Jasper reached the docks. It was barely sunrise. The front sail was square, not unlike the *Wind Chaser's*, but the rear sail was a lateen mizzen, one that resembled an oddly shaped triangle. The ship was eighty-five feet long, with a thirty-foot beam.

The ship was in good repair, its hull recently painted a dark green and its deck trimmed in red. A new name had been painted on the bow—*Flint's Anvil.*

"A bigger ship would've been better," Rig noted from halfway up the forward mast. "One with a deeper keel and a third mast, and a less heavy-sounding name."

"Change your mind?" Dhamon called.

"No. Just warning you she's going to feel the waves a little more than I'd like—and definitely more than you and Jasper would appreciate. Hope you don't get seasick and decorate my deck."

Dhamon made sure the supplies were aboard, including a dozen barrels of fresh water that were stacked in a pyramid near the rear mast. He still had about fifty steel coins left, more than enough to buy more food at a port along the way. He wasn't sure what he would do when he was out of money. Maybe this Palin Majere is wealthy, he mused.

Shaon had arranged for four crew members, three of whom were busying themselves making final adjustments to the rigging. The fourth came on board while Jasper was arguing with Shaon about cabin assignments. The new crew member walked with a wolf at his side.

"No animals," Dhamon said brusquely.

The wolf stood about three and a half feet tall at the shoulder and had thick red fur and golden eyes. The man stood twice as tall. He was tanned and burly and had rough features—a wide forehead, a puglike face and wide-set black eyes. He wore a vest without a shirt beneath it and the rest of his clothes were worn and tattered. A gleaming gold hoop that dangled from his right ear looked to be the most valuable item he owned.

"Half-ogre," Jasper muttered.

"The wolf goes," Dhamon called.

"Dhamon, meet Groller Dagmar," Rig returned. "I'd return the introduction, but he can't hear you. He's deaf.

And next to me and Shaon, he's the most competent seaman you have. I want him, so he stays—and that means his wolf does, too. Unless, of course, you want to find yourself another captain."

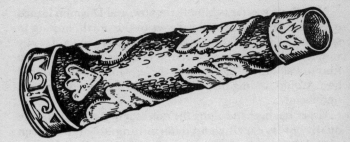

Chapter 17

Lessons

Dawn arrived with a slight breeze, barely enough to coax
Flint's Anvil out of the harbor. By late that afternoon the
wind was gusty and billowed the sails enough to make the
masts creak. They were making good time. Rig was at the
wheel, and the half-ogre, Groller, was with him. There was no
sign of the red wolf.

Dhamon and Jasper were doing their best to get acquainted
with the ship as it weaved across the bay. And the dwarf was
trying hard to get accustomed to the constant pitching.

"I feel horrible, like my stomach's climbed into my throat,"
Jasper grumbled. "Never been on a ship that rocked so much."

"That's only because you've never been on a ship when the

wind was blowing this strong," Dhamon returned. "I'll grant you the waves are pretty high, but it could be a lot worse. You'd better prepare for the Gale."

"It was always calm on the way to Schallsea," the dwarf said wistfully.

New Ports was far behind them now, and Dhamon leaned over the rail and strained his eyes to the north, hoping to spot Port O' Call. All he saw was the turbulent water. He idly wondered how many weeks they'd be at sea and what they'd find in Palanthas. "Evil breeds there," Goldmoon had told him. Would finding that evil be difficult? Or might the evil find them?

Jasper ran his hand along the rail, as if he were judging the quality of its carving and determining how it had been routed. Perhaps he was trying to keep his mind off the constant motion. A soft tinkling noise interrupted his inspection. He turned and frowned.

"Interesting name you chose for her, Jasper," Shaon observed. "Let's hope she's sturdy enough and doesn't sink like one."

"It was called *Melancholy Morkoth* before I bought it. I didn't like the sound of riding on a ship named after an ugly sea monster, so I renamed it after my uncle."

The dark-skinned woman shook her head. "Never cared much for relatives."

She was wearing a crisp white shirt, unbuttoned halfway to her waist, and tight black pants she'd bunched up to her knees. She was barefoot, and a thick gold chain she wore around her right ankle sported a double row of tiny bells that jingled merrily when she walked.

"I cared about Flint," Jasper muttered. "I cared enough to make a promise to him in a dream, that I'd help his friend Goldmoon, study from her too. Didn't figure being on a ship would be part of it." The dwarf gripped his stomach as the ship surged over a tall wave. His complexion was pale, and he grabbed the railing to steady himself. He stared at the water for a moment, closed his eyes, and turned around so his back was to the sea. "What's that?" he asked Shaon as he pointed at a taut rope.

Dhamon smiled. "Most people call it a rope," Shaon replied.

"Oh."

"But sailors call it a forestay. It's the line that runs from the mainmast to the bow. And you have to make sure it doesn't fray."

"And this?" The dwarf glowered and waggled his fingers at the mast.

"Well, the whole thing—the mast, boom, and gaff—is called a spar."

"This isn't so hard," Jasper grumbled. "Forestay, mast, spar, starboard, stern, rudder, rigging, keel, kender."

"Kender?" Dhamon turned away from the rail and followed the dwarf's gaze. He scowled as he spotted Raph and Blister climbing up the ladder from below deck. "I thought you two stayed in New Ports!"

"I wanted to," Blister sputtered, as she balanced herself on the rolling deck. "But Raph insisted on tagging along. I couldn't talk him out of it, so I figured I'd better come, too. Someone has to watch out for him and keep him out of trouble."

Dhamon groaned and strode toward the bow, away from the gathering.

Raph immediately spotted Shaon's ankle bracelet. He shuffled closer for a better look, the half-dozen pouches tied to his waist clinking and rustling as he went.

"How come you wear bells?" the kender asked.

"Rig gave them to me. Gold from Karthay."

"Why's your hair so short?"

"So it won't blow in my eyes."

"Why—"

Jasper positioned himself between Shaon and Raph, his back to the kender. He was still careful to keep one hand on the railing to help his balance. "Where do you think you and Rig'll go after you leave us in Palanthas?" he asked.

"We discussed it quite a bit last night. Rig didn't sleep much. I think he was excited to have his own ship. It's something he's always wanted. We might take her up and around the Northern Wastes and eventually back to the Blood Sea of Istar. That area's home for us."

Blister nudged her way into the conversation, and Jasper sighed in resignation and strode away, lurching toward a collection of crates near the capstan. The dwarf sat on the lowest one and grabbed his head as the ship rose over another swell.

"I've been there," she said. The kender was wearing an unusual pair of gloves this morning. They were green leather, and had small hooks on the thumbs.

Shaon glanced over her shoulder and stared dreamily at the water. "That's where I met Rig Mer-Krel—on a big carrack on the Blood Sea. The ship I was sailing on hit a reef. We took on water too fast, and a lot of men were trapped below deck and drowned. Sharks had already taken more than half of the rest of the crew when the *Sanguine Lady* pulled alongside. Rig was second mate on the *Lady*. He fished me out of the water. Those of us who lived signed on."

"That sounds exciting," Raph said. "You two married?"

"No. Not yet, anyway. But he's not looking elsewhere, so I'm satisfied."

"Why'd you end up way over here? The Blood Sea's practically a world away," the kender prattled.

"Shaon!" Rig looked sternly at the foursome. "Enough chatter. It's your turn at the wheel."

Rig drew Shaon aside, while Groller took the helm. Blister spotted Dhamon at the bow and headed toward him. Left alone, Raph became curious about the water barrels at the ship's stern.

* * * * *

Blister and Dhamon stood quietly for a long time, listening to the water breaking against the hull and the snapping of the sails. The sun was edging toward the horizon. It would set soon.

"You know, you never told me what brought you to the tomb, then to Schallsea," said the kender, finally breaking the spell.

"No, I didn't."

"And you're not going to, are you?"

Dhamon fixed his eyes on a large swordfish that arced above the water, then disappeared.

"You know, Mr. Grimwulf, if you're not going to tell the truth—or tell anything, for that matter—you better learn how to lie. I don't think you're very good at it."

"And I suppose you are?"

"I don't know about the lying part. But I'm good at telling stories—most kender are. Let me give you a lesson. If someone, like me for instance, asks you why you came to the Tomb of the Last Heroes, and you didn't want to tell them why you *really* did, you might tell them a story. You might say, 'I came to the tomb because I heard the dwarves from Thorbardin brought the stones that were used in its construction. I'm a student of dwarven architecture, and with the dwarven kingdom being sealed, I figured the tomb was my best chance to get a look at a recent work.' There's a gram of truth in that—you did come to the tomb."

"I see."

"And if they ask where you originally came from, you can say 'I came from Crossing, to the north of Solace. It's a fine port town known for its spiced ale and famous shipwrights. You should visit it some time.' That wouldn't be a lie, exactly. You did land in Crossing before you came to Solace. You just came from somewhere else before that."

"I see."

"And if they ask you about your profession, whatever it really happens to be, you tell them—"

"Look at me! Everybody, look at me!" Raph's high-pitched voice ended Blister's lesson. The young kender instantly had everyone's attention, save Groller's. The half-ogre stood at the wheel, oblivious to the noise.

Raph was standing at the top of a pyramid of water barrels. There were five barrels on the first tier, lying on their sides and lashed together to keep them from rolling. There were four on the second tier, two on the third, and one on top. Raph balanced precariously on the top one.

Satisfied that he had an audience, the little kender leaned forward until his fingers touched the wood of the barrel, then he kicked off with his legs until he was standing on his hands. His sandaled feet waved at those on deck below. The ship rolled to the starboard to meet a wave, and Raph happily held his position. His pouches clinked in protest.

"This is fun!" he hollered.

"Raph! Get down from there. That's dangerous!" Blister scolded. Her little feet pounded over the deck as she closed the distance to the water barrel pyramid. For a change, Dhamon was on her heels.

"You're always so worried, Blister. Always too careful. You never have any fun. Look at this." Raph tucked his right arm in toward his chest and was standing on one hand now. "I could be in a circus."

"You could be in the sea, which is where I'll toss you if you don't get off of our water barrels!" Rig cursed.

Jasper, who'd moved up to the mariner's side, scowled at the kender's antics. Shaon, who stood by the dwarf, was amused but mainly by the sight of Rig's cross expression.

The ship hit another swell, and the young kender dizzily swayed on his perch. A brief look of worry crossed his little face, and he put his other hand down to steady himself.

Shaon gasped and sucked on her lower lip. It suddenly wasn't funny anymore. The ship lurched again, and Raph's bag of spoons fell free—a few dozen steel and silver soupspoons and ladles—and went spinning toward the deck.

"Don't worry. I've got perfect balance!" the kender bragged.

"Balance yourself off those barrels!" Rig commanded.

"Wonder what this rope is for?"

"It ties the barrels together. Leave it alone," Rig spat. "And get down, now!"

But the big mariner's words were a heartbeat too late. Raph maneuvered back to his feet and brought his hands down to the rope and tugged. A smile stretched wide across his cherubic face.

"No!" Blister screamed.

Dhamon rushed forward just as the pyramid of barrels groaned and the rope came free. The bottom tier spread, separating and rolling to port and starboard, and the tiers on top of them shifted and toppled forward.

Raph was a cloud of color and waving hands and feet. He tried to somersault forward, pushing off the falling top barrel and attempting to clear the collapsing pyramid. But the rope he'd untied was whipping about in the wind like an angry serpent. An end struck his face with a sharp *snap!* Surprised, the kender faltered in midair and landed hard on his back on the deck. The wind rushed from his lungs and he was momentarily stunned. Before he could rise, the topmost barrel slammed into his slight frame.

Raph's eyes grew wide and he opened his mouth to scream. His words were drowned out by the crash of another barrel on top of him, and another.

Dhamon slipped on the spewed contents and fell to the deck. He looked up and instantly threw an arm in front of his face. Slats of wood went flying and struck his hand as another barrel broke. More water gushed across the rolling deck, but

Dhamon scrambled forward.

Somehow Rig had reached the kender first. A splintered barrel still lay on top of Raph. Its broken iron band was over his chest like a trap, pinning him to the deck. The other half of the band was imbedded in his leg.

The mariner rolled the barrel off Raph and tugged the pieces of iron loose.

"He's dead," Rig announced. "His chest is crushed. And now we have only one intact barrel of water. Wonderful."

The mariner cursed and stomped toward the wheel. "One barrel! It'll only last us a couple of days. We'll have to ration it!" he called over his shoulder. "Then we'll have to pull into Caergoth and get more."

"Dead?" Blister picked her way through the broken barrels and slumped beside Raph's body. She used the hooks on her glove to move the shattered pieces of wood aside. Ignoring the pain in her hands, she cradled his head. A trickle of blood ran out of his mouth.

"I came along to keep him out of trouble," she whispered.

* * * * *

They buried Raph at sea, wrapping his body in a colorful blanket, and weighing it down so it would sink. Blister said only a few words to honor the young kender. She hadn't known him long, and she was at a loss for something to say. A dull ache spread from her fingers and into her arms as her gloved hands clasped a silver spoon to her breast.

"I told him I'd take care of him," she whispered.

* * * * *

Sorrow over Raph's sudden death was soon outweighed by fear for their own lives when the crew of *Flint's Anvil* encountered the Gale. The storm was no surprise—the clashing air masses of glacial Southern Ergoth and the temperate main continent created a constant tempest in the Straits of Algoni—but there was no way to be completely prepared for a force of nature as volatile and unpredictable as the Gale.

As soon as they entered the deeper, colder waters of the Straits, Rig instructed the crew to take down all of the sails; they would be going under bare poles in order to provide the least resistance to the wind. The task was barely completed before icy, white-capped waves began crashing over the bow and Rig ordered Jasper, Blister, and Dhamon to go below deck.

The dwarf and the kender rushed toward the hatch, slipping a few times as the wooden planks grew wet and the ship lurched. The *Anvil* rose to the top of a large swell. Jasper watched as they were lifted high only to plummet immediately down the other side of the wave. Suddenly it was as if he were standing in a valley between navy blue mountains. He could see nothing but the curving dark water on either side of him. Where was the sky? The ship began to ascend the next wave, a rolling wall of water many times his height. Jasper threw open the hatch and descended the ladder. Blister stepped on the dwarf's head as she hurriedly followed.

Dhamon stood his ground, his arms wrapped around the mainmast.

"Go!" Rig shouted over the increasing wind.

Dhamon shook his head no, his eyes stinging from the salty spray as he tried to glare at the captain.

Shaon approached him, her body shaking and thinly coated with drenched cloth. "We'll need your strength later!" she said, her voice pleading. The ship pitched to the side and she fell back, sliding away from him across the deck toward the side of the ship that was tilted dangerously close to the angry water. Her descent was stopped as the rope around her waist snapped taut and the ship lurched to the other side. Icy water slid over the side of the ship and onto the deck, lifting her off the wooden planks and hurtling her toward the main-mast.

Shaon scrambled to her feet, wiped at her eyes furiously and then steadied herself. She extended her hand to Dhamon. She was shouting something but her words were lost in the howl of the tempest. Cold, pelting rain came at the ship sideways now, rushing down in sheets parallel to the water because the wind was blowing so.

Dhamon reluctantly let go of the mainmast and clasped Shaon's cold, wet hand. The ship pitched to the side again and the two fell to their knees, crawling toward the hatch. Shaon's icy grip remained firm until Dhamon was able to reach the opening. He dove headfirst into the darkness below deck as the hatch banged closed after him.

He could not be sure of how many hours of pitching and rolling, of being thrown into the sides of the hull and other crew members, of listening to every single creak and groan of the ship as it struggled to stay intact passed before he heard hurried footsteps above and a sopping cold rope was dropped down through the hatch. He could not be sure of whose voice it was that called his name from the raging blackness above.

Chapter 18

A Knightly Confrontation

Caergoth's harbor was considerably larger than the one in New Ports. Banks of docks stretched out into a bay deep enough to accommodate galleons, drakkars, galleys, and dromonds. The harbor was filled with ships in various states of repair, and most of them had been damaged after a run-in with the Gale.

Rig pointed to a galleon in dry dock that had a gaping hole in its bow near the waterline. He said he was surprised it hadn't sunk before reaching the harbor; probably it had hit an iceberg. The crew must've had to pitch cargo overboard to keep its bow high enough to make it into port.

After her harrowing encounter with the Gale, *Flint's Anvil* also had a narrow brush with an iceberg. The strait between Southlund and the White's territory was filled with bergs and blocks of ice that looked like tiny islands. Navigating around the ice was difficult, especially considering that the blocks on top of the water might be only a fraction of the size of the ice just below the surface. Rig was up to the task, however, and Dhamon and Jasper thought the mariner attacked the predicament with cautious enthusiasm. Under Rig's guidance, the *Anvil* eased its way through the frigid obstacle course and around a particularly threatening iceberg without putting a single scratch on the hull.

The ship was assigned a spot at the western end of the harbor, and soon she was lashed to the dock with her sails down. Blister asked to stay on the ship with Shaon. The two were becoming friends, and the dark-skinned woman said she could use help checking all the lines and sails. The kender put on brown leather gloves that had a magnifying lens attached to the thumb of the right hand, "to make examining the ropes easier," she explained.

Groller was appointed the task of purchasing barrels for fresh water and having them filled and delivered. The red-haired wolf, which had been hiding somewhere below deck for most of the trip, was at his side when he left the ship. Jasper decided to tag along, pleased at the prospect of being on solid ground and mildly curious how a deaf half-ogre, if he truly was deaf, would make a commercial transaction. The dwarf grimly suspected he'd end up making the arrangements himself. He scowled and fished about in his pocket to be sure he had enough coins for the barrels.

The three other deckhands were granted a few hours leave, but Rig gave them strict orders that they were to report back well before sunset. The *Anvil* wouldn't be staying the night in Caergoth.

That left Dhamon and Rig standing at the railing, looking toward the shore. It was an old port, from the look of the faded and chipping paint on the wharf and many of the taverns and inns that dotted it. And though it was a busy one, and likely a profitable one, it didn't look like the building owners were reinvesting any of their gains in maintaining their establishments. The newest structures were tall wooden towers, three of them, perched near the shore and stretching high into the air. Poised on platforms at the top were men who looked toward Southern Ergoth, spyglasses to their eyes. They were looking for signs of trouble, namely from the White who lived there.

The people who walked up and down the wharf were mostly sailors and deckhands on leave or on errands. There were several who looked like businessmen with work to conduct along the shore, and there were small groups of travelers who had just gotten off of ships or who were looking to book passage. A few women moved between them all, their attention fixed on the smattering of stalls that sold clams and shell fish.

A pair of fishmongers walked near the buildings and at the edge of the docks—trying to sell to anyone whose clothes looked reasonably intact and therefore might have coins in their pockets.

"Seems someone who had enough gold to sail to Schallsea would have enough to buy some decent clothes," Rig muttered. The sea barbarian was clad in dark green leather pants, and a pale yellow silk shirt with voluminous sleeves. He wore a band about the top of his head that was made of braided red leather that nearly matched the sash about his waist. The headband had thin tails that hung down to his shoulder blades and flapped in the gentle breeze.

Dhamon shrugged indifferently.

"Can't catch the ladies' eyes looking like you do."

"Maybe I'm not trying to." Dhamon stepped back from the rail and looked up into the cloudy sky.

Rig followed his gaze. "I don't like the look of them," the big mariner stated flatly. "That's why we're not staying."

"Clouds are clouds. What's wrong with them? Are they too worn for your taste?"

"The sky always carries a message, Dhamon—for those of us smart enough to read it. And that message is usually written in the clouds. When the clouds are flat, like sheets, the air is calm and the temperature's stable. The journey'll be easy. These clouds are bloated, and they're gray at the bottom. That means they're filled with rain, and it's only a matter of time before they let it loose. The only question is, will it be a simple downpour? Or will it be a big storm?"

Dhamon slipped his hand into his pocket and felt the silk banner Goldmoon had given him. He remained silent.

"I don't mind rain, and a little squall never hurt any decent sailor. But we've still got a way to go to get by Frost's territory—and a potential storm with icebergs thrown in the mix is something I'd rather not deal with. This will be my ship after I drop you in Palanthas, and I want it in one piece." He glanced at the dry-docked galleon. "So, we leave before sunset."

Dhamon padded past the mariner and followed the plank down to the dock.

"Hey! Where are you going? We'll be leaving in a couple of hours."

"I'm going to talk to some of the sailors. Maybe they came from the north. And maybe they were smart enough to read the clouds there. Might give us an edge."

"Shaon! Mind our ship!" Rig bellowed. "Wait, Dhamon. I'll join you."

As he brushed by Blister, the mariner added, "I'm really sorry about your little friend."

* * * * *

Jasper and Groller stood on a wood-plank sidewalk that stretched along the street just beyond the docks. Caergoth was Southlund's capital, and as such it was a good-sized city with an enticing waterfront. Several of the buildings had colorful awnings spread over the walk in order to keep the rain or sun off the shoppers, depending on the weather. Other businesses had signs in their windows advertising specials that might lure potential buyers inside—clam chowder, bitter grog, eelskin boots, dyed leather tunics, and the like.

The dwarf stared at the half-ogre. "You really can't hear me, can you?" Jasper asked.

Groller stared back and raised an eyebrow. The half-ogre couldn't *hear* anything, but his other senses worked. His eyes took in the exasperated expression on the dwarf's face. Groller pursed his lips and brought his arms out in front of his body, forming a circle with them parallel to the ground. Then he nodded toward a barrelwright a half-block away. Jasper hadn't noticed the sign that displayed a stack of wooden barrels until the half-ogre pointed it out.

Without waiting for a reply, and since he couldn't have heard one anyway, Groller turned and began walking toward the shop. The red wolf padded at his side and drew the stares of passersby.

Jasper started to call out, to ask Groller to walk slower. But he stopped himself. "Yelling at a deaf man," he muttered. He cursed softly and hurried to catch up, which was not an easy feat given the quick, long stride of the seven-foot-tall half-ogre.

Just outside the shop, Jasper managed to close the distance. Panting, he tugged on Groller's vest, and the half-ogre turned and looked down.

"Mmm. How do I do this?" Jasper grumbled to himself. "We need eleven barrels. Did Rig tell you how many? Of course he couldn't have. You wouldn't have been able to hear him. Good thing I came along." He made a motion with his arms, like Groller had, forming a circle in front of his chest. Next, he formed a cup with his hand and pretended to drink.

The half-ogre grinned and nodded.

"So you can understand me," Jasper said. "Or, at least I *think* you can." He held up his hands and spread his fingers wide. Then he formed fists and let one index finger stand up.

"Ee-lef-en," Groller answered. "Burls. Ino. Em not stooped. Jus def."

His words were difficult to make out. But Jasper caught the gist and nodded furiously. The pair went inside.

Groller strolled up to the counter, and a thin, elderly shopkeeper emerged almost immediately from behind a curtain. The dwarf, who stood at the back of the shop to watch, suspected the shopkeeper was alerted by the creaking of the floor beneath the half-ogre's feet.

"No animals in here!" the thin man shouted. He stood just barely over five feet, and he wore a shirt that was a couple of sizes too big. A leather apron hung from his neck. "I mean it. No—"

The red wolf's ears flattened against his head and he growled softly, and the shopkeeper stopped protesting. Groller pointed to a row of barrels stacked against the wall. He pulled a small hunk of slate from a deep pocket and fumbled with a piece of chalk. He held it before the shopkeeper.

The man shook his head. "I can't read."

Groller returned the slate to his pocket. "Ee-lef-en," he said slowly. The half-ogre thrust his thick fingers into his vest pocket and pulled out a few coins. "Ee-lef-en burls fild wid wadder." He handed the coins over. "Livered to docks—Flindsez And-val."

The shopkeeper looked at him quizzically and ran his fingers through his thinning hair. "Eleven barrels?"

The wolf barked and wagged its tail.

"Delivered to the docks?"

The wolf barked.

"The ship's name?"

"*Flint's Anvil*," Jasper offered.

The wolf barked again.

"So you haven't been deaf your whole life," Jasper observed, following Groller out of the shop. "You had normal hearing—at least for a while. Otherwise, you couldn't talk. I suspect you talked better at one time. Probably hard to make the words sound right if you can't hear them." He tugged on the half-ogre's sash to get his attention.

Jasper pointed to his own ear, then balled his fist and made a motion as if he were wadding something up and throwing it away. Then he pointed to Groller and shrugged his shoulders.

"Def tree years," Groller answered.

The dwarf pointed to a man and woman who were entering a leatherworker's shop. A young boy trotted behind them. Then Jasper pointed to the half-ogre.

"No fam-lee. No more. Allufum ded." The half-ogre's scarred face grew sad, and he bent to scratch behind the wolf's ears. "Ohnlee Feweree."

Jasper cocked his head, not understanding the last bit.

Groller drew his lips into a thin line, squinted as if he was mad. Then he curved the fingers of his right hand and held them over his heart. His hand flew up violently, suddenly. Then Groller's face softened, and he reached down to pet the wolf again.

"Angry. Mad," the dwarf muttered. "Fury! The wolf's name is Fury. I understand." Jasper grinned and realized it was his first smile in days.

Groller, not hearing Jasper, nudged the wolf along and shuffled past the dwarf. Jasper watched him saunter into an inn that advertised a special on clam chowder and dark rum. The red wolf dutifully sat outside to wait. The dwarf licked his lips and felt for the steel in his pockets. "Plenty of coins," he whispered. "And I am hungry." He glanced at the harbor for a moment and then joined Groller.

* * * * *

Dhamon stopped to talk to the first mate of a carrack. The man was standing on the shore, looking toward a row of stone and wood buildings that were near the docks. He was eyeing one in particular. It had a large sign above the door that depicted an overflowing tankard of ale. The mate cleared his throat, licked his dry lips, and mentioned he was thirsty, but he continued chatting with Dhamon. Rig was quick to step between the pair.

"We're heading up the coast," Rig interjected. "I overheard you tell Dhamon that your ship came down from there yesterday."

The mate nodded. "Weather's holding," he said. "Or it was. Our last stop was Starport, about ninety miles to the north. Those men pulled out several hours after us—judging by the time they got here. Maybe you should talk to them."

He pointed at a group of uniformly-clad men about a hundred and fifty yards away. There were a dozen of them; all wore steel armor that had been painted black. From their vantage point on the *Anvil's* deck, Dhamon and Rig hadn't been able to see them.

Over his armor, each man wore a dark blue tabard with a gray skull and a white death lily embroidered on the front and back. They were huddled together, as if deep in discussion.

"Knights of Takhisis," Dhamon whispered.

Though the Dark Queen of Krynn vanished with the rest of the gods, her knighthood had remained intact. It was one large order, but it had also fragmented into various divisions that fell under the auspices of powerful commanders who were spread across Ansalon. The knights still fought battles to defend the land their commanders claimed or to enlarge territories. Some worked as military forces for cities, and the commanders had prestigious positions in the

government. A few groups had overrun cities and claimed
them for the knighthood.

"They're still in considerable numbers, even though their
goddess is gone," Rig mused. "I wonder which petty general
these work for. At least with their factions divided, they're no
real threat anymore."

Dhamon shook his head. "They're armed and armored.
They're a threat."

"There's a ship full of 'em," the mate cut in. "That small
galley over there. They might have better information for
you."

"You could be right. Thanks." Rig tossed him a copper
coin. "Your next drink's on me." Then he strode toward the
group.

"I don't think this is a good idea," Dhamon called.
"They've probably got things on their mind other than talking to us."

Rig either didn't hear him or chose to ignore him. Dhamon's fingers slid to the pommel of his sheathed sword, and
he followed a few yards behind.

"Heard your ship came down from the north!" Rig's deep
voice cut across the sand that separated him from the
knights.

The men turned and revealed what had been at the center
of their huddle—a young elven woman.

"My, my," Rig said in a low voice. "I think I'm in love."

"I thought you were in love with Shaon," Dhamon whispered.

"I am. Or close to it."

The woman was tanned and shapely, dressed in tight dun-
colored leggings, and a sleeveless, fringed chestnut tunic that
clung to her slightly muscular frame. Her long, light brown
hair was thick and curly and flared away from her face, covering up her shoulders and looking like a lion's mane.

She sported several tattoos. On her face was an artfully-painted orange and yellow oak leaf. The stem curved around and above her right eye, and the leaf draped over her cheek, with the tip extending to the corner of her mouth. A red lightning bolt stretched across her forehead. From a distance it looked like a headband. Finally, on her right arm, from the elbow to the wrist, was a blue and green feather. The tattoos marked her as a Kagonesti, a wild elf.

She glanced briefly at Rig and Dhamon, then stared into the face of one of the knights. A band on his arm indicated he was an officer and in charge of the group.

"The dragon won't stop with Southern Ergoth," she was saying. "You have to realize that."

Rig and Dhamon were close enough now to hear her words.

"If something isn't done, if someone doesn't stand up to him . . ."

"What?" the officer returned. "The Kagonesti will never get their homeland back?"

There was muffled snickering from a handful of the knights.

"He's corrupted nature," she continued. "Southern Ergoth is an icy wasteland. Nothing grows there anymore. What if he travels here next?"

"I think he likes Southern Ergoth just fine," the youngest knight said. "I think he's satisfied and will stay put."

"Besides," the officer said. "We've our orders to consider, and they don't include dealing with a dragon."

She inhaled sharply. "But what if Frost doesn't stay put? He truly might come here next—or menace some other land. You could help me." The Kagonesti stared at the officer. "Please. You could take your ship there. Together maybe we could—"

"What? Together we could die? I understand your concern, but there's nothing I can do. We're here to recruit more knights, miss, and that's a task I'd rather concentrate on. It's

160

good for our order."

The Kagonesti's shoulders slumped, and she turned to walk away. One of the knights took a step after her and grabbed the back of her tunic. He spun her around, and moved in closer. "Why don't you join us?" he asked. He brought his other hand up to her mane of curls. "We'd make room for you on the ship."

Behind him, the officer frowned and ordered him back into line. The young knight hesitated, and the Kagonesti kicked at his ankles. "Join you? Never," she hissed. "I've more important things to deal with."

He released her hair, and the Kagonesti started to walk away. But the young knight followed her, slamming his shoulder into her back and knocking her face first into the sand.

"Can't even stand on your feet. How can you stand up to a dragon?" he taunted. The knights on either side of him laughed loudly.

Dhamon heard the officer reprimand the young knight. He also heard the shushing sound a blade makes when it's being drawn. Rig took a step forward and brought his right arm up, raising his cutlass level with the offending knight's throat.

"Apologize to the lady!" Rig demanded.

"Apologize? Because she's clumsy?"

There was more laughter. And another reprimand.

"Rig," Dhamon's tone was soft, but insistent. "There's a dozen of them and one of you. Bad odds—even if you're good with that blade."

The mariner hesitated. The elf rose to her feet, grabbed her pack, and scampered away from the knights. Rig saw that she was safe, then he lowered his weapon.

"Come on. Let's get out of here," Dhamon suggested. "No one's been hurt."

Rig took a step back, and in that instant the young knight

took a step forward. Itching for a confrontation, he drew his long sword, spread his legs for balance, and eyed the mariner. "Afraid to defend a woman?" he sneered. "Or maybe elves aren't worth it."

Rig raised his sword again.

"Don't do it," Dhamon pleaded.

"I know you!" the officer exclaimed. He was pointing at Dhamon and ignoring the upstart knight in his charge. The officer's eyes grew wide. "Last year in Kyre, near Solanthus. At the home of the old Solamnic knight. You were . . . "

"You must be mistaken," Dhamon said tersely.

"I don't think so. I saw you! Subcommander Mullor was there. You killed him."

"*I said*, you must have been mistaken."

"I don't think so, I . . . "

"The lady's with me!" the young knight barked, drowning out his superior's words. "Run back to your ship while you've the chance, you dark excuse for a frightened gully dwarf!"

"Run? Frightened?" Rig erupted. "Never!"

Out of the corner of his eye, Dhamon saw Rig and the young knight close. The big mariner parried the knight's awkward swing. Four other knights drew their blades but held their positions.

"Fight!" someone yelled from a distance. "Come on!"

The young knight raised his long sword high over his head and brought it down hard, trying to land a blow on Rig's shoulder. The mariner was fast and brought his cutlass up to parry the attack. The knight's blade clanged harmlessly away, and Rig countered with a swing aimed at the young man's thigh. Dhamon breathed a sigh of relief that the mariner was only trying to wound—not kill.

The knight had some skill, and he stepped back and met the mariner's blow with his own sword, catching it just below its hilt. The tactic kept the knight from getting hurt, but his long sword snapped from the angle of impact, and the blade spun to the sand. Cursing, the knight threw the useless pommel to the ground and glared at Rig.

Again, Rig lowered his blade, if only for an instant. Two more knights strode forward. The first circled to the mariner's right. The other met him head-on and swung in a wide arc aimed at his chest.

Rig dropped to a crouch as the blade passed above him, and plucked two daggers from the cuff of his boot with his left hand. He stuck one dagger between his teeth, the other he gripped and waved at the advancing knight.

"I am *not* mistaken!" The words exploded from the officer's mouth, and Dhamon swiveled his head in time to see the officer jabbing a finger at him. "Your hair's longer, but I *do* remember you. Get him!" The officer yanked his long sword free and rushed forward. The knight near him followed his lead.

"Look!" bellowed a voice from somewhere on the docks. "There really is a fight!"

In one fluid motion, Dhamon drew his sword and met the charge of the lead knight. Their swords clashed loudly. He whirled in the sand and met the second knight's swing just in time to keep his sword arm from being severed.

The officer darted in, slashing, and Dhamon tensed his leg muscles and leapt straight up, tucking his legs in toward his chest. The blade sliced just below the toes of his boots. As he came down, Dhamon shot his right leg forward, striking the officer hard in the chest and knocking him down.

Graceful as a dancer, Dhamon landed on his left foot and spun to meet the second knight's rush. The man's charge was slowed over the sand, and Dhamon was able to dodge the wide swing.

Dhamon slashed at the knight, but the blow rebounded off the black armor. His second swing fared better, and his blade sank deep between the knight's shoulder and chest plates. With a groan, the knight fell forward. Dhamon pulled hard to free his blade.

Behind him, the officer was rising and reaching for his fallen sword. Dhamon dashed forward and kicked the blade away, then slammed his boot heel into the man's stomach to keep him down. Two more knights advanced on him.

"My money's on the knights!" someone called.

"I'll take the long odds on the black man!"

Dhamon watched one of the knights rush in. Drawing his blade back over his shoulder, he spun as he sliced ahead. The blade connected with the knight's neck, instantly decapitating him.

"Double my money on the blond!" someone cried. "The beggar was just playing with 'em!"

A crowd was forming around the combatants, and the clinking of steel coins mingled with the clanking of swords.

Risking a glance toward Rig, Dhamon saw that the mariner was barely working up a sweat. Two knights were on the ground, a dagger in each of their throats. Two more knights faced him. Never more than two on a single foe, Dhamon knew. Greater odds would be dishonorable.

The mariner waved his sword about to meet the charge of his attackers. The fingers of his left hand flew to his waist and tugged free his red sash. He began making wide circles in the air, the sash whipping and whistling. It was weighted, like a bolo, and too late the knight darting forward realized the mariner's intent.

Rig tossed the sash forward. Spinning, it wrapped about the sword arm and head of the closest knight. The man paused to untangle himself, and in that moment, Rig darted forward and rammed his cutlass between a thin gap in the knight's breastplate. The man pitched backward, the sword lodged deep in his stomach.

Seemingly weaponless, Rig dropped to the sand, avoiding a mad slash by his second foe. At the same time, he reached into the V of his silk shirt, and his fingers came away with three more daggers. The first he hurled at the foe towering above him. The dagger skewered the knight's hand, causing him to drop the long sword.

The other two daggers Rig held in his right hand. As he jumped to his feet, he flung his left hand forward, releasing a shower of sand into the weaponless knight's face. Blinded, the man cast his head about and stepped back, but Rig pressed the attack and jammed the twin daggers into his side.

"No!" Dhamon cried. He darted below the swing of his own closest foe and waved his sword to catch Rig's attention. "These are knights!" he bellowed. Again he dodged a well-timed attack. "They fight honorably! No more than two on you at a time. And you should fight honorably too!"

Two knights pressed their attack against Dhamon, drawing his attention away from the mariner. One of them, a stout, muscular man, lunged to the left, but it was a false attack. He quickly stepped right and thrust forward at Dhamon's unprotected chest.

Dhamon pivoted just in time to avoid being run through, but the stocky knight's blade sliced his tunic. A thin line of red appeared and soaked through the worn cloth. Dhamon stepped back to avoid another swing and found himself in the path of the second knight's blade. Though not as skilled as his fellow, the knight's aim was lucky, and his sword sliced into Dhamon's arm, just below his elbow.

Dhamon gritted his teeth. The cut was deep, and he felt the warmth of his blood. He fought to ignore the pain and tightened his grip on the pommel of his sword.

The stout man thrust again. Dhamon dropped to his knees and felt the air ripple above his head from the strength of the man's swing. Without hesitation, he drove his blade upward, impaling the muscular knight. In the same instant, he slammed his elbow into the second knight to force him back.

The second knight moaned and retreated a step, and

watched the expert swordsman fall forward, driving Dhamon's blade even farther into his gut as his body struck the sand.

Someone in the growing throng yelled "Bravo!" And a cheer from the onlookers went up. "Pay up! The beggar killed another one!" someone yelled.

"Let's call an end this!" Dhamon hollered above the applause. "Now!"

He spied the officer struggling to his feet, aided by the knight who'd just fought Dhamon.

"No one else has to die!" he said. He rolled the body of the stout knight over, planted a foot on his stomach, and pulled his long sword free. He waved the blade menacingly in an arc over the fallen man.

The two men fighting Rig stepped back, watching Dhamon. But they kept their swords up, ready to resume the battle.

Four men lay dead at the big mariner's feet, all with blades sticking out of their still forms. Dhamon's sword had claimed three. Of the five remaining knights, one looked seriously injured and probably wouldn't live—one of Rig's daggers was embedded near his neck. The knight who had started the fray was still weaponless and unharmed.

"Rig!" Dhamon called.

"You're hurt!" the mariner returned. "But we can still take 'em! Easy!"

"No! It's over."

Rig cursed and held his position. Then he grudgingly nodded and lowered the daggers he held in each hand.

The Knights of Takhisis relaxed, but only a little. At their officer's orders, they guardedly sheathed their long swords.

"Pay up!" someone in the crowd called. "The knights lost."

"But they're not all dead!" someone else countered.

Rig started retrieving his weapons, tugging them free from the fallen knights. He wrapped the sash around his waist and stuck daggers in each of his boots and under his shirt. He grasped his cutlass firmly, then stuck it in the band of his sash.

Dhamon dropped to his knees on the sand. He laid his sword in front of him and bowed his head, mumbling a prayer for the dead men as drops of his own blood spattered on the ground. He had several deep cuts on his arm and chest, and his shirt was more red than ivory now.

"Dhamon," Rig hissed. "What are you doing? Let's get out of here." The mariner had spied more knights filing off the ship. The numbers were considerable. "Dhamon!"

The prayer finished, Dhamon stood. "We're sailing out soon," he told the officer. "We don't want any more trouble."

"You'll get none." The officer nodded and instructed his men to collect the dead. He fixed Dhamon with a steady stare. "But I wasn't mistaken about you."

Dhamon looked at his blade, covered with blood. He didn't sheath it, but he carried it low and to his side so it couldn't be misconstrued as a threat. He turned toward the *Anvil's* dock. Rig followed.

"All this talk of honor, Dhamon," Rig clucked. "Were you a knight?"

"Well, no. I always wanted to be a knight," Dhamon answered, fixing his gaze on the tips of his boots and remembering Blister's lesson. "My uncle was a knight. I guess I wanted to be like him."

"You're good in a fight," the Kagonesti said. She'd come up behind the pair, and now touched Rig's shoulder to get his attention. "It was amazing."

"I've never lost a fight," the mariner boasted.

"I'm trying to gather some men," she began, "to go after the White. I know some nature-magic, but I can't do it alone. I could use your help."

"We're going north," Rig said.

"We need to tend to something in Palanthas," Dhamon

added. "I promised to deal with it first. You're welcome to join us."

"Then perhaps you'll help with the dragon?"

"Maybe," Dhamon answered. He'd reached the dock and knelt next to it at the water's edge to clean his sword.

"I would like to leave this place," she admitted. She glanced over her shoulder, toward where the fight had taken place. The crowd was finally breaking up, but one of the knights stood, watching the trio.

"Another mouth to feed and water," Rig muttered. "At least it's a very pretty one."

"Ferilleeagh Dawnsprinter, once of the Foghaven Vale tribe," she said, extending a slender hand to the mariner. "Please call me Feril."

"Rig Mer-Krel," the mariner said. He bowed deeply and swept his hand in a gracious arc, then captured hers and brought it to his lips. He gently released it and motioned to Dhamon. "This is Dhamon Grimwulf, an *honorable* fighter. And there is my ship—the *Anvil*."

She arched an eyebrow at the carrack's name, but smiled. "It's a fine ship."

Rig cast his head skyward, then scowled. The clouds had grown darker. "Dhamon, won't you show the lady on board? I'm going to find my men. I think we'd better set sail as soon as possible."

* * * * *

Blister fretted over Dhamon, and—with Shaon's and Feril's help—finally coaxed him to sit on a coil of rope that was lying against the rear mast. He wasn't used to so much attention, but the Kagonesti's fingers stroking his forehead felt good.

The kender turned her back to him, and fumbled with one of her pouches. When she spun around, he could see that she'd changed gloves. She had on a white pair that had especially thick pads at the fingertips. The kender reached up and prodded the gash on his arm, and the blood quickly turned the finger pads red. He saw her wince, but he thought it was from the sight of his wound. He didn't know moving her fingers caused her pain.

"The shirt's gotta go," Blister ordered.

At Feril's insistence, Dhamon raised his arms, and the Kagonesti gently tugged the tunic off. Shaon scowled at the bloodied garment, then picked it up and threw it over the side. Like a dying bird, it fluttered to the dock below.

"Didn't look good on you anyway," Shaon complained.

Dhamon resignedly leaned back against the mast and tried to relax. It didn't work but he was grateful for the kender's ministrations. His blood loss was making him feel light-headed.

He watched Blister place the other glove over the line on his chest. It absorbed some of the blood and helped to clean the wound. So the gloves were specifically designed to tend to the injured, Dhamon mused. He idly wondered how many more pairs she had.

"What happened?" she asked as she continued to work.

"Just a little scuffle," Dhamon replied.

"You're learning to be a better liar," Blister said crossly. "But you've got to work on being more believable."

Feril recounted the story of the fight with the Knights of Takhisis, while Blister continued to fuss over him.

"I'll need some water to clean this better," the kender muttered. "We've plenty of barrels now."

"I'm fine, Blister, really," Dhamon groaned.

"No, you're not." The voice was deep. Jasper had returned. Groller and the red wolf were behind him.

Dhamon cocked his head and sniffed the air.

"We ah . . . stopped at an inn," Jasper said as he came closer and grimaced. The scent of rum was strong on the dwarf's breath. "Heard that a pair of . . . let's see, foolish upstarts I think they called 'em . . . picked a fight with a unit of Knights of Takhisis."

"That's not exactly how it happened. Ouch!"

The dwarf's fingers weren't as gentle as Blister's gloves.

"Did Rig fare worse?" Jasper's voice was tinged with the slightest bit of concern.

"He didn't get a scratch," Feril replied. She quickly introduced herself and once again recounted the tale of the battle.

The dwarf looked closer at Dhamon's wounds. "Not too terribly bad, but if I don't do something, they'll get infected. Can't have you getting sick on us." He knelt before Dhamon and closed his eyes. "Something Goldmoon taught me."

With a new pair of gloves that were spongy, especially at the palms, Blister wiped at the wounds. Jasper mumbled some singsong words none of the others could make out. A line of sweat broke out across his wide forehead, and his thick lips trembled. He grew pale, and Dhamon's arm and chest grew irritatingly hot.

"Oh!" the kender squealed.

Dhamon glanced down at his chest and saw the line of red fading, the rawness of the wound vanishing. He looked at his arm and watched the blood congeal.

Groller, eyes wide over the entire incident, helped Jasper to his feet.

"You will have scars," Jasper said. "But you won't get an infection." The dwarf turned to Groller and touched the half-ogre's sash. He pointed to the spot where Dhamon was injured, touched the sash again, and then used a finger to indicate a wrapping motion. His finger orbited the area of Dhamon's injury several times.

The half-ogre spun on his heels and headed below deck. Fury sat back and continued to watch.

"Groller's going to get some bandages," the dwarf explained. "And I'm going to get some rest."

By the time Rig and the other crewmen returned to *Flint's Anvil*, Dhamon's wounds were dressed. Shirtless, and with his long hair whipping about his face and neck, he stood at the rail and nodded to the mariner.

"Next port we'll have to get you a few new shirts," said Rig.

Dhamon rolled his eyes. "*We?*"

The mariner ignored him and moved toward the wheel. "Shaon, raise the sails! We're leaving!"

Chapter 19

Tempest

Groller's big hands gripped the spokes of the wheel, and his eyes scanned the horizon to memorize the positions of the small icebergs that dotted the water. Jasper hovered near him, grumbling to himself about the possibility of the ship striking one and sinking, and alternately proclaiming *Flint's Anvil* to be capable of withstanding anything. The dwarf knew Groller couldn't hear him, but he prattled on anyway, as if the sound of his own voice gave him some measure of assurance against the rough water.

Both wore a few layers of clothes to help ward off the bitter wind that whipped across the sea from the White's territory. The chill had reddened their faces, and each gust birthed new shivers.

The dwarf occasionally grabbed onto this or that protuberance to steady himself—especially when the half-ogre's hard turns to port or starboard to avoid a block of ice sent the ship reeling. The breeze was strong, and the ship was rolling with the high waves. Jasper didn't think the deck had been level since they pulled away from the Caergoth port. Nor did he think it had been dry. One wave after another poured sheets of water across it.

The dwarf was doing his best to keep the clam chowder and dark rum—the first meal he had been able to keep down since their encounter with the Gale—quiescent in his belly. To chase away the queasiness he decided to try a new tactic: keeping himself completely occupied. He vowed to teach himself more of the rudimentary sign language Groller employed.

So far Jasper had picked up a dozen gestures. And though he didn't especially like the sea, the dwarf had mastered the sign for "sea" first. Holding his hand with the palm parallel to the deck, he made up and down movements with his wrist and short fingers to simulate a wave. When Jasper tugged on Groller's vest, the half-ogre glanced down stoically. The dwarf pointed to his stomach, then made the wavy motion again—just as his cheeks puffed out. His stubby arms flung themselves around Groller's leg for support.

"Jaz-pear sea sick," Groller chuckled. The half-ogre proceeded to show him gestures for cloud, wind, and storm.

Jasper twirled his fingers in the air above his head. "Cloud," he said proudly. He fluttered his hands back and forth in front of his chest to imitate the wind. Then he fluttered them faster and more pronounced and shifted back and forth on his feet, "Storm."

Jasper glanced back at the storm brewing far behind them. The ship had outdistanced it.

The *Anvil* rose over a swell, and Jasper grabbed the half-ogre's leg again. When his stomach—and the ship—settled, the dwarf released his hold and gazed up at Groller. The half-ogre's attention was again fixed on the water.

"I wonder what it would be like," Jasper mused, "not to be able to hear. I can't imagine not being able to listen to the waves or the birds. Or people talking." The dwarf thought that the gestures the half-ogre used, and that Rig and Shaon seemed reasonably versed in, were a remarkable form of communication, beautiful in a way and incredibly visual. But he didn't consider them an adequate substitute for sound.

"When I know enough of these hand gestures," Jasper said to himself, "I can ask him what it's like to live behind walls of silence."

Blister was asleep, curled up with a shawl near the capstan, her head nestled on a coil of rope. Fury had wrapped himself around her for a while, though he kept his eyes open. The wolf was restless, and later took to pacing the deck, eventually settling near the Kagonesti, who stood against the rail at midship.

"No one in Caergoth would listen to me." Feril was saying to Dhamon, who stood a few feet behind her. She leaned against the rail ar.d looked west across the waves, at the setting sun and her former homeland. "I couldn't rally anyone. Not even those Knights of Takhisis would go after such a fearsome dragon. But I won't give up."

Her gaze fixed on the tallest mountain peaks. Like dripping watercolors, the sun's fiery-orange glow spilled down the snow-covered summits. Somehow the added color only made the land look colder—empty and forbidding.

Feril shivered as Dhamon stepped closer. He reached out to put his arm around her shoulders, but stopped himself.

"I lived in Southern Ergoth when it snowed only in the winter," the Kagonesti said softly. "I lived in the north, near the ruins of Hie, on the coast."

"I didn't think there were many people on the barrens," Dhamon observed.

"I didn't live with people. I was born in the Vale, in a Kagonesti village at the foot of the mountains," she continued. "I was happy there, at least, when I was young. But as I got older, I found myself preferring solitude to the company of my kinsmen."

She sighed wistfully, reaching down to scratch Fury's ears. "So I headed north and explored the mountains and the barrens near Hie, and my path crossed with a pack of red wolves—like this one. I studied them, from a distance at first, and I guess maybe they studied me. Ultimately the distance shrank, and one day I approached them. I dwelled with them for about five years."

Dhamon stared at her in astonishment. The sun softly highlighted the edges of her blowing curls, creating a shifting, pale orange halo about her head. "You *lived* with wolves?"

Feril nodded. "I think I was closer to them than to the people I'd left behind. The wolves taught me a lot. I learned I had an affinity for nature magic during those years, and that influenced my choice of markings. Even though I'd left my people, I still considered myself a Kagonesti, and I wanted to be marked as one."

"The oak leaf?"

"That represents my favorite season, fall, and it's curled to symbolize that it has been long absent from the tree, just as I've been away from my tribe for some time. The jay feather symbolizes my tendency to wander, like a feather blown by the breeze, and it marks my love of birds."

"And the lightning bolt?"

"It's red to symbolize the color of the wolves I ran with. The pack moved fast when hunting, like a flash storm, and its prey had little if any warning."

"So it hunted like a stroke of lightning?" Dhamon asked.

She laughed and nodded. "That's right. I learned how to communicate with the wolves, and eventually with a lot of other wild creatures. Words—people have so many of them for the same thing. A ship isn't just a ship. It's a galleon or a carrack. The land isn't just land. It's plains or scrub or tundra. To the wolves, the concepts and the objects are important, not the words. I learned how to see through their eyes, and merge my senses with theirs—a frightening sensation at first, but wonderful. That kind of magic hasn't faded from Krynn. It's not easy to find, but it's still around in abundance."

Dhamon took a step closer. "Didn't you miss your people?"

She shrugged. "I returned to the Vale from time to time, and traveled across other areas of Southern Ergoth—partly out of curiosity and partly to renew acquaintances with the few friends I'd left behind. My last trip was . . . well, it was spring, and the land had been changing, getting gradually colder. The wolves were nervous; they sensed something was wrong."

Feril recalled that the trip to the village took more than two weeks, and the farther south she journeyed, the worse the weather became. Travel through the mountains was treacherous, as winter was hanging on with a vengeance. But at last she reached her destination—though it took her a few days to realize it.

"At first I couldn't find the village. White stretched in all directions. The snow had drifted so high up the trees that it looked like they had no trunks. There were no signs of people, no homes, no tracks. But I searched," she said. "And when I had moved enough of the snow away, I nearly went mad from what I found."

She paused before a flood of memories brought the words rushing from her lips. "The ruins of the village lay beneath the blanket of snow; wood houses had been torn into pieces. Frozen parts of bodies were scattered beneath boards and broken furniture. There were great claw marks in the ground. I tried to backtrack and follow them to their point of origin.

"But it was hopeless. There was too much snow and ice covering everything. There were a few animals about—rabbits, badgers, elk—so I exhausted myself using my nature magic to see through their eyes, to find some trace of the creature responsible."

"Did you?"

She turned to face Dhamon, and a lone tear rolled down her cheek, following the curve of the oak leaf. "I was able to contact an elk who had just cleared a rise more than a dozen miles south of the village. It sensed something, and I could feel the fear as it rose in its heart. It started to bolt, but my mind shared its body, and I convinced it to stay. At first all we saw was snow, high drifts that practically buried a small glade. But then we saw twin ice-blue pools, and stretching behind them a jagged ridge of ice. I wondered why the pools hadn't frozen over. But then the pools blinked. They were eyes, and the jagged ridge of ice was the spine that ran down the behemoth's neck and back. As the elk stared, the creature—a dragon—rose from the snow and charged.

"I urged the elk to react with speed, but fear had locked its legs. The dragon was a mountain of white, taller at the shoulders than the great firs. When the creature opened its mouth, all the elk and I saw was a black cave filled with teeth that looked like icicles. The cave came closer, then there was blackness and pain. The elk died, and for an instant I felt as though I was being swallowed, too. I turned and ran."

"How did you reach Caergoth?"

She turned back to the rail, staring at the water. "I swam—for a very long time. An enchantment I cast let me breathe water. I slept along the sea bottom, near coral ridges at night where I would be safe. Eventually, I reached the port. But no one in Caergoth would listen to me. I guess I can't blame them. Dragons are formidable."

* * * * *

Shortly after midnight, the storm suddenly caught up with *Flint's Anvil*.

Shaon tied herself to the wheel, both to keep herself from being tossed over the side, and to make sure there would be someone steering. Rig worked the sails, which were alternately billowing and sagging from the erratic wind. The masts, groaning in protest from the constant battering, threatened to snap.

Dhamon and Blister were on the lines. Roused from below decks by the excessive yaw and pitch of the ship, they did their best to follow Rig's instructions, but the howling wind often drowned out the mariner's orders and they had to guess at his words.

The rain disguised Blister's tears, as the kender closed her gloved hands about a broken line and tried to draw it taut. The rope, like everything and everyone else on deck, was slippery with salt water. It resisted her efforts. Needles of hot and cold pain pulsed into her wrists and up her arms, and she bit her lip to keep from crying out. Move! she commanded her fingers. No matter how much it hurts, please, please move! At last she was rewarded—and punished. An agonizing jolt shot from her fingertips into her spine, but her hands held firm—and she was able to tie off the errant line.

The waves surged high and encompassed the bow of the ship, threatening to pull the *Anvil* to the bottom. Blister wrapped her arms about the base of the capstan as another wave washed across the deck. She winced as she had to move her fingers to seek a better grip. She wished she could huddle below deck as she had done during their voyage through the Gale, but she knew she was needed.

Feril scrambled up to the deck just as a breaker cut across midship. The water struck her and sent her skidding to the port side. She flailed about, trying to find anything to grab onto, before her fingers closed about a length of rope. Another wave buffeted her, and the rope flew from her grasp and whipped her face. She felt herself being pushed across the deck, and her back slammed hard against the railing. Air rushed from her lungs, and a sensation of dizziness swept over her. She locked her arms around a spoke in the rail. Again the water pounded her, but she managed to hold on, barely conscious.

From somewhere ahead, toward the bow of the ship, she thought she heard a cry. It was so difficult to pick out the words amid the howling wind and snapping sails.

Then she felt the *Anvil* list, and she had to concentrate on her own survival. The ship lurched until it was nearly turned on its side, and the rail she was holding onto was practically riding on the water. She closed her eyes and coaxed a spell to mind—words that would trigger an enchantment to let her breathe water. But the waves lashing her broke her concentration, and she gagged on the salt water that filled her mouth.

The waves crashing against the ship were practically deafening now, as the storm's intensity increased. Through a haze of salt water and tears, Feril wondered for a brief instant what Groller was experiencing—the cacophony of a raging storm would be nothing to him. Again the ship listed, this time to starboard. Feril felt herself buoyed upward, then a strong hand gripped her arm and pulled her to her feet.

Rig tugged her away from the rail. He was yelling at her, saying something she couldn't understand, trying to make himself be heard above the din. Then he was shoving her toward the forward mast. Her fingers fumbled for a hand-hold, and she ended up grabbing a rope that was wrapped around the mast.

Then she heard another cry, faint, but certain this time it was a human sound. Rig heard it too, and she watched as the mariner closed his eyes and let out a long breath. Somehow he never lost his footing. He balanced himself like a cat, flexing his legs when the ship rocked, never losing his footing. "Stay here!" he yelled.

Rig found Dhamon wrestling with a line that had pulled free from the main sail. The mariner grabbed him about the waist to keep him from washing away, and between the two of them they tied it off again. Dhamon turned to attend to another line threatening to pull loose, while Rig fought his way to the wheel, breathing a sigh of relief to discover that Shaon was still there.

"We lost two deck hands!" she called as she yanked the wheel hard to port. "They were near the bowsprit. I watched them go over. I couldn't do anything. I think the wolf went over, too."

"What about Groller?" Rig's voice was hoarse from shouting so loud.

"Groller's at the rear mast—at least he was!"

"The dwarf?"

"I'm not sure!" she shouted.

"If the weather doesn't break, we're done for! We're free of the icebergs. But according to the charts, there are some tiny islands out here, and some shoals. We could end up smashing into them or beaching ourselves!"

"I can't see anything," Shaon gasped. She shook her head to clear the water from her eyes. Her clothes and hair were plastered against her body. She was shivering uncontrollably from fear and the cold.

Rig's hand brushed her shoulder, then he was gone—making his way back to midship to check on Dhamon and

Feril. Through the sheets of rain, he spied Groller's big form at the mizzen sail and breathed another sigh of relief.

"Should've stayed in port!" Rig shouted to Dhamon as the mariner crept by him. "We can't see where we're going, and we're liable to run aground! I've already lost two men!"

Feril's keen elven ears made out the words, and she realized that running aground would likely mean all of their deaths. I have to do something, she thought. Have to . . . She wrapped the rope around her waist and dropped to the deck. The water rushed over her as she placed her hands on the wood so her fingers could feel the water's force.

She closed her eyes and murmured words that sounded like the susseration of peaceful waves against the hull. The Kagonesti's head pounded from the effort to keep calm. She concentrated on the water, what it felt like, smelled like. The movement, the coolness of it.

At last she was rewarded. She sensed herself slip away, submerged, with the water flowing all about her, caressing her, urging her to come with it, be a part of it. She allowed herself to be drawn along with the waves—which were no longer threatening, but pleasurable. Power seemed to surge through her as the *Anvil* rolled and tossed. Then she concentrated on extending her vision beyond the ship, below the white caps and away from the hammering wind. The darkness didn't bother her; she was water, and water didn't need the sun or the moon. She reached out and touched coral ridges, her senses caressing the colorful growths, then stretched forward to locate a lone rock that jutted up from the sea, hidden by the high waves. The formation was as black as night, and Feril knew Shaon would not be able to spot it. And it lay directly in the *Anvil's* path.

"To the right!" the Kagonesti screamed.

"What?" she heard Rig holler back.

"Take the ship fast to the right or we'll crash! Do it now!"

The mariner somehow trusted her and yelled to Dhamon,

who in turn called to Shaon to swing the wheel hard to starboard. Within the space of a few heartbeats, the *Anvil* angled and missed the jutting rock by scant inches.

Feril breathed a sigh of relief and let her mind range farther ahead of the ship. Beyond the coral a school of dolphins swam nervously about. They were far enough below the waves not to be worried by the storm. Yet something was bothering them. The Kagonesti plunged deeper until she was in their midst and searching for the source of their distress. Sharks, perhaps? She reached out with her mind, trying to touch one of the dolphins, but in that instant the dolphins appeared to panic and began to swim in a dozen different directions. All around her the water churned.

Feril felt the water being displaced by something large. A trio of dolphins swam madly toward her. Then she saw only blackness. A stream of air bubbles surrounded her as the water seemed to thicken and become warmer. Blood! She pulled back from the site until she was beyond the darkness, until her senses could pinpoint a row of icicle shaped teeth. "The dragon!" she screamed inside her head. The words tumbled from her lips above deck, too. "The White is down there! Feasting in the storm!"

She watched it devour the dolphins, overtaking and swallowing them as a sea bass might swallow the smallest of minnows. The great beast spun about in the water, its giant tail lashing behind it and striking a rocky spire that went toppling to the sea floor. She felt her heart hammer inside her chest, frightened though she knew the dragon couldn't see her—her body was safely on deck. Feril tried to calm herself, then saw the dragon look up. Its massive white head was aimed toward something above it. The Kagonesti followed its gaze and saw the bottom of the *Anvil*, being tossed in the water like mere flotsam. She shivered. The sea had grown terribly cold around the beast.

Then she watched in horror as the dragon tucked its

wings against its sides and its thick leg muscles churned through the water and propelled it toward the ship. It opened its maw and a jet of ice shot out, striking the *Anvil* with such force that the ship burst out of the water.

The ship listed to the right as it came down hard, water spraying everywhere. Dhamon hugged the mast to keep from getting swept overboard, and Rig hovered near Feril. "What was that?" the Kagonesti heard him bellow.

"Left!" she screamed, as she sensed the dragon moving toward the right, following the ship.

Rig relayed the order to Shaon, and the ship lurched to the port side as the White passed beneath it. The beast's spiky back cut above the water like a line of shark fins, then the dragon dove down and banked through the water for another pass.

The *Anvil* couldn't outrace the dragon, Feril knew. It was only a matter of minutes before the ship was crushed. Still, she continued to shout directions to Rig. Again the dragon swept its huge body around, but this time it didn't rise toward the surface. It dove deeper, as a surprised Kagonesti scoured the boiling sand of the sea floor. A giant octopus, cutting across the bottom, propelled itself quickly away. The dragon had decided to pursue it, suddenly interested in the flesh of a meal.

The White disappeared from view, lost in an eruption of sand and ink. On deck, Feril bit her lip so hard she felt the warmth of her blood spill into her mouth. Would the dragon return? Her senses roamed beneath the still-tossing *Anvil*. How much time passed, she couldn't say. She spent the next two hours scrying through the water and directing the ship around underwater ridges, small islands, shoals, and waterspouts. The dragon did not reappear. And at last the storm subsided, and the sea calmed.

"Minimal damage," Shaon huffed as she untied herself and stumbled toward Rig and Dhamon, who were inspecting the mainmast. "But we're down two men."

"They knew that there'd be risks where we were heading," Rig growled. "I never made them any false promises. I just hope we can pick up one or two more in the next port. I don't like being shorthanded." The mariner inhaled sharply. Inwardly, he may have grieved for the men, but the code of the sea rejected shows of sentimentality. "Just be thankful we're not all at the bottom. When that dragon surfaced, I thought we were finished."

He grimaced and cast a glance at the sleeping Kagonesti. Feril had collapsed from exhaustion, after doing her job so well. The rope was still tied around her waist, her brown curls were plastered to the sides of her head, and her clothes were painted to her body. A trickle of blood escaped from her lip. Water still pooled around her. The waves hadn't washed away the tattoos on her face or arm. She looked like a painted rag doll, discarded and laying in a heap.

"Could've been much worse," he said, nodding toward Feril. "She kept us in one piece."

Shaon balled her fists and set them on her hips. "I didn't see her at the wheel!" she fumed. The dark-skinned woman glared at Rig, then strode by him and started down the stairs, stepping aside briefly to let Jasper pass as he climbed up. "I'm changing clothes," she called. "I'll be back in a while—unless you don't need me."

The mariner sighed. "I better go unruffle her feathers." Rig started to follow her, but paused when he spied Groller at the rear mast. The half-ogre was still untangling the rope from the mizzen sail. The mariner clenched his hands, held them at shoulder height, then alternately moved them in an arc. The half-ogre nodded.

"Groller'll take the wheel," Rig told Dhamon. "See if you can clear the rope on the mizzen sail. Then untie Feril. I'll be back topside in a while." He quietly disappeared below deck.

Meanwhile, Blister eased herself away from the capstan.

Her soaked gloves were no longer warm and they were spotted with blood. She thrust her aching hands into her pockets so no one would see, and she skittered below to find another pair to put on.

Chapter 20

To Palanthas

"What's the matter?" Feril spotted Dhamon near the bow, scowling and looking out over the small whitecaps.

He shook his head. "Nothing. I was just thinking about . . . things." He was, in fact, thinking about Feril. She'd been occupying most of his thoughts lately.

"Thinking about the dragons?"

He nodded.

"Some say there's only a few dozen dragons left," she said. "At least, that was the talk in the Caergoth harbor. There were hundreds just a few decades ago. I talked to an old sailor who said the bigger dragons have killed off the smaller ones. The big ones that remain have territories, like the great Red that rules the east, or the Black down by the New Sea." She paused and looked down into the water. "And then there's the White."

"Dragons seem every bit as strong, maybe stronger, than before. The White magically altered Southern Ergoth. They have most of the magic now.

"I've never put much trust in magic," Dhamon stated. "I prefer to put my faith in something substantial, like my sword. Magic is gone, for the most part."

Feril frowned. "Pity you believe that," she said softly. "Magic is still very important to some."

Dhamon felt the red rising to his cheeks. He hadn't meant to upset her. That was the last thing he wanted to do. He opened his mouth to apologize, but her words came faster.

"How long before we reach Palanthas?"

"A few weeks. We only just passed Starport yesterday."

Rig had gone ashore to conduct some business. He didn't want a repeat of the altercation at Caergoth and instructed everyone else to wait on board ship. Several hours later he had returned with two hired mates, some supplies and several colorful shirts for Dhamon.

"Red looks good on you," Feril said, fingering his shirt and laughing as she whirled away.

She found Rig at the wheel nearby. "I overheard you talking about magic," the mariner told her. His deep voice cut across the deck. "Magic fascinates me."

I'll bet it does, Dhamon said to himself. He was looking over his shoulder at Feril standing next to the big sea barbarian.

"The magic I prefer to use lets me assume the form of an animal," Feril said. "But it's very tiring, and afterward I feel as though I've run for miles. I can also just look through their eyes."

"How do you take an animal's form?" The mariner seemed genuinely interested.

Feril grinned, reaching for a small leather pouch at her side. Tugging on the drawstring, she slipped her slender fingers inside and retrieved a lump of clay. "Like this," she explained as she worked the clay with her thumbs. Overhead a gull cried and she worked the clay faster, forming the crude shape of a bird with a thin tail and a dully pointed beak. She used her thumbnail to give the piece the semblance of eyes and wings tucked against its body. It wasn't an especially artistic rendering, but it seemed to satisfy her. "The gull," she said.

The Kagonesti held the clay image in the palm of her right hand and closed her eyes. She began humming, a melody that the bird overhead echoed with its cries. The distance between her and the bird evaporated, as her mind soared toward it, the air rushing all around her. Suddenly, she stiffened, and a smile played across her face.

She was looking down at herself and the mariner. "I'm high above the ship," she whispered. "I see the lump of clay in my hand. And I see Dhamon watching us, moving toward us. Jasper is back by the capstan. He's frowning and shaking his head. Shaon is watching him. I see the flag fluttering at the top of the sail. The bird likes to watch the sails."

"Do you know what the bird's thinking?"

Again she nodded. "It's like I'm inside his head. He's curious about us, about ships. He likes to follow fishing boats, and he wonders why we're not fishing. He likes to dart to the decks and snatch something to eat. It's a game with him, and he doesn't understand why we're not playing along."

"Can he see ahead of us? Are there other ships out on the water?"

Feril started humming again, and Rig glanced up in time to see the bird bank away. "I'm sending him north," she said.

"You're controlling the bird?"

I won't do that again, not after the elk, she thought. "I'm asking nicely," she answered. "And he's agreeable. There is a ship in the distance. Three masts. And there's another. There are other dots of white farther away—perhaps sails, perhaps white caps. And there's a smaller ship. They're all a long way off. The bird sees very far. One is a fishing boat. He wants to go closer."

The Kagonesti opened her eyes with a grin. "I guess he found someone who'll play his game," she sighed. Balling her fist, she squashed the lump of clay into a misshapen blob and returned it to her pouch.

"Perhaps you could teach me to do that," Rig ventured.

"Perhaps tomorrow," she answered.

* * * * *

Several weeks passed and *Flint's Anvil* eased around the tip of Tanith. The Gates of Paladine, the opening of the wide, deep Bay of Branchala, lay before them. Beyond that stretched the country and city of Palanthas.

The coastline was striking, and Dhamon found himself in Feril's company admiring the shore. The Kagonesti pointed toward the west.

"Sand," she whispered. "So much of it. White like snow."

"I didn't know the desert ran this far," Dhamon said. "But I've never been in these parts before."

"It looks like the only thing keeping the sky and sea apart is that thin strip of sand," Feril said. "I think I'd like to sail so far that I couldn't see any land. To be where the sky and sea meet, and to sail on toward an infinity of blue . . . "

The bright blue of the morning sky reached down to touch the white sand of Palanthas, making it look like a white ribbon waving slowing in the breeze. The sapphire water of the bay extended to the horizon, slowly rocking the ship.

"It is beautiful," Dhamon said.

"There's always beauty in nature," Feril agreed. "Even in Southern Ergoth. The snow was beautiful, cold and endless and quiet. The sheets of ice mirrored the sky. It wasn't natural, but it was difficult not to appreciate its beauty."

Dhamon stared at the horizon. And you're beautiful too, he thought. "I'd like to hear more about Southern Ergoth," he said. Actually, he just wanted to hear her talk.

"Feril!" boomed Rig's voice. "There are birds all around. Maybe I could try some of that magic again!"

Feril grinned and hurried off toward the mariner.

"Magic," Dhamon grumbled.

Shortly before dawn the next day, they eased into the city of Palanthas's deep harbor.

Chapter 21

Sapphire Schemes

The blue spawn stood on a ridge above Khellendros's underground lair. Its stubby tail twitched, miniature bolts of lightning danced between its clawed fingers, and its head slowly turned to take in the barren expanse.

Sand spread away from it in all directions. It was fine, white sand, not the coarse brown grains that covered the ground a few months ago. The white sand contrasted sharply with the color of the spawn, and with the Blue. Rich sapphire against glistening white.

A pale, cloudless blue sky reached overhead, and the sun hung suspended in the center of it, white-hot and merciless heat. Blessed heat, the spawn thought. Like its creator, it reveled in the blazing warmth.

Khellendros had been sculpting his land, as the other dragon overlords had been doing. But he didn't create any mountains or lakes or coax plants to grow in such great profusion. And he didn't make the desert much bigger than it was before. He left the terrain largely as it was—he had little inclination to significantly alter the physical features of the Northern Wastes. The dragon liked his home the way it was. He had simply changed the color and texture of the sand.

Khellendros believed the white grains stored the heat better. He loved to feel the intense warmth beneath the pads of his massive feet or beneath his belly when he stretched out in the middle of the day—the hottest time in the desert—as he was stretching out now. The warmth permeated every scale, soaked into his thick muscles, and massaged the ridge that ran along his back.

The white sand held the water better when he unleashed a storm to wet his hide and soak his domain. The dragon needed to be cooled off on occasion, if only because when the water dissipated and the heat returned he could more appreciate it, bask in it anew.

Ah, this glorious heat!

The dragon rumbled, purring like a cat, and the spawn turned to glance at him. Khellendros stared at his sapphire creation, and, as usual, found that he was staring at a miniature doppleganger of himself.

"Master? You wish something of me?"

"No," Khellendros growled, as he continued to stare. He cocked his head. "I wish to sleep. Wake me if you spy trespassers."

The blue spawn turned its head, and the dragon saw the scene shift away from himself and to the south. Khellendros was still getting used to this ability to see what any designated spawn saw—to see, hear, and feel. This spawn, and the others below in his lair, were extensions of himself. He closed his eyes and thought of the hot sand, and as he did so his senses pulled away from the blue spawn.

"*Two-legged* trespassers," the dragon softly added.

The spawn had previously—and needlessly—woken him when a wild camel plodded by. Trespassers, to the young, mentally-childish creation, seemed to mean anything that wasn't itself or Khellendros. The dragon knew the spawn would learn. The creature had the capacity for genius. Khellendros simply had to fill its mind and give it direction.

The blue spawn continued to survey its master's domain. It glanced at each cactus, every patch of scrub grass, ignored the large scorpions that skittered about, and paid little attention to the thin, brown snakes that worked their way across the land, leaving curved shapes behind them. The spawn knew when its master awoke, he would erase the S-shaped designs and restore the desert to blankness once again. It watched the air shimmer, the currents of heat rising from the master's bed of white. And it watched the tiny, two-legged trespasser approach. Khellendros was not allowed to sleep long.

"Master?"

The dragon rumbled. He irately rose on his haunches and looked past the spawn. Another camel? A giant scorpion perhaps? Maybe a small sandstorm? For an instant the dragon wondered if he had made an error in designating this blue spawn a sentry before it had been thoroughly educated. The dragon had been promised other sentries, suitable guards so that his spawn could remain a secret while he taught them. But the huldrefolk's promise of sentries remained unfulfilled, and Khellendros was constantly being awakened from his needed sleep.

The dragon's misgivings were quickly set aside. "I am pleased with you, blue spawn," he said. "You are serving me well."

The diminutive gray-skinned man, who a moment before

was only a speck on the horizon, strode persistently forward, apparently unbothered by the heat.

"Fissure," Khellendros hissed. He opened his maw, just enough so his tongue could edge out.

Away from the shadows of his lair and the black skies of Nightlund, the dark huldrefolk's features were revealed in all their blandness. Though Fissure had no ears, Khellendros could see small holes in the sides of his smooth, hairless head. In their earlier meetings, the dragon had thought the huldrefolk's eyes had no pupils. But now the sun exposed small black pupils set into deep violet eyes. And the weird eyes returned Khellendros's stare.

"Could you make the sand any color you wanted?" Fissure asked.

Khellendros raised a scaly eyebrow and growled. His tongue ran across his bottom lip. The huldrefolk would be an insignificant speck in the dragon's massive belly, but the thought of swallowing the impudent faerie gave him some satisfaction.

"Could you make it green or blue or purple? After all, I can make myself any color I choose."

"You came here to bother me about sand?" Khellendros slid forward, noiselessly.

"Actually, I came here to bother you about colors."

Khellendros snarled and the sky rumbled. Fissure looked up and noticed a cloud overhead, where none had been a heartbeat before.

"One color in particular," the huldrefolk continued.

The rumbling grew louder, and suddenly the light blue sky was darkening, becoming instantly overcast. Fissure thought he saw a flicker of lightning amid the gathering multitude of clouds. He certainly saw lightning crackle around the dragon's teeth.

"Gray," he continued unperturbed and unworried. "*The Gray* to be specific."

The rumbling lessened, though the sky remained ominous. The huldrefolk reached a reed-thin finger to his chin. "Interested?"

The rumbling stopped. Fissure padded forward, slipping by the spawn, which bared its razor teeth at the small man. He stopped about a dozen feet in front of Khellendros.

"I've been doing some research—about magic. It seems that tapping magic stored in items can augment any dragon or human's magic."

Khellendros drew his eyes into thin slits. "I knew that," he hissed. "That is why I first sought the magic held in the tower in Palanthas."

"Ah, but the humans do not know what I know, that certain old, magical baubles: swords, scepters,—the nature of the thing really doesn't matter—can release more force than others."

"Go on," the dragon coaxed.

"Things from the Age of Dreams," Fissure said.

"That was a long time ago," Khellendros snarled. "Before the gods began truly meddling in the affairs of Krynn."

"Yes, before the Time of Light, before Reorx was tricked into forging a stone that he left on the moon of Lunitari. While Reorx wasn't looking, the gods of magic, who had been banished from Krynn filled the stone with their very beings. These scheming gods tricked a Chosen of Reorx, into stealing the stone. The Chosen—accidentally perhaps— dropped the stone onto Krynn. And with that one act, magic reentered the world."

"I know all of that, faerie." Khellendros said with irritation. "But magic from the Age of Dreams—"

"Magical baubles from that age are not nearly so plentiful as the baubles that were created since, fashioned after the gods of magic started dabbling and spreading their trinkets around. Those ancient things are more powerful than all the baubles created since."

"Perhaps they could be used to reopen the portals," the dragon mused.

"That is my point. I think it is worth trying in any event. Now all that remains is to find one or more of those moldy baubles," Fissure continued, "which I suspect might take a considerable amount of time. Months, maybe years."

"Time matters little to me," Khellendros said. *Only Kitiara matters*, he added to himself, *and her spirit is timeless while it floats in The Gray.* "You will search for this magic." It was an order, not a request.

"Of course," the huldrefolk replied. "I want access to The Gray as much as you do. But first, I have a gift for you."

"The sentries you promised?"

Fissure nodded and gestured toward the sky. He opened his mouth, revealing a row of small, pointed teeth, and whistled shrilly.

At first Khellendros saw nothing, just the dark clouds he had summoned into existence minutes ago. Then his keen eyes picked out twin shadows amid the gray billows, shadows shaped like dragons, though not as large. The shapes dropped through the clouds, and—drawing their wings near to their bodies—plummeted toward the desert floor.

The creatures were dark brown and only partially-scaly, with wingspans of nearly fifty feet. The heads of the two looked as if they had been snatched from twin giant lizards, but they were filled with triple rows of long teeth, and curving fangs that edged over their lower lips. Their wings were batlike and leathery, not at all as enormous as a dragon's. And also unlike a dragon, they possessed no front legs. Their three-clawed hind feet opened as they landed, and their whiplike tails thrashed wildly, stirring up sand. The dragon spied a knot of cartilage near the end of each of their tails, from which protruded needlelike barbs that glistened with moist venom.

The larger of the two creatures opened its maw wide and emitted a loud hiss, a noise that sounded like a newly forged blade being thrust in cooling water. The other lowered its head and released a deep-throated growl that sounded more like the snarl of a great crocodile.

"Wyverns," the dragon observed.

"From Nightlund," Fissure added proudly, puffing out his small, gray chest. "They like the forests the best, where there's plenty of shade. But I finally persuaded them to come here. And I . . . enhanced them."

The dragon cocked his head. "Explain."

"Wyverns cannot normally talk," the huldrefolk stated. "But these can, courtesy of me. It was no small effort on my part, mind you. Lots of time, energy—nothing but the best for you. They can warn you of intruders, alert you to things going on in the desert, or they can travel wherever you choose to send them. And when they come back, they can report what they saw. I give them to you as a gesture of my good faith—a gift, a token of my friendship. They will loyally follow your instructions."

Khellendros narrowed his eyes. He doubted Fissure had any faith—good or ill, but he accepted the wyverns. The new sentries would allow him to keep the majority of his spawn below ground, and to use only a carefully chosen few as scouts. He could devote more time to tutoring his scaly off-spring.

"Aren't you touched?" Fissure asked.

The dragon rumbled. "I am satisfied."

"Do now what?" the largest wyvern asked. Its big black eyes blinked, and its nose quivered. It shifted its weight back and forth on its feet, never keeping one claw on the steamy sand for too long.

"Don't know do now what," the other answered, as it began to shift like its brother. It blew at its feet in a futile effort to cool them. "Ask do now what."

The pair looked to Khellendros as they continued their odd dance.

"Do now what?" they queried, practically in unison.

"They're not especially bright, are they?"

Fissure dug his smooth foot into the sand. "They possess some amount of intelligence . . . just not a lot of it."

The sky grew darker and a bolt of lightning raced to the ground behind the dragon's lair. Sand erupted over the dragon, the surprised wyverns, and the nervous huldrefolk.

"But I bet they'll get smarter. And I'll enhance a few more sentries for you just in case they don't," Fissure quickly offered.

"See that you do," Khellendros replied. "Ones with more intelligence."

"I'll see to that right now."

"No."

"No?"

"Not yet." The Blue edged forward, sliding over the sand like a snake. When he was inches from the huldrefolk, he said, "I need to create more blue spawn."

"More? Why? I thought you had dozens."

"I need to create an army, for protection and as a show of force. And to create an army, I shall need people. Bodies to corrupt and mold."

"Oh." The huldrefolk swallowed hard.

"Humans, preferably."

Fissure relaxed, if only a little. "Any kind of humans? Short? Tall? Fat? Men or women?"

The dragon ignored his questions. "First, you will travel to the hills south of the Plains of Solamnia. There are ogres there, my allies. I usually have brutes handle the actual extractions, but it is time I get use from other beholden followers. Find them, and direct the ogres to collect some people."

The faerie relaxed. "So I don't have to gather them myself. That's good. Well, where should I tell the ogres to get these . . . uhm, people?"

"There is a large city nearby. Palanthas, the humans call it. The ogres can take people entering and leaving that city, people passing through, those laden with burdens and who look like travelers or strangers."

"I don't understand."

"The residents of Palanthas will not care so much about the fate of strangers. They will be less likely to pursue, to search for the missing, and I will have less chance of being discovered. I prefer not to have fingers pointed at me yet. Contact the Knights of Takhisis in Palanthas. They have been most helpful in administering my realm. They can quietly aid the ogres in their mission and the brutes will receive the captured humans. If anything should go awry, blame will be placed on the ogres. They are expendable.

"My brutes have been raiding barbarian villages to the northeast of the city. But they haven't been bringing enough humans. And there are not many villages left to plunder.

"All right," Fissure answered. "I'll tell the ogres. And I'll meet with the Dark Knights. You can trust me."

"That task finished, you will attend to creating better sentries."

"Of course. Ones with more intelligence."

The dragon nodded. "You will deal with these matters quickly. Then you will start searching for this ancient magic you mentioned."

"From the Age of Dreams."

"Yes."

The huldrefolk drew his lips into a thin line, bowed his head, and melted into the desert floor. A small pile of sand materialized where his feet had stood a moment ago. The pile shimmered, then moved away from the dragon like a mole burrowing through a garden. It headed toward the southwest, in the direction of the hills.

"Do now what?" the large wyvern asked again.

"Do nothing?" the other posed a related question.

"Follow me," Khellendros rumbled.

"Good. Here hot."

"Hot too much," the smaller added. "Follow you colder?"

The dragon snarled as he guided the wyverns into his underground lair. The spawn took a last look at the horizon, and the mounting storm, then also disappeared into the cavern.

Chapter 22

The Trail of Evil

Blister strolled across the deck of Flint's Anvil. Her skin was nut-brown now, darkened from the weeks she'd spent on the ship, and it made her blue eyes stand out more, seem a little brighter.

The kender was wearing a dark blue tunic and matching gloves that had sharp metal nibs at the knuckles and along the fingertips. Her hair had been painstakingly arranged, and a painted seashell affixed to a small comb sat on the right side of her head, midway between her ear and her topknot. She was going into a large, new city, and she wanted to look her best.

"Dhamon, now that we're in Palanthas, what are we supposed to do? You've been awfully tight-lipped about what

Goldmoon told you." She adjusted her belt with her thumbs. A chapak hung in a loop off the blue leather belt, between two bulging bags. A weapon of kender design that she'd previously kept hidden in one of her packs, the chapak was a small single-bladed hand axe, the back of which was pronged and sported a slingshot.

"Goldmoon said that evil breeds near Palanthas," Dhamon replied, as he eyed her up and down, pausing to stare at the axe. He was wearing his black leather trousers and a forest green shirt Rig had picked out for him in Portsmith. The collar was open and trimmed in silvery-gray thread, and the sleeves were billowy. It was, in Dhamon's opinion, the most functional and the least showy of the three Rig had gotten for him. His sword was strapped to his left side. He'd been polishing it, and the old pommel gleamed in the early morning sun.

"And . . . " Blister coaxed.

"And I'd like to find just what that evil might be," he answered. "But we've a stop to make first. A place called the Lonely Refuge."

"Maybe we should just walk around the city, first—before we go anywhere," the kender happily suggested. "Maybe we'll notice something evil. Maybe we'll overhear someone talking about something sinister. Or maybe someone will try to steal from us. We could follow them to an entire gang of thieves. Besides, look at the size of this place. It looks wonderful. We should explore it. All of it. Of course, we'll have to be careful."

Dhamon followed Blister's gaze. *Flint's Anvil* sat near the northwesternmost point of a horseshoe-shaped maze of docks that clung to Palanthas's shore. The buildings nearest the shore were stone. Other than signs and shutters, they had little painted trim—not much for the salt air to eat away at. Their roofs were tile—greens, reds, and grays mostly—and the walkways between them were made of tamped-down earth with planks here and there.

Glancing toward the heart of the city, he could see the more impressive buildings—towers made of pale gray stone, and the ivory and rose spires of the palace. The edge of an old, circular wall seemed to cut through the center of the town.

"The city used to be that big." The mariner had silently crept up behind him and now stretched an arm toward the western edge of the old wall. "When the city kept growing, they had to build outside the wall and knock a few holes in it to accommodate more streets and buildings. Now the city extends to the mountains. There's really no other direction for it to grow. Maybe a little more to the east. Maybe."

Dhamon could see the mountains rising behind the buildings. It was as if Palanthas—all its homes, businesses, and empty temples—was cradled in a giant palm, ridged by mountains. "How do you know so much about the city?"

"I really don't know all that much. I visited Palanthas about a dozen years ago, when I wasn't much more than a kid. I don't remember there being near as many docks then. But I remember a place call Myrtal's Roost. Delicious steak. Had my first mug of rum there. I'll have me another one there today—if the place is still standing." Rig pursed his lips and shook his head, as if shaking away an old, stubborn memory. "I hope you're done pretty soon, so I can have my ship back. No offense if I change the name to something a bit lighter-sounding afterward?"

"Wait a minute." Dhamon's eyes narrowed. "It *is* your ship, and I could care less what you do with the name—after Jasper and I are gone. But the deal is, you agree to stick around for a while, remember? Just in case we need a ride out of here."

"How long?"

"A few days. Maybe a week. Just to be safe."

The mariner moaned.

"Can you trust him?" Blister cut in. "If we take off strolling through the city, he might just leave."

"I trust him," Dhamon returned as he stepped on the plank leading to the dock. "I believe he's a man of honor."

"Honor again," Rig groaned. His eyes met Dhamon's. "Okay, I'll wait—at least for a while."

"Wait!" Feril rushed up the steps from below deck, Jasper on her heels. "I'm coming with you."

"I'm not," Jasper grumbled. "It's too long a walk to the Lonely Refuge. And I don't intend to tire myself out unnecessarily. Besides, something tells me I should stick around here."

"But Goldmoon said you knew how to get there," Dhamon curtly noted. "She said you'd help."

"Oh, I'm helping all right. Here's a map I drew. Follow it, and you'll find the spot. Consider it a bit of insurance if I choose to rest up on the ship. I'll make sure it stays in port."

"I said I'd wait," Rig snapped.

"And just in case, I'll make sure you do," Jasper said. The dwarf nodded to the Kagonesti, who slipped past Dhamon and hurried ahead. Blister followed her.

Dhamon hurriedly glanced at the map, cut a glowering look at the dwarf, and joined Feril and Blister, who were already plunging into the bustle on the docks.

On the deck of the *Anvil*, Flint, Rig, Groller, and Fury watched the trio go. Shaon padded up behind them. "I think I should go with them," she pointed out.

"What?" the mariner said. "But you don't even like land— at least that's what you've always told me."

"You know I'd rather be at sea," she returned sharply. "And that's precisely why I'm going with them. I want to help them find whatever it is they're looking for—as soon as feasible. I'll hurry them along. Then we can hurry back here, and the ship will be ours to reckon with that much sooner."

Without waiting for his reply, she strapped on the sword the kender had used to pay for passage to Schallsea, then donned one of Rig's voluminous yellow shirts. "Don't leave port without me," she said with a chuckle, as she went by.

Rig's arm shot out and caught her wrist. He pulled her

close. "What makes you so sure I wouldn't?"

Her wide eyes fixed onto his, and she grinned. "Miss me, okay?"

"Miss you? I'd rather come with you."

"And who would mind the *Anvil*? Groller, who can't hear anyone? And Jasper, who doesn't know anything about ships? You're certainly not going to leave this ship in the hands of those two—or two hired mates we know little about." Her lips formed a pout. "Besides, I don't intend to be gone all that long. You know I don't trust my footing on solid ground."

"Then be careful," he warned. "And be quick about it."

"I will. I'd better go, before they get out of sight."

Rig tugged on her wrist again, and his other arm circled her waist and pressed her to him. His lips closed tightly over hers, as he held her for a moment. "Stay out of trouble, Shaon," he whispered.

She slowly withdrew from his embrace, offered him a sly smile, and hurried down the plank. Fury quietly slipped off the ship, following her.

"So something told you to stay here, huh?" Rig asked Jasper.

The dwarf had found an empty crate to sit on near the rear mast, and was sunning himself. "Yep."

"Don't trust me?"

"Trust has nothing to do with it," Jasper replied. "Besides, It'll give me a chance to learn more of Groller's sign language."

The mariner growled and pulled up a crate. "I know what's not a good sign. When Dhamon left the ship, all the women went with him."

* * * * *

The group's first stop was an unexpected one. Before they could exit the harbor area, they had to undergo inspection by

Dark Knight sentries.

Feril, who was ahead of everyone else, was the first to be stopped. When Dhamon saw the cluster of Dark Knights forming around the Kagonesti, he rushed forward, his hand dropping to the hilt of his sword.

Shaon caught up to him, taking his hand in hers so he couldn't draw his sword. "Mind if I join you?" she asked. "Thought I'd stretch my legs."

"We aren't looking for any trouble," Feril quickly interjected.

"Good," said a tall Dark Knight as he scanned the group with a critical eye. His left eyebrow arched when his gaze fell on Feril. "Now what is it you *are* looking for?" he asked, stepping closer to the Kagonesti.

"Who wants to know?" asked Blister, placing her gloved hands on her hips.

The three other Dark Knights moved toward the feisty kender but they halted when the tall one raised his hand as if to silence them. "Khellendros wants to know," he said. "Any more questions and you'll pay double the harbor tax."

"The harbor tax?" Shaon asked.

"Triple," said the Dark Knight.

Dhamon glared at his companions. "I'll speak for my group," he said, moving Feril aside and taking her place in front of the tall Dark Knight.

As the others were searched one at a time, Dhamon answered questions from the apparent leader of the sentries, who procured the triple harbor tax when he was finished.

Blister's search took the longest. They kept finding more pouches and pockets—more things—much to her delight.

When they had finally cleared the Dark Knights' checkpoint, Blister could no longer remain silent. "You should have let me do the talking. You're still no good at lying. And why's the Blue so concerned with our comings and goings? And . . . where are we going anyway?"

"The Lonely Refuge," Dhamon answered, pausing in front of a cartographer's shop that he had spotted from the shore.

Jasper's map was all right, but incomplete. Dhamon wanted something a little more detailed and authoritative. Jasper's map, which he waved at Blister, consisted of little more than the horseshoe-shaped harbor, an X indicating Palanthas, and a dotted line leading to another X northeast of the city. There was no scale, nor other points of reference. He stuffed the map in his front pocket and slipped inside the shop. Blister was one step behind him.

Shaon and the Kagonesti stood outside on the polished plank sidewalk. They drew appreciative and curious stares from passersby.

"C'mon," Shaon said. She pointed to a tavern nearby. "I'm going to quench my thirst while I'm waiting."

Feril wrinkled her nose, but joined the female barbarian out of curiosity.

* * * * *

Inside the shop, Dhamon stepped up to a low counter, the top of which was littered with rolled pieces of parchment and vials of ink. The walls of the business were covered with maps, old and yellowed, of buildings, towns, sea coasts, and islands. Behind a piece of glass, there was a rendering of Palanthas before the city spread beyond the circular stone wall. Only a handful of docks stretched out into the harbor, and a legend along the side indicated important places, such as the Tower of High Sorcery, the Great Library, and Nobles' Hill. Next to it were city maps of Neraka, Qualinost, and Tarsis, all expertly sketched down to the tiniest landmarks.

"Look at that," Blister pointed at the ceiling.

A map that was roughly six feet square was tacked directly overhead. It was a drawing of a hill, executed in black, brown, and green ink. Inside the hill were levels upon levels—thirty-five in all—of twisting stairways, large and small rooms, giant gears, and much more. A lower section was labeled "garbage dump," and a squinting Dhamon could make out a tiny broken chair atop a pile of indistinguishable shattered odds and ends. Nearby were other labeled areas—agriculture, geothermal station, research, and gnomeflinger control room. Pipes ran from the adjacent "Crater Lake" and seemed to feed into every level of the mountain.

"Mount Nevermind."

The voice was the proprietor's, an elderly, stoop-shouldered man with a spattering of liver spots on his near-bald head. He stepped from behind a canvas curtain and up to the counter, dabbing at a spot of ink on his white tunic as he continued. "Probably the most accurate map on all of Krynn that you'll find of the place, even with all of the rebuilding the gnomes have been doing."

"Did you yourself draw it?" Blister was fascinated by the complicated map, and studied it with her head thrown back and her topknot dangling down behind her."

"A gnome who used to work for me was born there. He drew it, and some of the other maps in the shop." The man sighed as he waved his hand at some of the more elaborate charts. "Passed on a couple of years back. Still miss him."

Dhamon stared at a map on the wall behind the old proprietor. It showed a V-shaped piece of land with the barrens of Tanith making up the left side, mountains forming the bottom of the V, and the coastline of Palanthas making up the right. The right tip was marked "Northern Wastes."

"With all these maps, you must know a lot about the area," Dhamon said. "Seen a lot."

"I've lived here my whole life," the man returned. "Never traveled much, but I vouch for my maps as accurate."

"So you're well-versed in the city."

"I've seen Palanthas prosper, and I've seen it grieve. I watched the Tower of High Sorcery get swallowed up by a strange earthquake just about thirty years ago. I had a map of the Tower. No use now. No one needs a map of a black spot. Lots of things have gone away since . . ."

"You've got some interesting maps." Dhamon broke in, changing the subject. "Would you happen to have one to a place called the Lonely Refuge?"

The man raised a snow-white eyebrow. "It's just an old ruin. Why would you want to go there?"

"To see Palin Majere," Blister cut in. She stepped quickly aside, evading Dhamon's attempt to elbow her sharply. "We're supposed to go there to find him. At least, that's what I overheard Goldmoon tell Dhamon."

The old man stared at Dhamon and whistled softly. "Palin Majere. There ain't much magic left on Krynn, but what little is left, he'd know about. A sorcerer, one of the few that's left—and one of the most powerful."

"You know him?" Blister asked, though her eyes were fixed on the wondrous outline of Mount Nevermind's massive outer hall.

"No. But I saw him a couple of times. He lived in the Tower of High Sorcery after the War of the Lance."

"The Lonely Refuge?" Dhamon prompted.

"Oh, yes. Well, a desert sits on three sides of the Refuge, and a rocky coast that plunges to the sea is on the fourth. I've a map of the area, and it shows where the ruin is—but I couldn't guarantee you the place is still standing. Five steel pieces."

Dhamon reacted with visible surprise at the high sum.

"Taxes," said the old man, pointing to a group of Dark Knights that was passing by the front of the store.

Dhamon fished into his pocket and set the coins on the counter.

"Three," Blister bargained.

"I already paid the man, Blister." Dhamon stuck the parchment into his backpack. "Let's go."

"To the Lonely Refuge?"

"After we get some supplies."

The kender grinned. She'd get to explore a little more of the city.

* * * * *

Despite the brightness of the morning outside, the interior of the tavern was dark, and the shades were drawn on its few windows. The tavern was open and busy, catering to sailors, who always seemed in the mood for ale—no matter the time of day.

The place was a single room crowded with old tables and chairs. It smelled heavily of spirits and sweat. Ships' wheels, small rusted anchors, lanterns, broken spyglasses, and an assortment of belaying pins hung from the walls as decoration. Nets were draped here and there from the ceiling, and a big wrought iron chandelier that was ringed with thick candles hung in the middle.

The salty air that wafted in through the front door only added to the discordant scents. Rum, sweat, frying wheatcakes, and pipe smoke, competed for Shaon and Feril's attention.

A half-dozen sailors sat around a table just inside the door. Four were attempting to play a dice game, the other two were facedown and snoring. A pair of rough-looking men with sun-weathered skin sat nearby, watching the sailors and working on a large plate of eggs and beef. They wore lizard-skin vests, homespun breeches, and sandals, and their hair was long and unruly.

Feril grimaced. "Smells worse than a weasel hole," she whispered.

"Well, you'll find a good share of weasels here," Shaon retorted. The sea barbarian glided to the back of the room, where a long bar of deep mahogany stretched along the wall. Behind it, a young man polished glasses.

"Morning, ladies!" he chirped. His eyes quickly fixed on Shaon and her flamboyant garb, then they roamed to take in the striking Kagonesti. "What'll it be?"

Shaon laid a steel piece on the bar. "Ale."

"This early?" Feril whispered. The Kagonesti wriggled her nose in distaste.

The barkeep's fingers snatched the coin. "The best I have," he said as he filled a mug and sat it in front of the sea barbarian. "The best for my prettiest customer. Customers," he corrected himself.

Shaon took a gulp and let the warm liquid run around her mouth before she swallowed. "It's good," she pronounced. "Hear of a place called the Lonely Refuge? It's outside the city somewhere."

The barkeep shook his head. "Don't have any call to go outside Palanthas. And I wouldn't advise you venturing outside the city limits either."

The dark-skinned woman cocked her head, raising an eyebrow.

The barkeep leaned closer, his voice barely a whisper. "I'd advise leaving Palanthas altogether. Ladies like you are bound to attract attention, and people have been disappearing from the city—*travelers* mostly."

The barkeep pointed to the pair of ruddy men in the lizardskin vests. "Ask them. They're from northeast of town. They say people livin' around there are getting scared. Very scared."

Shaon walked over toward the two and pulled up a chair. Feril stayed close to the bar. The scent of the polish used to shine the dark wood eased the stench.

* * * * *

"There they are!" Blister cried. The kender pointed a metal-tipped finger down the street.

Shaon and Feril were strolling out of the tavern.

"We're going shopping," the kender explained. "For supplies."

"Got your map?" Shaon asked.

Dhamon nodded, and the sea barbarian reached for it. "Let me see." She unfolded the clothlike parchment and traced her finger along a line of villages that led to the northeast. "There," she said, pointing at one village in particular. "The barbarians who live in the barrens are disappearing. So are travelers, and some of the goatherders who live in the foothills. A tiny village between Palanthas and a place called Ash—it must be this one here—is deserted. No one knows where the people went. It wasn't a dragonstrike; everything is in perfect shape, undisturbed. Just the people are gone. And those outside of Palanthas aren't the only ones who disappear."

"How'd you learn all that so fast?" Blister huffed, her pride a little wounded.

"Two men from Ash told us," Feril answered. "Ash is apparently a good-sized barbarian village about a hundred miles from here."

"The men we talked to have no plans of ever going back home," Shaon added. "They're scared."

"Ash is on the way to the Refuge," Dhamon mused. "We could stop and take a look around. There are several other small villages marked between here and the Refuge. It won't take that long to investigate them, maybe two days, two and a half. Worth the time." He replaced the map and fumbled in his pocket to add up the rest of his coins. "I'll see how expensive horses are. If you're coming with me, I'll meet you at the west gate in an hour."

"A deserted village," the kender wondered aloud. "Sounds kind of spooky. Of course, I don't mind a good scare now and then but. . . ."

Chapter 23

The Calm Before the Storm

"**I've reached my decision, Majere.**" The individual called the Shadow Sorcerer spoke barely above a whisper. The sorcerer was dressed in the same black robe Palin had seen him in when they first met nearly three decades ago. It wasn't worn or faded, and it never showed signs of dirt. It was always clean, and it always entirely cloaked the features of the person who wore it. His silver metallic mask revealed no emotion.

Palin had given up wondering just who the sorcerer was, or whether the individual in question was male or female. The Shadow Sorcerer had proven an apt ally and an able researcher, and Palin, in all these years, had not pried. His Uncle Raistlin had been secretive enough, and if the Shadow Sorcerer still desired anonymity, Palin wasn't about to argue. Sorcerers were often a mysterious lot, wrapping themselves in peculiarities. Palin, on the other hand, was usually open about everything. Dealing in secrets was not his customary practice.

"It was not an easy decision," the Shadow Sorcerer continued.

"And it is not to release any information about our discovery," Palin sadly guessed. Palin's eyes were intense and sparkling, and there was only a hint of wrinkles on his face, despite his age. Usha liked to tell him they were worry lines, and he agreed with her. He worried often enough. His skin was quite tanned, as he made it a point to venture outside several times a day—even if only to meditate.

"You are perceptive, Palin," the Shadow Sorcerer said. "Though I must admit I was unsure of my decision until yesterday. But you are correct. I'm siding with the Master. The secret stays with us."

"I saw this coming. I could have guessed the outcome." Palin walked away from the long ebonwood table, at which sat the Shadow Sorcerer and the Master of the Tower.

"I truly considered your stance," Palin heard the Shadow Sorcerer say. "But it is not a prudent course at this time."

When will it be prudent? Palin wondered. When I am too old to care or when it no longer matters?

Palin drew in a deep breath and stared out the window, the highest one in the Tower of Wayreth. At least Ansalon had rediscovered magic through sorcery. Palin was teaching magic at his Academy of Sorcery near Solace. Still, he wanted to do more. He hoped that either he or Goldmoon's heroes would stumble across some chink in the dragons' armor that would render all the anxiety unnecessary.

The sorcerers had been scrying into Malys's realm. There was one particularly large mountaintop that drew Palin's attention. It sat between Flotsam and Farholm, and spiky rock fingers seemed to ring it like a crown. He stared at it now and wondered what manner of beings were making their way there. He'd observed a parade of goblins winding their way to the top about a month ago. He wanted to investigate, but so far his companions had urged caution. "Watch from a distance," the Master said. It was wise advice, he was forced to agree.

"In your heart you knew there could be no other decision," the Shadow Sorcerer continued, interrupting Palin's thoughts. "We've studied this area for nearly two months now. This Red has transformed the very land, something not even the gods would have done. All the magical items we control or can get our hands on must be kept at our disposal—and ours alone—in case we are threatened by her or by any other of the dragon overlords. We will use the items wisely. We can't vouch for how others would use them."

"I will abide by this Conclave's vote," Palin said. But privately he thought it almost presumptuous that only three wizards could dare to decide something so important.

"But realize that if we discovered the secret of destroying magical items to fuel powerful spells, it is possible other sorcerers will also," Palin felt compelled to add.

"Doubtful, Majere," the Shadow Sorcerer said. "None are as strong as we are, or as experienced."

"Unfortunately, a great many of the young believe the study of magic is a hopeless endeavor," the Master of the Tower added. "The new order of magic will need time to flourish."

Not all the young believe that, Palin mused, thinking of his own sorcerer son, Ulin, at the Academy. "We may not have time," he said, to no one in particular.

He had been able to see Malys only once while scrying. Palin had watched as she silently skimmed over the trees, coming in from the west. But he hadn't seen her since, not for nearly two months. Her absence, *her invisibility*, bothered him. It teased the hairs on the nape of his neck and drew him to his crystal ball. It kept him up all hours, and it kept him away from his wife. He'd spent so little time with Usha lately. How long would she be so understanding?

"Where is the Red?" he asked aloud.

"Maybe she's elsewhere, taking over some other country," the Shadow Sorcerer suggested.

Palin ran his slender fingers through his long, graying hair and yawned. "I don't think so. My divinations tell me she's still in her realm. What is she up to?"

He was achingly tired. He'd been pushing himself hard, staying up well into the early morning hours, sleeping very little, while poring over his Uncle Raistlin's tomes, looking for clues to power, hints at something that might be used against the dragons, some grain of knowledge about magic that had previously escaped him. His companions tended to keep the same hours, but not always, and they were sensible enough to retire to bed before being forced to cast minor magical spells to keep themselves from nodding off.

"I think she's probably just curious. Why kill us, when she can study us, learn from us?" The Shadow Sorcerer leaned forward intently. "Learn our weaknesses, the shortcomings of humankind. Perhaps she listens to us even now."

"Perhaps," Palin said. "We should leave."

"And go where, Majere?"

"To the Northern Wastes. Goldmoon sent some people there to meet me."

"Yes, I recall," the Master said. "They were to look for you at the Lonely Refuge."

"We must go to the Wastes."

"Just for Goldmoon's wishful heroes, Majere?" the Shadow Sorcerer's soft voice was laced with doubt. "Do you truly think they can accomplish anything? What can they do that we can't? And what can you do, what can any of us do, to help them?"

Palin stepped back from the window and returned to his seat at the head of the long table. He rested his elbows on the tabletop, steepled his fingers, and glanced down. His troubled reflection was mirrored in the polished dark wood.

"Everyone looks at the world differently, my friend," Palin finally returned. "They might see something we haven't, discover something we've overlooked. They're not like us—entrenched in a tower going through musty, old books and guessing what the dragons will do next. Besides, Goldmoon has faith in them. And I have faith in her."

"We will summon ourselves there, then," the Master said. "And we will do our best to help them."

"But I won't be going," the Shadow Sorcerer said. "Perhaps you are right. Perhaps one individual—not entrenched in a massive tower—can see the Red. If she is indeed, as we suspect, the most powerful and dangerous of the dragon overlords, someone needs to watch her, discover her plans."

"It could be risky," Palin warned.

"I know that."

"You'll rejoin us?" the Master asked.

"Of course. I'll find you in the Northern Wastes."

"Good luck to you," Palin said as he rose from the table and rotated his head, working a crick out of his neck. "Now, if you will excuse me." He strode from the room and climbed one more set of stairs, throwing back a heavy wooden door and climbing out onto the roof.

He inhaled deeply and gazed about, then padded near the edge. The air was still and warm. He closed his eyes and tilted his chin toward the sun, focusing his energy. Several moments passed, his breathing slowed, and he felt a soft breeze play over his skin.

"Goldmoon," he whispered.

"It has been too long since we talked," replied a wispy image.

Goldmoon hovered several feet in front of him, her feet

floating in the air off the edge of the parapet. She was nearly translucent, but Palin could make out her flawless face and starlike eyes. Her golden hair slowly writhed in the breeze created by magic.

"We will be going to the Wastes late tonight to await your champions," he began. "The Lonely Refuge is—"

"The haft?" the image interrupted.

"Has been retrieved," Palin added. "After I meet your champions, I will go into Palanthas with them. Goldmoon, do you think your plan will work?"

"The new heroes are made of sturdy stuff," she answered. "As is the lance. But they can't set things aright on Krynn by themselves."

"But they are a beginning . . . " Palin finished.

Then the breeze picked up and blew the image away.

* * * * *

Later that night Palin put away his uncle's books, returned to the Academy and found Usha. She was diligently painting a scene she'd remembered from her childhood. A dense forest of oak and pine was taking shape, and next to the largest tree stood an incredibly handsome man of indeterminate age, an Irda that Usha called the Protector. The man had raised her, taken care of her, and sent her away when the rest of the Irda deemed it time for her to rejoin her own people. If he hadn't sent her away, she would have died with the Irda on their idyllic island when the Graygem exploded.

Usha had been toiling over the painting for a few weeks, and it was nearly finished, one of her best.

"It's beautiful," Palin said, coming up silently behind her.

"But it doesn't do him justice," she said. "His eyes. They burned with hope. They laughed at me when I did something foolish. They scolded me when I was wrong. And they cried when I left. His eyes spoke to me. I just can't capture that."

"Maybe he wouldn't have wanted you to," Palin offered. "Maybe the meaning of his eyes was for you alone, and not for whoever admires his image hanging on a wall. The painting is beautiful. Exquisite."

Usha had started painting after the children were grown, and after Palin started spending an increasing amount of time studying the dragons and Raistlin's notes. She had to have something to occupy herself, and that something now decorated several walls in the Academy. She'd improved with each painting, teaching herself subtle techniques to shade and highlight and add texture. There were paintings of Ulin and Linsha, friends she and Palin had met, fantastical creatures they'd witnessed, and sunsets viewed from Solace. This was the only one she'd attempted of an Irda.

"Beautiful, maybe. But I still don't think it does him justice." Backing away from the easel, she swirled the brush in a mug of water, shook it clean, and set it gingerly on a tray. "He was a wonderful man."

"More wonderful for sending you to me." Palin took her hands and pulled her close. He kissed her gently.

"I've missed you," she whispered. "I haven't seen you for days, locked in that room with those men."

"We've been . . . "

"I know, the dragons."

"We'll be heading for the Northern Wastes tomorrow," he said, looking to her hopefully.

She sighed heavily. "We?"

"It might not be safe. When we find a means to combat the dragons, we will become targets."

Usha pursed her lips. "Can you tell me that any place is truly safe, Palin Majere?"

Palin scowled.

"Well, can you?"

"Some places are safer than others," he said tersely. Palin drew her toward the stairs. "I need to know you are looking after the Academy. I need to know you are here. I continue to have dreams about the Blue. Now I am finally going to his realm."

"Maybe if you see Khellendros in the flesh and scales, you'll quit dreaming about him," she said with a chuckle.

Palin pursed his lips. "The Blue is nearly as powerful as the Red."

She edged up the stairs ahead of him. "Maybe I could paint him," she mused. "I have lots of blue paint."

When they reached the landing, he paused before an oak door. "I *have* talked you into staying, haven't I?"

She shook her head "yes" and said, "I can talk you into something, Palin Majere."

Usha smiled slyly, opened the door, and gently tugged him inside.

Chapter 24

Blister's Gloves

Dhamon led three dun-colored mares, two of them saddled, to the western gate of Palanthas. The largest carried packs that bulged with dried meat, cheese, and waterskins.

"Three horses. Four of us," Blister dryly commented. "And I don't see any pony."

"I didn't have enough coins. I couldn't even buy a third saddle."

"Well, you could have asked us to help," the kender said huffily. "I've some coins left—and Raph's spoon collection." She demonstrated by jiggling one of her pouches and the coins inside clinked together.

Dhamon offered her a weak smile. "Maybe it's better if we

have a few coins to spare among us, Blister. Just in case other expenses arise," he said. "You'll have to double up with Shaon or Feril. Sorry."

He vaulted onto the saddleless horse.

"You're used to riding," Blister observed caustically. Her eyes narrowed, and she said more softly, "I'm used to riding, too—at least I could've ridden a pony bareback."

Feril took the smaller of the two remaining horses, and settled the kender in front of her. The Kagonesti ran her fingers along the horse's flank and made soft clucking noises. The horse responded with a whinny.

"These horses are old, Dhamon," she said.

"They were all I could afford," he replied testily.

Dhamon's gaze drifted to Shaon. The sea barbarian was staring at her mare, looking from the saddle to the stirrup to the bulging pack. She shifted her weight back and forth on the balls of her feet and toyed with the reins.

"I think I'd rather walk for a while," Shaon said. "If the horse is old, it doesn't need me weighing it down. No need to hurt it. Besides, I could use the exercise, and—"

"Don't worry about that," Feril was quick to interject. "These horses might be old, but they are in very good condition. They're strong, and they're happy to be out of the pen. They're definitely used to riders. And I'll make sure that they'll tell me when they're tired."

"Still, I think I'll walk."

Dhamon slipped from his horse's back and walked toward her. "Haven't ridden before?"

"Of course I have," Shaon replied a bit too quickly. "I'm just not in the mood right now."

"It's not difficult," he said softly. "Let me help you up."

"I don't need help—see!" Shaon put her right foot in the stirrup and hoisted herself up and over. It was an expert maneuver but she was facing backward. Frowning, she tried to change stirrups and turn around, but the horse balked,

THE DAWNING OF A NEW AGE

and she was thrown to the ground.

"Ouch! Damn horse! See, it doesn't want a rider. It *wants* me to walk."

Dhamon bent to help her, but Shaon slapped his hand away and jumped up. "I don't need help."

"But we need to get moving." Dhamon's voice was tinged with annoyance. "And I'm not planning to be slowed down by your walking."

"Maybe I'll just stick with the ship. Then Blister won't have to share a horse."

"And tell Rig that you changed your mind because of a horse?" Blister asked. "Besides, my feet wouldn't begin to reach those stirrups."

Shaon looked unmoved.

"Suit yourself," Dhamon snapped, striding away.

Shaon brushed the dirt from her clothing. She cursed when she saw that Rig's shirt had been soiled, maybe ruined. He'd be upset. Drawing her lips into a thin line, she grabbed the reins and hoisted herself up properly this time, easing into the saddle. "See, I told you I don't need any help," she called to Dhamon.

He gave her a smile before mounting his own horse. A moment later, Dhamon was leading the small procession away from the city.

Feril clucked softly to Shaon's big horse, and it neighed in response. The Kagonesti seemed engrossed in communicating with the horse, listening attentively to its noises.

"What'd you tell her?" Blister whispered.

"That's between me and the horse," Feril whispered back.

"Oh, come on, Feril," Blister encouraged.

"Ask Palla if you're that curious," the Kagonesti returned, cocking her head toward Shaon's mount. "I don't spill any secrets."

Blister glowered. However, as the miles passed, the kender noted that Shaon's horse was providing an especially gentle

223

ride. Blister suspected the Kagonesti had told the horse to go easy on the sea barbarian.

They spent the night in a small barbarian village called Orok's Clay. They learned it was named after a long-dead chieftain who was determined to build homes out of the earth. Indeed, many of the homes were domes shaped of clay and dung, and they were cool inside—at least compared to the uncomfortable heat of the barrens. The people were guardedly friendly, and after sharing their food they admitted they hadn't heard much lately from the nearest village, Dolor. It was several miles to the northwest, and a report from the elder there was long overdue. They hadn't sent someone to the village to investigate. There were reports of brown lizards flying across the sand—lizards with very large wingspans.

A few of their own hunters had disappeared—why or how, they couldn't say, though they feared the brown lizards or the Blue might be responsible. And because of the mysterious disappearances, they suspected something bad had happened to Dolor—and perhaps to other neighboring villages farther north.

The quartet left shortly after dawn, Blister riding with Shaon this time. The dark-skinned woman groaned as she planted herself in the saddle. Her legs and back were sore from the unaccustomed position of riding for so many hours.

"Why the gloves?" the sea barbarian asked Blister. Shaon was trying to take her mind off her aching thighs. "I've never seen you without a pair, and you must have at least a dozen."

Blister wore a pair of tan leather gloves this morning. Surprisingly, they bore no attachments or odd decorations.

"Did you ever ride a horse before yesterday?" the kender countered.

"No," Shaon said with a groan.

"Then I'll tell you why I wear gloves." Blister decided to be honest with her riding companion. "I had an accident about thirty years ago," she began. "I didn't used to be such a cautious sort. I guess I was a lot like Raph."

The years melted away as Blister reminisced about Calinhand, a city on the southern coast of Balifor, a country that bordered to the east of her native land of Kendermore. Calinhand was a bustling port city filled with wonderful sounds and so many things to investigate—though not nearly so big as Palanthas.

While visiting the city, she became particularly interested in the merchant ships along the docks that kept loading and unloading crates—and taking a large number of them to Hosam's Imports.

She snuck inside the place late one afternoon when there were plenty of shadows to hide in. The back room was large, and everything in it seemed to be some type of container—crates, bins, elaborate chests, coffers, bags, satchels, and barrels. There were mysteries everywhere, discoveries to be made.

"And you found a crate full of kender-sized gloves?" Shaon speculated.

Blister shook her head. "But I found this." The kender pointed to one of the pouches that hung from her belt. It was a heavy dark green net, tightly woven.

"Which is?"

"A magic pouch. It doesn't get dirty. It doesn't snag. I can put sharp things inside, and nothing breaks it. Someone told me once it was made out of seaweed, and maybe it was magic. After all this time, I'm certain it is."

The kender recounted exploring the insides of a few bags and bins that were blocking her path to a large black chest. It was smooth, polished and expensive-looking. Surely what was inside was also expensive.

"Well, what was inside?" Shaon had become engrossed.

"I didn't find out." Blister hung her head. "There were words on the chest, and I guess they were some kind of a magic spell. As I played with the lock, the letters suddenly slid down off the chest and on to my hands. They wrapped tightly around my fingers and palms, almost cutting off the circulation at my wrists. Their acidic touch ate away at my skin. It hurt bad, and I couldn't shake them off. I guess I cried out. And then *he* came."

She recollected that Hosam, the portly old merchant himself, rushed into the back room. He saw her and started screaming and waving his fists at her. Blister wasn't paying attention to what he was saying, her hands hurt too much, feeling like they'd been thrust in a pot of boiling water. She backed away, with Hosam chasing her, but he was slow because of his size. He raised his meaty fists and screamed as she raced through the alley and stumbled face first into a puddle of rainwater. She stuck her hands in it, hoping the water would take away the pain, but it didn't. The magical letters kept chewing away at her fingers for what seemed like hours. The pain didn't stop until sometime very late that night.

She tugged a glove free and held the hand out to her side so the sea barbarian could get a better look. Her small fingers were bent, misshapen, and they were covered with dozens of tiny blisters and rough splotches.

Shaon winced. "Oh, does it hurt?"

"Only when I bend them, which I try to avoid. And the more I bend them, the more it hurts." She gingerly replaced the glove.

"So that's why you're so cautious about your fingers all the time."

The kender nodded.

"And that's why you're called Blister," Shaon figured out. "Because of what happened."

"Well, there's more to the story." The kender shifted on her perch. "But I'll save that for another time."

Shaon laughed. "So what's your real name?"

"Vera-Jay Nimblefingers."

"Know what? I like Blister better."

The kender heartily agreed and as the miles passed, she continued to regale the sea barbarian with tales of her exploits in Balifor and Kendermore. Dhamon and Feril rode in silence, listening also, until the outskirts of Dolor came into view.

It was shortly past noon, and the day showed no promise of cooling off. Feril brushed the sweat off her forehead, squinted, and looked at the collection of clay-domed houses and wooden buildings erected against the sides of some low hills. There was no sign of people. It was just as the barbarians in the tavern had said it would be.

The Kagonesti inhaled deeply, then coughed. The air was tinged with the musky rot of death. A shiver raced down her spine, and she cast her gaze about, looking for the corpses she knew must be near.

"I feel like we're being watched," Shaon whispered. "I wonder if there are any ghosts about . . . ."

Chapter 25

The Death of Dolor

Feril dismounted and headed toward the village, the horse following her. The mare whinnied softly.

"I know it smells bad," Feril hushed. "Stay here."

Metal cooking pots sat by cold firepits outside many of the earthen, dome-shaped homes. She idly wondered if Orok's Clay was patterned to be like Dolor, or if this village was the later of the two and had borrowed Orok's building techniques, and improved on them. Some of the domes looked more elaborate, and decorations were etched into the sides of some—plants, animals, circular and zigzag patterns.

A loom that held a partially finished ocher and black blanket sat just beyond the doorway of the closest structure.

Inside another she saw clean clothes folded on a high shelf and dirty plates on a table. One home had an empty child's bed in view, a red wooden ball and some other toys underneath it. Behind a small dome was a pen filled with pigs. They huddled in the scant shade thrown from the building and showed only mild curiosity at her presence.

The scent of death remained heavy, but the Kagonesti still didn't spot any bodies. She saw that a section of the pen's fence was broken and guessed they were probably coming and going, foraging for food. She doubted the pigs ate the dead, however. There would be some bones scattered about, and there were none that she could see.

She followed a curving path that cut through the center of the village, and she passed by a larger pen, for horses or cattle, she guessed. It was empty.

Dhamon and Shaon came closer, but as their horses passed by the first few homes, the Kagonesti held up her hand, silently warning them to keep their distance. She didn't want any noise or scents to interfere and confuse her.

She heard a shuffling ahead. Someone moving? Something? She peered to her left and saw a canvas sheet over a doorway, rustling in the slight breeze. She relaxed, creeping forward.

She passed the middle of the village, where the path turned and the crude homes were the largest. She spotted what she believed was the central lodge. From here, she could better see the far end of the village—and a fresh row of graves at the edge of a graveyard.

There were more than a dozen recent graves. Who dug them? Who buried the people? Feril continued slowly down the path. She stopped a few feet from the new graves and dropped to her knees. Her hands touched the ground at the mounds' edges, and she started sketching, her fingers digging into the soft, dry earth.

Dhamon and Shaon rode in as far as the central lodge, watching her.

"What's she doing?" Blister whispered. The kender's question went unanswered.

Dhamon slid from his horse and edged ahead. The sun was high and behind him. His shadow stretched in a line toward the elf. It looked as though she was sifting dirt through her fingers and tracing a pattern in the ground. Through the still air, he heard her softly humming.

Blister nudged Shaon, and the sea barbarian jumped from her horse and plucked the kender from the saddle. She handled Blister gingerly, as if she were a porcelain doll that might brake. Shaon didn't want the kender's fingers to bump against anything.

"What's she doing?" the kender asked again.

Feril counted fifteen new graves, all small, as if Dolor's recently deceased residents had been dwarves or kender—although the homes' doorways were obviously tall enough to accommodate humans. A few of the graves had been freshly dug, she could tell by the looseness and color of the dirt on top of them. From the dome to her right drifted the odor of rotting bodies. There were some dead that were not yet buried.

No one left to put them in the ground? the elf wondered. Was a plague to blame? She couldn't pick up the scent of anyone living, not even of any of her companions. The smell of decay was too potent.

She continued to draw in the dirt, tracing twin patterns to a simple spell that would permit her to see through the soil, learn what it knew, see who was buried here and what had happened to them. She hummed louder, the enchantment nearing its completion. Then suddenly she cried out as an arrow struck the dirt in front of her. A second one followed swiftly, lodging itself deep in her arm.

Dhamon ran forward, dirt showering the air behind him. He drew his sword, running toward the far building on the Kagonesti's right. He saw arrows coming from the doorway.

"Get down, Feril!" he hollered as he darted inside.

The Kagonesti dove forward, as two arrows cut through the air where her head had been just a heartbeat before. She lay between the mounds of two graves. Turning to her left, she stretched her hand across her chest, bit her lip, and tugged the arrow free.

Now I know what a hunted deer feels like, she thought. Only a deer doesn't have hands to get the arrow out. Warm blood spilled from the wound, darkening the sleeve of her soft leather tunic.

She heard a thud behind her. Dhamon? Risking a glance, she poked her head above the mound and saw Shaon and Blister racing down the center path. There was no sign of Dhamon, though she heard another thud from inside the hut.

"Why did you shoot her?" she heard Dhamon shout.

Shaon drew her sword and crouched just beyond the door, then her eyes opened in surprise and she stepped back. In that instant a boy was pushed outside. The force of Dhamon's shove knocked him down. Caught off-balance, his head slammed back and hit the ground. He groaned and struggled to get up, but Dhamon followed and planted a foot on his stomach. Shaon dashed forward and held her blade at his neck.

Feril stood and slowly walked toward them. She cradled her arm against her chest. The wound throbbed as blood poured from it, but she thrust the pain to the back of her mind and concentrated on the boy. She guessed he was nine or ten. His chest was bare and slick with sweat, and he smelled of death. His lips were cracked and bleeding where Dhamon had punched him in the mouth.

"I'm all right," the Kagonesti offered. She glanced around at the doorways to the other homes, watching to see if anyone would come to the youngster's defense.

Dhamon backed away from the boy and was at Feril's side

231

in two steps. Behind him, Shaon kept her sword leveled threateningly.

"Why'd you shoot her?" Blister asked. "She didn't do anything to you."

"Answer us!" Shaon spat. "Give me a reason why I shouldn't run you through!"

"She must die! She meant to disturb the graves!" he cursed. *"Defilers!"*

"So he does have a tongue," Dhamon muttered. He sheathed his sword and pulled a small knife from his belt and started to cut at Feril's sleeve. "At least he also has bad aim."

"Where are the others?" Shaon kept the sword inches from his throat.

"There are no others," the boy responded. "They're all dead, just like you'll soon be. The sky monsters will carry you away, kill you!"

"Sky monsters?" Blister glanced up at Shaon as the sea barbarian took a step back.

"Get up!" Shaon snapped. "Blister, check that building."

The kender scurried through the doorway. "It stinks in here." She disappeared in the shadows and began rummaging around.

"I don't care what it smells like. This whole village stinks. Is anyone else in there?" The sea barbarian lowered her voice, speaking to Dhamon next. "Is Feril all right?"

"Yes," the Kagonesti answered for herself. "I'm fine. It just got my arm."

"No. She's not fine," Dhamon disagreed. "She's lost quite a bit of blood. And the wound's dirty."

"'Cause the arrows are dirty," Blister added. She emerged from the hut, grimacing with her fingers clutching a handful of arrows. She kicked a leather quiver in front of her, and more dirty arrows spilled out. "They stink, too" she said, extending them to Shaon.

"Coated in dung," Dhamon swore.

"Yuck," the kender said. She dropped the arrows, glaring at the boy. "And there's blankets in there, covering up stuff that stinks worse—bodies."

"Leave them alone!" the boy shrieked.

"Are they your people? Did the sky monsters kill them?" Shaon asked.

The boy nodded.

"Why were you spared?"

He hung his head, mumbling something. The sea barbarian stepped closer so she could hear.

Meanwhile, Dhamon led Feril away toward his horse. "This will help," Dhamon said softly, as he tugged free a waterskin. "But I want to start a fire, burn the wound a little to make sure it doesn't get infected and so the bleeding will stop. It'll hurt."

The Kagonesti pursed her lips. "I wish Jasper was here," she said, recalling how the dwarf had healed Dhamon's wounds by casting a spell.

They sat on the ground next to a small fire pit, and Dhamon used the legs of a crude chair for kindling. He held the blade of his knife in the flames, turning it over and over until the edge glowed from the heat.

"I hope you didn't hurt the boy," she said.

"He tried to kill you."

She shrugged. "He thought I was going to defile—" The hot metal hurt worse than the arrow, and Feril clenched her teeth and dug her fingers into the dirt at her sides as Dhamon probed the wound. She felt tears spill out over her cheeks. Finally finished, Dhamon doused the wound with water again. He'd found some clean clothes inside one of the homes and had torn up a child's shirt to make a bandage. She watched him wrap her arm. He was thorough, practiced.

"You're used to tending to the injured, aren't you?"

He stared into her eyes. "I've had some training. I know how to dress wounds."

She inched closer. "Where'd you learn how?" Her legs brushed his as she rested her injured arm on his knee. "Good in a fight and a good medic. I'll bet you served in an army somewhere. Tended the wounded on a battlefield?"

"In a manner of speaking, I . . ." He brought his face close to hers, felt her breath on his cheek.

"I got some answers from the boy!" Shaon interrupted.

Dhamon reluctantly turned to face the sea barbarian. He felt the red warmth of embarrassment, and Shaon's wide grin and quick wink didn't help matters. The boy was standing in front of her, looking down at the dirt near his feet.

"He'd run away from his chores," Shaon said.

"That's why he wasn't killed," Blister added. Having said this, the kender trotted over to inspect Feril's bandage. "He was behind those hills when a big storm hit, and he stayed there until the rain stopped," Blister added.

"When he came back, all he saw were bodies." The sea barbarian scowled. "He says he doesn't know what happened to them, but he claims there were claw marks on some, like a wild animal got them. Says others had burns on their hands and chests."

"It was the sky monsters," the boy whispered defiantly. "They came with the storm."

"He's been burying the bodies," Blister said. "Three a day. Said he couldn't bury more 'cause the digging made him tired. I told him we'd help bury the rest."

Dhamon stood and brushed the dirt off his breeches and counted the grave mounds. "So this happened five days ago?"

The boy nodded.

"Everyone but you died?"

"No," the boy whispered. "Most of the people, more than thirty, are missing. The sky monsters took them."

"I'll check for tracks," Feril offered. She stretched an arm toward Dhamon, and he gently pulled her to her feet. She winced, but the pain had already lessened.

"You won't find any tracks," the boy said. "I already looked. The monsters fed my people to the storm."

"Maybe they rode away on the horses," she suggested.

"No. I told you, they were from the sky."

"But you didn't see these monsters," the Kagonesti persisted. "So you can't really know what happened."

He shook his head. "I didn't see them. It stormed and the adults vanished."

"I guess I'll just have to chat with the pigs to be certain," said Feril. "They might have actually *seen* what happened."

"How many are left to bury?" Dhamon asked. He watched Feril walk toward the pen. His face reddened again as he noticed Shaon watching him with interest.

"Four," the boy said. "Children. They weren't big enough to eat."

Shaon shivered, staring at the youth. She wished she had stayed with Rig. Maybe the sky monsters were the growing evil Dhamon was always talking about. "Where are the shovels?" she asked, wanting to leave as soon as possible.

The boy pointed toward the largest clay home and started in that direction. He glanced over his shoulder to make sure she was following him.

"I'm coming," the sea barbarian said. "Hey, what are you doing here?"

Dhamon, Feril, and Blister followed her gaze. At the western edge of the village, Fury stood panting. The red wolf wagged its tail, and barked a greeting.

"At least you didn't bring Rig and Groller," she said huffily, as she squinted and looked behind him just to make sure. Then she pivoted on her heels. "About those shovels?"

* * * * *

Feril leaned over the rail, studying the pigs. A large spotted black one regarded her intently, while the others busily rooted around in the dirt. Wriggling her nose and making snuffling sounds, she coaxed it near and reached into the leather pouch at her side. Her fingers closed around a lump of soft clay.

The pig looked at the proffered clay and sniffed the air, thinking it might be a treat. Deciding it wasn't, the pig snuffled dejectedly and looked at its fellows.

"I have nothing," Feril whispered. "But don't leave."

The pig snorted, then slowly turned to face her. She worked the clay with the fingers of her left hand. Her arm ached, and made the process difficult.

Fury trotted around the side of the small home, sending the pigs scurrying toward the far end of the pen. Feril frowned and called the black and white one back. "Fury won't hurt you," she assured it.

The wolf barked, as if to agree with her, then brushed against her leg and looked up devotedly. She worked the clay faster, giving it a snout and four legs. She used her small fingernail to etch out a curly tail.

"I want to talk to you later," she told the wolf. "Right now, I'm busy." She smoothed the clay, making it even and slick like the pig's hide, then she began to snuffle, her soft snorts sounding faintly musical.

The pig squealed excitedly, and Feril felt her mind reaching toward it. Hot air streamed around her as her senses focused on the pig. Its grunts were starting to sound like words inside her head, the nature magic translating them into terms she could understand.

"There were people here," she began, using grunts that caught the attention of the other pigs. A few shuffled closer, their gazes drifting between her and the wolf.

"Many people," the spotted pig answered. "People who fed us and chased the flies away."

"Where did they go, these people?"

"All gone," the pig grunted sadly. "All but the boy. He feeds us small things and doesn't scratch us at all. The boy has no time for us."

"Where did all the people go? Maybe if you tell me, I can bring them back. You'll get more attention."

"They won't be back."

She gestured for the pig to continue, translating its grunts and the subtle gestures of its ears and nose.

"The sky flashes came for the people."

"The lightning," Feril murmured to herself.

"The flashes killed the little ones. The bigger ones were pulled into the sky."

Feril scratched her head. "What pulled them?"

"The ugly men."

She cocked her head. The pig snuffled louder. "The many ugly men who rained from the sky."

Feril stepped away from the pen, promising the pigs they'd be rewarded with good food and plenty of scratching tonight. Then she remembered the wolf. "Why did you follow us? Is Groller all right? Jasper and Rig?" she asked Fury.

The wolf barked and wagged his tail, then loped away from the pen toward the graveyard.

Yes, we might need help, Feril interpreted. She watched his retreating form. She felt suddenly alone and rushed to catch up with him and join the others waiting by the graveyard.

The Kagonesti told them what she had learned from the pig as they buried the rest of the children. The shoveling obviously hurt Blister's fingers. She refused to stand back and simply observe, however. Even Fury helped, digging with his forepaws and sending clumps of dirt flying behind him.

The last child was buried shortly before sunset. To the west, miles away, there was a flicker of lightning. The grave diggers looked toward the dark clouds. The breeze was heavy with the scent of water and hinted a storm would descend on them soon.

The boy was trembling, and Blister reached up and gingerly patted his back. "We'll protect you," she promised.

"Let's get some rest," Dhamon suggested.

"But it's dinner time," the kender protested, her stomach grumbling.

"I want to be on our way in a few hours," Dhamon said. He eyed the clay domes, selecting a small one for Feril and Fury, who followed him inside. Shaon and Blister chose the central lodge.

"We can't leave the boy here," Feril said, as she stretched out on her back on a wide straw mattress covered with blankets.

Dhamon draped a thin blanket over her. He noticed there was a shelf covered with carefully folded clothes above the bed. They would be able to find clean things to wear before they left.

"The boy's safer here than with us," he returned. "Besides, his monsters have no reason to come back here. There's nothing left for them to take."

Feril nodded reluctantly and then yawned. "You should go find a hut and get some rest." Within moments she was sleeping soundly, the wolf curled at her side.

Dhamon watched her for a while, then went outside and selected a nearby dome. His sleep was troubled, filled with flashes of lightning and charred bodies. He awoke a few hours later to the sound of rain splattering against the clay roof.

Chapter 26

Blue Death

Judging by how rested he felt, Dhamon guessed it was near midnight. He stepped outside and tipped his face toward the sky. It was so overcast that no stars poked through. Dark clouds stretched in all directions, and the rain that continued to fall was heavy and warm. He closed his eyes and let the drops wash over him. After several minutes, he padded to Feril's dome. He glanced in just as the Kagonesti was rising. The wolf was nowhere to be seen.

He found clothes roughly Feril's size and handed them to her. He spotted a child's tunic that would do for Blister, and a large shirt could replace the yellow one of Rig's that Shaon had torn and dirtied. His own clothes were in reasonably good repair, but he picked out a soft leather shirt for himself and tucked it under his arm. He might need it later.

The Kagonesti joined him outside, wearing her tan leggings and a dark green tunic that hung below her hips. Through the darkness he tried to examine her bandage, but she wasn't cooperating much. She slowly spun about, obviously enjoying the rain, throwing her head back and letting the drops splash into her mouth. Every time he moved closer, she took a few steps away, as if playing a game. Finally he grabbed her good shoulder and tugged her closer to the dome, where the doorway offered a little shelter.

"You two have a good sleep?" Shaon purred as she poked her head out of the central lodge. As she walked closer, Dhamon saw that the female barbarian's dark eyes sparkled with meaning. Blister followed her, yawning and shuffling.

When he finally he got a look at Feril's arm, there was no sign of fresh blood. The wound was healing. Satisfied, he handed the spare clothes to Shaon and busied himself organizing and saddling the horses.

"The mares aren't happy about traveling in this weather," the Kagonesti said. She listened sympathetically to their whinnies and scratched a spot between her horse's eyes.

"I'm not especially happy about it, either," Dhamon said. He was thoroughly soaked already, and his clothes felt heavy and cumbersome. Dhamon helped the Kagonesti onto her horse and wedged his new shirt under the saddle. Feril's dripping curls were plastered practically flat against her head. He reached up and traced the oak leaf on her cheek.

"That tattoo's there for good," she said. "No amount of water is going to wash it away."

"You two want to turn back?" Shaon asked pointedly. "I won't object if you want to call it quits. Rig and I can drop you somewhere cozy along the coast." That's what Shaon wanted certainly—to go back to the *Anvil*. She'd spent the night dreaming of sky monsters and dragons and being crushed by giant jaws. She wanted nothing more than to be back lying in Rig's arms on a boat rocking miles from land.

"No. I can't turn back." Dhamon leapt on the back of his horse. He untied his hair and whipped it about his face. Below him, Fury shook, too, emerging from somewhere. The wolf threw water off his thick coat in all directions. It was a futile gesture, as the rain continued to drench them. "You're welcome to stay here with the boy until I come back. Or to return to Palanthas. But I wouldn't suggest that. You might get lost."

"You realize we don't know where to look for these . . . monsters," Shaon grumbled. "We could be riding around these barrens for hours. Days even."

"We're looking for the Lonely Refuge," Dhamon returned. "But if the boy's sky monsters materialize at night during a storm, now's the time to look for clues."

"Provided you believe a pig and a little boy." The sea barbarian sighed. She didn't want to stay with the boy, who stood in a doorway watching them, and she didn't intend to go back to the Palanthas harbor by herself. She knew Dhamon was right—without the visibility of the stars, she'd likely get lost, and she didn't want to risk bumping into any sky monsters on her own.

Shaon ran her fingers over the wet pommel of her sword and adjusted the brown shirt that hung in wet folds over her. "Well, I've never lost a fight, yet. And they might need me," she whispered to herself. "All right, let's go," she said loudly. She helped the kender on the horse. "The sooner we're done with this, the sooner I can get back to the ship."

"We'll send someone for you," Dhamon called to the boy. "But it might be several days. Be careful." He tossed him a sack filled with dried beef and nuts, a fair amount of the rations he'd purchased.

Dhamon's course took him past Dolor's graveyard. His horse's back was slick and slippery from the rain, but he was a practiced rider, and he nudged it into an easy gallop. The map showed that there was another village better than a dozen miles ahead, almost in a direct line with the Lonely Refuge. Maybe the sky monsters had moved there. It was as good as any place to look, and it wouldn't take them out of their way. He hoped they wouldn't miss the village entirely because of the darkness and the sheets of rain coming down.

Shaon and Feril paced him, and the red wolf ran alongside, sometimes darting ahead, sometimes falling back to sniff at patches of scrub grass. The Kagonesti made clucking sounds to encourage the mares, and glanced from time to time at the female sea barbarian to make sure Shaon was managing the horse all right.

"I think the rain feels good. It makes me feel clean," Feril told Shaon. "But the mares are complaining about it." She had to practically shout to be heard above the incessant rain and clomping hooves.

"You haven't heard complaining until you've heard mine!" Shaon retorted. "If I'm going to get wet, I'd rather be at sea. Water doesn't mix too well with dry land. And land—dry or muddy—never agrees with me."

"Then why'd you come along?" Feril wondered.

Shaon shrugged. "The sooner Dhamon finds what he's looking for, the sooner Rig and I can reclaim our ship and leave."

Blister was miserable too, but the kender kept uncharacteristically quiet. Grousing wouldn't make her any drier. She couldn't decide which she hated worse—the extreme heat of the midday sun or this driving downpour. At least she was getting to see some of the countryside. She gritted her teeth and reached into her pack. It took a little work, but she managed to pull out a pair of sealskin gloves to help repel the water a little.

Less than an hour later, the rain stopped. The sky was still black, but there were thin spots in the clouds here and there, and a few stars shone through. A breeze had picked up, and it blew over them, drying them a little.

Dhamon frowned and pulled on the reins, bringing his horse to a stop. There'd be no sky monsters tonight, not with the storm ending. He glanced at his companions, who had likewise halted. Shaon and Blister were grinning, pleased at the improving weather. Water ran in rivulets from Feril's tight curls. She offered him a weak smile as she patted her horse's neck.

"The next village is still a few miles ahead." He pointed a finger toward the northeast. "Somewhere over there."

"Somewhere?" Shaon laughed. "It's so dark we can hardly see where we're going. Who knows if we're even headed in the right direction?"

"But it will be getting lighter shortly," he said. "The clouds are thinning, and dawn's not far away." Dhamon shifted on his horse's back, peering to the north. Among the varying shades of gray and black, he spotted a low rise. He nudged his horse, which started off again slowly.

Feril was quick to catch up, and Shaon grudgingly trailed behind. "I'm not getting left alone in this place," the sea barbarian muttered. "And Rig had better be waiting for me."

"Sorry, can't hear you," Blister said.

"I said it's great it stopped raining."

"The rain is good for this land," Feril was saying to Dhamon. "The ground was so dry back at Dolor. By the way, my arm is feeling much better. Thank you. Where did you say you learned how to heal people?"

"Several years ago, just east of Solamnia." Dhamon paused. "I was traveling with an army, and the commander saw to it that everyone in his unit knew how to dress wounds. It's a skill that comes in handy on a battlefield."

"So you left the army, obviously. But what brought you here?"

"It's a complicated story."

"I've got time," she coaxed. "You said it's going to be a long ride. Were you ever in a battle? Was . . ." Feril's words faded as her horse whinnied loudly. Her mare stopped, its eyes widening.

Dhamon and Shaon's horses stopped, too. They snorted and nervously pawed at the ground, shifting back and forth. The sea barbarian's mount seemed especially jittery and was tossing its head from side to side.

"What should I do?" Shaon blurted out as she fumbled with the reins.

Blister grabbed the horse's mane to keep from falling off. The sea barbarian struggled to remain erect behind the kender.

"Something's wrong," the Kagonesti said in a hush. "The horses smell something." Feril's nostrils quivered, trying to pick up the scent that was making the mounts nervous. She did smell something odd, something unfamiliar.

Fury sensed a problem, too. The wolf threw back his head and howled, just as a bolt of lightning cut through the air— sideways, like a thrown spear. It pierced the neck of Feril's horse, which slumped and died before it even hit the ground.

The Kagonesti vaulted from her saddle as the horse fell. Agile as a cat, she landed on her feet in a crouch. Her eyes scanned the horizon to the north, but all she could see was darkness, shadows, and low-hanging clouds. Fury crept up beside her with a growl. His coat of red hair stood in a wet, spiky ridge along his back.

"Down!" Dhamon barked to Blister and Shaon. He too leapt from his mount and drew his sword.

Shaon slipped on the wet saddle and fell hard to the mud as another bolt of lightning flashed through the air, just missing her. The horse reared back and Blister was thrown from her perch. The kender whirled head over feet and landed on top of the sea barbarian, leaving both of them momentarily dazed. The mare bucked madly and dashed headlong into the darkness, churning up clumps of mud in its wake. Dhamon's horse followed.

"I saw where the bolt came from," Dhamon hissed. "Over there, that small hill." He crept toward the Kagonesti. "You all right?"

Feril nodded, then looked where he had pointed, slightly to the east. She concentrated, and her keen elven vision parted the darkness, helping her distinguish the shadowy, moving shapes from the stationary ones of the low hills nearby. What she first thought were bushes were giving off more heat than they should. Then they started to move forward.

"There's three of them, Dhamon! I don't know what they are, but they're coming closer!" She reached into her pouch, and her fingers quickly touched feathers and clay and passed over them, searching for something else.

Dhamon crouched and raised his sword, as one of the shadows stepped forward. Pointed white teeth stood out from the inky background. Blister and Shaon struggled to their feet. The sea barbarian drew her sword and ducked, just as another bolt of lightning shot overhead. It came from one of the grinning shadows! The sea barbarian hurried to stand with Dhamon.

More stars fought their way through the thinning clouds, shedding just enough light now for Dhamon to get a look at the approaching creature. Its shape was distinct.

"A draconian," he whispered breathlessly. "Feril, be careful! These things aren't sky monsters, but they're dangerous!"

"Deadly," the lead creature corrected Dhamon. It was larger than the other two, practically seven feet tall. "We are spawn. And you are ours." It closed the distance to Dhamon, flapping its wings to speed its course.

Dhamon slashed at the thing, but it was quick and anticipated his move. It flapped its wings and glided above him, hovering, until suddenly it balled its fists and slammed them down into his chest. Dhamon fell backward, his sword flying from his hand. The thing jumped on his chest and pinned him to the ground. It brought its face close to his, and Dhamon watched in horror as tiny bolts of lightning flitted between its sharp teeth, illuminating the draconian's features.

Its scales glistened in the scant light. Its sapphire arms and legs were muscular and thick, and its tail beat against Dhamon's thighs. The draconian's wings buffeted him, shooting a fusillade of mud at his face and momentarily blinding him. Its sharp nails dug into his collar bone.

Dhamon gasped as pain coursed through him, and he renewed his attempts to shove the thing away. It snarled at his feeble efforts and dug its claws in deeper. Suddenly the creature opened its black maw and screamed, jerking upward to confront a new foe.

Shaon had rushed forward and had brought her sword down hard across the thing's back. She'd managed to slice through one of its wings, which now flapped uselessly, spraying blood and scales. It hissed and skittered toward her, no longer able to fly. Lightning arced around its claws, and its eyes glowed golden yellow.

"Come and get me, you ugly beast!" the sea barbarian taunted. She danced back and forth, and effortlessly ducked just as it opened its mouth and a bolt of lightning shot out. Shaon slashed upward and her blade pierced the scales on the creature's abdomen. It screamed again, unaccustomed to the novel sensation of pain, and brought its claws down hard. Miniature lightning bolts leapt from its fingers and grazed the top of her head.

Shaon fell back, moaning, her hair singed and her scalp tingling. Her clothes were covered with the creature's blood, and she grimaced at the stench and stickiness of it. The creature stared at her for a moment, looked down at its wounded abdomen, then growled as it advanced. She jumped to her feet and threateningly waved her sword.

"Get out of here!" she shouted. "I'll cut you again! I'll kill you!"

Dhamon scrambled to his feet, saw the tall blue draconian keeping its distance from Shaon, and quickly looked about for his own sword. His eyes grew wide as he saw it under the foot of one of the creatures. This one was broad, thick about the chest and heavily muscled. It grinned at him, then turned its head toward Blister, who was several yards away, and opened its horrible mouth. Dhamon saw the lightning around the thing's teeth spark, and in that instant he darted forward, his feet scrabbling over the mud. He barreled into the creature and knocked it to its scaly knees, just as a thick bolt of lightning erupted from its mouth. The bolt struck the damp ground, sending up a shower of dirt and mud.

Blister ran forward, waving her chapak in her right hand. Gripping a weapon so tightly hurt her, but she told herself it would hurt a lot worse if the creature cooked her alive with its lightning breath. Still on its knees, it was an easy target for her. She dodged its claws, which were slashing at her. She darted beneath the creature's grasp, spun around behind it, and attacked the back of its thighs.

Dhamon used the kender's distraction to pull his blade out from under the creature. His fingers closed on the pommel and he brought the sword up, but the beast was flapping its wings fast and furiously. Dhamon cursed and leapt after it, thrusting upward. His blade managed to slice the dense flesh just above its ankle. The thing squealed loudly as it rose up.

Dhamon pulled back as the creature climbed higher into the sky, out of his reach. He glanced over his shoulder, worried for Feril. The Kagonesti was behind him on her knees, humming and swaying, moving her head in circles and dropping her chin down to her chest. She waggled her fingers in front of her, holding her arms parallel to the ground. As her humming grew louder she raised her arms, still twirling her fingers as if she were working a marionette. The mud in front of her started churning and rising, as if pulled by her invisible strings. It buckled and arrowed away from her, as if a giant gopher was burrowing underneath madly charging the smallest blue creature.

Fury was barking and circling the beast's legs, dashing in and snapping while keeping an eye on the approaching mud missile. The creature flapped its wings to hover several feet above the ground. It stared at Feril and opened its mouth. Lightning flickered around its teeth.

"No!" Dhamon shouted. He saw the Kagonesti leap out of the first bolt's way just as a second was released. Dhamon swiveled his head to see the broad-chested beast gliding to the ground, another lightning bolt snaking from its mouth straight toward his blade. When the bolt touched the metal, crackling and hissing, the jolt ricocheted off the sword and into his arm. The sword grew incredibly hot, the pommel scorching his hand. The intense shock raced from his fingers to his chest, then down his legs. His muscles twitched wildly as he fought to maintain his footing.

"Can't drop it again," he growled. Gritting his teeth, he tightened his grip on the searing pommel and drove the sword forward and straight up. The blade sank into the advancing creature's abdomen. He pulled it free and drew it behind his head, then followed through with a wild swing that struck the broad-chested beast just below its kneecap. It had launched itself into the air, escaping a lethal blow, but the tip of Dhamon's sword cut through bone. The creature screamed furiously and began flapping harder.

Dhamon tried to pull his blade free, but this time it was firmly lodged and wouldn't budge. He felt himself being lifted up. He yanked harder and harder on the pommel, but the beast was bearing him aloft. An image of the boy from the village flashed into Dhamon's mind. Sky monsters. Dhamon thought of jumping but could not see the ground below so he could judge the distance he would fall.

Holding onto the sword with his right hand, he flailed about with his left until he found a grip on the thing's scaly ankle. Somehow he managed to climb the creature's leg as it writhed more than a dozen feet above the ground, trying to dislodge him.

Below, Blister was using her chapak as a slingshot, pelting the draconian with well-aimed rocks. They harmlessly bounced off the creature's chest, however, and only seemed to fuel its anger.

"That's no help!" Dhamon yelled to the kender. "Defend Feril! She doesn't have a weapon!" He had inched his arms up to the beast's waist and was holding on fiercely. The thing was having a hard time craning its neck so it could shoot a bolt of lightning at him. Instead, it clawed Dhamon's shoulders and the miniature bolts that arced downward struck his wet shirt and quickly penetrated to the skin.

He nearly lost his grip as the electricity wracked his body. His hair, practically dry now, stood on end—a puffball mane. He felt as if he were dying. Once, a few years before, he had experienced a similar sensation. Dhamon had been ready to die then, but not now. He fought to remain clear-headed and conscious. Continuing to hang on to the beast with his right arm, he slipped his left hand down to his belt, where his knife hung.

His fingers clutched the handle, then drove upward, slamming the small blade repeatedly into the thing's side. The draconian gyrated in the air, trying futilely to dislodge its unwanted passenger. It was all Dhamon could do to hold on as the battle continued.

Below, he could see Feril still trying to work her nature magic. She gestured with her fingers, weaving a pale green pattern in the air. As the design brightened and began glowing wildly, she threw back her head and howled. Dhamon blinked in astonishment. She sounded exactly like Fury!

As her cry died, the earth missile she'd been crafting

exploded into the air and struck the small draconian in front of her. The wet earth projectile caught the thing off guard, slamming into the center of its chest. It was thrown backward through the air from the terrific impact. Its wings no longer flapping, it struck the ground, and was immediately cornered by the red wolf, which barked and snapped at it.

Meanwhile Shaon was advancing on the tall beast she'd been keeping at bay. The thing regarded her cautiously. Lightning crackled from its hands, but the sea barbarian was too quick for the miniature bolts. She darted forward and sliced through its remaining good wing, ensuring that the creature would stay hopelessly earthbound and not be able to escape her. The sea barbarian nimbly avoided the next barrage of lightning that sprang from the beast, though it was clear she hadn't avoided all the bolts. Her shirt and the black tunic hung on her in singed tatters.

Dhamon's attention was forced back to his own enemy as it began climbing higher. Its sharp claws raked into his back, sending a wave of pain through him. The creature was trying to pull him off, but Dhamon wrapped his legs even more strongly about the its calves, giving him a better purchase. He felt the thing's claws rake his skin again, ripping his flesh, and then he felt the warm puddle of blood on his back.

Again, Dhamon drove his knife into the creature, this time higher on its chest, just under its breastbone. The blade sank in, and he tugged it free and plunged it in once more.

"You've got to have a heart inside you someplace," he cursed. Again his hand flashed as the stickiness of the creature's blood ran down his fingers. The thing yowled, this time sounding almost pathetic, and Dhamon summoned all his strength as he drove the blade in deeper than seemed possible. This time it lodged in bone and Dhamon couldn't yank it free.

The beast shuddered, then it seemed to disappear, and Dhamon's fingers closed around air. A flash filled the sky, taking the creature's place. A bright golden light filled Dhamon's senses as a ball of lightning burst where the thing had been present a moment before. The air crackled and then the ground rushed up to meet him, and he struck the earth hard, the air exploding from his lungs. Dazed, he glanced up. He could see only the night sky and a few stars twinkling down at him.

"Die!" Shaon was shouting at her opponent. The sea barbarian lunged forward, shoving her sword into her foe's belly. At the same time its maw opened and a bolt of crackling lightning raced to strike her chest. She was knocked back several feet.

The creature looked down at the sword buried in its body. Its claws fumbled with the pommel, found a grip, then tugged it free. The beast seemed oddly energized by its wound. It held the weapon up, and lightning from its claws raced up the hilt and along the blade, flashing and sparkling like a fireworks show. Grinning, it advanced on her, waving the crackling weapon.

Fury raced toward it. The red wolf darted inside of its reach and sank its teeth into the beast's calf. The creature gave a shriek and brought the sparking blade down on the wolf. But Fury was quicker and raced around behind it. The blade cleaved only red hair.

Dhamon struggled to his knees, risking a glance behind him. Feril was using the mud to bury her draconian opponent, pin it to the ground. Blister stood over it, whacking at its chest with her chapak. The creature harmlessly spewed lightning. Overhead, the sky thundered in response.

Forcing himself to his feet, Dhamon grabbed his blade, then took a deep breath and rushed to stand with Shaon. The beast sidestepped the wolf and was closing.

"I can fight my own battles, Dhamon!" Shaon yelled. "I don't need any help!"

"Maybe so, but you can't fight very well without a sword!" he called back.

The sea barbarian stubbornly dodged around Dhamon and claimed the creature's attention. It lunged toward her. Distracted by her movements, it forgot about the wolf. A fatal mistake. Fury leapt on its back, and the beast plunged face-forward into the mud.

Shaon slammed her heel down hard on the back of its scaly hand. It released the grip on her sword. As she bent to scoop it up, the creature twisted around and angled its claws at Shaon, sending an electrical charge her way.

Shaon screamed, dropping to her knees. She shut her eyes to try to keep out the bright burning light, but still the jagged flickers danced everywhere. Fumbling about on the ground, her fingers brushed across the hilt of her sword. She grabbed it and blindly swung it where she thought the creature's head was.

"Watch out!" a nearby Dhamon snapped. "You almost skewered me!" He'd lunged toward the thing and now had joined the close-quarters fighting.

"Then get back! This thing's mine!" Shaon had to crawl away, however, blinking to clear her vision.

From behind, Fury closed his jaws on the beast's neck. The creature howled as it pushed itself to its knees. The wolf dug his teeth in deeper. Dhamon lashed out at the thing and his sword cut through the dense flesh of its arm. The creature fell forward again amid a bright flash—a burst of lightning that sent Fury yelping.

Dhamon's arm shot up just in time to cover his eyes, but the electricity rushed out to envelop him and Shaon. It burned and made their teeth chatter with shock. Then as quick as the sensation surrounded them, it seemed to dissipate.

"What's happening?" the sea barbarian cried. "I can barely see anything!"

"Look! It exploded!" the kender squealed. "Dhamon killed it!"

Fury growled and stood up, shaking himself. His red hair

was standing on end, making him appear fluffy and nearly half-again his size. The creature was gone, but there was a bowl-shaped depression in the mud where it had been. Shaon knelt just beyond it, still blinking wildy.

Looking over his shoulder, Dhamon could see Feril was in no real danger, so he helped the sea barbarian up. Her vision was slowly returning.

"It was mine to finish," she complained. Shaon frowned and felt about her face and head. Her short hair was singed, and a scorch mark ran nearly the entire length of her left arm. "It'll scar," Shaon mumbled. "A little souvenir of tonight."

Dhamon pointed toward Feril and Blister.

"We really caught it!" Blister said breathlessly. The kender leveled her chapak over the thing's face. "You open your mouth and breathe lightning, and I'll cut your head in two!"

The beast struggled, but Feril had piled enough mud on top of it that it wouldn't be going anywhere anytime soon.

"Why'd you attack us?" Dhamon demanded.

The blue thing locked its eyes onto his and hissed. "Master's orders."

"Your master ordered you to attack us?"

"Attack humans," it sneered. "Capture humans."

"I guess we taught you a lesson," Blister taunted. "Hey, Dhamon, how'd you know this thing could talk? Wow, you're hurt pretty bad."

"All draconians talk," Dhamon answered. "And this one had better talk a little more unless it wants to join its fellows in oblivion."

"Spawn," the creature hissed. "We are not draconians. We are better, stronger, more. We are spawn."

"Who is this supposed master?" Dhamon stood above the creature now, his hand tightly gripping his sword's pommel. Blister stood opposite him. Both of them stared down into the spawn's face.

"The Portal Master," it hissed. "Only he commands me."

"Gibberish," Dhamon cursed.

"The Storm made us," the spawn continued. "Shaped us from flesh and tears, made us creatures of lightning. And the Storm shall slay you."

"Why does your master command you to attack people?" Blister asked. She winced as she switched her chapak to her other hand and waved the kender weapon for effect.

"Doesn't want kender. Only humans," it hissed. "The Master only wants humans."

"I see," she said offended. "So you would have captured Dhamon and Shaon and left me and Feril alone."

"You and the elf," it sneered, as lightning flickered along its lips, "we would have killed you."

"The village," Dhamon said, drawing the thing's attention. He pointed in the direction from which they'd come. "Did you take all the people from that village?"

What approximated a smile spread across the blue spawn's scaly face. "That village, and others. For the glory of the Portal Master. Our master and sire."

That answered the grim mystery. Dhamon looked at the thing in horror.

"What shall we do with it?" Feril asked Dhamon. "We can't let it loose. It'll only go after more people."

"I say we kill it!" Shaon suggested eagerly. The sea barbarian stepped closer and shouldered her sword. Her dark eyes were rimmed by red. "I'm willing to do the job. Step back."

"No!" Dhamon held a hand out to stop her.

"No?" Blister asked incredulously. "If we leave it here, it'll dig itself out eventually."

The creature grinned, showing its sharp, glowing teeth.

"I want to take it with us, to Palin's."

Shaon groaned. "You're crazy, Dhamon."

"Palin's supposedly a sorcerer, and the Lonely Refuge can't be that far away. We can herd it there. If you kill it, the thing will disappear and we'll have nothing, no evidence to study."

"Fine," the sea barbarian said with supreme annoyance. "We don't have any rope. It's miles to the next village—which might be deserted. And we don't have any horses. Yours and mine ran off. Feril's is buzzard food."

The Kagonesti shot her a vexed look.

"We'll use our belts to tie it," Dhamon suggested.

"Brilliant," Shaon retorted. "Don't you think it's strong enough to snap them?"

"I have an idea." Feril knelt on the ground by the creature and thrust her fingers into her pouch. She pulled out a dried bean seed. "I don't know if I have enough energy, but I'll try."

"Try what?" Blister wondered aloud. The kender stepped away from the spawn and stood behind the elf, where she could take in the whole show.

Feril held the seed above the creature's mud-covered chest. "As tiny as this seed is, so shall you be." She made a small impression in the mud with her thumb, placed the seed gently inside, and brushed a bit of mud over the top to cover it.

Then she rocked back on her heels, closed her eyes, and sang. The words were elvish, something Dhamon, Blister, and Shaon couldn't make out. Throaty and rich, the song's melody was soft and slow, and the breeze that rustled their tattered clothes seemed an apt accompaniment to it. As the tempo increased, Feril's skin took on a soft sheen, practically glowing. Her fingertips glistened, and she moved them over the spawn's form.

She drew her hands together, as if she were praying, and the glow intensified. Then she separated them and placed her palms a few inches above the seed. The glow spread to the mud, centered on the spot where the bean was buried.

Blister gasped. The seed began to sprout, a small green nub emerging from the earth. Beneath it, the spawn struggled more fiercely. The nub grew longer, a thin tendril rose toward Feril's hands. When it was several inches long, the Kagonesti withdrew her hands. In that instant, the green shoot curled over and plunged into the mud near to where its seed had been planted.

Feril continued singing. She pictured the thing shrinking, folding in on itself. But it wasn't working quite correctly. She had to stop her song, and as she did so, the shoot began to wither. "It's no use."

"Try again," Dhamon urged. "Please."

She sighed and resumed her song, which seemed much sadder now. Again she held her palms over the bean seed. Fury came over next to her. But the red wolf wasn't lending morale support. It yawned, stretched and lay down, resting its head on her leg and idly watching what she was doing.

"As tiny as this seed is, so shall you be." Again she closed her eyes. This time the energy was there. She felt it pulsing all around her. It ran from her toes to her fingertips. She sang louder, and the small plant grew a darker green and burrowed deeper toward the blue spawn.

"Look!" the kender exclaimed. "The creature's getting smaller."

A surprised look crossed the spawn's lizardlike visage. It renewed its struggles, thrashing about in vain as it slowly disappeared beneath the mound of mud. Dhamon dropped his sword and started digging. Shaon joined him.

Within moments, the mud had been cleared away, and a spawn no taller than a man's hand was uncovered. The thing furiously flapped its wings, and shot upward. But the sea barbarian was quicker, and her fingers closed about its tiny legs.

Lightning exploded from its mouth and bounced across her arm, but it only stung her with the force of a spider bite. Shaon laughed and shook the thing. It feebly clawed at her hand, scratching it no worse than a small cat.

"Are you going to carry it all the way to Palin's?" Blister asked.

"Only if you give me your net bag," Shaon returned.

The kender's eyes opened wide. "Of course! My unbreakable bag. My magic seaweed bag." She hooked the chapak to her belt and tugged free the bag. When she upended it, several of Raph's spoons, a couple of spools of thread, a handful of marbles, a pair of lime-green gloves, and a ball of yarn fell out. She proudly handed the bag to the sea barbarian, then fell to the task of collecting her dropped belongings into another bag.

Shaon thrust the struggling spawn inside, then held the drawstring bag up to her face. The green weave was tight, but she could see its eyes gleaming dully through a small gap. The bag wiggled, and she saw it glow with light as the creature attempted to use its lightning breath to break free.

"What do you know, Blister," Shaon grinned. "I think this really is magical. It can't get out."

Dhamon helped the Kagonesti to her feet. "Are you all right?"

Feril nodded. "A little sore, but I think I fared better than you and Shaon. You two need some serious tending."

The kender, finished with her task, sat back and sighed. Her fingers ached terribly. But she glanced up at the sea barbarian and Dhamon and giggled. "You're a mess!" she chuckled. "I wouldn't dress a scarecrow like either one of you!"

Dhamon's shirt hung on him in strips, as did Shaon's. Their pants were ripped, and mud and scorch marks dotted their exposed skin.

Dhamon had to smile. He had no more coins. No horse. No food. But there was the spare shirt beneath the saddle of Feril's dead horse. He retrieved it and passed it to Shaon.

"Maybe Palin's got some extra clothes in the Lonely Refuge," Blister added.

"It was going to be a long ride by horse," Shaon grumbled. "Now your Lonely Refuge is going to be a very long walk." Under her breath she added, "Rig had better wait for me."

"I can find us food and water along the way," Feril volunteered. She fussed over Dhamon and Shaon for the next several minutes, binding their wounds with the tattered remnants of Dhamon's shirt.

"To the Lonely Refuge, then," Dhamon said. He sheathed his sword, motioned to Feril, and started north. Fury walked at his side. "Hopefully we'll come across another village and can send someone for the boy in Dolor. We'll travel by night. I don't want to be sleeping when these things are around."

"Who said they only come out at night?" Blister asked, as she hurried to catch up. "It can storm during the daytime, too."

"Wonderful," the sea barbarian said. Shaon held the net bag close to her face and watched a tiny grin spread across the creature's sapphire visage. She shivered and fell in step with the others.

Chapter 27

Blue Spy

Khellendros had watched from the bowels of his lair
deep beneath the desert. He had watched as one of his children was slain in midair by an audacious human who refused
to give in to its sharp claws and lightning. The man was tall,
broad-shouldered, with wheat-colored hair that blew in the
breeze about his intense face.

Khellendros had watched the man repeatedly drive a blade
into the blue spawn's chest. The spawn was in an agony that
Khellendros shared. He had felt the lifeblood of his first successful creation ebb away. He had felt his child gasp for
breath and discover blood, not air, in its lungs.

The dragon had pulled himself back, detached his senses—

not wanting to feel his first offspring's death, not wanting to know what death was like, what Kitiara experienced so long ago when he had failed her and her body died.

But his concentration had been interrupted by the death of another blue spawn, this also at the hands of the wheat-haired man.

"No!" the dragon had shouted. The walls of his cavern shook and grains of sand had rained down like falling snow through the cracks in the stone ceiling overhead. The wyvern sentries had stared blankly at him.

"Do what?" the larger had asked.

"Do nothing," the other had suggested.

The Blue's ranting and raving had gone on for several minutes.

Now more than two dozen spawn watched and waited behind the wyverns. They looked past the dull-witted guards, watched their master, but kept wisely silent and did nothing as the sand continued to rain down.

"I shall not be bested!" Khellendros cursed. "Not by a handful of mortals. I shall send more spawn. I shall . . ." The dragon paused, sensing a third child in the barrens, one the humans had not killed. It was relatively uninjured, but it was frightened, and it was . . . trapped?

Through the eyes of his mud-encased spawn, Khellendros saw faces framed in green. A kender, one well into life and with thick streaks of gray in her hair. The man was there, too, looking down with his wheat-hair fluttering about his face. The man was saying something, but Khellendros couldn't quite make it out. And the blue spawn was getting more frightened with each passing moment. The thunderous beating of its heart drowned out practically all else.

"Calm," the dragon communicated to the creature. "Show no fear."

The spawn relaxed, but only a little. With the dragon's persistent coaxing, its heart slowed, quieted. Then Khellendros heard a word.

". . . Palin's," a man said.

Palin? The dragon furrowed his brow. The name was vexingly familiar. A human name that had significance. Ah, yes. Palin Majere, a baby born to Caramon and Tika Majere, humans who meddled in dragon affairs and angered Kitiara—Heroes of the Lance, their brethren called them.

Kitiara's nephew?

And the man was also called a hero himself for managing to survive the Chaos War and for founding the Academy of Sorcery. He was a recurring problem.

The dragon was curious, wanting to see this offspring, learn how his parents died—if they were dead. Caramon and Tika were often a bane to Kitiara, which meant they were a bane to Khellendros. He would learn what happened to them, share the news with Kitiara when he recovered her spirit. Perhaps he would kill them all, Caramon and Tika if they still lived, and their whelp—show Kitiara their bodies as a homecoming present.

"They think you a common draconian, my spawn," Khellendros hissed conspiratorially. "They think you a simple creature, not a complex being born of a draconian and a human and given life by my essence. *I* am a part of you." The dragon was immensely pleased with himself, relishing the prospect of seeing this Palin Majere—being taken to him via the blue spawn.

"A fine spy, you will be, my spawn," Khellendros continued. He felt his creation's heart beat with pride now, happy that it could satisfy its master.

The Blue instructed his spawn to test the prison. It was a strong net, but not truly magical. With only a minimal amount of effort, the creature could tear its way free. Its talons were sharp enough to slice through the seaweed. Its nails crackled with lightning, sparking against the tight weave and threatening to sunder it so it could fly free.

"Stop!" Khellendros ordered. "You must not free yourself—not yet."

The spawn settled back, confused and trying to make itself comfortable. It feebly wrestled with the net now and then to make the bag jiggle and to keep up the illusion of captivity.

This kept its master happy.

Chapter 28

Uninvited Visitors

Muglor was in the lead boat. Chieftain of the Strongfist Tribe of ogres in the hills near Palanthas, he'd chosen the largest longboat to ride in, as was his right. It was the boat that was most recently stolen and seemed the safest. Muglor didn't care for the water, though he knew how to swim. The water only served to clean his hair and skin and chase away the smell of himself, of which he was quite fond and proud.

Muglor was a little larger than the ogres he commanded, his size being one of the reasons he had been put in charge. He was ten feet tall and weighed more than four hundred pounds. Like his fellows, his skin had a dull, dark yellow cast. It was inordinately warty, and sickly-looking violet patches dotted his shoulders, elbows, and fell across the backs of his big hands. His long, greasy hair was forest green, though it looked black this night, as the moon was hidden by clouds and obscured some of his more interesting features.

The darkness didn't bother Muglor or his fellows. The ogres' large, purple eyes were keen, easily taking in the peaceful Palanthas harbor and all the ships docked there—and the few men who strolled about on the decks.

Muglor motioned for the rowers to stop, to let the longboats drift in. Though it was late, and though nearly all of the sailors would be sleeping or carousing in town, the ogre chieftain didn't want to take any chances that those few awake would sound an alarm and ruin their mission.

The ogre wasn't so much worried about the townsfolk. He and his fellows could easily bash in the heads of those who might foolishly attack them. But he was concerned about the Blue.

The Storm Over Krynn wanted humans, and the Storm wanted the ogres to obtain them. Muglor had no desire to disappoint the dragon. Muglor wanted the Storm to be happy. And making the dragon happy would mean Muglor could continue to live and lord it over his tribe.

He knew the Dark Knights would help if it became necessary, but he wanted to do this job alone. They had already been insulted when they were instructed to bring the captured humans to a camp set up by brutes. Apparently the ogre camp was not good enough. The clannish brutes had moved right in on the ogres' territory, accompanied by a few Knights of Takhisis. The tall skinny creatures were at the beck and call of the Dark Knights and even painted their skin blue. As if someone would mistake them for a blue dragon!

Muglor's thoughts were disturbed as the lead longboat brushed up against a green-hulled carrack. There were words painted on the side, and Muglor strained to read them. *Flint's Anvil.* He raised his greasy eyebrows. Had he read that right?

Flint was a piece of rock used to help start fires, and anvils sank. Of course he read it correctly—the humans simply chose a stupid name for their big boat. Muglor was also the rare chieftain who could read and who was intelligent—at least as far as ogres were concerned. He was the smartest member of the Strongfist Tribe.

With choreographed waves of his big shaggy arms, he directed the other longboats to different targets. Satisfied everyone was following his orders and being reasonably quiet, Muglor stood and tossed a net over one arm. He stuck a crude club, a carefully selected piece of hardwood he'd affixed spikes to, in his belt. Convinced it wouldn't fall out and make a racket, he dug his claws into the side of the *Anvil* and started climbing. One ogre remained in the longboat to make sure it wouldn't drift away. Three others accompanied Muglor. They were laden with nets and weapons and tried very hard not to make the slightest sound.

The dragon had asked for humans who were strangers to Palanthas, people whom the locals wouldn't be attached to and wouldn't be terribly concerned about if they happened to disappear. Muglor, being particularly smart, figured the best place to find such strangers would be at the port. The stupid people of Palanthas would think the missing sailors had drowned or left for work elsewhere—or were kidnapped by pirates, which they'd be afraid to pursue. No one would be the wiser if the ogres plucked up only a few, and the Blue—and Muglor—would be happy.

Muglor effortlessly vaulted the *Anvil's* rail and landed with a thump on the deck. Squinting through the darkness, his eyes separating the shadows and locking onto objects that generated heat, he found a man. Sleeping? Must be, Muglor thought. He didn't hear me. The chieftain and his fellows crept forward.

Groller sat facing the shore, his back against the mainmast. His neck brushed up against the wood and was sufficiently scratched to feel good. He was thinking about Fury, his friend who'd run off a few days ago. He knew the red wolf would be back soon. The wolf was prone to disappearances, sometimes for days or weeks, and he always managed to return.

The half-ogre sighed and inhaled the salty air. Tomorrow he would go back into the city, to the place Rig took him that was called Myrtal's Roost. The steak he and Rig had there two days ago was delicious, and Groller had more than enough coins for several more. Maybe he would treat Jasper, teach him hand signs for different types of food.

Rig promised once they left the harbor they'd run along the coast of Northern Ergoth, stop at Hylo and pick up a hauling contract or two. The sea barbarian claimed the money would be good. The half-ogre grinned. He'd drink the best ale that coins could buy and live on a feast of steaks. He'd even buy some for Fury.

Suddenly, he stiffened, his wide nostrils picking up the scent of something unfamiliar and out of place. He stood and sniffed again, then whirled to face the *Anvil's* starboard side.

Ogres! He reached for the belaying pin that always hung from his waist. But he was too late. The biggest ogre, a disgusting-looking yellow brute, was already on him, wrestling him to the deck and striking him with a club. Groller grunted and fought hard, but his foe was heavy and had the advantage of surprise. The club cracked up against the side of his head, and he felt himself falling, sinking. He felt a tide of warm darkness rushing in to cover him as if he were a rock along the shore being covered by the tide. Then he felt his hands being bound, his body being wrapped in something—a fishing net?

If I wasn't deaf, he thought as the black tide continued to sweep around him. *If I wasn't deaf, perhaps I would have heard them, and I could have warned Rig and Jasper.* Then the tide swept away his consciousness and blackness claimed him.

"He be human?" The smallest ogre posed a question, pointing at Groller.

Muglor bent over to scrutinize their prisoner more closely. "Be part human, at least. He'll do," the chieftain passed judgment. "Below you go. Find more."

Muglor scooped up Groller under one arm and half-carried, half-dragged him to the rail. The chieftain pitched his burden over the side of the *Anvil*, and the ogre below caught him and arranged him roughly in the bottom of the longboat. Looking across the harbor, the chieftain watched other netted sailors being deposited into boats. He grinned, revealing a row of pointed black teeth.

"The Storm Over Krynn be happy," Muglor beamed. He patted an empty sack that hung from his side and trundled below deck to see if there was anything other than humans worth taking, too.

Less than an hour later, Muglor and his flotilla of longboats sailed from the Bay of Branchala. The boats sat heavy in the water, laden with netted prisoners.

"He not be human," Muglor said, pointing at an unconscious short-haired dwarf who lay on the bottom of the boat.

"Sorry," a young ogre apologized.

Maybe the brutes won't notice, Muglor thought. He'll be put in the center of the pen.

The flotilla headed toward the northeast, toward the hills where the ogres made their home. Once ashore, the longboats would be carried to their camp. No evidence would be left along the water's edge—in the event one of their prisoners might turn out not to be a stranger and someone in Palanthas would try to take steps to find him.

Chapter 29

In the Desert

Midway through the next morning, they stopped walking. They were sore, tired, and thirsty. Their stomachs growled incessantly. Feril volunteered to hunt, but Dhamon argued that rest was more important right now. He'd found a small hill with a slight outcropping—enough to provide a little shade from the sun that was high overhead and beating down on them.

Shaon plopped to the sand and dropped the net bag at her feet. Fury stretched out beside her and stared at the tiny creature who peered back at him through gaps in the dark green net.

The sea barbarian winced as she reached out to pet Fury.

Her arm was branded, burned from the bolt of lightning she'd been the target of last night. It would likely leave a lengthy, ugly scar. "Why did I come along?" she whispered to the wolf. "Did I really think I could speed them up? Help them? Or did I just want Rig to miss me for a while?"

Again she thought about the big mariner, wondered what he was doing and wondered if he was thinking about her. She closed her eyes, leaned back, and imagined she was on the deck of the *Anvil*. She was going to have to change that name as soon as she got back, even if Jasper protested. The dwarf would be gone soon enough anyway.

Dhamon sat next to the Kagonesti. Feril tried to fuss over the claw marks on his back, but he brushed away the attention. There was no water to clean the wound, and if they made any more bandages out of their clothes, they wouldn't have anything left to wear. The kender, perhaps because she was small—or lucky—had the least damage. She had managed to only get her topknot singed.

"Dhamon, how long do you think it will take to reach the Lonely Refuge?"

He shrugged. "I don't know. Several days, maybe—if we're lucky. The map was in the pack on my horse, and the horse is probably miles and miles from here. Sorry you came along?"

Feril grinned and shook her head. "We'll find the Refuge. And I'll find us something to eat in a little while. I'm a good hunter. Maybe I'll take Fury with me. I wonder if he can hunt? Or has living with people made him soft?"

"I just wonder where we are," Blister interposed distractedly.

Feril glanced at the kender. Blister had been mumbling and pacing, periodically stopping to kick at the sand, trace circles in it with the heel of her boot. Her bottom lip protruded in concentration, and her arms swung at her sides. She wore gray canvas gloves today. There were some sort of odd attachments on them—a button and hook contraption on each thumb and larger buttons on the palms.

"I know all about draconians," the kender was babbling to herself. "I read about them somewhere. They're copper, bronze, brass, silver, and gold. They don't come in blue. At least they didn't before. These have got to be new. Hey! Dhamon, look! There's a building!"

Dhamon leapt to his feet, his mouth gaping. The kender was right! There was a tower, tall and distinct, sitting about a half-mile away. Had it been there a moment ago? He wasn't sure. He'd been looking off in that direction.

"Is it a mirage?" Blister wondered aloud. "I've heard about the heat on the sand playing tricks on your mind."

"No," Dhamon said. He extended a hand toward the Kagonesti, offering to help her up. She leapt to her feet without any help, and started toward the structure.

"It's not hot enough yet for mirages," Feril said. "At least, I don't think it is. And it's casting a shadow. Mirages don't do that. I'm betting it's magic." She cast a curious look at Dhamon. "And some of us have faith in magic."

Shaon, roused from her daydreams about a carrack named after herself, roughly snatched up the spawn's bag, nudged the wolf, and followed. "Come on, Blister, Fury," she urged. "If it's not a mirage, I'm going to be inside it in a few minutes—and filling my stomach with whatever food I can find."

The tower was made of smooth stone, a simple, gray granite. It was massive, shedding a long shadow across their path.

Dhamon guessed there were eight or nine levels to it. Perhaps more extended below the sand. Had it been here all along and something only now allowed them to see it? A few yards from the door, he stiffened and held up a hand to stop the others. Maybe this was where the blue draconians, the spawn, came from. There were no tracks around the structure. The spawn flew and didn't have to leave any.

Then the door soundlessly opened, and a figure draped in silver and black appeared in the entranceway. A voluminous hood obscured the face in its shadowy recesses, and the sleeves dangled just below where the tips of fingers would be. The figure could be a man—or a ghost, even a spawn.

It beckoned them forward. But Dhamon made them hold their place.

"You must be Goldmoon's champions," the figure said. His voice was soft and scratchy. "I am the Master. Palin is inside. He has been waiting for you."

"Is this the Lonely Refuge?" Blister asked excitedly. The kender had run to catch up with her long-limbed companions. She took a step closer.

Dhamon looked intently—skeptically—at the silvery-robed man.

"Please, come in. There's no need to stand out in the heat. I'll tell Palin you're here."

"I don't know," Blister babbled. "Maybe he killed Palin. Maybe he's only pretending Palin's inside. Maybe he wants to kill us, and he just wants to do it in there—where it's probably cooler. Maybe he's the you-know-what—The Storm Over Krynn."

Fury padded up to the door, sniffed at the man. Then with a wag of his red-haired tail, the wolf disappeared inside.

"I think it's all right," Feril whispered.

Dhamon nodded, but his hand drifted to the pommel of his sword. He strode into the tower, Feril and Shaon on his heels. The door started to close as Blister took a last nervous look at the sandy waste, then also rushed inside.

The large, open room they stood in was cool and pleasant. A thick rug stretched across the center of it, which soothed the kender's aching feet and made her feel a little better.

The walls were covered with tapestries and exquisite paintings that depicted beautiful countrysides, faces of distinguished people, ships, unicorns, and windswept coastlines. A polished stone staircase wound up the side of the room, and more paintings led upward, each one seemingly more striking and expertly rendered than its predecessor.

A man came down the steps. He was tall, dressed in dark green leggings with a lighter green tunic. A white sash was wrapped around his waist, and designs embroidered in red and black crowded it. His graying auburn hair was long, his eyes intense but tired-looking, and he had the start of a beard shadowing his lean face.

The kender guessed him to be roughly her age, perhaps older but in remarkably good health if so. He walked straight, his head held high and his shoulders squared. She judged him handsome and intriguing for a human. She decided immediately that she liked him.

"Goldmoon's champions," the Master of the Tower announced, as he extended a sweeping arm toward Dhamon and his companions. "This is Palin Majere," he softly added. "Our host."

Silence filled the room. Dhamon wasn't sure how to begin, and Feril was too busy ogling the surroundings to say anything. Blister edged forward and nodded a greeting, knowing better than to extend her hand for fear he might actually shake it and hurt her.

"Pleased to meet you, sir. Jasper Fireforge told me all about you. Well, some about you anyway. But Jasper's not here. He's on the ship—in Palanthas. I think he was afraid it might sail away if he left. Of course, it wouldn't, even if he did. It's waiting for us. I'm Blister."

"I am pleased to meet you, Blister. Goldmoon said you would be coming. Follow me, we have much to discuss."

"Take a look at this," Shaon said, suddenly rushing forward. She held the jiggling net bag toward Palin. "It calls

275

itself a spawn. We were attacked by three of these things last night. Only they were a lot larger and meaner at the time."

Palin took the bag from her and peered through the net. The spawn stopped wriggling and stared back through a small hole in the weave.

* * * * *

From his lair beneath the desert, many miles to the north, Khellendros gazed through the eyes of his spawn.

So this is Palin Majere, the Blue thought. Not so old or feeble as I had anticipated, and his allies are powerful. I shall study this Palin Majere, Kitiara's nephew, as he studies my spawn. And I shall learn what happened to his parents. Perhaps they still live, and I can use him to get to them. Such a fine sacrifice all of them would make.

* * * * *

"Goldmoon said she sensed a growing evil near Palanthas. And I think these are definitely evil," Dhamon began. "They're like draconians, though a little different."

"They explode into balls of lightning when they die," Blister cut in. "Of course, they can shoot lightning bolts at you when they're alive. And they can fly. This one said its master is a big storm."

The sorcerer stroked his chin. "The Master of the Tower and I will study this spawn. Won't you join us upstairs after you've had time to refresh yourselves? Please, take your time. This," he said, indicating the net bag, "will take a considerable amount of study. We will be on the top floor." The sorcerer turned and retraced his steps up the stairs.

* * * * *

They were given a chance to bathe and eat, to tend to their wounds and put on clean clothes that were provided for them. Their old garments were discarded into a fireplace. Fury contentedly curled up in front of the hearth. Despite the heat outside, the interior of the tower stayed pleasantly cool.

They sat at a round birch table, on birch chairs that were thickly padded and comfortable. They drank peach cider from tall crystal goblets and enjoyed the silence. The room was elegant, yet simply furnished, white wood everywhere. The china cabinet and the long, low buffet near it were respectively filled and covered with white dishes and vases. It was a welcome change of pace from the desert.

Blister upended her drink, licked her lips and slipped from her chair so she could better admire the dark orange tunic she was wearing. It was one of Linsha Majere's discarded shirts that was gathered and belted, and it looked more like a long gown with the tip of its tail dragging on the floor. It had tiny seed pearls along the collar, and as the kender ran her white-gloved thumb across them she smiled.

Dhamon was roughly Palin's size, and borrowed a pair of dark brown leggings and a white silk shirt that fit him almost perfectly. He was pleased at its relative plainness, and the soft material felt good against his body.

Shaon and Feril wore clothes kept on hand for needy travellers, which were far removed from what either woman was used to. Shaon's dress was a pale lilac trimmed in ivory lace around a high neck. It was a little short and draped only to the tops of her ankles, as Shaon was quite tall. The sea barbarian nonetheless looked stunning, and to her surprise found herself staring in the mirror.

Feril's was a forest-green flowing gown with roses embroidered in dark red thread along the bodice. The sleeves came to her elbows and fluttered like butterfly wings when she walked. Following Blister's lead, she got up from the table. She whirled in front of Dhamon, laughing softly. "Do you approve?" Her hair was full again, like a lion's mane.

Dhamon stared at her. "You're beautiful," Dhamon said in a hushed voice. She looked surprised. It was one of those rare times when she couldn't think of anything to say.

Shaon cleared her throat loudly and walked toward the stairs. "I want to check on my creature," she said.

"Your creature?" Blister grumbled. "It's *my* magic bag. And Feril shrank the nasty thing." The kender stuck her chin in the air. "It's *our* creature." But the sea barbarian was long gone, and the kender's words were wasted.

Dhamon moved toward the stairs, but Feril's hand on his shoulder stopped him. "Wait," she began. "You were traveling to the Lonely Refuge for something." She gestured to a polished walnut box nearly two feet long and half as wide that sat in the center of the table.

"Was that there before?" he asked. Dhamon stepped closer and ran his fingers across the lid, and carefully opened it. Inside was a piece of steel, dented in places, and festooned with bits of brass and gold.

It was a lance handle, old and ornate, with intricate whorls and designs along its surface. He pulled the handle out and inspected the hole for the lance. Dhamon held it with his right hand, the way someone wielding the completed weapon might. The thing felt impossibly light.

Dhamon turned it over and spotted twin hooks. He reached inside his pocket, where he'd slipped the silk banner after changing clothes, and fastened the flag in place. "Only one part is missing now," he said. "And Palin will take us to it." He looked to Feril, who was smiling at him proudly.

"One of the original dragonlances," Dhamon said reverently. "I wondered if these things were simply legends."

Feril laughed. "They were real all right—and I guess a

couple of them are still around."

Dhamon nodded and gently replaced the lance handle and banner in its box. "I don't know if even a magical lance could kill something as big as the White you saw."

"You have to have faith," Feril countered. "Magic, if it's powerful enough, could make the size of something irrelevant," she said. "And speaking of magic, I think I'll see what Palin is doing with the spawn."

Feril, her butterfly sleeves billowing, seemed to float toward the stairs. As she started up, Blister, who had been so still and silent they had forgotten she was there, followed her. The kender glanced at the big steps, and scowled. "Everything's built for humans," Blister muttered. She knew Feril would get to the top long before her.

* * * * *

"Goldmoon's champions are a rather ragtag lot," the Master said. He sat at a long polished table, opposite Palin.

"I remember my father telling me stories about he and Uncle Raistlin, Tas, and everyone. I suppose you could have called them ragtag, too—especially after they'd been in a fight."

The blue spawn stood in the center of the table inside a bell-shaped piece of glass with a thick cork stopper at the top. It intently regarded the two men. Then, ultimately bored, it paced back and forth, hissing and spitting lightning. The bolts bounced off the sides and ricocheted into a dazzling light show.

"And I suspect Goldmoon chose wisely," Palin continued. "If they bested three of these things—these new draconians—they must be formidable."

"Or lucky." The Master edged his head closer to the jar and nudged the cowl back slightly, yet still his face was hidden. "Indeed, it looks like a draconian, but there are differences."

Palin leaned closer and stared at the spawn. The room fell silent. Suddenly, he reached forward and gripped the bottle tightly. "It's the eyes! Look at them!"

The Master gently pried Palin's fingers from the jar and leaned in to study the spawn intently. "They are not entirely reptilian," he said in agreement.

"I don't just mean the large round pupils or the placement of the eyes closer to the front of the head instead of toward the sides, I mean what's *behind* them. They have depth. They're soft and sad, almost . . ."

"Human," finished the Master. He regarded Palin's sudden ashen pallor and waited silently for a few moments.

"What is going on?" Palin cried. "What is happening to us? What are we becoming"

"Not *we*," said the Master. "We are going to figure this out." He put his hand on Palin's shoulder. "The spawn has a thinner tail than a draconian, and it is capable of flight. Only sivaks could fly before. Could this creature have come from the egg of a blue dragon?"

Palin nodded. "The lightning would be consistent with a blue dragon's breath weapon, but Takhisis created the other draconians. With her gone, who created this?"

"Let's find out."

Palin stood and walked to a bank of cabinets that stretched the length of the room. Built into the wall, and made of the same wood as the table, it contained a few dozen different drawers of varying size with assorted nobs and handles. He opened a drawer and extracted a few sheets of parchment, a quill and a vial of ink. "I will record our observations," he explained as he arranged the objects on the table.

The Master left the room for a moment, his dark robe silently trailing behind him. When he returned, he was carrying a copper basin filled to the rim with water. He placed it on the table and seated himself there. Placing his hands on either side of the basin, he leaned forward as if he meant to drink from it. Words tumbled from his lips. Soft and craggy, his voice sounded like a breeze rustling papers.

Palin watched the Master, realizing he was casting a spell of divination that would allow them to see the birth of the creature, the process that created it, and who was responsible. Without taking his eyes off the water's surface, Palin reached for the quill and the first sheet of parchment.

The Master's words became softer and softer, until Palin could barely hear them anymore. The water shimmered slightly, reminiscent of rays of sun hitting the smooth surface of a lake. An ethereal, rippled image of a haggard-looking youth with a tangled mane of black hair appeared. Broad shouldered, scantily dressed, and weathered from the sun, he was likely a barbarian.

"I'd say he was from the Northern Wastes," the Master whispered. "Look at the markings on his belt."

"Yes, and by their indications he wasn't from too far to the north of here."

"Where are you, man or spawn? Show us your surroundings, the place you were born," the Master insisted.

The water rippled around the image of the man, its currents shifting and reforming into a frame that resembled stone.

"He's in a cave," Palin said. There were shadowing images against the cavern wall—people of various sizes and shapes, though the sorcerers could not make out enough of their features to guess their ages.

The image on the water's surface shifted again, the man's muscles receding, then expanding, becoming coppery and scaly. Wings sprouted from his back, revealing a kapak, a rather witless draconian that cringed and looked furtively about the false cave.

"This is interesting. Perhaps a kapak was merged with the man," Palin speculated. "But how? And why would it turn blue?"

Again the image rippled and shifted form, the kapaklike image starting to grow, seeming to fill the entire cavern in which it had stood. The water turned completely blue and the two sorcerers leaned closer toward the basin.

"What happened?" asked Palin.

"Perhaps it is the sky," answered the Master, leaning still closer to search for a small figure in flight or a cloud.

Suddenly the water parted in the center, revealing a huge glowing orb. A blue dragon had just opened his eye.

The two sorcerers quickly backed away from the basin and looked at each other. "Skie," said Palin.

They watched together as the reptilian eye rotated around its bulbous socket, seeming to look around the room. Its baleful gaze fixed on them and the eye narrowed. The image began to ripple. The water grew turbulent, roiled and then boiled away. The copper basin was empty.

"What does all of that mean?"

The voice was Shaon's. The sea barbarian stood in the doorway, glancing at the basin and then at the jar containing the trapped spawn. She shuffled into the room and leaned over the table, staring at the creature. It returned her gaze.

Palin scratched furiously on the parchment, wanting to record every observation before time passed and chased away even the merest recollection.

"It means that Goldmoon chose her champions wisely," the Master said. His voice was softer than before, the ordeal of the spell wearing on him. He leaned back in his chair, exhaled slowly. "For all our magic and books and hours of study, you and your fellows were able to discover something about the dragons that Palin and I, and our associate who is elsewhere, could not. If the dragons—if even one of the dragons—found a way to create new draconians, spawn— then . . ." His voice trailed off.

"Then Krynn is in worse trouble than any of us feared,"

Dhamon finished. He had stepped into the room behind
Feril.

The Master agreed. "The dragons are enough of a menace
on their own. And if we have to deal with the Blue's spawn
before we can defeat the dragons, I don't know if we have a
chance."

"There is always a chance," Palin said, laying down the
quill. "I'm going with you back to Palanthas. We'll pick up
the final piece of the lance there."

"The Dark Knights—the Blue's agents—will be watching
us," Blister added. The kender had finally made it up the
stairs and was panting from the exertion. She wondered
how many trips the sorcerers made up and down the stairs
each day. Maybe mages kept their important rooms at the
top so they would force themselves to get exercise, she
thought.

"Still, we must go to Palanthas. I believe we can find more
answers there than we can by sitting here." Palin thrust his
hand into a deep pocket. He retrieved Blister's net bag and
handed it to the kender. "It's not magic," he told her. "Sorry.
And it's not especially strong. I suspect the spawn must have
been injured in your battle with it, unable to summon the
strength to break out. We'll keep it in the jar to be safe."

"Won't it die in there, without air?" the kender wondered.

Palin shook his head. "The jar *is* magical. I don't want this
thing escaping." He glanced at Feril. "When did you study
mysticism with Goldmoon?"

"I didn't," she said, looking down.

Intrigued, Palin turned toward her. "And the shrinking of
the spawn, your magic?"

"It's just something I can do. I've been able to use magic
all my life."

"Inherent magic," Palin said, smiling and turning to look
at the Master. "When we have time," he added, "I'd like to
discuss your magic with you."

She nodded. "I'd be honored."

"Can we make a . . . side trip?" Feril asked. "There's a young boy in a village. He's all alone. The spawn took all the adults in his village."

"How many adults?" The words erupted out of Palin's mouth.

"A few dozen were taken, from what we understand," she replied.

"The Blue could indeed be making an army of these things," the Master said. "And an army is never without a purpose."

"Well, the spawn are not unbeatable," Palin returned, pointing at the trapped creature.

"Neither are we," Blister said.

* * * * *

Khellendros purred. He looked out through the eyes of his blue spawn, studying Palin, the Master, and the others. "By taking my spawn with them, they are taking me."

The Blue was pleased. He would know everywhere they went, whatever they were working on, and all they discovered—without leaving his comfortable lair. In the process, he'd learn all there was to know about their weaknesses and drives. And when the time was right, he vowed to strike against them.

"Perhaps I shall worry them first," he hissed. "Threaten them, frighten them. Perhaps make a game of it." His mouth curled upward in the approximation of a grin, and he crooked a claw in the air, beckoning the wyvern guards.

"Do what now?" the larger asked.

"Do something?" the other echoed.

"Yes," Khellendros intoned. "My lieutenant, Gale, find him. His lair is to the north. Bring him here."

"Do now? Sun out now."

"Hot out now," the larger complained.

Khellendros growled as the wyverns hurried out into the hateful desert afternoon.

Chapter 30

Secrets
___

It was late that night, and they had not yet departed for
Palanthas. Under the light of several tall, thick candles that
warmly lit the bell-shaped jar and bounced off the polished
table, Palin continued to study the spawn. His copious and
detailed notes were spread out nearby; some were on the
floor. Stacks of unused sheets occupied an adjacent chair.

A stubble was flourishing across his face, the true makings of
a beard, and his eyes were shadowed by fatigue. His stomach
quietly rumbled—he'd been so absorbed with the operation
that he passed on dinner. The Master had brought him a plate
of bread and cheese, a small bowl of sugared berries, and a glass
of wine. All of it sat untouched. The spawn eyed it hungrily.

The Master of the Tower was with Dhamon and his companions several levels below now, quizzing them about their encounter with the creatures, and using a few simple spells to recreate the battle—phantasmal ghosts playacting against the dining room wall, replaying the struggle again and again.

Dhamon watched, his fists clenched. He did not enjoy experiencing scenes of battle. He wondered if the threat of a new draconian army was the precursor to something more horrific than he had ever experienced.

High overhead, Palin shook the jar until the angry spawn let loose with another barrage of miniature lightning bolts.

"Interesting creature, Majere."

Palin turned. From the darkest corner of the room, the black-cloaked Shadow Sorcerer emerged. The figure separated itself from the room's shadows and edged toward the table, its metallic mask sparkling in the candlelight. The Shadow Sorcerer scanned the sheets of parchment, as Palin explained his findings at length.

"I saw the Red," the Shadow Sorcerer said. "She is a huge female, larger than any other dragon we've observed, perhaps as large as Takhisis. She had no . . . spawn, as you call it, no draconians. However, she did have a growing army of creatures—goblins and hobgoblins."

"Perhaps all the dragon overlords are amassing armies," Palin explained. "If they were doing so to fight amongst themselves, I would not be as concerned. But the Dragon Purge is long over—not for several years has there been any fighting each other. And there's no arguing that their war is against us now. The good dragons are doing what they can, but they have to work in secret."

The black-cloaked figure nodded. "Secrets are sometimes necessary."

Palin looked at the Sorcerer for a moment, then went back to arranging his notes. "I am concerned about the spawn."

"Indeed." As the sorcerer leaned closer to the jar, the

spawn in turn peered into the shadowy recesses of the figure's hood.

"We are leaving for Palanthas, a spot outside the city."

"When?" the Shadow Sorcerer asked.

"Now. After I saw to the care of a boy whose village had been attacked, we had only to wait for you." Palin rose from his chair. "I will gather the others together for transport. We can waste no more time." He descended the stairs, pausing by a painting of his Uncle Raistlin. He gave everything for magic, for his art, Palin thought. Am I sacrificing myself, too?

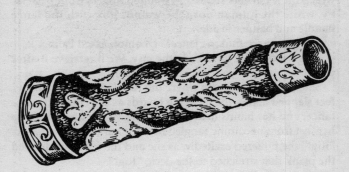

Chapter 31

Against the Ogres

After bidding goodbye to the Master and the Shadow Sorcerer, who suddenly changed their minds about accompanying the group to Palanthas, Palin magically transported the adventurers and himself. Shaon led the way to the city, her footfalls light and hurried. She was spurred by the scent of sea air and the thought of being with Rig again. She kept pace with Fury, and the two of them easily left the others behind.

Blister bounced along at Palin's side, pestering her patient companion with seemingly unending questions about all the places he'd been and what the Abyss looked and smelled like and were there very many kender there. Palin answered what he could until he was practically out of breath.

Dhamon and Feril quietly walked several yards behind; the Kagonesti was carefully carrying the spawn in the bottle, which drew curious stares and pointed fingers from passersby, while the human bore the walnut box with the lance handle and banner inside.

"Where do we find the lance?" Dhamon asked Palin.

"It's waiting for us here in the city. We'll retrieve it after you've reported to your friends on the ship."

Shaon reached the slip where the *Anvil* was anchored. Her feet slapped across the creaking boards as she closed the distance, and her hands held her skirt above her knees to keep her feet from becoming tangled in the luxurious violet fabric. "Rig!" she hollered excitedly, as she and the red wolf climbed the plank that stretched to the deck. "Rig?"

Fury sniffed the railing and threw back his head with a howl. Though half the length of the waterfront separated them from Shaon, Dhamon and the others could see her darting about the deck and hear Fury's cries.

Dhamon whirled and thrust the walnut box into Palin's hands. He drew his sword and rushed toward the ship. Had the creatures been here, too?

He raced down the dock and onto the ship—just as Shaon's head disappeared below deck. "Rig?" she kept calling, her voice becoming softer the deeper she went. Dhamon added his voice, but still there was no reply.

"No one's on board," Palin observed, as he, Feril, and Blister approached the green carrack, bringing up the rear. The sorcerer closed his eyes, concentrating. "There hasn't been anyone here for a few days." Glancing over his shoulder at a knarr, a small cargo ship moored nearby, he saw an old sailor leaning on a weathered rail and caught his eyes. The sailor shook his head sadly.

Blister and Feril climbed onto the *Anvil*, while Palin turned back toward the old man.

"Groller's," Dhamon whispered, as he bent and snatched

up a belaying pin and showed it to Feril. She sat the spawn jar by the mainmast, and started searching about.

"Rig!" Shaon shouted one last time as she clambered up from below. "Dhamon, he's not here!"

Dhamon put a hand on her shoulder. "Calm down, he might be in town." Out of the corner of his eye he noticed Fury pacing nervously, the wolf's agitation silently undercutting his words.

"You don't understand!" the sea barbarian insisted. "No one's here. Not the deck hands. Not Jasper. Not Groller. Rig wouldn't leave any ship unattended, let alone his. I know him. And there's other things missing. My jewelry, for example." Her eyes were wide and glistening. She glanced at the belaying pin Dhamon had found and sucked in her lower lip. "I half expected the ship to be gone, that Rig wouldn't wait for me. I didn't expect the ship to be here without them. Something terrible must have happened."

"Aye, girl. Something very bad's happened. T'were beasties."

Palin was leading the stumbling old sailor onto the deck. "Saw 'em, I did. Nobody 'lieves me, though. Big beasties. Late at night they came."

Shaon towered over the newcomer, and he took a step back, intimidated. He stared up at her, his rheumy blue eyes blinking over a bulbous red-veined nose.

"What are you saying?" she demanded to know.

"Beasties—I told ye." The sailor stroked his stubble-covered chin and grinned and winked at Feril, who'd come up behind to join the sea barbarian. "Took yer men. Got lotsa men. Nobody 'lieves me, though. But I'm still here—if ye need a man."

Shaon inhaled sharply. "You're drunk." His breath and clothing reeked of ale, as much as if he'd mopped up a floor of a tavern with his body.

"Aye, girl. S'why nobody 'lieves me." He punctuated the

remark with a loud burp. "But I sees 'em, drunk er no. I was layin' on the deck of *The Hunter* over there. Me face hangin' over the side 'cause I'd had me a mite too much to swallow. They sailed right in, bold as ye please, an' started haulin' men off ships. Didn't want me."

"I can't imagine why," Shaon growled.

"Where'd they take the men?" Dhamon interjected.

"Sailed right out agin." The old sailor swayed, and Feril stepped in to help prop him up. "Took 'em out to sea, the beasties did. Sailed 'round the point over there. Probably ate 'em. Beasties eat men, you know. They each had three heads and lotsa arms. Their feet were as big as anchors. An' their hair was seaweed. Their eyes glowed like fire, like they came from the Abyss."

Shaon shuddered. "I don't believe you." But part of her had to. The sea barbarian had seen some strange things recently—an empty village, spawn, buildings that suddenly appeared. Monsters—they were not entirely out of the realm of possibility.

"I can find out if his story is true." Feril sat on the edge of the deck, near a section of rail with deep scratches in it. Claw marks, perhaps, the Kagonesti thought, as she reached into her bag and pulled out a lump of clay. She worked it with her fingers as she hummed, rocking back and forth. Within moments, it resembled a small boat.

She stared over the side of the ship, the still water reflecting her tattooed face. She drew her lips into a straight line and hummed louder. The magic was difficult today, the spell seemed to tease her from afar. Still, she persisted, her mind groping for the connection to the energy.

Finally, Feril's mind located the energy and found the strength to draw out the enchantment. The water below her shimmered and rippled, and a mirror-image of the *Anvil* appeared. Groller was on the deck—surrounded by a foursome of ugly ogres. They quickly subdued him, then went below and kidnapped the others. The whole scene played out on the water as all of the companions watched.

"Thems what I saw," the old man said blusteringly, waving his hand at the water. " 'Cept they were big as life, the beasties were, not pictures on the water. Mean looking, too, they were, and with eight eyes each and lotsa teeth."

Shaon gripped the rail as the water calmed and Feril returned the clay to her pouch. "They might be unharmed," the Kagonesti offered. "They're tough, Rig and Groller, and Jasper seems resourceful. The boats seem too small to be sea vessels. Therefore, the ogres would've had to land somewhere nearby. They couldn't last long out on open water."

"Why would these ogres be kidnapping sailors?" Blister wondered.

"Ogres keep slaves," Palin answered. "Sailors are strong and would make good laborers. But the ogres won't have them for long. We'll get them back." If they're alive, he added to himself. He pointed to the belaying pin Dhamon still held. "Perhaps I can try some of my magic to track them down."

The sorcerer handed the walnut box to Shaon. "Guard this with your life, as the lives of many others might depend on it," he said. Then he took the belaying pin, held it in the palm of his right hand, and concentrated his gaze, as the others watched.

The words Palin spoke were distinct, though they were of a tongue unknown to the others on deck. As they fell from his lips, the belaying pin quavered and took on a different shape, looking like a doll-sized replicate of Groller. Beads of sweat dotted the sorcerer's brow. His hands glistened with moisture. The words continued to spill from his lips, faster now. Then they abruptly stopped and the image of Groller became the belaying pin once again, though it had two imprints, or scars, where the doll's eyes had been.

Palin inhaled deeply, shook his head, and hefted the pin.

"This will act as a magnet and lead us to your friend. He knelt and called to Fury. The wolf dutifully trotted over and sat patiently while Palin tugged the sash free from around his waist and looped it several times around the wolf's neck. He stuck the belaying pin beneath the makeshift collar.

"Fury! Find them!" Palin commanded. The sorcerer watched the wolf's gold eyes sparkle with an unusual light. Then Fury barked loudly, and took off loping down the plank. Palin rushed after him, leaving the old sailor staring mutely at him and the others while weaving precariously on the *Anvil's* deck.

"Now where's he runnin' off to?" the old man wondered aloud. "Didn't like me company?"

"Feril, come on!" Dhamon called.

The Kagonesti leapt to her feet. Shaon started down the plank too, but Feril caught her arm. "Someone has to stay here," she reminded, "in case Rig and the others escape and come back. Besides, you have to guard the box." Shaon agreed, and Feril raced after Dhamon.

"Rig wouldn't want anything to happen to this ship," Blister added. "Someone might steal it if nobody's here." The kender grimaced as her fingers closed about Shaon's hand, and she led the sea barbarian back onto the deck. "I'll stay here with you."

"What about me?" the old drunk belched.

"Go home," Shaon snapped.

He shrugged and awkwardly lumbered down the plank, muttering about yellow beasties with tentacle tails and lovely rude women who didn't appreciate his obvious charms.

The sea barbarian fidgeted with her lace collar of her gown. It suddenly seemed tight and scratchy, uncomfortable, and her eyes had become irritated, filled with water. She'd so wanted Rig to see her like this, beautiful.

* * * * *

The wolf led Palin, Feril, and Dhamon beyond the city, east toward the foothills of the mountains. For hours they walked, until the day melted away and Palin's chest began to heave from the exertion. The sorcerer was accustomed to walking up and down seemingly endless stairs in the Tower of Wayreth. But he was far from the young man who journeyed for an extended time across the country with his cousin, Steel Brightblade, and who then fought against Chaos in the Abyss. This journey was long and taxing, and his pride prevented him from staying behind or asking the others to slow their pace. He tried to ignore the tightening feelings in his chest, to concentrate on magical theories, the threat of the dragon overlords, and to think about Usha.

Feril and Dhamon seemed tireless. The Kagonesti had shortened the long skirt, and expeditiously created a ragged green dress that hung just above her knees. She apologized to Palin for ruining the gown but he shook his head and said he understood. Feril's pace was quicker without the long folds about her legs.

Sunset found them many miles from Palanthas's outer guard posts, sitting on the damp ground and relaxing against the massive trunk of a dead tree. Palin closed his eyes. The muscles in his legs ached, his feet throbbed, and he imagined he had blisters upon blisters on his soles. Despite his soreness and the roughness of the bark against his back, sleep quickly claimed him.

Dhamon sat next to Feril, looking sadly into her eyes. "Ogres can be awful. I've been in their camps before, and I know they don't treat prisoners well. They're malicious. Our friends might not be whole—or alive."

"Let's hope for the best," she whispered. "With Palin and me, there's magic on our side. Things might work out. They have to work out—I couldn't bring myself to deliver any bad news to Shaon."

The Kagonesti snuggled closer and rested her head on

Dhamon's shoulder. A gracefully pointed ear edged out between her curls and tickled his cheek. He sighed and laid his head back against the tree, quietly slipping his arm around her shoulders. I might not have much faith in magic, Feril, he mused, but I have faith in you. The two fell asleep quickly, their soft snores mingling with Palin's.

Shortly after midnight, the wolf slipped away.

* * * * *

Feril followed Fury's tracks in the morning, only slightly perturbed that the wolf hadn't waited for them. His tracks were plain enough in the patches of mud and stretches of sandy soil. Even Palin and Dhamon could read them without much trouble.

The next nightfall found them reunited with Fury and hiding behind a low hill while spying through a gap in the rocks. The sky was cloudless, and the stars glimmered down on a disheartening scene several yards distant—a pen full of captured people.

The people milled about, their sullen faces lit by a campfire that burned nearby. An ogre with dark yellow skin and stringy green hair sat in front of the flames, turning a charred deer leg over and over and mumbling to himself.

"There must be fifty or sixty in the pen," Feril whispered. There were so many that few had enough room to sit or lay down. She saw some sleeping on their feet, leaning against the rail. "I think I see Groller. But I only see the one ogre in front of the fire. We could easily take care of him."

"There's bound to be more than one," Palin quietly returned. "They're brutal and strong but they never travel alone." He craned his neck above the rise, risking being spotted. "Over there. I count eight figures against the far hill. I'm not sure they're ogres, they look less bulky. They might be humans. There's a tent nearby, and there's probably more inside it. Getting your friends out isn't going to be easy." The sorcerer drew back and looked thoughtfully at his traveling companions.

"I want everybody freed," Dhamon whispered, "not just our friends. I'll go around to the other side, see if I can slip into the tent and deal with any ogres there."

"I think I can sneak into the camp and make sure Rig, Groller, and Jasper are in the pen," Feril whispered.

"Be careful," Dhamon cautioned.

She nodded and offered him a slight smile, then she slipped away.

"I'll try to hold the ogres outside at bay," Palin said.

"You don't have a weapon," Dhamon warned.

"I don't need one," Palin replied. He mentally rehearsed a series of enchantments, trying to select which one would be the most appropriate.

Fury followed Dhamon's retreating form, but the Kagonesti continued to stalk forward. A dozen different scents assailed her. The stench of the captives, their sweat and fear, the rankness of the ogres who apparently went months without bathing. There was a dung pile nearby, and as she darted behind it, the ogre at the campfire looked up and sniffed. He grunted, then he eyed his blackened deer meat and fell to devouring it. Feril edged forward.

She passed by a mound of discarded antelope and deer carcasses. The wind shifted, and she nearly gagged on the scent of rotting flesh that still clung to the animals' bones. She also picked up the strong odor of mead. The ogres were drinking, at least some of them. Perhaps they'd imbibed enough to dull their senses and make our job easier, she thought.

The Kagonesti hurried toward the pen, crossing an open area. Her heart raced as she saw the eight figures Palin had spotted. They were most definitely not ogres. There were two Dark Knights and six manlike creatures who were quite tall.

Their thick hair hung in twisted locks and was decorated with feathers. Their long-limbed, muscular bodies were streaked with blue paint.

She also saw a group of ogres, a little more than a dozen, leaning against an embankment and chewing on haunches of animal flesh. Palin couldn't have counted them. They were behind the tent Dhamon was heading toward. He'd see them, of course, but there were simply too many to handle. She hoped he wouldn't try anything foolhardy. She reached the pen, rolled under a low rail, and quickly lost herself in the crowd.

"Feril!" The hushed voice was Jasper's. His stubby hands tugged at her dress. "What are you doing here?"

"Rescuing you," she replied. "Is Rig alive?"

The dwarf nodded toward the center of the pen. Groller stood next to Rig, who towered above most of the people. The big mariner grabbed her shoulders and positioned his body to help hide her from the ogre who'd just finished his meal and was sauntering toward the pen. The other prisoners pressed in closer, curious about the newcomer.

"No!" Rig spat. "Keep back. The ogre will figure out something's wrong." The big mariner's fierce look and Groller's stance forced half of the other prisoners away. "Where's Shaon?"

"On the ship," Feril quickly explained. "Someone had to stay behind and look after the *Anvil*. But Dhamon's here. So is Palin Majere."

"Who?"

A boom rocked the campsite, a thunderous noise that jarred everyone and brought gasps to the lips of most prisoners. The odor of charred flesh filled the air to such an extent that it made Feril's eyes water.

"That would be Palin's doing," she whispered. "He's a sorcerer. Come on, we're all getting out of here." She rushed toward the railing and hesitated when she spotted a gaping hole in the center of the campsite—where the eight figures had been. A curl of smoke drifted upward. The lone ogre that had been approaching the pen also stared at the crater. The slack-jawed ogre was taken by surprise when the prisoners broke through the railing and quickly trampled over him.

The dozen ogres left alive were running toward her and the escaping mob. A Dark Knight was still alive, too, and was barking orders—a few of which Feril could make out. "Don't kill them! Grab them!" he yelled.

Fury was racing toward the lead ogre, snapping and growling. The wolf pushed off against the ground and flew upward, striking the ogre's chest and throwing him on his back.

Through a gap in the ugly yellow bodies, Feril saw Dhamon. He was surrounded by ogres.

"Toward the rocks!" Feril directed the fleeing prisoners. She gestured wildly at the gray-haired sorcerer who was standing ahead on a flat, tablelike stone. His hands were a flutter of movement, his fingers a blur as he weaved a pattern of pale yellow light in the air. "Hurry!" she cried in encouragement. Then she whirled on her heels to face the charging ogres. Rig was right next to her.

"They stashed our weapons in the tent!" he growled. "We'll be cut down without them!" With that, he dashed toward the charging ogres, barely managing to evade them and slip inside the tent.

Feril reached into her pouch and ran her fingers across an assortment of objects. She selected a polished pebble and held it out as she started to sing. A trio of ogres headed her way, and she quickened her song. The remainder of the ogres had peeled off to pursue the prisoners.

"Come on, Feril," she heard Jasper urge behind her. But she ignored him. Out of the corner of her eye, she saw Groller dashing forward. He'd grabbed a piece of the railing to use as a club. He met the charge of the largest ogre, and slammed the makeshift club into its ugly yellow stomach. The ogre doubled over, and Groller swung again, this time hitting the brute on the back of the head and knocking him to the earth.

Feril's song was heard above the pounding of feet. It was an old elvish tune about the woods and the land. The breeze stopped as the song crescendoed, and then the last note died away. She hurled the pebble at the two ogres still running her way. As the rock spun toward them, it glowed and enlarged— first to the size of a man's fist, then bigger still. It struck the smaller of the two in the chest. Caught by surprise, he lost his footing and fell backward. Groller was on him in a heartbeat, driving the club into his skull.

The third ogre sprung on the Kagonesti. His filthy claws closed about her waist and dug in as he forced her to the ground. The nails cut through her dress and raked her sides. Then all of a sudden he stiffened, his grip relaxed and he fell forward with a groan, his great weight pinning her. The foulness of his breath made her gasp. Blood trickled from his mouth and onto her cheek. She rolled out from underneath him to see Jasper standing there, his stubby fingers bloody, and a grim look on his face. A wooden stake protruded from the ogre's back.

She leapt to her feet, surveying the scene. Groller was swinging his club in a wide circle, keeping a quartet of ogres at a distance. Another four were closing on the escaping prisoners. As she watched, bright shards of light flew from Palin's fingertips and struck the creatures, buying time for the prisoners to race to the safety of the rocks. The ogres pitched forward, almost in unison, grabbing their glowing stomachs and howling in agony.

The largest of the lot, the one she guessed to be the leader, writhed and cursed as Fury continued to grapple with him. But the wolf seemed in little danger.

She cast her gaze back to the tent and started off in that

direction, the pounding footfalls of Jasper behind her. Dhamon, his shirt crimson with blood, had his back to the tent and was swinging his sword in a high arc over his head. Five ogres pressed toward him, cursing and growling. He pulled the blade hard to his right, just as one of the ogres darted in. Then he lunged forward. The sword connected with the creature's neck and cut through the tough muscle and bone. Blood spurted in the air, and the decapitated brute fell to his knees before pitching forward.

The remaining ogres hesitated, and Dhamon used the moment to his advantage. He pressed forward, jabbing his sword like a spear, and pushing it through the belly of one of the brutes. The blade sank all the way in and protruded from the ogre's back as Dhamon brought his leg up to shove the beast away and free his sword. The ogre toppled over, nearly in the path of the mariner, who was emerging from the tent.

Two ogres remained focused on Dhamon, but the third turned its attention to Rig. It glowered at the mariner and charged the big man, growling and dripping foul-smelling saliva. Rig was ready. A dagger was gripped in his left hand, and his rapier was balanced in his right. "I'm not a sleeping target now," the mariner taunted. "You won't find me such an easy mark."

The ogre barreled in, and Rig slashed at him. His blade slid into the creature's throat, but it kept coming, its long arms reaching out for him, and its claws raking his chest. Simultaneously, the mariner plunged his blade into the beast's side, withdrew it, and thrust again. The ogre fell, taking the mariner down with him. Rig cursed and pushed the dying creature off him before lumbering to his feet.

Dhamon's eyes were blazing and locked onto the larger of the two creatures still hounding him. He feinted to his right, dropped to his knees, and slashed his sword forward and up, cleaving an appendage off of the large ogre. The beast howled and pulled the bloody stump against its chest as its fellow ogres surged forward, angry and spitting. Dhamon's sword slashed again into the smaller ogre's leg, cutting through the dirty yellow flesh and exposing bone. But the ogre ignored its wound and lunged forward, slamming its shaggy shoulder into Dhamon's chest and knocking him back into the tent. The old canvas billowed around them, sagged and groaned, spilling human and ogre to the ground.

A Dark Knight crawled out of the sagging tent's collapsed entry. "Incompetent beasts!" he shouted. The larger ogre with the severed hand took a few steps back, apprehensively watching the man.

"Kill them!" commanded the Knight, gesturing toward the three companions who were fast approaching.

"Run or die!" Rig shouted, rushing forward.

Confused, the beast froze for a moment. But when Jasper snarled and stepped forward with a makeshift club, the ogre turned and stumbled off into the darkness, still moaning and holding its bloody stump. When the three turned their attention to the Dark Knight, they found he had disappeared.

Rig and Feril ran to the collapsed tent, furiously pulling at the canvas. A bloody yellow claw reached up to strike a blow, but Rig managed to grab the ogre's arm. As the mariner struggled with it, he felt the thing shudder. Its muscles bunched, then relaxed. Rig released the arm and stepped back as Dhamon crawled out of the canvas.

Feril was at his side in an instant, helping him up. "So much blood," she said in an awed voice.

"It's not mine." He sheathed his sword and tore the silk shirt from his back. Feril breathed a sigh of relief to realize that he wasn't badly injured.

"Thanks for the rescue," Rig said.

Dhamon nodded an acknowledgment, then his eyes widened as he took in all of the carnage. Groller had taken out four ogres singlehandedly with his club, and now was plodding toward another group that was struggling to their feet—the ogres Palin had momentarily downed with his magical shards of light. Fury stood on the chest of the largest ogre, blood dripping from his fangs. He cast his head to the sky and emitted a howl.

Dhamon slipped past the mariner and Feril and he rushed toward Groller. Jasper followed. Groller charged one of the four remaining ogres, abandoning his club and leaping on the brute's back. The pair rolled over and over, dust flying, and the commotion drew the attention of the other three. Leaderless, they were confused. Outnumbered, they were frightened.

Dhamon waved his sword in the air. "Surrender!" he called to the few still standing. "If you value your lives, yield now!"

A cracking noise echoed through the campsite. Groller had snapped the neck of his foe and now was rising to his feet.

"We give," one of the ogres said. "No kill us. We give."

Jasper stepped forward. "Why'd you kidnap us?" The angry dwarf shook his small fist at them.

The ogres stared dumbly at their ruined campsite, their fallen comrades. "For the Dark Knights," the spokesman said finally. "The dragon wanted people."

Dhamon strode up to the ogre, flashing his sword. The light from the still-blazing campfire caught the blade and made it gleam threateningly. "The Blue?"

The ogre looked to its brethren and then up at the sky. "Don't know."

That was answer enough for Dhamon. "Where's Skie?"

"Don't know. Don't want to know. Somewhere in the desert, but don't know where. Muglor know. But Muglor dead." The ogre glanced toward Fury, who was pawing over the large, dead ogre. "That Muglor."

Dhamon sighed. "Why'd skie want these particular men?"

The ogres looked at each other and shook their heads dumbly.

"Then for what?" Dhamon persisted. "You don't kidnap people for no reason."

"Don't know," one ogre stammered. "Muglor said the Blue wants more spawn things."

"Spawn?"

"Don't know!" shouted the original spokesman.

Jasper tugged on Dhamon's sword belt. "You got any idea what spawn is?"

"We'll tell you later," Feril said. She and Rig had come up behind them.

"Get out of here!" Dhamon screamed at the ogres. "Before I change my mind and decide to finish off each and every one of you anyway."

The ogres turned and ran, too frightened to look back.

Meanwhile, Palin had climbed down from the large, flat rock. His face was flushed, his breathing labored. The few spells he'd cast were potent and took quite a bit of energy out of him. "Let's get out of here," the sorcerer said softly. He turned and headed toward the men who waited among the rocks. Dhamon was the only one who lingered, praying briefly over the bodies of those who had died.

* * * * *

They traveled only a few miles, just far enough to put some distance between them and the camp. There were nearly six dozen freed prisoners. Only half of the men were sailors who had been taken from ships in the Palanthas harbor. The rest were farmers, traveling merchants, and visitors to the city—all who had been attacked before they reached the city gates.

They were ravenously hungry, and Feril, who had been healed by a spell from Jasper, had all she could do to scrounge up enough food to take the edge off their hunger. Dhamon occupied himself talking to Palin about the dragons and spawn, and what their next step ought to be in combating the menace.

The sorcerer rubbed his chin. A short, though uneven, beard had sprouted from his face, making him look almost distinguished. "We'll assemble the lance and talk with Goldmoon before we decide on a course of action. I trust her counsel, but I suspect the decision will be to go after the Blue that's nearby."

Across their makeshift camp, Rig was rubbing the Kagonesti's shoulders. "I thought I was done for," the mariner admitted. "It's funny. I can remember only one other time in my life when I really feared for myself . . ."

Feril turned her head and glanced up, her eyes encouraging him to continue.

"Shaon and I once sailed on a ship called the *Sanguine Lady* in the Blood Sea. There'd been a mutiny. It was supposed to be bloodless, and I was designated the new first mate. I had a lot of respect for the captain, and I thought the others did, too. We agreed to set him ashore with a few coins and enough food to last him until another ship came by. I myself went in the longboat with the captain and a handful of others.

After we landed, I watched as the others fell on him, cutting and beating him until long after he was dead. I couldn't do anything—not unless I wanted to die with him. We rowed back to the boat in silence. I never told Shaon what really happened. And the next time the *Lady* made port, I grabbed Shaon and we disappeared. We kept low for a while, and I'm sure she was curious why. But she knew better than to press me. Eventually we found our way to New Ports."

"You must really care about her," Feril said. "It's obvious she cares for you."

The mariner's hands lingered on Feril's shoulders. "We're good *friends*," he said.

Dhamon was looking for the Kagonesti and spotted her

across the camp. Rig was hovering closely, touching Feril. Dhamon felt a surge of jealousy. He'd thought Feril had been showing interest in him. She'd only been teasing, he decided. Dhamon balled his hands into fists, but didn't budge from Palin's side, where their discussion continued.

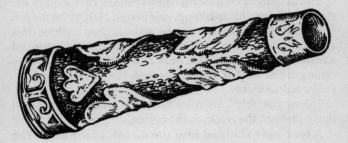

Chapter 32

Fissure's Grim Tidings

Khellendros stretched as comfortably as the confines of his underground lair allowed, his muscles rippling, his tail twitching like a contented cat's. He'd slept the better part of eight days, replenishing his energies, and now was ready to devote himself to creating more blue spawn. The ingredients should be arriving soon, herded across the desert to their doom. After that, he intended to enlarge his lair—to give himself more room to relax and to provide an underground barracks for his growing army.

The dragon flexed his claws and rumbled happily, the sound growing loud enough to vibrate the cavern's walls. The regiment of blue spawn that stood behind him looked warily toward the ceiling and at the sand that spilled down through the cracks. The floor was covered with more than an inch of fine, white sand now, for the dragon's agitation had continually weakened the lair.

The dragon eased forward. It was time to bask a bit in the sun, luxuriate in his sparkling, pale desert. He'd lie on the hot sand while he waited for the new arrivals. Two or three days at the most, he suspected, and they'd be here. He moved ahead slowly, extended his neck and rubbed it against the ceiling to ease an itch. Then he paused. His vast nostrils quivered uncomfortably.

"Show yourself!" his voice boomed. More sand trickled down through the cracks in the ceiling.

A lone ogre shuffled into the mouth of the cave. The dragon shot a claw out, intending to smash this insolent creature who dared to defile the sanctity of his lair. Then Khellendros paused. Perhaps this was a messenger from the Strongfist Tribe, announcing the arrival of the ingredients. But even as he entertained this thought, the ogre's form shimmered and melted away, replaced by the tiny body of the shapeshifting huldrefolk.

"I was with the ogres," Fissure began.

"As I ordered," the dragon returned. "My ingredients?"

The huldrefolk seemed uncharacteristically nervous, and the dragon could smell the faerie's apprehension. Something had gone wrong, and this displeased The Storm Over Krynn.

"Well . . ." Fissure started over.

"Well . . ." Khellendros pressed, his displeasure mounting and made the worse for the bother of coaxing bad news from his ally.

"The humans the ogres captured . . . well, they were rescued."

"Rescued!" The dragon's voice filled the underground chamber, the waves of sound hurling the huldrefolk back several paces. More sand filtered down.

310

Fissure feigned bravery and was quick to describe the unexpected assault on the ogre camp and to recount in detail the incident—giving special attention to the gray-haired mage in the tunic and leggings who cast spells and cut down the brutes and Dark Knights.

"Palin Majere," Khellendros hissed, fixating right away on the huldrefolk's description of the sorcerer. "I underestimated him and his fellows. But I shall not do so again. And . . . I shall make them pay for this affront."

"I guess some of the captives must have been friends of this Palin," Fissure mumbled. "I guess he thought he had to—"

"Majere." The word rolled like thunder, a curse slipping off the dragon's tongue. "Kitiara's brothers. The Majeres were a bane to Kitiara. And their offspring has become a bane to me."

"Well you still have all of your Dark Knights and brutes and I can find more ogres—"

"Silence!"

The blue spawn pressed back into a shadowy recess, avoiding the savagely flicking tail of their master.

"Palin Majere must be punished. I must hurt him," the dragon mused. "And the best way to hurt him is to hurt those he cares about."

"What do you want me to do?" Fissure whispered.

"I'll tend to Palin Majere. Revenge will be mine, and it will be sweet. Kitiara will be pleased."

The huldrefolk hurriedly vanished into the floor, a raised line in the sand the only hint of his incarnation.

"Yes, I shall tend to . . . "

A shimmering in the air interrupted the dragon's retaliatory reverie. The shimmering spot grew to form a large circle that practically filled the chamber, floor to ceiling, then it sparked red and coalesced into a near-transparent visage of a red dragon—and a very angry red dragon indeed.

"Malys," Khellendros said. His anger doubled. The Red

had never contacted him here before. It was a violation of his privacy.

"Traitor!" the image ranted. "You make a creature—secretly—one sleek and powerful." Malystryx's apparition spat and hissed, flames writhing like serpents from its nostrils. "Blue spawn, you call it. But you don't tell me!"

The Red's image continued to fume and berate the Blue, and all the while Khellendros's mind schemed. Words came to him, and he mentally rehearsed them, waiting for a break in the tirade. The apparition could do nothing to him, and he was not afraid of Malys. But he respected her power, and he knew he could not afford to have her as an enemy. Dealing with an enemy like her would keep him away from his true work.

"I demand to know why you kept this secret from me!" the Malys image hissed.

"Pity you discovered it so soon," Khellendros purred. "And pity that you felt you had to spy on me and ruin my so carefully planned surprise. I thought we trusted each other, Malys. I had intended to present the spawn to you as a gift. I've been working hard perfecting the creatures, wanting to make sure they were a suitable present for the most powerful dragon overlord, the dragon who perpetually occupies my waking thoughts."

The Malys image quavered. "A gift?"

"For the dragon I most revere on this world," he silkily continued. He was speaking the truth in that respect. He did admire Malys, her brawn and ambition, her ability to manipulate the other dragons and the humanoids in her region. "Though I am not yet satisfied with the spawn, I shall share my secret now—if that is your wish, Malys. Anything I have is yours, of course. *Anything.*"

The image nodded, accepting Khellendros's flattery. The Blue knew reds basked in adulation, and Malys was not an exception. The Storm Over Krynn proceeded to explain the grisly process for creating spawn—the draconian, human, and dragon essence required. The Malys image was rapt with attention.

"You must shed a tear?" Maly's voice was filled with curiosity. "That must be hard for you. It would be impossible for me." The image deepened, becoming a dark haughty crimson, and the phantom flames rose higher, until they dissipated against the cavern ceiling. "I shall use blood to birth my spawn. Blood is more powerful than water. And together, we shall create armies. Then, when the time is right, and when our forces are great, we shall spill this secret to the other overlords. Though they shall never have as many spawn as us—nor ones as powerful."

"As you wish." Khellendros bowed, then the image of the Red disappeared.

Cursing, the Blue moved out of his lair and into the blessed sun. That Malys knew of his spawn was an unforseen complication. She would have found out eventually, he knew, when he sent his forces out to conquer something, to gather magical items. He decided her learning the secret early was better. He raised a blue snout in the approximation of a smile.

Khellendros still wished to keep a low profile in the Northern Wastes, to have others do the drudge work. Let the humans' attentions be focused on Malys and on Beryl and Frost to the south and west, he thought.

He concentrated on a lone blue spawn, the one hungry and angry, the one trapped in a magical bottle on a green carrack. The spawn was sitting on a desk in a cramped cabin below deck. The dark-skinned woman with close-cropped hair was staring at it. Behind her, a kender paced and mumbled words he couldn't quite pick up. The damnable glass was muffling everything.

Khellendros stared back through his creation's eyes. He watched the pair intently, and he plotted. *You may break free now,* the dragon mentally told his offspring. *I don't need you as a spy any longer. I know where they are, that Palin Majere is coming back to the ship with his followers.*

The blue spawn's heart beat stronger. "Free!" it cried, in its parched voice. It beat its wings and shot upward toward the cork stopper. Its claws were extended and drove into the soft substance—and lodged there. The spawn hung, suspended, too weak from lack of food and water to go any further.

Khellendros closed his eyes and pulled back, silently and briefly grieving for the offspring he now counted as dead.

* * * * *

Hours later the wyverns returned, a blue dragon flying behind them.

"Do right?" The large one posed a question as it landed less than gracefully on the steamy desert floor.

The smaller sent a shower of sand into Khellendros's face as it touched down. "Do right?" it echoed. "Done? Do now what? Do cooler place something?"

"Do darker place something?" the tall one almost begged. It shifted back and forth on its clawed feet, not wanting to keep any part of itself too long on the hateful sand.

Khellendros growled and flicked his tail toward the entrance of his lair. The wyverns stared at each other, then trundled into the darkness, thankful to be out of the heat and brightness.

The blue dragon glided toward the sand, landing several yards in front of Khellendros. He was roughly half the size of the Storm Over Krynn. Still, he was impressive, his long horns curling in an unusual spiral. He lowered his head so it was below Khellendros's.

"Gale," Khellendros hissed. "I am pleased you came."

The lesser blue dragon nodded. "Yours to command," Gale returned. "As always while I breathe."

Khellendros knew his lieutenant was not as servile as he let on, yet he knew he had Gale's temporary loyalty. The Storm had not destroyed the lesser dragon during the Dragon Purge, though he easily could have, and he kept the other overlords from doing the same. He had kept the smaller dragon safe. In return, Gale had vowed fealty, much as a knight would swear allegiance to a lord. Khellendros trusted Gale more than most.

"I've an errand for you," Khellendros began. "One that will not take much of your time, and one that you might enjoy. Have you ever heard of Palin Majere?"

Gale nodded, a sly grin playing across his blue face.

315

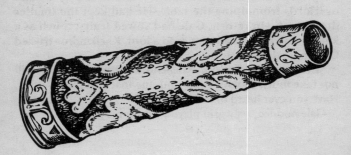

Chapter 33

A Brief Repast

They ate breakfast at Myrtal's Roost—Palin at the head of the table. Dhamon, Rig, Shaon, Feril, Groller, Blister, and Jasper filled the rest of the chairs. The polished walnut box with the lance handle sat at Dhamon's side. Everyone was in clean clothes, and looked more rested and presentable than they had in days.

Fury sat on the steps outside and sniffed at the wonderful aromas seeping from the crack under the door. His golden eyes sparkled hungrily as his tail thumped against the door. But the door stayed shut.

The captives had been returned to their ships, farms and businesses, grateful for their freedom. But their abuse at the hands of the ogres was something they never would be able to put behind them entirely. They'd forever be looking over their shoulders, cautious. They'd forever wonder what might have become of them if their rescuers hadn't arrived.

Blister concentrated on a piece of sausage skewered by a corkscrew attachment on her black dress gloves. Feril sat next to her and frequently glanced at Dhamon. His eyes never met hers. He stared at the cider in his glass and busied himself with the food Palin had so generously provided for everyone.

"So what do we do now? Where do we go?" the kender asked between bites. "And how are we going to get where we're going?"

Palin stroked his neatly trimmed, short beard and pushed his plate away. "Dhamon and I are going to the inn down the street to . . . pick something up. Then I suspect we'll head toward the tip of the Northern Wastes."

"The Blue," Jasper cut in. He took a long draw from his cider mug and nodded for Palin to continue.

"And the spawn," Shaon added.

"I think we should rent a ship to take us there, around the point past the Palanthas harbor," the sorcerer said. "We'll need a base from which to operate."

"We should take the *Anvil*," Rig said quickly, surprising everyone. All eyes were on the big mariner, even Shaon's.

"I'm a part of this, now," Rig explained. "I guess I was only kidding myself that I could sail away and ignore what was going on around me. The dragons and all. It's not safe for anyone anymore."

Jasper's fingers twirled in the air, making silent gestures to Groller so the half-ogre could understand the conversation.

"Thank you," Palin said. "The Shadow Sorcerer and the Master have learned that Malys is up to something. She's the largest dragon on Krynn, likely more formidable than the Blue in the Wastes. She bears watching, and that's just what they're doing."

Palin smiled and looked at Rig. "It's been a long time since I've been on a ship. I think it will feel good to travel someplace without having to employ magic to do so."

Groller motioned to Jasper, forming a cup with his hands and tossing it back to his mouth. Then he made the sign for "ship," another for "food," and he rustled his pocket to indicate money. The dwarf quickly caught his meaning.

"We'll need substantial supplies," Jasper translated.

"But we don't have any steel to buy them," Dhamon said. He glanced up, caught Feril looking at him, then focused his attention on the eggs on his plate.

"I still have Raph's spoons," Blister said. "They must be worth something."

"I'll take care of the supplies," Palin offered, as he tossed a small sack to the dwarf. "It's the least I can do."

Jasper looked inside the sack. It was filled with steel pieces. He nodded his thanks to Palin. "This will be more than enough," he said.

"Then the least I can do is buy Dhamon a shirt," the kender suggested. "He goes through clothes awfully fast." She passed the bag of spoons across the table. "Dhamon, use these to buy something *you* like," she laughed, looking directly at Rig.

"Rig and I will ready the ship," Shaon volunteered. Jasper, Blister, and Groller agreed to help.

The half-ogre filled his napkin with a handful of sausages, stuffed it in his pocket, and strolled out to present Fury with a treat. Within moments, Dhamon, Palin, and Feril were left alone at the table.

Palin eyed his companions. A grand journey was in the offing, and it had been decades since he had involved himself in such an adventure—too long. Studying tomes and scrying were one thing, but plunging into a quest and personally dealing with dangerous matters himself was something he had to confess he had missed.

"Even with Goldmoon's counsel—and the lance—we could die in the trying, you realize," said Palin.

"Everyone dies," Dhamon said. "It's only a matter of when." He edged away from the table and toward the door. Jangling the spoons, and tucking the walnut box under his arm, he looked over his shoulder at the sorcerer. "I've some clothes to replace. I'll meet you at the inn down the street shortly." The door closed softly behind him.

Palin glanced at Feril. The Kagonesti was eyeing the door.

"I speak from experience," the sorcerer began. "Life is too short, even for an elf, not to fill it with something or someone important to you. My uncle was always alone. He filled his life with magic, but he still had this emptiness. I fill my life with magic, too. But I have Usha and my family. I don't think my magic would be as strong if they weren't there. I wouldn't be as strong, and I wouldn't have the same convictions."

The Kagonesti offered him a slight smile, then rushed after Dhamon. She caught up with him outside. "Wait!"

"Feril, I . . . "

"I think I'm in love with you," the Kagonesti blurted out.

Dhamon closed his eyes and shook his head. "Don't. . . ."

"Don't you feel anything toward me?" The elf stepped in front of him, blocked his way.

"What I feel, or what I think I might feel, doesn't matter," he began. "Besides, there's Rig to consider."

"Rig? Because he fussed over me after we rescued him?" She sighed, putting her hands on her hips. The mariner had kept close company with her all the way back to Palanthas. She hadn't minded the attention. Dhamon had been preoccupied with Palin—and at the time she thought it was because they were discussing the spawn or speculating about the Blue. Now she realized it was also because he had noticed Rig's attention.

"You're jealous," she finally said. "Rig is just a friend. He flirts, that's all. And if you weren't so jealous you could see that. And if you *are* jealous that means you're feeling something."

"All right, I feel *something*," Dhamon confessed.

"*Something?* That's it?" The Kagonesti glanced toward the harbor and caught sight of the *Anvil's* mainmast. "Well, when you decide just what it is you feel, let me know. Maybe I'll still be interested."

As she whirled on her heels, he closed his hand around the crook of her arm and pulled her close. His hand drifted up and cupped the back of her head, his fingers entwining in her soft hair, becoming trapped in the curls. He brought his lips down to smother hers hungrily. The force of his emotions surprised him, but she returned his kiss, wrapping her arms around him and hugging him fiercely. They were oblivious to the stares of the passersby, and to the bemused expressions of those in the shops who watched from behind windows. After several long moments, they released each other.

"*Something*, huh?" Feril teased silkily. "I think I could get used to *something*." She playfully tugged on his tattered collar, bringing his face close to hers. This time she initiated the kiss, and again it was several moments before their lips separated.

"I'll see you on the *Anvil*," she whispered into his ear.

Chapter 34

Retribution

Gale skimmed low over the desert sands, letting the heat rise up and soak into the undersides of his blue wings. Soon the heat would be behind him and he'd have to contend with the uncomfortable coolness of the Palanthas countryside.

But it won't be for long, the dragon thought as he passed beyond the edge of the Northern Wastes and headed toward the city. After he had finished this particular task for Khellendros, he could return to the blessed heat and his own lair.

Gale's quarry was on a ship in the harbor—that much The Storm Over Krynn had explained. Well, there would be streets and buildings and all manner of things between himself and the harbor—all manner of things waiting to be destroyed. After all, Gale considered, Khellendros did not say he was to deal *only* with the ship and that *only* Palin Majere should feel the Portal Master's wrath.

The dragon's sapphire lip curled upward in a smile. If he was to be bothered by running an errand, he'd make sure he got some enjoyment out of it. Gale pumped his wings faster, and the miles melted away below his striking form. His mind reached out to touch the wind that played over his scales.

Obey me, Gale coaxed. The breeze picked up in response.

*   *   *   *   *

Groller and Jasper quickly arranged for a dozen barrels of fresh water, and a good supply of dried fruits and meats. They selected several bolts of canvas, in the event the sails might need mending along the way, and a half-dozen coils of new rope.

There were plenty of steel coins left over, but the half-ogre made it clear he wanted to keep some in reserve—in the event they needed more supplies later.

They made arrangements for everything to be delivered this afternoon to the *Anvil*, and then the pair, accompanied by Fury, headed toward the docks.

"Windy," the dwarf said. He tugged on the half-ogre's sleeve and made the sign for "wind."

Groller nodded, made the sign for storm, then drew his hands close together.

"A storm is coming," Jasper translated. "I hope you're wrong. I hope instead we . . . " The wind howled, drowning out the rest of the dwarf's words, and the sky darkened.

A ridge of hair stood up on Fury's back, and the wolf growled softly.

*   *   *   *   *

Dhamon's hair whipped about his face, and he turned his head this way and that to keep it from streaming into his eyes. He had the walnut box under one arm, and a paper-wrapped bundle of clothes tucked under the other. The paper made crinkling and snapping sounds in the strong breeze, as he walked toward an inn named the Feather Rest.

Palin was waiting for him.

"The lance is in here?" Dhamon looked through the window. It was a rather plush establishment, with a lobby full of overstuffed chairs.

"On the second floor," Palin answered. The sorcerer smiled. "In good hands, rest assured. Follow me."

He led Dhamon up a wide, gently curving staircase with a peach-colored carpet runner tacked to the middle. A brass chandelier hung from the ceiling above the landing. Its candles were not lit; enough light spilled in from a window at the end of the hall. Palin strode to the nearest door, knocked once, and entered. Dhamon hesitated for a moment, then stepped inside.

The room was finely furnished, with a large four-poster bed, an oak cabinet, and several comfortable-looking chairs. Standing midway in the room, Palin was hugging an old woman. Near her, an elderly man looked on and smiled. Dhamon stared at the threesome.

The old woman was slight, with short, curly white hair and flashing eyes that complimented her bright blue dress. The wrinkles on her face were not deep, though they seemed more pronounced around her eyes and lips when she smiled. The man looked familiar somehow. He was big, broad-shouldered, and had a wide girth. His thick hair, an equal mix of steel-gray and white, fell to his shoulders. He was wearing a pair of light brown trousers over which hung an ivory tunic. His meaty, weathered hand patted Palin on the back.

"Son, it is good to see you," the old man boomed.

"Caramon Majere," Dhamon whispered. "You're Caramon

Majere, and you're . . . ." He turned to the old woman, who had disentangled herself from Palin.

"I'm Tika." Her voice was clear and soft. She smiled warmly as she took Dhamon's hand. "We've been waiting for you and Palin for several days. We were beginning to worry."

"*You* were beginning to worry," Caramon corrected. "I knew Palin would be along. I figured he was busy."

Dhamon stared at the two. Heroes of the Lance, soldiers in a long-ago war, he thought they'd have been dead. Caramon must be near ninety, he suspected, though the man looked to be twenty years younger than that. He was obviously fit, with no stoop to his shoulders. Tika also wore her age well. Perhaps they'd been blessed by the gods—decades ago, when the gods were still around.

"The Inn of the Last Home?" Palin queried.

"Is in good hands," Tika replied. "But we should be getting back there. Business always drops off when we disappear for a while." She turned to her husband. "Caramon, don't you think you should retrieve what this young man came for?"

The elderly man nodded and walked over toward the bed. He knelt, lifted up the quilt, then retrieved a long, canvas-wrapped bundle.

"A friend of mine carried this, and it served him well." He rose and placed it almost reverently on the bed, at an angle because of its length. He began untying the cords.

"I remember it all as if it happened yesterday—not a lifetime ago," Caramon continued. "Sturm Brightblade wielded this. He was a very good friend. Sturm was strong and determined. I guess we all were, confident in our youth. Somehow our weapons and wits were enough during the War of the Lance. But the dragons are larger now. Things are different."

Palin nudged Dhamon closer, taking the package of clothes from beneath his arm. Caramon continued to talk as Dhamon sat the walnut box at the foot of the bed.

"Goldmoon contacted us many weeks ago," Caramon went

on. "She was with us during those years. She fought beside us and encouraged us when things seemed impossible. I think we all owed her our lives at one time or another." His fingers fumbled for a moment with the cord's last knot, before it finally yielded. "She said there'd be new champions in need of old weapons. Well, this is a very old weapon." He drew back the canvas, revealing a silver lance that shone softly in the light that drifted in from the open window.

The wind picked up, making the curtains flutter wildly. It was a cool wind, and it whistled as it washed over the lance.

Dhamon bent over the weapon. It was so polished and well-cared for that it looked newly forged. It had tiny etchings along its widest part, the images of dragons circling, some flying. The shadows cast by the waving curtains made it seem as if the dragons were moving. He touched the metal and was surprised that it felt warm. His fingertips tingled.

"We'd kept it in pieces, I guess because we all wanted a piece of history, a trophy from the war. This hung above the mantle in our inn. Tika and I gave the haft to Sturm, our oldest son, whom we named after Sturm Brightblade." Caramon's shoulders slouched. "Sturm and Tanin, another of our sons, died a long time ago. The haft passed to Palin, our youngest."

"Young," Palin chuckled. "Not anymore, father."

"Goldmoon kept the banner," Caramon added. He nodded toward the walnut box. "Is it in there?"

"Yes." Dhamon quickly retrieved the haft. Its silk banner fluttered in the wind, which was even stronger now. He handed it to Caramon, who expertly joined it to the lance.

Tika drew a shawl about her and glanced out the window. The sky was darkening, and she saw a flicker of lightning in the clouds.

"It's yours now," Caramon said, hefting the weapon and passing it to Dhamon.

The weapon felt lighter than it should be, yet it was

superbly balanced. "I don't know what to say," Dhamon began. He looked back and forth between Tika and Caramon. "To give me this. I don't know if I—"

"Promise you'll slay a dragon with it," Caramon interrupted. "That's what it was made for. And there's certainly a few dragons on Krynn needing to be slain."

A thick bolt of lightning shot from the clouds and touched down in the city. The ground shook, the vibrations felt even in the inn room, and thunder filled the air. Another bolt followed it, slicing through the corner of a balcony down the street, at the edge of Tika's vision. Tile and stones rained down onto the sidewalk below. Tika quickly stepped away from the window and looked at Caramon.

"We'd better get going," Palin said.

"Always in a hurry," Tika said. "But I suppose Caramon and I were always in a hurry years ago." She took the sorcerer's face between her small hands and kissed his cheek. "The storm is a bad one. All this lightning. I wish you'd stay until it passes. Your ship can't leave during a storm."

Palin backed toward the door. "Mother, Father, I'll see you again—soon. Next time it will be at home. I won't ask you to do any more traveling . . ."

"Nonsense!" Caramon interrupted. "Checking out other inns is good for us. Gives us ideas for the Last Home. Besides, we—"

Lightning crackled sharply and thunder boomed, louder this time. Again the inn shook, and screams cut through the air—coming from somewhere outside on the street. Palin rushed to the window and looked out. He saw a building in the distance collapse as lightning repeatedly struck it. A wave of people were coming down the street, running away from something.

"The storm's not natural!" Palin shouted over the thunder. "No rain! The lightning seems directed!"

Dhamon moved to the door. "Feril and the others . . ."

Palin drew back and nodded. "I know, let's go."

"Dragon!" they all heard someone scream.

"I'm going with you!" Caramon announced. "Let me get my sword."

Tika grabbed her husband's arm as Dhamon and Palin dashed out into the hallway. "Not this time, Caramon," she admonished. "Stay here and protect me."

The big man knew his wife didn't need protecting, but he nodded and joined her at the window.

Chapter 35

Reunion

Palin found himself hurrying to keep up with Dhamon. He had to stop several times to duck or dodge flying debris. The wind was howling down the street, blowing shutters and signs off buildings, overturning benches and flowerpots. Lightning continued to flash, striking near enough to make the cobblestones shake beneath their feet. They could hear glass breaking, masonry striking the street.

Screams were coming from the docks—a cacophony of shouts, barked orders and shrill cries. As the two rounded a corner, they were nearly barreled over by a crowd of sailors and dock workers running toward them. They could barely see through the gaps in the mass of panicked people.

"Run!" a fisherman bellowed as he shouldered his way past Dhamon.

"Skie!" cried another, red-faced and clutching at his chest as he rushed by.

Palin and Dhamon pushed through the crowd and saw what was responsible for the panic—a large blue dragon that hovered directly above *Flint's Anvil.*

"Feril!" Dhamon yelled. He gripped the lance tighter, shouldering it as he increased his pace, leaving Palin behind.

The sorcerer dropped Dhamon's clothes bundle. He thrust his hands into the folds of his robe and grasped the first magical item he touched, a small brooch. He began mouthing the words to a powerful spell, one that would destroy the bauble and most certainly leave him practically helpless afterward. But it was a strong enchantment, one he hoped would force the dragon away.

Dhamon's feet pounded against the docks. "Feril!"

On the deck of the *Anvil,* Rig stood by the railing, slicing at the blue's flailing tail. Blister and Jasper were perched by the capstan. The dwarf's fingers glowed with the makings of some clerical enchantment aimed at Groller, who lay twisted and bloody at his feet—the first to fall to the dragon.

Shaon had climbed the mainmast and, from her precarious perch, she was swinging her sword at one of the dragon's rear legs. Her violet dress billowed about her long dark legs. Lightning arced from the sky, making her blade practically glow.

Feril was clutched in the dragon's claw. The Kagonesti's arm pumped up and down as she repeatedly stabbed at the dragon with a knife. The dragon's flesh was dense, and the blade merely bounced off the sapphire scales and finally shattered, shards of metal falling to the planks below.

Shaon's sword struck successfully, however, cleaving scales and skin and causing the dragon to roar in surprise. The blue beat his wings to carry himself higher, just beyond the female sea barbarian's reach.

The Kagonesti closed her eyes and concentrated, thought about her homeland of Southern Ergoth—the ice that covered the land, the snow that fell every day and every night and pressed down on the earth, smothering it. The dragon's claw was pressing in on her. She dropped the knife pommel and spread her fingers wide, touching the dragon's paw and making him feel the terrible cold she envisioned.

Caught off guard by the frigid sensation, the dragon released Feril, and she plummeted toward the dock far below. In the same instant, the blue dragon opened his maw and delivered a bolt of lightning, a thin stroke that cut through the mainmast and sent the mast and Shaon flying toward the deck. But the dragon's claw was quick. He stretched down and caught the sea barbarian in midair. The sword she'd injured him with clattered harmlessly to the deck.

Then the great beast raised his head to the growing clouds and released another bolt, this one echoed with a great boom by the sky. He flapped his wings to again move higher.

Rain began to fall, soft at first, pattering down on the ships, the planks, and the harbor. But within the span of a few heartbeats, the tempo quickened.

Feril managed to spin about and landed crouched on the dock, on her hands and feet as if she were a cat. She sprang toward the *Anvil's* railing and vaulted onto the deck. She reached into her bag, her fingers searching for the clay.

Dhamon scrambled up the plank that led to the *Anvil's* deck. He quickly glanced at Feril to make sure she was all right, then he shouldered the lance and peered through the sheet of rain at the dragon. The beast was too high up, beyond Dhamon's reach. He squinted through the rain, trying to get a better look at the dragon. Something about it seemed familiar.

Palin's thumb ran over the smooth stone in the center of the brooch as his words and his pulse quickened. He stood on the shore, his feet touching the edge of the dock. His voice rose as the incantation concluded, and the brooch shattered in his hand. A streak of pale green light rushed from his palm and through the sky as if it were an arrow. It unerringly struck the dragon in the center of his chest, and scales and blood fell like leaves from a shaken tree.

The dragon howled in pain as blood spurted from his belly. He beat his wings to make himself ascend, the sea barbarian still clutched in his claw.

"Shaon! No!" the big mariner bellowed. He leapt to the rail, balancing himself like an acrobat. His fingers found the daggers strapped to his chest, and he began heaving them at the rising dragon. Rig's aim was true, but the beast's hide was too thick. The daggers glanced off and fell benignly into the sea.

"Dark human!" the dragon hissed at Rig as he flapped his wings harder and craned his neck. "You want this woman?"

"Shaon!" Rig bellowed again. He jumped down to the deck, no longer able to balance himself in the tremendous winds created by the blue's wings. The ship rocked wildly in its slip.

The sea barbarian wriggled in the dragon's grasp, trying futilely to pry a claw open so she could fall free. But her fingers could find no purchase.

"You want this woman?" the dragon raged.

Palin had finally made his way to the *Anvil's* slip, and standing next to the post to which it was moored, he had begun another incantation. His fingers clutched a gold coin. It was a token his Uncle Raistlin had enchanted and given to him when he was little more than a child, and he'd treasured it all these years. The coin vibrated in his hand.

The dragon's eyes narrowed. "Palin Majere," he hissed. "Palin Majere—is this your woman? Does she mean something to you?"

Palin paused in his spell, surprised the dragon knew his

name. "Let her go!" he cried.

"You can have her!" the dragon spat.

Shaon screamed, a white-hot sensation of pain shooting through her as one of the dragon's claws pierced her stomach, nearly cutting her in two. Then the dragon dropped her. She fell like a broken doll, and her motionless body struck the *Anvil's* deck. The mariner rushed to her.

"Gale!" The word erupted from Dhamon's mouth. The dragon was indeed familiar! Dhamon's eyes widened with recognition of the dragon's visage. The long curling horns, the ridge above the dragon's malevolently gleaming eyes— the features were distinct. He swallowed hard. "Stop this! Gale!"

The dragon glanced down, spied Dhamon toting the lance, saw his own blood hitting the deck and painting the wood crimson. The blue paused in his assault and scrutinized the man, his wings slowing as he hovered above the dock.

"Dhamon?" the blue hissed. "Dhamon Grimwulf?"

Palin's concentration faltered, ending the spell. The sorcerer looked incredulously at Dhamon. Feril and Jasper were staring at him, too. Blister was slack-jawed and speechless.

Dhamon nodded. "That's right, Gale. It's me. You don't have to do this. These people have done nothing to you. And you have no reason to fight them."

"Dhamon, join me!" The dragon's voice cut through the rain and thunder. "Together again, we can serve a new master!"

"No!" Dhamon retorted. "I'm through with that life!"

"Fool!" Gale hissed. "A grand war is in the offing, Dhamon, and if you side against me, you will be on the losing side."

"Don't be certain about that, Gale," Dhamon said. He held the lance up.

The dragon threw back his head and roared, sending a thick bolt of sizzling lightning skyward. Thunder rocked the harbor. "You're through with that life? Then you'll soon be through with life!" the dragon roared. "I'll spare you for the moment, for old time's sake. When next we meet, I will not be so charitable."

The dragon raised his head to the sky and released another barrage of lightning, then he pumped his wings and rose to the clouds, banking toward the western hills.

The rain increased, hammering against the docks and ships. The wind howled like a beast, the ships in the bay crashed into piers.

Palin, fighting against the unnatural weather, thrust the unused coin into his pocket and struggled up the slippery plank to the *Anvil's* deck. He headed toward Shaon.

Rig held Shaon's body, as Jasper, Blister, and Feril crowded around. Dhamon slowly approached them. The big mariner's eyes were filled with tears, his chest heaving with deep sobs. His dark shoulders shook.

"Shaon," he moaned. "Why?" He turned to see Dhamon and his eyes narrowed. He gently lowered Shaon's body to the deck and stood up. "You! You have a lot of explaining to do!"

"You know the dragon?" Feril's voice was thick with disbelief. "You know the dragon that killed Shaon?"

"Groller?" Dhamon swallowed hard. "Is he dead, too?"

"He'll live," Jasper answered. "But he's hurt badly."

"Answer me, Dhamon!" Feril insisted. "You know the dragon—how?"

"He was my partner. Years ago," Dhamon began. "When I was a Knight of Takhisis . . . "

"No!" the mariner wailed. He charged forward, slamming into Dhamon. The lance fell from Dhamon's hands, clattering, as the pair toppled to the deck. Rig's hands closed around Dhamon's neck.

Feril pulled at the mariner. "Stop!" she screamed. "No more killing!" It took her, as well as Palin, to pull the big mariner off.

Dhamon rolled away. He gasped and grabbed his throat, coughed and inhaled deeply as he pushed himself to his knees. "I'm sorry!" His voice was hoarse. "I left Gale years ago."

"If you hadn't left him maybe Shaon would still be alive!" Rig spat.

"You don't know that," Palin whispered.

Feril took a step toward Dhamon. "Why didn't you tell us? How could you keep something like this from us?"

"Feril, I . . ." He stood up and reached out to her, but she recoiled and stepped back. "I'm sorry," he repeated. Dhamon closed his eyes, trying to control his tears, but they spilled down his cheeks, mingling with the rain.

"Sorry? You're sorry?" Rig fumed. "Sorry won't bring Shaon back! You should be dead—not her!"

Dhamon's gaze met the mariner's. "Look after Feril—please. I'll deal with Gale. I'll make sure he never hurts anyone again." He hurried down the plank that lead to the dock.

"Dhamon!" Palin called. The sorcerer retrieved the lance and held it out. "You'll need this."

Dhamon shook his head. "No I won't." He quickly lost himself in the crowd that had gathered to stare at the battered *Anvil*.

Chapter 36

Severing Ties

The rain fell, ceaselessly. The sky was gray, the clouds thick, hanging dismally over the entire scene.

Rig held Shaon's body close, rocking back and forth as he sat on deck with his back against the broken mainmast. He whispered to her, as if her spirit might be comforted. He whispered about how sorry he was, how beautiful she had looked in the violet dress, how much he loved her, how he didn't know if he could go on living without her.

Jasper and Blister helped Groller to his feet, and Fury paced around the half-ogre, whimpering nervously.

"Below deck with him," the dwarf said. "I want him in bed, then I'll see what else I can do for him."

Blister chewed her lip as her fingers painfully closed about Groller's big hand. She and the dwarf slowly helped the half-ogre to the hatch. The red wolf was close on their heels.

Feril gazed toward the shore, but saw no sign of Dhamon. There was a crowd growing along the bank. She felt very alone.

Palin looked toward the hills, to the west, while the mariner continued his tirade against the former Knight of Takhisis. "Dhamon's responsible for all of this! Let the dragon kill him, too!"

"Perhaps you are wrong in your anger," Palin said, not turning around to face Rig. His voice was soft, but the words were forceful enough to give the mariner pause. "A blue dragon killed Shaon, and the dragons are responsible for most of the pain on Krynn."

"But he knew the dragon—rode it himself!" Rig ranted. "When he was a Knight of Takhisis. He called the dragon his partner!"

"When he *was* a Knight of Takhisis," Palin returned. "*Was*—your word. And I thought he was your friend. He rescued you from the ogres."

Rig's shoulders sagged. "Shaon is dead."

"She should be mourned, but not forgotten," Palin continued, his back still to the mariner. "It would not be honorable to blame Dhamon for her death. How can you condemn a man for a life he left behind? How can you blame him for the despicable deeds of a dragon? Isn't there anything in your past you want to leave behind and bury?"

The mutiny, Rig thought, as he continued to cradle Shaon's form. But I couldn't have prevented the death of my captain. This is different.

"Isn't there anything you prefer to leave behind?" Palin persisted.

Through a haze of tears Rig gazed at Shaon's still form. Maybe Dhamon couldn't have done anything else. . . .

"I'm going after Dhamon," Feril, who had been watching, announced. "He can't take on that blue dragon alone. And he's why we came here to fight the dragons."

"I'm coming with you," Palin said, turning to face his companions. I'll inform the others below.

"Let's hurry," Feril urged.

The rain continued to fall as they wedged their way through the crowd on the shore and struck off toward the western hills. The sorcerer moved quickly, despite his years and the fatigue he felt. Still, his pace was not as fast as the mariner's. Rig had caught up with them before they reached the edge of town. He carried the lance.

"Damning him won't bring Shaon back," Rig admitted to Feril. Then to Palin, he said, "I guess you're right. Sometimes pasts were meant to be buried."

* * * * *

Dhamon scrabbled up the mountainside. The rocks were slick with rain, and more than once he almost lost his footing. The storm continued to rage around him, and the lightning illuminated the dragon perched high above him.

Gale watched his former partner approach, and he flapped his great wings to create a strong wind to complicate Dhamon's climb. Lightning flickered about the blue dragon's teeth, and he sent a thin bolt down.

Rock shattered near Dhamon's feet, pelting the backs of his legs and causing him to scramble for better purchase.

"Change your mind?" the dragon boomed. "Come to apologize? Come to seek my forgiveness and ask to ride with me again?"

Dhamon didn't answer. He gritted his teeth and continued his ascent. Gale's form loomed closer.

The dragon waited patiently and continued to orchestrate the storm. Gale willed a gust of wind to rush down the mountainside, and the dragon watched with amusement as Dhamon's feet flew out behind him, his hands the only things anchoring him to the rocks.

"Persistent," Gale observed. "But you were always persistent."

At last Dhamon reached the top and stood in the blue dragon's shadow. "You didn't have to kill her," he said. "She'd done nothing to you."

"Nothing but befriend Palin Majere," the dragon returned. "And killing her hurt him."

"He barely knew her," Dhamon said crossly.

"Then I erred in my target. Help me pick another, one that will have more meaning to the sorcerer."

"There'll be no other targets," he told the dragon.

"I no longer take my orders from you."

Dhamon stared up into the large eyes of his once-friend, then he reached for his sword and stepped closer.

Gale's eyes grew wide. "You mean to fight me?"

"I mean to kill you," Dhamon said as he rushed forward.

The blue dragon tensed his leg muscles, pushed off, and flapped his wings to take him skyward. In that instant, Dhamon sprang up and swung his sword. The blade sunk deep into Gale's rear leg.

Dhamon held tight to the pommel as he felt himself being lifted. His legs dangled in the air as he struggled to pull himself up.

"We were allies once," the dragon hissed. He slowly turned his head over his great scaly shoulder and opened his maw. "We were more than friends, we were brothers. Don't force me to kill you."

Dhamon held tight to Gale's leg, finding handholds on the blue scales. He tugged free his sword, sheathed it, and climbed higher, over the dragon's haunch and to his back. Dhamon knew Gale could have easily tossed him from his precarious perch. The dragon was being magnanimous, but not overly so. He saw Gale glance backward at him, felt the dragon inhale, and he held tight to the spiked ridge as a bolt of lighting shot out between the dragon's fangs. Electricity raced harmlessly along Gale's scales, but not so harmlessly into Dhamon. The painful sensation jarred him. He closed his eyes, gritted his teeth, and tried to block out the pain.

It was a warning, Dhamon knew.

"We were allies," the dragon repeated.

"Allies in the past!" Dhamon yelled over the storm. "That life is dead to me!"

The dragon closed his eyes and sadly shook his head. "Then, you are dead, too." Gale beat his wings fiercely now, trying to throw Dhamon from his back. But Dhamon held on as his left hand closed around a dragon scale. The sharp edge sliced into his hand, and he felt the blood rush down his palm, but still he maintained his grip.

"Why didn't you stay in the city? I would have let you live—for old times, for past pleasures," the dragon cried.

"You killed a friend of mine!" Dhamon cursed. "You destroyed a new life I have been building!"

"I was following orders," Gale boomed. The dragon again released his lightning breath along his back. This time it was not a warning.

Dhamon cringed as the pain from the bolt sent numbing heat through him. He felt his muscles relaxing, his legs and fingers releasing their hold on the dragon.

"No!" he cried as he scampered for another purchase. His hands flailed about, meeting only slick scales. He was sliding off. At last his elbow locked around a spiked scale on the ridge of the dragon's back.

He climbed up, hand over hand. Gale rolled in the air, turning on his back and nearly toppling him. But the former knight was dogged. He ignored the pain and continued his climb. The dragon righted himself, soaring higher. Dhamon was nearly up to Gale's neck by now. Locking his legs around

a spiked scale and holding onto another with his left hand, he
drew his sword and raised it. He plunged it down into the
base of the dragon's thick neck. The blade sank in deep, and
Dhamon grabbed the pommel with both hands to hold on.

Gale roared and the sky reverberated. The rain lashed sideways—tossed by the fierce wind, spurred on by the drum of
thunder. The dragon dipped over a rise, dropped and pulled
his wings close to his sides. Dhamon held on desperately as
his legs flew free behind him.

* * * * *

Feril reached the top of a hill. It was all she could do to
stand there against the roaring wind and rain. She screamed
when she realized it was blood that splattered her tunic. In
horror, she watched the injured dragon pass overhead and
dive toward a lake nestled among a ring of hills. Then all of a
sudden the dragon pulled up, and his claws grazed the water.
He climbed higher and higher.

She saw the tiny form of a man hanging on, and heard the
thunder fill the air.

* * * * *

"I had no closer friend once," Dhamon said.

"But you deserted me!" the dragon hissed, his words all
but drowned out in the roaring wind.

"I abandoned that life of evil."

"And when you left the Knights of Takhisis, I resigned too!
I couldn't go on with another partner!" the dragon cried.
"Now I serve a better master. I serve the Storm Over Krynn!"

The dragon rolled onto his back. Dhamon gripped the
pommel of his sword and flailed about, trying to find something his legs could hold onto. At last the dragon righted
himself, and Dhamon's legs closed about a scaly spike at the

base of Gale's neck. He tugged the sword free.

"Your master?" Dhamon asked with contempt.

"The Portal Master. The Storm Over Krynn. Khellendros!" Gale cried. The dragon sent a lightning bolt skyward, and a myriad of strokes issued earthward in response. The ground rocked far below.

"Khellendros is the greatest blue dragon Krynn has seen! There is none larger! None more powerful!" Gale roared. "Together, my master and I could shatter Palanthas!"

Dhamon gritted his teeth and drove the sword in again. The blade sank in halfway to the pommel, and the dragon let out a scream.

Far below, Palin and Rig stood with Feril, squinting through the driving rain. The mariner hefted the lance and looked up, hoping for an opportunity.

"The dragon is seriously hurt," Palin said. "I have spells that could reach him, though I don't know if they'd be enough to finish him. And if they were, he would land on the rocks. Dhamon wouldn't stand a chance of surviving the fall."

High above them, Dhamon drove the sword in again. "You'll serve no master of evil!" he shouted. "You'll kill no one else again!"

Gale thrashed about and flapped his wings furiously, trying to dislodge Dhamon. He brought his tail up and lashed it wildly.

The tail struck the rider, and Dhamon howled in agony. Still, he would not let go. He managed to yank the sword free one more time, blood showering his face. Shaking his head and blinking to clear his eyes, he swung wide, and he felt the blade carve through Gale's huge leathery wing.

The dragon screeched again and breathed his lightning, but the bolt shot away harmlessly, striking a hill far below. Again Dhamon's blade flashed, cutting through more of the wing, slicing away at Gale's weakness.

Then Dhamon felt himself falling. The dragon was plummeting, uncontrollably spiraling down. Dhamon saw a lake rushing up from below. He closed his eyes and for a moment thought about Gale, about the time they'd spent together, about the men they'd slain. He felt the sword slide from his fingers, then he felt consciousness slip from his grasp.

"No!" Feril screamed, as she watched the dragon plunge into the lake. The water rose up in a great tower. She scrambled down the hill, her feet flying over the slick rocks and mud. Rig and Palin followed, tumbling and sliding.

The rain was softer by the time they reached the shore. The wind was dying down. The clouds were thinning, letting the blue of the sky peek through and reflect itself in the lake's roiling surface. The water was just starting to calm itself.

Feril stood at the shore, water gently lapping around her feet. She took a few steps out, until the water was just below her knees, then she extended her senses into the water, trying to find Dhamon, the dragon, any hint of life.

Palin moved up behind her, knelt, and touched his fingers to the water's edge. He murmured words to a simple enchantment, and ripples raced away from him. "Dhamon," Palin whispered. "Find Dhamon." But the spell found no living trace of the former knight. The ripples dissipated.

Rig placed a hand on Feril's shoulder, every bit as concerned as Palin and the Kagonesti.

A bubble formed in the center of the lake, then another and another, until Feril's heart began to beat with faint hope. But then the bubbles stopped, as did the rain. The wind ceased. And hope died.

Palin stood and tugged her toward the shore. She buried her face in his shoulder. The sorcerer wrapped his arms comfortingly around her.

"He killed the dragon," Palin said simply.

"That dragon had to be the Blue from the Northern Wastes," Rig said quickly. "The one that created the spawn, controlled the ogres. Left alive, it could have destroyed Palanthas—and more. Dhamon won."

"At the cost of his life," Feril sobbed.

And Shaon's life, the mariner silently added. Rig shouldered the lance. He guessed the weapon was his now to use against another dragon, perhaps the White in Southern Ergoth. He felt numb, and useless, however. And he couldn't bring himself to leave the spot.

"Victory rarely comes without a considerable cost," the mariner said, finally breaking the silence. He reached out and touched Feril. "I'm going to honor Shaon and Dhamon by continuing the struggle—whatever the cost."

Feril nodded and looked up into Palin's eyes.

"We've a mast to mend," the sorcerer said, as he glanced toward Palanthas. "We've fallen friends to honor. And we've many more battles ahead of us."

Feril edged away from him. Tears continued to spill from her cheeks, and her slight frame trembled.

Palin Majere took a last look at the lake, then turned toward the city. Rig and Feril fell in place behind him.

All-new editions from Margaret Weis & Tracy Hickman

The Second Generation

Meet them again for the first time – the children of the
Heroes of the Lance, those who inherited the sword, the staff,
and the legacy of the heroes who came before them. This
all-new paperback edition features stunning cover art from
DRAGONLANCE® artist Matt Stawicki.

February 2002

Dragons of Summer Flame

When the father of the gods returns to Krynn, the world
is shaken to its core. The battle that rages in this hottest of
summers will change the people and deities of Ansalon
forever. Striking cover art from Matt Stawicki graces this
all-new paperback edition!

February 2002

Legends Trilogy Gift Set

A handsome hardcover case surrounds this trilogy of classic
titles from the foundation of the DRAGONLANCE saga. Each title
in this collectible boxed set features paintings by Matt Stawicki
and is a must-have for any DRAGONLANCE fan.

September 2002

The Dhamon Saga
Jean Rabe

The sensational conclusion to the trilogy!

Redemption
Volume Three

Dhamon's dragon-scale curse forces him deep into evil territory, where he must follow the orders of an unknown entity. Time is running out for him and his motley companions—a mad Solamnic Knight, a wingless draconian, and a treacherous ogre mage. Is it too late for Dhamon to redeem his nefarious past?

July 2002

Now available in paperback

Betrayal
Volume Two

Haunted by the past, Dhamon Grimwulf suffers daily torture from the dragon scale attached to his leg. As he searches for a cure, he must venture into a treacherous black dragon's swamp. The swamp is filled with terrors bent on destroying him, but the true danger to Dhamon is much closer than he thinks.

April 2002